7/21

KEVIN J. ANDERSON

ROLL

HEX WORLD
BOOK 1

aethonbooks.com

ROLL (HEXWORLD BOOK 1)
© 2021, 1989 WordFire, Inc.

*A previous version of this book was published under the title Gamearth, but it has been revised and re-edited for this release.

ALSO IN SERIES

HEXWORLD

1: ROLL

2: PLAY

3: END

PROLOGUE

S unday night, like every Sunday night, they played the Game.

Melanie carried four glasses of soda to the table, hating the real-world role of hostess. "We can make popcorn later, if you guys want." She flipped a strand of brown hair behind her ear and stared at the master map on the table. Hexworld, their beautiful fantasy world....

"Forget popcorn—try my dip instead," Tyrone said. "Black bean and shrimp this week. And I brought some sesame crackers too."

David arrived, late as usual. He stuck the keys from his Mustang in the pocket of his denim jacket. His dark hair looked soft, but his eyes were hard. "We ready to play?" he asked, finding a seat at the table. He bent over to frown at the map and did not say hello. Melanie made him get his own glass of soda.

Her parents had found someplace else to go, as they always did when the group met at Melanie's house. At first, her mother and father had stood on the sidelines to watch, curious and condescending. But the concept of a role-playing game seemed beyond them—where it was all pretend and no one really won or lost. The group played the parts of characters through adventure after adventure in a world created from their own imaginations.

The colorful map beckoned from the table. Flat, with precise hexagonal sections of forest, grasslands, mountains, ocean. She touched the smooth paint and thought of the characters they had played, generation after generation after generation. In her father's study, she had used the computer to generate scores and to keep track of all their characters.

Scott cracked his knuckles. "Hey, Tyrone—you know when geese fly south for the winter, how they always fly in a V-formation, right? And one side of the V is always longer than the other, right? Why do you suppose that is?"

Tyrone pondered and shrugged. "Why don't you tell us, Mister Science?"

"Because there's more geese on that side!"

Tyrone coughed on his own dip. Melanie found Tyrone's reaction more amusing than the joke itself. Scott blinked behind his glasses, looking proud of himself but baffled, as if he hadn't considered the joke very funny in the first place.

Their group, the same group for two years, had started out playing with hexagonal graph paper, scrawling haphazard terrain markings with colored pencils. They were playing for fun, for something to do. But Melanie spent a month painting and color-coding each hexagon of terrain with bright acrylics to make a permanent master map on wood. She had looked at real maps to develop geography that made sense, deserts where the weather patterns might leave the air dry, forests where the climate should have been hospitable.

"Everybody's here. Can we start playing, then?" David drummed his fingers on the tabletop. "Where were we last week?"

Melanie talked as fast as she could, trying to outrun his impatience. "My characters Delrael and Vailret were just about to go into the swamp terrain to rescue their friend Bryl." Melanie pointed to the map. "He was captured by an ogre, remember?"

"Well, go ahead and play," David said.

Melanie looked at him, but he kept his expression neutral. His brown eyes contained no emotion, his face showed no smile whatsoever. Something was bothering him. She didn't know what it could be, but Melanie thought he might try to take it out on the Game.

She gripped the dice in her hand. Twenty-sided. Eight-sided. Six-sided. Four-sided. They seemed to exude a kind of power, so much that she almost dropped them in surprise.

Melanie marked on the graph paper where her characters would begin their movement. She threw the dice.

Always remember this: every character on Hexworld was created by the Outsiders. We exist solely for the amusement of those who Play our world. Our ambitions, our concerns mean nothing—everything is determined by the roll of the dice."

—The Book of Rules

CHAPTER 1
CESSPOOLS OF GAIROTH

RULE #1: Always have fun.
—The Book of Rules

A s they crossed the thick black line that separated one hexagon of terrain from the next, the forest suddenly became an oozing swamp. Even the fresh woodland smell changed to the festering dampness of decay.

"Bryl is supposed to be lost somewhere in here?" Vailret promptly sank up to the top of his boot in swamp muck.

His burly cousin Delrael strode over the sharp hexagon line into the swamp, heedless of where he put his foot. He walked confidently, ready for anything. "Good thing friendship runs deep—Bryl wasn't that much of a Sorcerer."

Vailret searched for a safer place to step, but it all looked the same to him. His eyes were weak from too much reading in dim rooms, though he found the reading much more interesting than questing from hexagon to hexagon.

"He hasn't had any training, Del. He's three times our age, but nobody's ever taught him worthwhile magic." He scratched through his spiky blond hair and thought of the manuscripts still waiting to be deciphered, chronologies of legends to be worked out. "You of all people know how important training is."

The thin mud slurped against Vailret's boot as he took another step. Running from quest to quest, exploring catacombs, searching for monsters and treasure—it struck him as being juvenile. The world had changed since all that. He wished the Outsiders could amuse themselves by playing more sophisticated games, like hexagon-chess.

Delrael slogged ahead. His leather armor covered broad shoulders, but he wore no helmet to protect his head. Vailret saw bits of forest debris clinging to his cousin's brown hair from sleeping on the ground the night before. Even on an adventure, Delrael wore his gold rings, badges, and especially the silver belt his father had given him.

Delrael sighed. "About time we had another quest together—it's been, what, six years? The world is settling down too much. I spend all my time down at the game tables or practicing with the trainees at the Stronghold, and you waste away poring over manuscripts. We should find us a good cave to explore, maybe even an ancient dungeon left over from the early days of the Game."

Vailret squinted into the hazy air, frowning. "Bryl was looking for the Air Stone, not just wandering around for fun."

"Well, I wish he'd waited for us to give him some reinforcements— whoever heard of going on a quest by yourself?" Delrael shouldered branches and weeds aside, grumbling. "And now we have to rescue him."

Delrael had plenty of strength, charisma, and endurance for situations like this. Vailret was by no means weak, but he had trouble doing anything graceful with a broadsword or a battle-axe; and with his weak eyesight, he made a poor archer. He could prove his worth if they needed some serious thinking or planning. He had not been born with any Sorcerer blood, so he could not use magic to defend them.

"Next time, we'll have to teach him to leave a trail of breadcrumbs." Vailret brushed aside a beard of Spanish moss and followed behind his cousin.

Delrael pushed ahead without slowing. "Come on, we should be able to cross another hex or two before nightfall."

As the swamp thickened and began to drool with humidity, clouds of starving mosquitoes feasted on the two men. The forest sank in on itself, separated by scattered pools of stagnant water the color of tea. Dusty brown butterflies flitted across the ground.

Wide-boled cypress trees dangled branches like fingers and thrust knobby knees upward as if trying to keep their balance in the muck. Huge pitcher plants, large enough to swallow a man, gaped with wide and colorful mouths, exuding a sweet aroma that made Vailret feel dizzy. Curious, he peered down the gullet of one plant and saw partially digested birds and a dead frog. He stumbled away, breathing deeply to clear his head.

"When is this swamp terrain going to end?" Vailret heaved in a lungful of the thick air. Sweat seemed to hang on him. He thought of his own dwelling with the scented candles lit, with the manuscripts of scribbled folktales stacked up, waiting to be read....

Around midmorning, they encountered a stench so overpowering that it hit them like a slap on the face. Vailret pushed his nose into the crook of his elbow.

Delrael blinked his watering eyes. "We have to investigate."

"Don't you dare, Del!"

"Anything out of the ordinary. You know how to Play the Game. We can't just ignore it. Besides, I'm a fighter, remember? We might find Bryl."

Vailret grumbled to himself. "I'd like to have a talk with whoever wrote the damned Rules."

Thorns lined the rim of a wide cesspool. Decomposing matter and stagnant water had condensed into one horrible battering ram of smell.

More mammoth pitcher plants clustered near the thorn bushes, but the cloying narcotic fragrance did little to abate the cesspool's miasma. The slime-covered surface of the pool stirred, as if something actually lived within it.

"So now what do we do?" Vailret asked, covering his nostrils. He spoke in a whisper as the sounds of the swamp hummed and faded into the background. He focused his attention. "Wait, I hear something."

Delrael cocked his head. "What?"

A rhythmic crashing grew louder, nearing the cesspool. *Bom bom bom BAM!* Delrael stood up and stared into the forest across from the cesspool until Vailret pulled him down to cover. They watched through the tangled peepholes in the thorns.

Something massive stomped toward the pool, rattled a chain, and grumbled, accompanied by splashing sounds. Vailret blinked his eyes, trying to see more details, squinting until he had a headache.

A burly ogre emerged from the trees, wiping gobs of mud from his dirty fur garments. As he strode forward, the ogre knocked his spiked club against the cypress trunks, keeping his beat and smashing against every fourth trunk. *Bom bom bom BAM!* The wobbly cypress trees shivered with the impact.

The ogre stood nine feet tall, with muscles big enough for him to break rocks. A nose the size of a potato peeped out from between strands of long black hair like hand-drawn wire. One of the ogre's eye-sockets was empty, and his pockmarked face sported a drooping overhung lip. Garments of brown furs held themselves together with crude stitches that were popping in many places. His big feet squished swamp mud between his toes.

In his free hand, the ogre clasped a rusty iron chain that led to a small dragon like a dog on a leash. A bulky iron collar throttled the dragon's neck, apparently put on years before and never replaced as the creature grew. The dragon panted and wheezed, lolling a purple forked tongue and looking more like an overgrown crocodile than a fearsome fire-breathing reptile. Two stubby wings stuck upward from its body like arthritic elbows. Many of the dragon's scales had fallen off, and its pointed teeth were brown and cracked.

"Doesn't look like much of a dragon," Delrael said. "Nothing we can't handle. It'll be fun."

Vailret squeezed his eyes shut. He felt his heart leap, then grow cold. "The ogres were supposed to have been wiped out in the Scouring." Vailret breathed in deeply. His stomach churned, and sweat popped out from his pores. "Your father said he killed them all."

Vailret felt a bitterness in his voice that surprised even him. He kept seeing visions, ghosts from his childhood. He had only been eight years old, but the sight of the ogre brought all of his memories into razor-sharp focus—

He stood just inside the gate of the Stronghold, a little boy with his mother and his Aunt Fielle. His father Cayon had gone hunting with Uncle Drodanis, Delrael's father. By the first weeks of spring, everyone in the Stronghold got tired of the old stores buried in the cellars, and fresh meat would make a good feast down at Jorte's gaming hall. They might even dig up an early barrel of spring cider.

Cayon and Drodanis were always competing with each other, in the true Game spirit—dicing, hunting, weaponry contests. They had adventures that were legendary in the Game lore. But this time, Drodanis came back alone. Young Vailret watched his uncle plodding up the path of Steep Hill to reach the Stronghold on top. Drodanis had marched in silent grief through the village, bearing Cayon's body in his arms, letting the villagers' questions bounce off him unheard. Young Vailret was afraid, but he kept himself quiet. He didn't understand.

Aunt Fielle shuddered. Vailret's mother, Siya, watched in horror. Drodanis did not speak until he had met them at the gates, gently placing Cayon's body on the ground in front of the already-weeping Siya. Drodanis untied a sack from his waist and tossed the bloated head of an ogre to the dirt.

"I'm going to wipe out all of the ogres," he said.

Drodanis gathered a small party of the Stronghold's best trainees, including his wife Fielle, and set off eastward. Two months later, another slow procession returned with the heads of five ogres Drodanis and his fighters had slain, along with the bodies of two trainees…

Now, though, the one-eyed ogre stopped in front of the cesspool and looked around, unaware of the two men. The dragon strained against its chain, tongue lolling as it tried to reach the cesspool.

Vailret made fists, as if he were trying to strangle his knuckles. He had only a dagger with him. He wished he could cast a spell that would make the ground open up beneath the ogre's feet, but he was only human.

Delrael reached forward to clasp his cousin's shoulder. He squeezed, making it more than just an empty gesture. "What if he's got Bryl?"

Two weeks before, Vailret had been studying in his rooms at the Stronghold. Several candles burned on his table, and he had all the windows open to let in as much light as possible. Otherwise, Siya would nag him about reading in the dimness and ruining his eyesight further. Vailret disliked the candles because the crumbling old manuscripts were highly flammable.

Old Bryl, the half-breed Sorcerer who lived at the Stronghold, came in to bother Vailret, bored from watching Delrael train his students at the chopping posts or the archery targets. "Nobody's ever going to read a history of Hexworld, Vailret. Why bother with all this work?"

"It's important to me." Vailret looked up at him over the candle. "Don't be so defeatist all the time."

Bryl was short and frail-looking. Gray hair and a narrow gray beard stuck out from his head and chin. He wore the scarlet hooded cloak his father Qonnar had given him. At one time, Bryl had claimed the slick and shiny fabric had been woven of the threads from caterpillar cocoons, but nobody in the gaming hall believed him.

Vailret touched his fingertips together and explained to Bryl as if he were lecturing to a child. "Someone should set down the events of the Game. To the Outsiders, we're just an amusement, adventures to free them from their ennui—everything must be too perfect in their world. But to us, that's our *history*. The Game is worth nothing if we don't learn from previous turns."

Bryl puttered around with the artifacts and manuscripts on Vailret's table. The young man eyed him, exasperated. "What do you *want*, Bryl? Go play a game or something."

The man born of half-Sorcerer race shrugged and picked up a worn scrap of sheepskin. On the rough side, tiny letters had been painstakingly scratched into the surface. "What's this?"

Vailret removed the scrap from Bryl's fingers. He brushed at smudges the old man had left on the edges. "Please be careful—do you know how much we have to pay Scavengers for any one of these scraps?"

"I'm sorry." Bryl didn't seem to care. "Well, what does it say?"

Vailret sighed and put his elbow on the table. "If I tell you, will you leave me in peace for a while?"

"Of course," Bryl looked away, uneasy. He mumbled, "I thought you'd be glad I'm showing interest."

Vailret scowled, mostly at himself, and tried to cover up his expression by studying the manuscript. "It tells how the four elemental Stones were created as a parting gift from the old Sorcerers before they went on the Transition. They made one Stone with special powers for each element—Air, Water, Fire, and Earth. The ones who stayed behind were supposed to use the Stones as weapons to protect the humans and half-breeds left on Hexworld after the rest of the Sorcerers had gone."

"Where are the Stones now?" Bryl asked. He reached for one of the other scraps of writing, but Vailret deftly moved it out of his reach.

"Why don't you pay attention to things like that, Bryl? How many full-blooded Sentinels are left in the world?" He held up three fingers, flaunting them in front of the half-Sorcerer's face. "Enrod, who lives far to the east in the rebuilt city of Tairé—he holds the Fire Stone. And Sardun keeps the Water Stone in his Ice Palace to the north. He lives with his daughter."

Bryl narrowed his eyes. "My parents never taught me anything like that—they killed themselves when I was a child. As you're so quick to point out, there aren't very many Sentinels left. Who was going to teach me?" He waited in silence for a moment, then pointed to the manuscript. "Well, what about the other two Stones?"

"As near as I can tell," Vailret considered the scratches on the leather, searching for details, "the Air Stone and the Earth Stone were both lost during the battles. The magic in the Stones helped us wipe out a lot of surviving monsters, but now those Stones are gone."

He waited for Bryl to remember his promise and leave, but the little half-breed sat watching the dancing flame on the candle. He seemed hypnotized by the trails of wax crawling down the candlestick. Then Bryl snapped his gaze away from the flame and stared eastward with glassy eyes, as if looking through the walls of Vailret's dwelling.

He said in a distracted voice, "I have to go now." Muttering something about the Air Stone, he stumbled toward the door. Vailret watched him, baffled, and turned back to his work.

Next morning, Bryl was gone from the Stronghold. He had left a clumsily scrawled note behind. Vailret could imagine the length of time it had taken him to remember how to write all the letters.

"Think I know where AIR STONE is. Vision yesterday while listening to V. tell story. East, 10–12 hexes. Swamp terrain (?). Stone is in eye of skull, on pile of bones. Adventure and treasure. Going to get it."

Bryl's father had been a full Sorcerer, and his mother was a half-breed herself, but they had died when he was young, many, many years before, and no other Sorcerer had given Bryl full instruction on how to use his magic. Not that Bryl ever seemed concerned about it. And he had seen a glimpse of where he could find the lost Air Stone. He could have the Sorcerous power immediately, with no hard training. Maybe Bryl thought it would make up for the magic he had never been able to use before. *Bryl*, a man who couldn't care less where the Stone came from or what its history was—

Vailret resented the way the Rules excluded him from such revelations. Being only a human, he had to sweat over old manuscripts, sift through folktales and remembrances, cramming his brain with details he hoped would come together. Bryl had such power handed to him on a serving platter. If the half-Sorcerer brought the precious Air Stone back to the Stronghold, Vailret could never use its magic, not even to study it.

Since then, two weeks had passed, and still Bryl did not return. Delrael decided to go find him, and Vailret followed.

At the cesspool, the dragon bounded forward, jerking the ogre's arm and nearly pulling him off his feet. The ogre grumbled and kicked the dragon, catching one of its back ridges with his bare toe.

Unconcerned, the dragon stopped at the brink of the cesspool and waited as the ogre scooped at the surface, exposing fresh bilge water.

"Aww, it shore be hot, Rognoth," he rumbled at the dragon, wiping his brow with a muddy finger. The ogre bent to scoop up a handful of the thick water, slurping it with satisfaction on his face. Green scum ran between his fingers to plop back into the water.

Vailret winced.

Rognoth the dragon bent to lap up some of the water as the ogre straightened and pointed a proud finger at himself. "Ahhhh! Gairoth knows how to keep his cesspool!" The dragon's tail twitched like a convulsing python.

"Ogres aren't supposed to be able to talk!" Vailret whispered.

"Maybe he's part human," Delrael said. "A human breeding with an ogre? That's disgusting."

Vailret scowled. "The Outsiders have a sick sense of humor sometimes."

The ogre rubbed his hands together, as if getting down to business. He raised the club over his head, bringing it down with a crash on the edge of the pool. A chain of shock-wave ripples marched across the coated surface of the water. Gairoth slammed his club down again and again, sending thunderclaps through the swamp.

"Wake up, you!" the ogre bellowed at the cesspool. The dragon bolted for the forest, slinking close to the ground, but Gairoth jerked on his chain. Rognoth whined miserably.

The ogre grinned as a translucent, spine-covered tentacle reached up from below the surface. The tentacle coiled in the air, reaching for Gairoth, but the ogre bent back out of the way. The pool stirred again, and more thin tentacles whipped in the air. The body sack of a gigantic jellyfish, hemispherical and milky translucent, broke through the scum. A lumpy ridge crowned the creature, speckled with dots of color. Deep inside the thing's skin, a splash of scarlet outlined a small human form.

Vailret stiffened, startled. Bryl! He tugged on his cousin's arm, and Delrael nodded.

The jellyfish churned in the water, waving tentacles. "In you go, Rognoth!" Gairoth caught the dragon as he made one last attempt to flee, then hurled him into the cesspool with a grunt of effort. The dragon paddled frantically back toward the shore.

The tentacled thing ejected the form of Bryl, apparently seeing more interesting prey. Gairoth rubbed his hands together as the jellyfish drifted toward the dragon, then he lumbered toward the other side of the pool where the red-cloaked Bryl floated face down in the bilge.

Rognoth whimpered as the first thin tentacles wrapped around his tail and lower body, but his patchy scales provided temporary protection from the paralyzing needles. Gairoth waded into the cesspool, fished out the half-Sorcerer, and sloshed back to shore before the jellyfish could notice him.

Finished with his work, Gairoth strode back to the dragon. The ogre dropped the slime-covered burden of Bryl and picked up his club. "Come on, Rognoth. We gots to go home."

Two more tentacles had coiled around the dragon's neck. Rognoth floundered in the water. Gairoth gave a sigh of disgust and fished in the pool for the end of the dragon's chain. He found it and pulled with enough force to stretch Rognoth's neck out of joint. The dragon ripped free, tearing off three of the jellyfish's tentacles in the process. Rognoth scrambled to the shore and collapsed, panting and wheezing. A laugh belched from Gairoth's lungs. "Haw! Haw!"

He grabbed Bryl's pale foot and dragged the half-Sorcerer behind him into the forest. A thin trail of slime trickled along the ground. Rognoth lay on the ground shivering, then got shakily to his feet, following the ogre into the trees.

Delrael sighed. "It's all part of the Game."

Vailret's anger bubbled up within him, but he brought it under control. He had never seen an ogre up close before, and now he wished he could destroy Gairoth and finish the job his uncle Drodanis had begun. Wheels turned in his head as he considered the possibilities. They would have to think of a sophisticated way to fight Gairoth. Vailret's father had pitted his luck and battle skill against an ogre—and he'd lost. This would take something more. A slow smile grew on his face.

"You're thinking of something, aren't you?" Delrael cocked an eyebrow and looked at him. "What are we going to do?"

"I always think of something." Vailret took a deep breath. "It's going to be good. Even the Outsiders might enjoy it."

"That's what we're here for." Delrael shrugged, ready for anything.

Gairoth's feet had left deep impressions in the soft ground. Following, Delrael bent low, taking one careful step at a time. Vailret tried to imitate him.

Up ahead, Gairoth snapped branches and grumbled curses. After a brief silence, Vailret and Delrael crept closer. Uneasy and afraid of what they would see, they slipped behind a large lichen-encrusted boulder and looked into Gairoth's encampment.

The ogre sat cross-legged in a small and cluttered clearing, munching on a bone torn from the rotting carcass of what appeared to be a goat with reptilian legs. The dragon drooled and fixed large yellow eyes on the oozing meat, intent on his master's jaws as they churned up and down. The spiked club lay close beside Gairoth's leg.

Behind the clearing stood the ogre's abode—the hollowed-out rib cage of some massive beast. Dried sinews and scattered furs covered the bones to provide some shelter but left plenty of gaps for flies to get in (and out again after they had smelled the stench). A small pile of treasure lay beside the tumbledown dwelling: jewel-studded weapons, gold artifacts, and gaudy ornaments.

Wedged into one of the monster ribs sat a small skull the size of a child's ... and inside the skull's eye-socket shone a fist-sized diamond, pyramid-shaped, like a four-sided die. It glinted in the hazy swamp light. Though Vailret's weak eyesight blurred the details, he remembered Bryl's vision of the diamond. "Stone is in eye of skull, on pile of bones."

Vailret's eyes reflected the splashes of sunlight shining through the woven swamp foliage. The Air Stone—he thought of holding something so old, so powerful in his hands. The old Sorcerers had made it before they left Hexworld.

He thought of all the stories he had heard about the Stone, its origin, its history—and the power of illusion it held. It was still the weakest of the four Stones, but it could be used very effectively with a little imagination.

But as far as Vailret was concerned, the Air Stone might as well be just another diamond. Without Sorcerer blood, he could not use the magic.

Bryl never worked at his abilities, nor did he know much about the background of his race. Vailret spent all his time staring at the legends, trying to uncover the reasons, straining his mind to be worthy, all in vain. He gritted his teeth.

Delrael tugged on Vailret's arm, pointing at a red-cloaked and dripping figure strung by his feet to a branch of an overhanging cypress. Vailret saw no signs of life in the half-Sorcerer's wet and grayish skin.

Gairoth pulled another appendage from the carcass, making a sucking pop as it separated from the rest of the meat. The ogre licked his lips and slurped oozing flesh off the bone. "Ahhh, aged perfect!" Gairoth sucked the last of the juices from the bone. Rognoth sat, entranced with his master's meal.

"Time for us to split up," Delrael whispered.

Vailret nodded. "Luck."

"Luck. We'll get the job done." Delrael left his cousin where he was and slipped off into the forest.

Delrael drew a deep breath, heady from the adventure. Vailret's plan buzzed through his head—everything seemed perfectly clear in his mind. Ah, it made him feel alive again, not stagnating in the interminable training classes that kept all the fighters in practice. The Outsiders had done little in years to make life interesting.

In the clearing, the ogre tossed a thick bone to Rognoth. The dragon snapped it up, cracking the bone open with a yellowed fang and spilling the runny marrow down his throat.

Delrael took five deep breaths, closing his eyes and coiling his muscles. *Ready, ready, ready*—wish me luck. This was what the Game was all about. With a grin on his mud-spattered face, he stood up and strode into the ogre's camp.

Rognoth let the bone fall from his mouth, snorting menacing clouds of smoke. His chain clanked as he took one step forward. With the instincts of a fighter, Delrael assessed how long it took for Gairoth's reflexes to react. The ogre dropped his meat and scrabbled for the club.

The man paid them no heed as he swaggered into the clearing, whistling to himself. He sat down and faced the astonished expressions of both the ogre and the dragon. "Howdy, neighbors."

Taken aback, Gairoth rubbed his thumb on the wood of his club and took one step forward. "What you be?"

"What you mean?" Delrael blinked his eyes innocently. He lowered his voice, speaking with a gruff and thick-lipped accent.

"Be you *human*?" The ogre's face brightened for an instant, then he frowned again. "You plenty bigger than him." He jerked his thumb over to waterlogged Bryl hanging from the tree.

Delrael laughed. "Naw—me not be human. Me be *ogre*, like you be." He smiled broadly, knowing Gairoth could never have seen his own reflection in the scum-covered cesspools. He held his impulses in check —his arms wanted to grab for the sword, lunge forward, and hack at the ogre. But he knew his uncle Cayon had failed, and if a fighter like Cayon had not been able to defeat an ogre with his strength, then Delrael had little chance.

Gairoth looked down at his dirty furs, brushing off cakes of dried mud. He scratched his scalp as he glared at the young man's own mud-stained clothes, the leather armor. Gairoth's mouth hung open as if he were going to say something but hadn't found the words yet. Delrael beat him to it.

"Gairoth's furs better than mine be. Me bonked another human, took his clothes. But don't worry. Me ogre too."

The ogre blinked his eyes. "Uh ..."

Delrael jabbed a finger at himself. "Me be in swamp all these years. Never bothered to say Howdy! Watched you long time, though, Gairoth. Uh, I be—" (Gairoth, Rognoth ... what's in a name?) "Delroth."

The ogre hadn't moved or relaxed his grip on the club. "How come you *talk*, Delroth?"

Delrael paused a moment. "Huh?"

"You be no ogre—you talk!"

"Ha!" Delrael felt a cold sweat. "You talk, Gairoth. You be ogre. How come you talk?" Judging from the monster's expression, Delrael saw he had struck a point of pride.

"Gairoth be an *in-tell-ee-gent* ogre. My Paw was Sorcerer, but he dead now. Paw give Gairoth smarts—Maw give Gairoth muscles!"

To emphasize his statement, he bashed his club against the dirt.

The stench from the rancid meat made Delrael feel queasy. Vailret had told him once how, near the end of their centuries-long wars, the desperate and dying Sorcerers had interbred with humans, whom they had created, to restore the strength of their race—but Delrael had no idea the Sorcerers had been driven to breed with their other creations, especially something so foul and ugly as a female ogre!

But the laws of probability allowed even the most unlikely dice rolls, given enough turns.

Delrael forced a yawn, trying to appear at ease. He looked at the grayish form of Bryl, hanging from the nearby tree. "What that be, Gairoth? Dessert?"

The ogre spoke around a dripping mouthful of meat. "Naw—he be Sorcerer too. He teach Gairoth how to use magic Stone." With his elbow, he indicated the gleaming diamond in the tiny skull's eye. Delrael saw the diamond and decided that it must be the Air Stone Vailret had gotten so excited about. He looked back at the half-Sorcerer.

"He be dead?" Delrael brushed a fly away from his face.

"Naw. He be awake soon enough."

"You feeds him to the thing in the cesspool? What for?"

The ogre shrugged. "Keeps him from running away. And makes him skeered of Gairoth."

"Thing don't hurt him? Just hold him there?"

Gairoth reached for his club again. "Questions! Talk!" he spat.

Delrael spread his hands. "Gairoth be in-tell-ee-gent ogre. You gots answers."

That did the trick. "Aaahhh. I dips him into a pitcher plant afore I feeds him to that thing. Jellyfish can't digest him then."

Delrael rubbed his hands together. "Real smart. Haw, haw!"

Vailret crouched in the underbrush as close to the half-Sorcerer as he dared to go. The hanging form of Bryl stirred, but Vailret couldn't risk making a move just yet. He wished Delrael would hurry up. He wanted to go home.

"So, Gairoth," Delrael leaned forward and lowered his voice. "How you keep treasure pile safe? I be scared someone steal mine. Humans, adventurers, quests—you know how the Game be. I works my fingers to the bone to get jewels, then can't never leave my camp. Afraid treasure might get stole."

Hidden in the underbrush, Vailret squirmed and motioned for his cousin to hurry. Delrael didn't notice him.

"Hey, you wants to see my treasure?" Delrael smiled, open and friendly. "Promise not to steal it? I gots no guards. But I trust Gairoth. You be good neighbor."

Even from his distant viewpoint, Vailret thought he could see the gleam in the ogre's eye. Soon … soon.

Gairoth stood up, ready to follow Delrael. Then, to Vailret's dismay, the ogre turned around and plucked the skull with the Air Stone from his dwelling. "Now we go."

No! I wanted the Stone! Vailret shouted in his mind.

Delrael looked at the pyramid-shaped diamond swallowed up in the ogre's hand and flicked a glance toward where Vailret hid. Vailret noticed his cousin heave a sigh as he motioned Gairoth to follow him into the swamp. The dragon bounded along, eager.

When the trees blocked them from sight, Vailret emerged from his hiding place, holding a hand to his stiff back. Flies buzzed around his head.

He cautiously went to where the half-Sorcerer hung dripping. Greenish-brown water puddled in the dirt below him. Bryl seemed to be regaining his consciousness and vitality, but too slowly to help. According to the Rules, he would take about a half-day to recover completely. Vailret scowled, knowing he'd have to carry the half-Sorcerer on his back. Bryl's red cloak and scraggly gray hair reeked like the loathsome cesspools, and the smell would soak into Vailret's jerkin.

He grumbled at the invisible Outsiders, knowing they would never listen. "Why don't you go play a game of hexagon-chess? Why don't you make me a magic user? Why can't you entertain yourselves and leave us alone?"

Vailret withdrew his knife and cut the rope, catching Bryl as he fell. He hiked the half-Sorcerer across his shoulder blades and stooped as he scuttled forward. Delrael was the one who had the strength score for this type of work, but he was preoccupied at the moment. Bryl stirred, and the smell of spoiled-everything rose into the air.

Vailret sighed. It was nearly over—all the Game adventures had become tedious. Predictable. Vailret would rather be finishing his history of Hexworld—not stuck with these frivolous, familiar quests the Outsiders played all the time.

Grunting with the effort, he shifted Bryl's bony body to a more comfortable position, then moved away from Gairoth's encampment toward the cesspool.

"It be gone!" Delrael wailed. "Stole!"

Rognoth nearly collapsed after the wild-goose chase the man had led through the swamp, circling back and forth, getting even the ogre hopelessly lost. But Delrael's tracker-sense would not let him get confused.

Delrael stared at the clearing they had stumbled upon, pointing an accusatory finger. He gaped at the ogre, incredulous. "Gold, gems—right here! All be gone! Someone stole it!" He switched his own dismayed expression for one of horror. "Oh, no! You be next, Gairoth! Hurry!"

The ogre looked as if he grasped what was going on. "Come on, Rognoth!" Gairoth smacked the dragon with the end of his club. "We gots to get home!"

Delrael crossed his fingers, hoping Vailret had done his part. Everything seemed to be going well, *too well* for a Game adventure, and he wondered how long the Outsiders would keep making dice rolls in his favor.

He sprinted after the alarmed ogre.

Vailret slogged through the swamp, stumbling with the added weight of the unconscious half-Sorcerer. Bryl hung like a half-full sack of wet flour on his shoulders, and Vailret's muscles felt as if they wanted to snap. Most of all, he ached for not being able to grab the Air Stone. Why had Gairoth taken it? Damned monster! Why hadn't Bryl managed to get it somehow? And the worst insult of all was that Gairoth—*Gairoth!*— had Sorcerer blood in him and could use the magic inside the diamond. It seemed ridiculously arbitrary.

The heavy stench made the air difficult to breathe near the cesspool. Vailret's eyes stung. He found a weed-sheltered place where he could set the half-Sorcerer down. The cesspool seemed quiet now, waiting.

Vailret peeled off Bryl's sopping scarlet cloak. He removed a blanket from his pack and tossed it on top of the half-Sorcerer.

Bryl snored softly.

In the background of the swamp, he could hear Gairoth bellowing. The insect songs fell silent for a moment, then continued.

Vailret crumpled the soggy cloak into a ball before tossing it onto the scum of the pool. Then he sat back to watch the tentacled thing rise to the surface, waving its whiplike appendages and curling around the scarlet fabric. The creature pulled the cloak beneath the scum, like new prey.

Lurching forward as fast as he could, Gairoth reached his camp and smashed the spiked club against a tree trunk. He roared a battle cry that made the air vibrate, holding high the skull with the Air Stone. Rognoth lunged to the end of his chain, snarling.

But they found no one to fight.

Rognoth blinked his eyes. Gairoth came to a full stop, confused. "Haw! We skeered 'em off! They gots none of my treasure! Haw!" Gairoth mopped his brow.

Breathless, Delrael reached the camp and flashed a glance to the trees. He saw the damp patch on the ground where cesspool water had dribbled from Bryl's cloak, but the half-Sorcerer was gone.

Rognoth raised his scaly nose in the air, looking around with runny yellow eyes. When he saw the spot where Bryl had been, he snorted clouds of black, oily smoke.

"Shut up, stupid dragon! Nothing be there!" Gairoth snatched up a bone from the ground and bounced it off Rognoth's head.

"Gairoth, they gots your magic man!" Delrael pointed to the severed rope hanging from the cypress branch.

The ogre let his mouth drop open. Rognoth leaped to his feet, but the chain strangled him and he wheezed. Gairoth turned around in circles, looking for someone to hit with his club.

Delrael saw that the ogre needed help. "Cesspool! But we catch 'em! Bonk! Quick!" He gave Gairoth a helpful shove in the right direction.

Rognoth galloped down the path as Gairoth stumbled after him, clinging to the iron chain. The ogre clutched the skull in his hand, holding the Air Stone in place with his thumb as he grasped the thick iron chain. But he didn't seem to know what to do with the diamond. Delrael ran behind.

The dragon reached the edge of the cesspool, with Gairoth fighting to keep his footing. They arrived just in time to see the tentacled creature swallow something bright and scarlet. Rognoth yelped and leaped ahead, not slowing down as he reached the bank.

"Stupid dragon!" Gairoth bellowed. He let go of the chain, but it became tangled around the Air Stone and the skull. Both the dragon and the ogre plunged into the cesspool, vanishing under the scum. Rognoth splashed to the surface, looking around, tongue lolling out. A whine broke from his throat as he realized where he had landed. Clawing at the thick water, he began to swim.

Gairoth emerged, pulling duckweed out of his eye and spitting green sludge from his mouth. Delrael saw with dismay that the skull in the ogre's hand had broken. The Air Stone had sunk to the bottom of the foul cesspool.

In the water, Gairoth's gaze settled on the pitiful dragon. His nostrils flared, and the cypress trees trembled as he roared his rage. "Rognoth!"

The dragon gulped as the ogre heaved the spiked club out of the cesspool and sloshed toward him. Threads of green slime dribbled from the club into the water, following Gairoth as he moved. Rognoth ducked under the deep water just as the ogre swung at him with a crashing blow.

Delrael sauntered up to the edge of the pool, chuckling. Vailret emerged from his hiding place but looked downcast at seeing the Air Stone gone. He watched Gairoth's struggles in the water without sympathy. Vailret heaved a limp and groggy Bryl to his feet, bringing him into view.

The ogre stopped splashing and glared at them, astonished and betrayed. Delrael couldn't resist adding a last comment. "Now you've gone and lost the Air Stone, you clod. But we've got your magic man!"

Gairoth exploded in fury and charged toward the young man, but he stumbled in the mire. The ogre scrambled to his feet again and shook his fist in the air. "Delroth! I gonna bash you!"

Spine-covered tentacles rose up and writhed around him, translucent and glinting in the slanting afternoon light. A tentacle slapped around

Gairoth's neck, and another slimy appendage grabbed his ankle and jerked him under the water.

Rognoth paddled toward the shore, but he could go no farther than his chain allowed.

The bulbous body sack of the jellyfish rose to the surface and burbled; more tentacles emerged, wrapping around Gairoth. The ogre thrashed right and left, annoyed and helpless.

Tentacles coiled around the dragon's tail, but Rognoth whirled and snapped at them, biting deeply into the translucent flesh.

"Time to get going, Vailret," Delrael said. "How's Bryl?"

Vailret shrugged but kept looking dejectedly at the cesspool. "Why did Gairoth have to drop the Air Stone? Now we've lost it all over again!"

Delrael smiled. "At least we know *where* it is. Maybe there's another quest in the offing?"

"It would keep the Outsiders satisfied, I guess." He picked up his pack and wrapped Bryl in the blanket. "You carry him, Del. Your strength score is a lot higher than mine."

Gairoth finally yanked his right hand free and with a thick slurping sound pulled the club out of the slime. Dragging himself toward the jellyfish with its own tentacles, the ogre bashed his club into the mass of the creature's head. More tentacles wrapped around the ogre's face, and both monsters went under the water thrashing.

Delrael hiked the half-Sorcerer over his shoulder. "Well, do you think the Outsiders enjoyed that one? The whole adventure?"

Vailret frowned at him, puzzled. "Why shouldn't they? It's the same type of stuff they've always liked."

They walked off, listening to the bellows and splashings from the cesspool until the sounds vanished into other swamp noises. Soon they would reach the hex-line and be back into forest terrain.

But Vailret kept thinking about Delrael's question. *What if the Outsiders are no longer interested?* It felt like a premonition.

INTERLUDE: OUTSIDE

David yawned, making sure everybody saw him. Tyrone smiled with delight at the adventure, but Melanie saw Scott fidgeting. He and David seemed … disinterested. She couldn't understand what had changed for them.

David picked at his fingernails.

Tyrone finally asked, "What's up your butt, David?"

Melanie nodded. "You've never been this bad before."

David looked at her, and suddenly, Melanie had a sinking feeling that they had done exactly what he wanted. Now he could always say *they* had raised the question.

"Since you ask—" David dropped a handful of dice on the table with a loud clatter, "there's something I'd like to bring up."

Melanie frowned as he looked at each of them in turn, like Charlie Chan about to announce his pick for the Murderer of the Month.

"I think we should quit playing the Game."

Even Tyrone, who was usually happy to play anything someone suggested, gasped in surprise.

"But why?" Melanie asked.

"It's boring. We've been at it too long. There's nothing left to it—it's not interesting anymore. Is that enough reasons? Look at the adventure we just finished: good, standard stuff. A big bad ogre, some treasure, an exciting chase. Your characters tricked their way out of it, as they always do, Melanie. It's like watching *Star Trek* reruns—they're great for a few years, but it gets old after a while." He brushed at the sleeve of his denim jacket.

"And aren't *we* getting a little old for this stuff too? Do you know how much crap I take from my parents about our stupid Game every week?"

Melanie stared at him, then at Scott and Tyrone, then at the dice scattered across the table. Anger kept her voice even. "Would you rather go out for sports, David? Be a jock? Or how about hanging around in video arcades turning into a joystick zombie? Would your parents prefer that?

"The Game makes us put *ourselves* into a world we made up. Think of all we've done, all the history we've made. That's a lot more important than bouncing a ball through a hoop."

Scott looked at her a bit in surprise. "Don't go overboard, Mel. This is just a game. It's nothing real."

"Are New York or the Rocky Mountains real? Have you ever been there? No! Then how do you know *they* exist? Huh?"

She thought of Hexworld, the villages, the characters. Every one of them seemed to be real to her. Couldn't the others see it? Or feel it? Scott blinked at her vehemence, which surprised even Melanie. She could feel something going on here, something important.

Since the four of them had equal experience in role-playing, they took turns acting as Game-master. Each of them ruled a particular section of the map and interacted with the other players.

"Why don't we just go back to exploring dungeons? That was fun," Tyrone said.

Scott made a rude noise. "*Those* were boring, Tyrone. Wandering through catacombs gets monotonous really quick. And what do all the monsters eat? What do they do all the time? You can't say they just stand there waiting for our characters to come along. How am I supposed to have fun if I can't *believe* any of it?"

Melanie grabbed at the idea. "But we outgrew the boxed dungeon adventures! We broadened the Game to cover an entire world. *Our* world. Didn't you enjoy the old Sorcerer wars, David? You thought of that."

Tyrone said, "I liked it when the old Sorcerers created all sorts of creatures to do their fighting, not just humans."

"Oh, you just like monsters," Scott said.

David used a cracker to scoop up some of Tyrone's dip. "Yes, and the fighting got boring too. Battle after battle in a war that was never going to end. What's the point?"

"We had the Sorcerers make peace between themselves. They used the rest of their magic to turn the race into six giant Spirits. The *Transition*. We should have known enough to end it there."

"There was more to the story!" Melanie said. Why weren't Scott and Tyrone helping? "How could you just stop the Game there?"

She began to feel clammy sweat on her back. What if they put Hexworld away to gather dust on a shelf, never to play it again? What about the world? What about the characters?

"I tried," David sighed.

"But I won. Roll of the dice."

"Yeah, Melanie," Scott added, "and we spent the past three months playing the Scouring of Hexworld. The humans and a few leftover Sorcerers hunted down surviving monsters to make the world safe for Mom, democracy, and apple pie. Tyrone had a lot of fun. But the humans are all settled down now. You've got your Stronghold established and safe. There's nothing else to play."

"I want to quit," David repeated.

"No." Melanie tried to glare him down.

"Doesn't matter to me," Tyrone said. "I thought even the dungeons were fun."

Scott pursed his lips, putting on his coldly logical "Mr. Science" persona again. "Settle it like we always settle disagreements. Why don't you two just roll for it instead of arguing?"

Tyrone shifted in his seat. "I'd like to play *something* tonight—it is Sunday, you know."

Melanie watched David, and they both reached for the twenty-sided die at the same time. David grabbed it first.

"If I beat you, we stop playing. We think of something else to do, or we stop meeting altogether. We've got our lives to live, you know."

Tyrone and Scott sat up straight. Melanie took a deep breath. David was serious—it meant more to him than she had thought. Something worse than this was bothering him.

But the Game meant even more to her. She wanted to hold on to the world they had created. Hexworld was a part of her and a part of them all. They couldn't just put it away and forget about it like a game of Monopoly.

David squeezed his hand around the die. He threw it down hard onto the smooth painted surface of the master map. The die bounced, but came to rest before it could fall off the table.

"18."

"Eighteen, Melanie. You won't beat it."

She picked up the twenty-sided die—the expensive transparent kind from the hobby shop. Each facet looked smooth and perfect, with a number etched in the center.

"But if I win the roll, we keep playing. We stay in Hexworld with all our characters there. No chickening out."

David bristled at that, but Scott and Tyrone remained silent.

As she leaned forward over the master map, Melanie felt that she could fall into the world.

She imagined the mountains, the forests, the islands, the frozen wasteland, vivid against a backdrop of the history they had played.

She closed her eyes, silently asked for help from whomever else watched over Hexworld, and tossed the twenty-sided die onto the table. "Come on!" she whispered. The die skittered and rolled and came to rest against the master map.

The "20" faced up.

"Yowza!" Tyrone clapped his hands.

"There." Scott sounded businesslike again. "Now can we get started? It's your turn next, isn't it, David?"

David glared at the twenty-sided die that had betrayed him.

"Come on, David. Don't be a sore loser."

He drank from his glass but continued to look at the map. "If we don't quit, I'm going to destroy Hexworld. I'll have my turn and I can set things in motion. There won't be anything left to play in. Then we'll have to stop."

"You've got to follow the rules," Scott said.

"I'm going to. But I'll unleash something so horrible upon this world that nothing can stop it. Your characters can try all they want. It won't work. I'm going to win."

Melanie stiffened. Scott and Tyrone seemed to be enjoying the friction. Melanie thought of the Game's characters, looked at their settlements, their lands, and felt a pang inside her. Something seemed to be calling out to her.

Melanie ran her fingertip over one of the smooth faces of the twenty-sided. She hoped she hadn't used up her luck for the evening. She wished the characters themselves could help in the fight—if only they knew what the stakes were.

She wanted to warn them somehow.

"The rules work both ways, you know. I can use them to *save* Hexworld." Melanie forced a smile, trying to look self-assured and a little wicked. "I'll beat you, David. You can count on it."

CHAPTER 2
ATTACK ON THE STRONGHOLD

Hexworld has been built around a precise set of Rules. Though we may find them restrictive at times, these Rules can never be broken, lest we invite chaos and anarchy into the world.
—Preface, *The Book of Rules*

Making good time, while carrying Bryl, Delrael and Vailret crossed nine hexagons of terrain. They reached the Stronghold by the evening of the third day.

Vailret wished he had remembered to bring map paper with him to mark the terrain and keep his bearings. Delrael claimed to have memorized the colorful mosaic master map inlaid into one wall back at the Stronghold.

The trees were thick and full, the undergrowth colorful and lush. Clear-cut paths wound through thick stands of oak, maple, and pine, leading off to various adventures. But all the terrain had been explored and mapped, all the dungeons uncovered, all the adventures played out and exhausted in days long past.

A clear stream followed the boundary between two hexes of forest terrain. One willow dangled over the bank, like a Medusa washing her hair in the water.

During the bloody Scouring, well-organized human armies and magic-using Sentinels had removed most of the enemy monsters from the map. The Outsiders had not seen fit to create any major new threats for more than a century. The forests had once been inhabited by ogres, sasquatches, packs of intelligent wolves, marauding bands of reptilian Slac—all descendants of monsters that the old Sorcerers had created to fight in their wars. Vailret's father had been killed by one of the surviving ogres.

Vailret imagined Cayon, a great fighter but hopelessly outclassed by the ogre in the early morning mists. Drodanis, his uncle, had told of awakening to the sounds of battle, seeing the campfire cold and his brother's blankets neatly folded. In a clearing, he had found Cayon and the ogre—two of Cayon's arrows protruded from the ogre's back.

Vailret tried to remember, but somehow he could not picture his father's face. He recalled only a few rare occasions when Cayon had focused attention on him; how frightening and godlike the great warrior had seemed. The memory of his father eluded him, but the ogre seemed real, vivid to the last wrinkle in his leathery skin.

Drodanis said he had drawn his bow to join in the fight. He thought Cayon had looked impish, as if trying to show off with his sword. *Why?* Vailret kept wanting to ask him. *It was so stupid! Because of that, you were killed! Who were you trying to impress? I was proud of you anyway.*

The ogre had swept his club sideways, breaking Cayon's wrist and knocking the sword from his hand. Drodanis sank an arrow into the ogre's chest, but the monster still drove at his first victim. Cayon stood ashen gray and tried to stumble backward, out of the way. The ogre smashed the twisted club across Cayon's chest, spraying blood into the forest. Drodanis roared in rage, sank three more arrows into the monster's back and neck, and then launched himself upon the wounded ogre, slashing with his sword from behind—

Vailret had heard the story many times from others in the gaming hall. Drodanis had completed his pogrom against the ogres, and then became a recluse behind the walls of the Stronghold. He had never spoken of Cayon's death after the first time, not once in all the hours he had spent staring at manuscripts with young Vailret....

About an hour after Vailret and Delrael had left the ogre's cesspool behind, Bryl came back to full consciousness. The half-Sorcerer walked by himself now. He moved a little slowly, but they made better time than when Delrael carried him. Bryl sulked, ashamed and grumbling to himself. "Wish we didn't have to leave the Air Stone there."

"It's at the bottom of the cesspool," Delrael said, turning around on the path. Vailret had watched Delrael's impatience with Bryl grow, watched him tense every time the half-Sorcerer said anything, but until now, he had been able to stifle his urge to speak out. "Do you want us to take you back so you can dive for it? Or maybe you'd like to ask Gairoth for help?"

Bryl moaned quietly. "I just wanted to have more magic. I don't know much—it could have helped us all." Delrael made a rude noise, and the half-Sorcerer turned to him, looking defensive. "Well, *you* imagine being trapped inside a giant jellyfish, just waiting to be digested —and your only hope of survival is a dim-witted ogre who might not remember to come back before it's too late." Bryl sounded indignant. "I was just trying to find the Air Stone. Gairoth tortured me! He made me teach him how to use the Stone!"

Vailret spoke softly but with enough seriousness to make Bryl pay attention. "By showing Gairoth how to unlock the magic, you've given an ogre one of the most powerful weapons left on Hexworld. A weapon that was specifically given to *humans*." He saw Delrael ball his fists.

Bryl looked broken and upset. "He shouldn't have been able to use the magic anyway. How was I supposed to know an ogre could have Sorcerer blood?"

Vailret scowled at him, beginning to lose patience himself. "You should have known something was wrong when an ogre could speak."

"You know I don't study things like that."

"Maybe you should consider it." Vailret sighed, letting his anger drain away. He squinted through the trees to see the boundary of the forest. The light had grown dim in the late afternoon, but he sensed they were near the Stronghold.

Bryl sounded close to despair. "What are we going to do?"

Delrael kept walking, plainly upset. "Good thing the Stronghold can keep Gairoth out if worse comes to worst." They came upon a cross path and Delrael paused, looking both ways to take his bearings. He turned left and set off. Vailret and Bryl followed.

The sun had set behind them as they crossed from the last hex of forest terrain to the flat agricultural areas. Narrow roads separated the hexagonal fields from the unclaimed areas, but the fields had expanded outward as more and more characters settled around the Stronghold. All the cropland had been reclaimed since the Scouring, and the human foothold had grown stronger as characters worked the land, tending to their own existence rather than questing for treasure or adventure.

Vailret could see the Stronghold perched on the crown of Steep Hill, overlooking the village and surrounding lands like a sleeping watchdog. The double-walled stockade appeared imposing even to Vailret. Just the sight of the structure evoked thoughts of epic adventures in his mind.

At the beginning of the Scouring, the great General Doril had built the Stronghold. He wanted to help protect the poor farmers and miners trying to make a life for themselves against the back-and-forth tides of the wars. Doril had chosen Steep Hill, which stood rugged and unscalable from the rear, cut off to the north by a swift stream, and open to assault only on the south and west sides. An attacking army would break most of its momentum charging up the abominably steep path.

A double wall of pointed logs surrounded the Stronghold proper. The villagers had packed the gaps between the outer and inner walls with dirt, more than doubling the strength of the barricade and making it almost fire proof at the same time. A steep trench encircled the Stronghold walls, as deep as a man stood tall. The trench was filled with pointed rocks and sharp sticks.

The Stronghold had withstood serious attacks during the long Scouring wars. Monstrous Slac armies had besieged it several times, but the Stronghold had never fallen. Now, few of the Slac still existed on Hexworld, and they hid themselves in the mountains to the east, letting humans live in peace. The Stronghold had not seen an enemy in years, and Vailret suspected that many of its defenses were obsolete.

The days of empty questing had faded away, leaving the characters to attend to problems of day-to-day survival. No one bothered to remember the old adventures.

Seven years before, more than half a decade after the death of Cayon, the peaceful times had lulled Drodanis out of his gloomy seclusion. Vailret liked to think that if an enemy had indeed threatened, Delrael's father would never have left the Stronghold in the hands of his eighteen-year-old son and a couple of old veterans from his early campaigns. Vailret had been only fourteen then, and he had wanted to accompany Drodanis on his self-indulgent quest to find the Rulewoman Melanie. But Drodanis had chosen someone else, leaving Vailret behind.

In the seven years since, Delrael had done little more than train the villagers and miners over and over again, killing time until something adventurous happened. It seemed that the Outsiders took little interest in Hexworld, tired of throwing threats at their hapless characters. This pleased Vailret, though—the characters could worry about their *lives*, instead of tedious adventures. He could go about writing down the history of the Game....

Dusk had set in as they started along the pathway up Steep Hill. Already Vailret could see Jorte getting his gaming hall ready for the evening, where the villagers would gather for dicing and other amusements. Characters in the village below had seen them return and they'd all want to hear the story of Bryl's rescue and the adventure with Gairoth. It would be their first quest-telling in a long time.

But Vailret didn't much like the loud gaming and conversation. He hoped he could talk Delrael into describing the adventure by himself—he only wanted to get back to his work on the old manuscripts. Documenting the quest on paper was as important as telling it. More important, in fact, because his original words could remain unexaggerated in telling after telling.

At the top of the hill, they crossed the split-log walkway spanning the trench and passed through the only gate in the Stronghold walls. Heavy wooden mallets hung on ropes next to the walkway, ready to knock out the pegs and sever the walkway in case of an invasion. Directly on the other side of the heavy gate was another hidden pit covered by a second walkway.

Vailret's mother, Siya, stood outside the main building. Her hair was dusted with early gray, and she wore it pulled back in a tight braid, which stretched her wrinkles tight but left her scowl firmly in place.

"It's about time," Siya said, but Vailret thought he saw genuine relief in her eyes.

"This time we beat the ogre, Mother," Vailret said.

Alarm flashed in her eyes. Delrael cut off any scolding as he offered to help her cook something. "I'm hungry. And I'm going to start heavy training again tomorrow with some of the best fighters."

Delrael turned to Vailret with a glint in his eyes. "After all, we know where the Air Stone is.

We know where a surviving ogre is—at last, we've got some questing to do again! Doesn't it make you feel alive? To have a purpose in life?" He patted his leather armor, the silver belt, the knife and sword at his side. "This is what we were made for."

Sounds from the gaming hall rang distant but clear in the damp night. At the edge of the trees, the veteran Tarne stood, preferring the silence and the dark. He kept watch in the muffled shadows, looking at the aurora overhead. To him, visions filled the night. He wondered if he would catch another glimpse of the future.

Tarne was one of the surviving warriors from the campaigns with Drodanis and Cayon. In his adventures, he had found more treasure, slain more monsters, explored more trails than any other character save Drodanis and Cayon. Tarne had accompanied Drodanis on his vendetta against the ogres, slaying half a dozen of them himself for the murder of Cayon.

But none of that mattered to him anymore.

Since those bygone days, Tarne had given time to reflecting on his life. Sometimes he reveled in the companionship of others, in the gatherings for the winter tales, telling story after story about the old campaigns. But other times, he spent weeks alone in the forests. He had shaved his head to let the thoughts flow unimpeded, exposing all the scars from battle injuries. An ogre's blow had knocked him unconscious many years before ... and had opened up his ability to see visions.

After ending his active service as a fighter, Tarne had become the village shearer and weaver. He was big enough to wrestle the sheep for shearing, and he also knew enough woodcraft to find the proper flowers and berries for dyeing the cloth he wove. It was a different life for him, but Hexworld itself had changed. He kept an old set of leather armor hidden in his dwelling along with his most precious possession, an ancient sword from the Sorcerer wars. Sometimes he took the old things out from under his table just to look at them.

Another round of laughter came from the gaming hall. He could discern the clatter of dice on tabletops, the tallying of points. Delrael and Vailret would likely come down to tell of their adventures, but the others had begun their amusements without them.

Tarne considered young Delrael for a moment, admiring him. Seven years before, he would not have guessed the young man could run the Stronghold so well in the absence of his father—but Drodanis had been a recluse for his last few years anyway, before he'd gone off in search of the legendary Rulewoman Melanie.

Even as he thought of Drodanis, Tarne felt an echo of the man's pain. Barely a year after the slaying of Cayon, Drodanis's wife Fielle died. A new fever spread its claws through the village, causing the villagers to hide in their homes. Drodanis lay sick for days as Fielle cared for him, nurturing him so closely that she fell ill herself. He recovered; she did not. They had been married fourteen years.

Drodanis had reacted to Fielle's death more strongly than he had to Cayon's. He and Fielle had been perfect for each other—only she could beat him in archery, only he could beat her in throwing knives at targets.

Drodanis grew more somber each day, leaving no one to attend the Stronghold duties. Training stopped. Tarne had helped when he could get away from his own shearing work. But for the most part, he could only watch Drodanis withdraw into himself.

Drodanis studied the legends of Hexworld. Roving Scavengers—the only characters still actively questing in the world—had found many papers and scrolls left behind by the Sentinels. Young Vailret also took an interest in the legends and spent much time looking over Drodanis's shoulders. He ran errands and helped decipher faded writing.

Drodanis had come across an obscure tale that fascinated him—a mysterious Rulewoman named Melanie, possibly a manifestation of one of the Outsiders, who watched over the Game and directed the characters that interested her. The legends said she could be found deep in the forests to the south, and whoever found her would know peace for the remainder of his days.

Drodanis became obsessed with the legend. For years, he searched for every scrap of knowledge concerning her. He wanted to find the Rulewoman so he could demand an explanation for the misery inflicted in his life. What had he done to offend the Outsiders so deeply?

Finally, when Delrael turned eighteen, Drodanis announced he would embark on a quest to find her. Tarne volunteered to accompany him, as did young Vailret, but Drodanis refused them both.

He took with him only Lellyn, Bryl's twelve-year-old apprentice. As if the old half-Sorcerer knew enough about magic to *teach* anything, Tarne thought. Lellyn, a boy from one of the northern mining villages, exhibited strong sorcerous powers, though he bore no trace of Sorcerer blood. Lellyn was a wild card, a manifestation of magic that should never have occurred. His use of magic broke all the Rules, but somehow Hexworld had allowed it to happen.

Drodanis said he would take only Lellyn with him on his quest because the boy was an *anomaly*. And if Drodanis was going to find the Rulewoman, he needed to have the help of someone who could break the Rules.

So Drodanis and Lellyn traveled south and disappeared into the deep forests. Seven years had gone by, but they sent no word. Most of the villagers believed them to be dead.

Tarne turned his eyes to the sky again, looking at the shimmering auroral curtains that called to him. The rippling light of Lady Maire's Wedding Veil painted the summer night in delicate pale colors, swathed across a great portion of the northeastern sky. Tarne stared at the hypnotic patterns that showed him visions of the future.

Like Lellyn, Tarne was an anomaly too, a Rule-breaker. After his head wound had healed, he found he could sometimes see things in the dance of the Veil. Though his ability was well known in the village, Tarne kept the details of his revelations to himself. He considered them to be private glimpses into the plans of the Outsiders. Only rarely did he weave the visions into special tapestries, which he explained to no one.

He had no Sorcerer blood either. Sometimes it seemed to him that Hexworld had a magic of its own, a magic that knew nothing of the Outsiders' Rules and acted only to preserve itself.

The Veil held Tarne's attention now. The revelations didn't always come, but he felt giddy this night, filled with a fuzzy claustrophobia that made him want to release whatever visions were trapped in his head.

As he watched, Tarne saw a claw-like tendril of greenish light reach from the east and stab into the rosy color of the main aurora. The shrouds of light changed, and the details of the future struck deep into his mind.

Tarne fell to the ground in awed dismay.

Behind his eyelids, the truth reeled. He lay against the cold grass for a long moment. He blinked his eyes open, and the Veil was a simple aurora again, lights painted on the sky, reflections from the Outside world. Tarne climbed to his feet, stiff and off-balance, and waited for his emotions to die down. He knew he could not keep this revelation to himself—or else the Stronghold was doomed.

Vailret held the wooden message stick in his hands, afraid that he might damage it. His eyes sparkled with wonder. "This wasn't here when we left, I swear it."

Delrael put his hands on his hips, resting thumbs against the silver belt. His hair hung wet and clean, and his face was shaved and scrubbed raw. "It's got my father's seal on it?"

"Look for yourself." Vailret passed the message stick to his cousin. The fireplace in his room burned with a hot new fire. The message stick had been waiting for him, prominent on the tabletop with his other papers.

"And my mother says no one came in here while we were gone."

"Maybe Drodanis really did find the Rulewoman." Bryl looked awed and frightened by the short, polished stick. "She's supposed to be an Outsider—she could have found a way to deliver the message stick."

"The Outsiders can't communicate directly with us—it's against their own Rules." Vailret frowned, more confused now than ever. "I don't know what's going on here."

Delrael shifted the message stick from one hand to the other, staring at it. "When the need is great enough, some people are willing to break the Rules."

That settled a blanket of silence on them, a few minutes thick.

A message from Drodanis....Vailret had spent five years with the older man, growing up as he helped Drodanis study, then deciphering scrolls himself. But when Drodanis left on his quest for the Rulewoman —after working beside Vailret for years, he took Lellyn with him instead. Vailret had begged to go along, but for some reason, Drodanis found Bryl's young apprentice more appropriate. It stung Vailret like an unexpected slap in the face.

The boy Lellyn had no Sorcerer blood, but he was remarkably adept with magic. He had the powers by accident. Vailret resented that, and he wanted to know how the Rules had been bent. It seemed unfair to him, arbitrary. Though seven years had passed, Vailret wasn't sure he wanted to know what the message stick said.

"Well, are we going to burn it or just look at it?" Bryl fidgeted.

Before Vailret could answer, a pounding on the main door of the Stronghold building distracted him. The veteran Tarne stood in the wide doorway, cocooned in the night. He shielded his eyes as Vailret swung open the door, then eased himself closer to the light. "I've been watching the Veil."

After Vailret had ushered the veteran inside, leading him along a corridor to the firelit chambers, Siya came down the hall, curious. Wax covered her fingertips; she had been dipping candles again. He motioned that everything was all right and closed the door of his room before she could make a fuss.

Tarne stepped forward to stare at the flames, warming his big hands in front of the hearth. The night was cool enough, but Tarne looked chilled to the bone. Vailret could see the map of pale scars on the veteran's bald head. Tarne rarely said anything about his visions, but Vailret coaxed him now, anxious to get a hint of what had frightened him. "Did you see something tonight?"

Tarne wiped the shine of sweat from his forehead. "The Stronghold is going to be captured. And I don't believe we can do anything about it."

"Attacked!" Delrael leaped to his feet. "By whom?"

After a moment of silence, Bryl said, "We've had peace for so long!"

Delrael's eyes went wide. "The Outsiders are probably getting bored with peace." He slammed one fist into his flat palm.

Vailret looked at the veteran, forcing himself to remain calm, to get the facts and try to come up with a solution. "Any other details, Tarne?"

The veteran shook his head. "The visions aren't like that. Just a certainty that we are going to be attacked in two days. I don't know who the enemy is. But the Stronghold will fall for the first time in its history."

Tarne stared down at his dye-stained hands. "I thought I saw something else to the east, though—terrible and growing, drinking all life in its wake. I feel so helpless! But the danger to the Stronghold is more immediate and drowned everything else out."

Vailret wished he could know what it *felt* like to have the power, even unbidden magic like Tarne's, singing through his body.

"I wonder if that has anything to do with my father's message?" Delrael held the carved stick up to the fire light. Vailret noted the expression of interest on Tarne's face.

Delrael took a step toward the fireplace. "We'll never find out if we don't get started. Tarne, you're welcome to stay—we'd like to hear your thoughts."

The veteran shrugged and remained standing by the table. He seemed uninterested in Vailret's scrolls and scraps of writing, though he was careful not to touch any of them.

Delrael closed his eyes for a moment, as if making a wish, then he tossed the message stick into the fire.

Vailret held his breath—Drodanis had put his seal on the stick. He had sent a message. Had he reached the end of his quest? Had he found the Rulewoman? Did Drodanis regret taking young Lellyn instead of him?

The flames attacked the wood, peeling away the outer spell and shelling the spoken words, sending them into the fire. The crackle of consumed wood rose to a hiss, then to whispered words. The flames climbed higher, dancing together, forming a memory-image of Drodanis.

Vailret's eyes glistened as he stared at the flickering silhouette of his uncle. Drodanis appeared older, but he wore the same clothes Vailret remembered him in. Drodanis's eyes were dim and downturned. He seemed content, not haunted as he had been—but he also seemed dead inside, with nothing left now that his sorrow was gone.

The spectre spoke from the glowing hearth.

"Delrael, Vailret—the Rulewoman Melanie is risking everything to let me send you this warning. She is bending her own Rules, hoping she does not get caught by the other Players.

"Hexworld is doomed—the Outsiders have grown tired of us. One of the Players has set events in motion to destroy our world.

"None of us is *real*. We exist only for the amusement of the Outsiders. You know that. But now the Outsider named David has planted a monstrous, growing thing far to the east. He wants to end the Game. As his creature sucks up life, it grows ever stronger and it will soon spread across the entire map. That will be the end of everything for us.

"The Outsider David is playing by the Rules. And the Rulewoman Melanie will try to fight him in the same way. But we must help as well. You must find some way to stop the enemy. We are the characters on this world, and we have a stake in it."

The fire popped and crackled, drowning some of Drodanis's words. Vailret watched, feeling numb from his uncle's warning. The image wavered, and Drodanis's tone changed.

"… Stronghold is in danger from an entirely different source. You must ignore that. Do not waste your time and effort trying to regain the Stronghold, should it fall. This is my warning—you must listen. The Outsiders have set up the second threat as a distraction, an adventure to amuse themselves. You know what is more important. The Stronghold will have no significance if Hexworld is destroyed."

The message stick crackled again. Layers of ash slid off, leaving little of the stick unconsumed. Drodanis's words became garbled, overwritten with a sound like frying fat.

"The other Outsiders do not know you are aware of their plans. The Rulewoman has slipped this message past them. But be prepared—if they find out, they will do everything to stop you.

"I am begging you to find a way to protect the world. Do not be side-tracked. This is the grandest quest in our history—not for entertainment, but survival."

The hissing grew louder, and chunks of words drifted up into the chimney. "I am well. Lellyn is ... gone. Preserve Hexworld."

The message stick crumbled in a final burst of light. The image of Drodanis scattered and vanished with the flames up the chimney, leaving only the logs and the low fire.

The morning air had a fuzziness to it, erasing sharp details of the forest and the countryside. Tarne kept watch at the Stronghold walls, looking down upon the few villagers who still tried to do field work in the rising midmorning heat. Other defenders moved within the empty Stronghold courtyard, waiting. Waiting.

Tarne could not be specific about the time of attack, nor could he even tell them what enemy they would face. He had gone out again later that night and stared at the aurora for hours. He rubbed his temples, trying to concentrate, willing the clues to come, but the Veil remained closed to him, nothing more than silent green-gray curtains suspended above the world.

After burning the message stick, the four of them had discussed possible solutions. Delrael had seemed upset at his father's instructions to ignore the threat to the Stronghold.

Tarne stood tall and stared at Delrael. "I will stay here and fight. This is my home. The Veil has given us a brief warning, and I will not waste it."

Delrael turned to watch the fire. He pounded a fist into his palm. "I hate to leave you, especially if you might have a battle—but you heard the Rulewoman's message. We have to go and confront the greater enemy, whatever it is."

"*How?*" Vailret had said. "We need to cut this thing off somehow, protect ourselves. But we know nothing about our enemy. It's hard to make a plan when you're blindfolded and have both hands tied behind your back."

Bryl hung his head and looked dejected. "If only we had the Air Stone."

"What about the other Stones?" Tarne asked. "Weren't there four of them?"

"Yes." Vailret furrowed his forehead. "The only one we could get to in a few days is the Water Stone. Sardun keeps it in his Ice Palace, north of us. That one controls the weather and water, and Sardun's a powerful Sorcerer himself."

Bryl scratched at his ears. "Maybe we should go and ask him for help."

Delrael looked at Vailret, who shrugged. "It's a start."

Tarne had rapped his knuckles on the table, feeling the charisma grow in him again. He remembered fighting with Drodanis; he remembered giving orders on the battlefield. "I will gather up all the fighters from the village. We'll be ready at dawn."

He had stared beyond the walls, pondering. "The others may have to leave the village for a time and hide in the forest. But don't worry—I will take care of them."

Before dawn, Delrael, Bryl, and Vailret set off northward, bearing their standard packs and the weapons they had chosen at random. Vailret's precious old manuscripts lay in a large buried chest sealed with wax to prevent dampness from getting in. Tarne had no idea when they would return. His world, his adventure focused on protecting the Stronghold.

Now, at dawn, other villagers furtively glanced up at the top of the Hill. The Stronghold had protected their homes for centuries. Tarne realized that most of them hoped his vision would prove false, but he knew better. He had never been so sure.

Each of his picked defenders had been armed, some with relics from the old Sorcerer wars, others with less ornate creations by Derow the blacksmith. Derow had little experience in making weapons and felt ashamed to see his swords next to the elaborate weapons used by the former warlords. But Tarne had seen how well Derow's blades cut—and little else mattered.

A hush fell over the abandoned Stronghold. Occasionally, the air rang with the distant clink of a hoe striking a rock, or a dissolving snatch of nervous laughter from the villagers far below.

"I thought I heard something," said the young farmer named Romm.

And suddenly, Gairoth, wearing the dazzling Air Stone set in an iron crown on his head, appeared on the Hill, stepping out of thin air and leading Rognoth the dragon—and an army of other ogres. Their combined howl of attack sounded like an avalanche.

In the instant of surprise, one thought shuttled through Tarne's brain: Ogres don't work together. Flashbacks of his campaign against the ogres came flooding back, hunting down the monsters one by one with Drodanis and the other fighters. Tarne could not imagine that so many of them had survived the Scouring, or that they would band together. But Vailret had already warned him that Gairoth was part Sorcerer himself, and no ordinary ogre.

The ogres roared and lurched up the hill path, gaining momentum in defiance of the steep slope.

"Sever the walkway!" Tarne cried. Romm was already there, picking up one of the dangling mallets and striking out the wooden pins that held the walkway across the stone-filled trench.

The ages-old bridge settled a little, but jammed in its supports. "It won't drop!"

The ogres had almost reached the top of the path, swinging their clubs in anticipation of wreaking havoc.

"It'll drop when they come across it! Secure the gates! Quick! Jorte, help him!"

The two men swung the heavy doors shut while others slammed the crossbars into place. A few defenders shot arrows at the oncoming giants. One arrow struck Gairoth's tree-trunk arm, but he plucked it out without a wince of pain. The monsters kept coming. Tarne had never believed there were so many ogres in the entire world, not even at the beginning of the Scouring.

Gairoth surged like a battering ram across the walkway, and still it did not fall. Rognoth crouched behind his master as the ogre took his club and pummeled the heavy doors. They splintered.

"Ready the trap inside the door. This one better work!"

With one massive final blow, Gairoth blasted the thick doors inward, sending spear-length splinters of wood flying into the courtyard. Arrows struck at him like lightning bolts, but bounced away like raindrops.

"What the hell?" Tarne looked at his bow as if it had betrayed him. "Arrows always worked before."

With the other attacking ogres behind him and Rognoth at his side, Gairoth strode into the courtyard wearing a smug and triumphant grin.

"Now!" Tarne bellowed, and Derow the blacksmith pulled the lever that would plunge the ogres into the pit inside the gate. With incredible agility for bodies so large, Gairoth and Rognoth simultaneously leaped to the side as the trap fell inward, exposing the deep pit. The other ogres roared, working their way around the trap and into the Stronghold courtyard.

"How can this be happening?" one of the men wailed in shock. Though the defenders launched volley after volley of arrows, not a single ogre appeared to be injured.

"Where is Delroth!" Gairoth bellowed. He leaped into the air and brought his club down on the ground for emphasis.

"We knew it would happen," Tarne said to the defenders. "And we were foolish enough to think we could prevent it. To the ladders! Everyone out!"

Ogres flooded into the courtyard as the defenders set up rickety wooden ladders against the northeastern wall of the Stronghold. The men scrambled over, dropping to the ground. They made their way through the thick forest toward the caves in the hills, hoping the ogres would not follow.

CHAPTER 3

SARDUN'S ICE PALACE

RULE #5: The speed at which a character may travel on foot is strictly limited. Characters may traverse no more than three hexagons of grassland, forest, or grassy hill terrain per day; two hexes of forested-hill, swamp, or wasteland; and one hexagon of mountain terrain. Once a party has covered the allowable distance, they must stop at the intervening hex-line.

Naturally, if characters have access to other modes of travel, such as horses or boats, the allowable distances are modified, as given in Table A-1....

—The Book of Rules

G ood thing we weren't there," Bryl said. "Try not to sulk so much."

"That was our home, and now Gairoth has it," Vailret answered. Delrael said nothing.

They had watched from the top of a hill shortly after sunrise. Delrael squinted into the long shadows of dawn, describing details that Vailret could not see. None of them could believe the ogre had won so easily.

Delrael finally shook his head. His eyes, Vailret saw, were heavy and red. "There's no excuse for how we've failed. We brought it on ourselves by being lazy. I wanted my father to be proud of me. What would he say now?"

They talked as they continued northward at a brisk pace. The Rules allowed them to travel three hexes per day in forest terrain and three in grassland. At one point, a panoramic view of grassland terrain bordered an abrupt line of forest. The black barrier was sharp and hard as a razor stretching off into the fuzzy distance; lush forest lay on one side of the line, vast grasslands on the other.

"Your father told us not to fight for the Stronghold, Del. He wouldn't consider you a failure. We're doing exactly what he wants by focusing on the main threat."

Delrael shook his head. "It's not that." He shifted his hunting bow, rubbing the red spot where the quiver strap had chafed his neck. "I mean we failed in a larger sense—the Outsiders got *bored* with us. We didn't perform like we were supposed to. That's why we were created in the first place—and they found Hexworld so tedious that they want to destroy it."

He shook his head, avoiding Vailret's gaze. "We should have gone questing more often, started some wars among ourselves." He made a distasteful noise. "Farming and training—even *I* found it boring. No wonder the Outsiders gave up on us."

Delrael kept moving along the trail. Vailret caught up and put a hand on his shoulder. Delrael seemed uncomfortable at being touched, but Vailret held him there anyway. "The Rulewoman Melanie is fighting on our side, too. Hexworld isn't a complete failure—she must be enjoying it."

Delrael didn't answer and pushed ahead.

For the rest of the day, Delrael kept to himself, brooding. Vailret remained busy planning how they might fight the Outsiders' threat. Bryl complained most of the time, but Vailret found him easy to ignore.

He doubted they could do any serious fighting. Delrael had only a bow and his leather armor; Vailret had only a dagger, and not much battle skill or training to go with it; Bryl never practiced his magic and knew few spells. The half-Sorcerer could work some useful everyday magic such as starting a camp fire and replenishing their packs with food and water, but his only unusual spells were that he could make flowers bloom on demand (a useless talent, Vailret thought) and that he could blunt or sharpen a blade, which might prove valuable in a battle. Bryl had no one to show him new, more powerful spells, and he did not have the ambition to learn them himself.

Vailret had always wanted to be a fighter, like his father Cayon—but he did not have the physical build or the skill in weaponry, and his weak eyesight spoiled him for anything but close combat. Or reading.

He remembered the days of training at the Stronghold. At daybreak, the other villager trainees would leave their homes and trudge up Steep Hill. Visiting trainees from other villages lived within the Stronghold walls and helped with some of the preparations for the day's instruction. Drodanis and Cayon would send everyone back down Steep Hill to come running up again, to strengthen their leg muscles. They made the trainees carry water up from the stream, whether the Stronghold needed it or not.

But after the deaths of Cayon and Fielle, Drodanis had done little training. Delrael, who was then fifteen, and the old veteran Tarne conducted the necessary exercises. Young Vailret had thought quests were old-fashioned and juvenile, and he spent much time with Drodanis, learning to think and read.

On Vailret's eleventh birthday—two years after the death of Fielle—Drodanis had led him outside, across the enclosed yard, to the small, windowless weapons storehouse in a corner by the double wall. The sky was gray, and Vailret could hear wind whipping in the trees of the hill, but the tall walls of the Stronghold sheltered them. Bryl waited for them at the storehouse door, looking bored.

"Has he agreed?" Bryl asked. "Do you think he's prepared enough?"

Drodanis shrugged and looked at young Vailret, who felt a touch of fear at the back of his curiosity. "I haven't even told him what we're going to do."

Without looking at Vailret, Drodanis opened the door of the weapons storehouse and stepped inside. Bryl looked at the boy, keeping a grave expression on his face.

Just inside the storehouse, Bryl snapped his fingers to light a single candle. Vailret looked around in the dim orange light. The dark interior of the storehouse seemed to be a haven for shadows and hidden fears. Spears, swords, arrows, and bows—mostly ancient Sorcerer artifacts sold by the Scavengers—lay stockpiled against the walls. Bryl's face wore a nasty grimace as he gestured the boy inside, then closed the door behind them. Vailret held his head up, trying to keep his composure. He knew Drodanis wouldn't hurt him.

"This is a role-playing game, Vailret. It is to be a test of your imagination," Drodanis said. "And also to see how quickly you can think, how adequate your solutions are, how well you react under pressure."

Bryl blew the candle out. Darkness swallowed all of them. The man's low voice resonated in the shadows.

"You are imprisoned in a Slac fortress. You have watched as the Slac cut your companions to pieces, one by one, for amusement—you heard the screams from your friends, the laughter from the Slac. You are the only one still alive. Two guards come and drag you out of your dank little cell. What do you do?"

Vailret didn't answer for a moment. "I don't understand. What am I supposed to do?"

"Pretend you're in the situation I just described. What would you do? The guards are taking you. Are you going to struggle, or come along peacefully?"

"I'll struggle!" Vailret said. "And then what?"

"And then run."

"Where? Back to your cell, or blindly through the tunnels?"

"Pick a number from one to ten," Bryl said.

"What?"

"Pick a number. If you guess the right one, I'll let you break free. If you guess wrong, the Slac keep their grip on you. It's like rolling dice."

"Three."

"Wrong." Drodanis picked up the story again. "A guard raps you on the side of the head, causing one damage point and knocking you nearly senseless. They laugh. You are being taken to an arena where you will be thrown in with the Akkar, an invisible spine-covered creature that feeds on Slac victims. They want to watch your death convulsions. Any questions?"

Vailret paused only a second. He had begun to feel the game now. He closed his eyes and imagined, seeing himself in the Slac tunnels. "Will I have any weapons to fight with?"

"You are given a small club. That's all."

"Do I have the club now?"

"No. When they get to the arena entrance—and you are almost there now—they will throw it into the arena and force you out there."

"How are the Slac guards armed?"

Drodanis paused. Bryl answered, "With spears."

"You see the end of the tunnel ahead. It opens into a wide area covered with sand and gravel.

All around the pit are jeering Slac, out of reach of the invisible Akkar. One Slac guard tosses your club out into the pit."

"I'm going to grab for that guard's spear and dash out into the arena with it. Then I'll have more than just a club," Vailret broke in.

Bryl and Drodanis looked at each other. "All right, pick a number between one and fifteen," Bryl said.

"He has the advantage, Bryl—he's surprising them," Drodanis said.

"All right, a number between one and twelve, then."

"Eight."

"Got it!" Bryl said, surprised.

Unseen in the blackness, Drodanis chuckled. "The Slac shout in anger, but they're not about to follow you to get the spear back. You have the spear in your hand. The club is about ten feet in front of you, lying on the bloodstained sand. Behind you, the Slac slam shut a heavy door, trapping you in the arena. You can hear a grunting noise, like something running. The sand and gravel is covered with broken bones, but you can see large footprints appearing as the Akkar charges toward you."

"I'm going to run and get the club. I'll pick it up off the ground and hold it in my hand, waiting to throw it as hard as I can at the front of the creature when it gets close to me." Vailret felt breathless, as if his life was really at stake.

"You get the club and you throw it. Pick a number between one and three."

"Two. There *is* only one number between one and three."

"Hah! Caught me. All right, then. You hit the beast with a loud thump, probably in its head. You can't see if it did any damage, but you have halted the creature's charge. For the moment."

"Now I'm going to try to stick it with my spear. Is it making any noises so I can find it easier?"

"Yes, you hear a snorting, breathing noise."

"I'm jabbing with my spear."

"Pick a number between one and seven."

"Five."

"Missed."

"I'm jabbing again! And again, until I hit something."

"You hit it. I'm thinking of four different sections of the creature's body. Pick numbers one, two, three, or four and I'll tell you where you hit."

Vailret paused in the darkness, concentrating. "One."

"You skewered the monster's throat! Several points of damage. Blood is gushing out—you can locate the Akkar easily now. But it is angry and charging."

"I'll dodge, now that I know where it is. Can I try to get my club again?"

"You can't get to the club," Bryl said flatly.

"You said there were lots of bones lying around. I'm going to run and pick up the first big one I find and throw it at the Akkar."

"All right. After you've done so, you see another blotch of blood appear in front of the spear wound—one more point of damage. This time, you hit the monster in the head."

Vailret paused again, considering his next course of action. "Is there one Slac around the pit who looks like a leader, like an overlord?"

Drodanis paused, but he did not ask what Vailret was considering. "Yes, one seems to be dressed more magnificently than the rest. He has a portion of the arena circle to himself."

"I'm going to steer the Akkar to get near the Slac warlord. I'll pick up another bone and throw it if I have to."

"You throw another skull. It misses, but the Akkar is getting cautious. It is still bleeding heavily from its neck wound."

"I'm up against the wall of the pit below the Slac warlord."

"The beast sees you cornered and charges."

"I'll plant my spear in the sand, bracing the haft and myself against the pit wall, sticking the point directly in front of me so the monster will charge into it."

"Good." Drodanis laughed. "Pick a number between one and five."

Vailret paused a long time, sweating. Two? Four? One? "Five!"

Drodanis laughed again. "The Akkar has impaled itself on your spear!"

In the darkness, Bryl's voice became serious. "Pick another number. Between one and ten."

Vailret picked five again.

"You have been gored by one of the many invisible spines on the Akkar in its death throes. Your side is laid open and you are bleeding badly."

Vailret let out a quiet cry. "Is it bad?"

"Very bad. If it isn't taken care of, you will soon bleed to death."

"The Slac will never take care of it, will they? I'm going to pull the spear free from the Akkar's body. Can I do that?"

"Yes."

"Remember I'm just below the Slac overlord in the pit. And he's alone in his own part of the circle, you said. I'm going to throw my spear directly at him to kill him!"

Drodanis apparently found this exciting and let him succeed. "The spear strikes him squarely in the chest! You know it is a mortal wound. The other Slac start shouting and screaming. They begin firing arrows at you."

"I'm going to take shelter behind the carcass of the Akkar!"

"It helps some, but not enough. You are hit by three arrows. A fourth," Drodanis said. "You are dead."

Vailret felt a cold lump form in his stomach.

Bryl lit the candle again, dazzling the three of them. Vailret felt confused but exhilarated. After a long silence, he finally asked the question that had been bothering him. "What should I have done to win?"

Drodanis looked at the boy, hiding a gleam of pride in his eyes, but Vailret saw it there. "Nothing. We left you no way out."

Vailret frowned, baffled. "Then why did I have to play the game? What did it teach me?"

Drodanis grinned. "It taught you never to let yourself get captured by Slac."

The three men traveled northward across hex after hex. The fifth day of walking took them over a ridge forming the southern rim of a bowl-shaped plain. They could see mountains on the near horizon. Vailret stopped to stare out across the grassland, but Delrael and Bryl plodded ahead. He hurried to catch up.

Overhead, the sky was clear. They saw no birds, no wildlife. The silence in the air started to bother Vailret as they marched out onto the lake of dry grass. The dead blades whispered against each other as if confiding secrets, but he could detect no breeze. Bryl stopped and spread his arms out in amazement. "Something happened here. I can still feel it."

Vailret scanned the valley, the mountains to the north, and the high grassy hills to the south. He sniffed the air but smelled only grass and dust. A memory skittered around the back of his mind.

Then it came to him, but the hissing sound of the wind in the grass covered his gasp of surprise.

"This is where the Transition took place!" He turned around, eyes wide and mouth open in wonder.

Delrael stopped, baffled. Bryl knelt down and touched his fingers to the ground, then looked up in childish delight. Vailret wondered what the half-Sorcerer could sense, what emanations the spectacular Transition had left behind, an echo that only a magic user could hear.

The valley did look large enough to hold the entire Sorcerer race. Vailret pictured in his mind all the surviving Sorcerers marching there to pool their magic, to transform themselves collectively into ... something else.

The silence buzzed around them, as if the valley itself was still stunned. Many of the Sorcerers would have been afraid, some of them eager. But they had summoned up all their magic, pooled it—it was something even the Rules did not know how to handle. The Sorcerer race had transformed themselves into six Spirits—three Earthspirits and three Deathspirits—leaving their bodies behind, fallen like scattered wheat.

Only pureblooded Sorcerers could join in the Transition. A few Sentinels had remained behind because of human or half-breed loved ones. The Sentinels had carried the fallen, dormant bodies into the mountains. They had erected the Ice Palace as a monument to their race.

Vailret shielded his eyes, trying to squint and focus on the high range standing ahead of them. "The Ice Palace must not be far from here."

Vailret thought he heard voices riding on the cool wind, Sorcerer ghosts trapped in the air and trying to get back into their empty bodies. He felt uneasy. The history fascinated him, but from a distance. He didn't like this place. Delrael and Bryl seemed uneasy as well. All three of them pushed forward at a faster pace to the mountains.

Sheer peaks stared down at them. At the black line separating the valley floor from the first hexagon of rugged mountain terrain, two statue sentries towered, thirty feel tall, carved from ice. Vailret stared at the monolithic sculptures—gaunt soldiers in full armor, with the insignia of the old Sorcerer race chiseled into their uniforms. They carried glistening icicle spears as weapons.

The silence pounded down on the travelers. The ice sentries stood in front of them, oozing cold, somehow casting crossed shadows on the road.

Slowly, the three men passed between the statues. Vailret looked to his companions. Delrael appeared calm, but Vailret could see tension in the way he walked. Bryl acted as if he were stepping on a giant mouse-trap. Vailret tried to ignore his own uneasiness.

As they stepped over the black hex-line, the chill around them grew distinctly worse. The wind itself carried an essence of absolute cold. Vailret's skin became numb, the feeling in his nerves snuffed out like an extinguished match. Flecks of snow danced in the silent air. Bryl tightened his sky-blue cloak around his shoulders, but he made no complaint.

"Sardun could be doing this with the Water Stone," Vailret said, uneasy about suggesting the possibility. "It controls the weather, you know."

"But he's a Sentinel!" Bryl's words were muffled around his cloak. "He's supposed to help people."

From behind came a loud clattering sound. They turned to see that the monolithic sentries had crossed their icicle spears on the return path. Then only the cold breeze broke the deathly hush.

Claws of wind slashed at the blankets, bleeding warmth away. The stars shone intensely bright in the sky as clear as black glass. The three travelers had stopped for the night, shivering under a sheltered rock over-hang, but they found nothing to burn for a fire, nothing to keep them warm. Bryl wasted one of his day's spells to force a small magical fire, but that did little to warm them. Delrael roused them before dawn. "We should have come more prepared. Come on—we'll freeze if we don't keep moving."

Handfuls of snow had collected in the tiny pockets and notches on the rock faces. Lady Maire's Veil cast auroral light down on the land-scape, enough to see by.

They plodded onward with sore feet and aching legs, but the cold had deadened most of their feeling. Vailret felt giddy and floating. Numbness roared in his ears. At dawn, they reached the top of a boulder-strewn rise in the path. Delrael looked northward, then extended his arm. "It's there! See that glint?"

Vailret could not see anything clearly enough; the peaks in the distance blurred out of focus, but he trusted Delrael's eyesight. They pushed on at a faster pace, and within an hour, even Vailret could discern the gleaming towers of the Ice Palace nestled in the rocks.

Then the sky smeared over with clouds, and sleet pelted down. Vail-ret's fingers were sluggish to respond when he tried to curl them inside a fold of his tunic.

Vailret squinted to see the Palace's structure made of clear blue ice. But the gray sleet kept details hidden. He had seen a few sketches showing the main building, a pyramid flanked by two thin spires capped with onion domes.

The vast Palace was inhabited by only one old Sentinel and his young daughter. They tended the frozen underground crypt that held the husks of Sorcerers who had departed in the Transition centuries before. The other Sentinels and half-breeds had once made pilgrimages to the monument, but as the Game slowly ground to a halt, few made the effort anymore.

Few human characters would appreciate the monument and its treasures, but Vailret felt his own excitement growing. He could now speak with Sardun himself, have access to the original source material, even the Water Stone. Vailret felt optimism creeping up on him again.

Tall cliffs closed in on either side, finally blocking off the sleet-wind. The Ice Palace loomed up in front of them, but it did not match Vailret's imagined picture at all. "Something's happened," Bryl exclaimed.

"Look at it!" Delrael craned his neck upward. Vailret stared, letting his mouth drop open.

The tall crystal spires were warped and drooping, with their decorative pinnacles melted away. A stumpy cascade of icicles ran like tears down the sides of the towers. Motionless frozen streams hung down the walls, stained black with a sooty residue. The structural blocks were now cloudy rather than transparent ice. The top of the main pyramid had been sheared off, blasted inward and leaving ragged, melted edges.

Vailret forced back a strong urge to cry. He felt angry and helpless. "What did this?"

"And what if it's still here?" Bryl mumbled. His wrinkled skin made him look parched and afraid.

Delrael narrowed his eyes and looked for enemies hiding in the rocks. He broke the astonished silence and nudged them toward the destroyed buildings. "Let's get out of this cold." He moved forward, ready with his hunting bow, though his fingers were probably too numb to use it.

The tunnel entrance to the main pyramid gaped like an abandoned trap. The Palace had no gates, no defenses at all.

"The whole point was that anyone could come here, whenever they wished," Vailret said with a note of despair. "It was a memorial—why would someone destroy it?"

Snow had piled up at the entrance. The ragged wind hooted through the hole. Everything inside lay desolate and untended, empty. Delrael led the way down an uneven, half-melted corridor, deeper into the main pyramid. The rough texture gave them footing on the ice walkway. The main tunnel spiraled around the outer wall of the pyramid, working its way toward the central chambers. Their boots sounded like thunderclaps on the frozen floor.

Refracted light seeping through the prismatic walls made unnatural rainbows, rippling and bathing them in color. Vailret looked from side to side, feeling the loneliness and emptiness gnaw into him.

The sound of the wind soon vanished behind the thick blocks of ice, but the cold itself seemed to focus and deepen as they neared the heart of the Palace. Up ahead, lights danced on the frozen walls, ricocheting and sparkling like tiny meteors. The wind returned, louder, from a source within the central chamber.

Intrigued but uneasy, Vailret pressed close to his cousin as they moved forward. A vaulted arch rose over the corridor, and the three of them emerged into the main reception room.

The entire ceiling of the central pyramid had been blasted away, and frigid air swirled out of the wide hole. Great rivers of ice streamed to the floor like petrified waterfalls. Snow drifted down to settle in a bull's-eye pattern of ripples in the floor where the ice had been melted and refrozen.

A blocky white throne stood in the center of the room. Encased in tendrils of frost, an old man sat staring mindlessly at the blasted walls.

Sardun the Sentinel looked shriveled, mummified by cold. A long gray mustache hung against the wrinkled folds of his face. Vailret stopped and stared, afraid to make any sound. Delrael looked at him, questioning. Sardun blinked.

"He's even older than Bryl!" Delrael whispered.

"He's old enough to be my father," Bryl said, annoyed.

The old Sentinel had plunged his left arm up to the elbow in the translucent ice of the throne's armrest, embedding it. Through the murky ice, Vailret could see Sardun's gnarled hand grasping the sapphire Water Stone. The Stone was a cube with a number etched on each face, shaped like a six-sided die, more powerful than the four-sided Air Stone. Unnatural cold spewed from the gem, swirling up and out into the world. "Sardun!" Vailret called. His voice cracked.

The Sentinel swung his eyes back to focus around him. The wind breathed a ragged gasp and failed as the blue glow in the Water Stone died away.

"Haven't I been wounded enough?" Sardun's high-pitched voice held a tone of condemnation, then he chuckled a little. Vailret noticed that the old Sentinel lisped. "What's left for you to destroy? There's no more damage you can do!"

Sardun heaved the Water Stone out of the frozen armrest of the throne, pulling it up through the solid ice. A few drops of water dripped off his hand and disappeared into the air. The cavity in the armrest filled again and solidified. Sardun glared at the three and leaned forward.

"Look out." Delrael edged back against the wall. "He's going to roll it." Unless Sardun rolled a "1," his spell would be successful and grow in power, depending on how high he rolled.

The Water Stone sapphire bounced twice on the ice floor. The number "4" came up.

A thin bolt of lightning shot from the Water Stone, striking at the three travelers. But the Sentinel's aim was skewed. The bolt pinged off the glistening walls several times before it dissipated.

Sardun did not pick up the Stone to roll again. His attack seemed halfhearted.

Vailret stood a moment in turmoil, knowing it might be safer to run away, but then he'd never know what had happened here. Nor could they ask for help to save Hexworld.

Confusion and indignation overcame Vailret's better judgment. He stepped into view and spoke quickly, hoping the Sentinel would hear his sincerity. "Wait! You're Sardun! You cherish the history of Hexworld as much as I do. Sentinels aren't supposed to destroy people!"

Sardun swung his gaze at Vailret and snatched up the Water Stone from the floor to roll it again. Vailret knew he had little chance of avoiding a direct strike. Lightning traced the gray veins under the skin of the Sentinel's hands.

Delrael shouted at him, but Vailret kept walking. He forced himself to be calm and brave, keeping his voice level. "We are friends, Sardun. You don't have to hurt us. I know about the old Sorcerers and the Transition. I know about the Sentinels, and how you built this Palace as a monument to your race. This was to be a place for pilgrimages, where all interested characters could come and see what had happened during the previous turns."

He gestured behind him, where Delrael and Bryl remained out of sight. "One of my companions is a half-Sorcerer, son of the Sentinels Qonnar and Tristane. My other companion, Delrael, runs the Stronghold. See, Delrael wears a silver belt that is an ancient Sorcerer relic. He and I are both descendants of the great General Doril, who fought in the Scouring."

Sardun watched Vailret with narrowed, watery eyes. Still holding his hunting bow in front of him, Delrael stood where he could be seen from the Sentinel's throne. The wind whistled over the wide opening in the ceiling.

Bryl also peeked around the corner and held his palms out to the Sentinel. Gray-haired and frail looking, Bryl posed no threat. "You can trust us."

Sardun sat for a moment, wavering on the edge of consciousness. His eyes seemed half-crazed with grief and desperation, but even that faded into listlessness. The Sentinel had surrendered. He said nothing.

Vailret undid the frozen straps on his pack and with drew a wadded second blanket. Feeling awe at approaching the legendary Sentinel, he delicately wrapped the blanket around Sardun's shoulders. He looked at the old man's fur-trimmed gray robe; snowflakes had been embroidered along the shoulders and down his sleeves.

The air in the main chamber had grown warmer. Outside, he could see the sun shining again as the Water Stone released its hold on the storm.

Delrael entered the chamber, looking from side to side with narrowed eyes. Vailret watched him inspect the corners and the openings of other passageways, as if expecting something monstrous to crawl out and attack. Bryl waited, fidgeting in uneasy confusion.

Vailret tucked the blanket around the Sentinel and discovered that his legs were frozen solid, like meat left too long out in the snow, as was his chest and his right arm. For a moment, Vailret was appalled that Sardun had been left alone like this, with no one to care for him. Then the other thing that nagged at the back of his mind snapped into place. "Sardun, where is your daughter?"

The old Sentinel was like a fragile clay pot, shattered by Vailret's question. He fell backward, almost drowning in the ice of his throne. "Tareah!" he said. "She's gone … gone." Tears ran down Sardun's face, branching in the network of wrinkles in his skin. As Vailret watched, the tears froze, then evaporated and were gone.

Delrael paused in his inspection of the room and then squinted at a thick, soot-covered icicle that looked like a maggot in the ceiling's wound. He wrinkled his nose, as if sniffing at a strange taint in the air. Delrael seemed lost in deep thought, then he stood with one word on his thin lips.

"Dragon."

Vailret looked up at his cousin's comment. His gaze drifted to the fangs of icicles running straight down toward the floor, at the hole that had been blasted through from the outside. "A dragon did this!" Delrael said.

Confused words spilled out of Sardun's mouth. "Yes, a dragon! Tryos, from the island of Rokanun, south of the city of Sitnalta, many hexes from here. He flew all the way … to steal Tareah! Oh, my Tareah."

Vailret stared at him, then rubbed the old Sentinel's shoulder. "You can tell us what happened. We might be able to help."

Sardun shuddered. "I couldn't stop him! The Water Stone was no help—dragons are not affected by magic." He stared down into the flat faces of the sapphire Stone. He rolled it in his hand, looking at the number engraved on each face. "That is why they caused so much destruction in the old Sorcerer wars."

He swallowed and looked up to meet Vailret's gaze. "Tryos came, blasted his way in here ... and took her."

"But why would a dragon want to do that? Why Tareah?"

Sardun glared at him. "Because dragons collect treasure! Tryos is very old and he is bored with colorful baubles. Gold, gems, silver—he already has enough of those. Now he collects anything that *others* place value on, anything precious or beautiful. He has stolen works of art, sculptures from the height of the Sorcerer days, precious relics.

"And now my treasure, my Tareah! I tried to defend her—I really tried. But I am weak. I have been here waiting one hundred and seventy years, tending this museum that no one ever comes to see....do I not have an excuse to grow weak?" His lisp grew worse as he became more distraught.

The Sentinel stared at the wall in his silent horror. His lips trembled, but he said nothing else. The three stood numb for several moments before Bryl finally spoke up. "But why would Tryos take *your* daughter?"

"Idiot! She is everything!" Sardun turned his head sharply, but the gesture was odd and jerky because of his frozen lower body. "She is our future! Tareah is the last full-blooded Sorcerer woman. One day, she may be strong enough to awaken all the sleeping Sorcerers in the vault below the Palace. Our race will rise again. She will shepherd them back to us, to make things the way they were. And now Tryos has taken her."

He hung his head, trapped and paralyzed on his throne. "Oh, why couldn't I have more strength? I used more magic than the Rules would allow. I sacrificed most of my body." He swiveled his head to indicate his frozen arm, his lifeless legs. "All for nothing."

"We might be able to rescue her," Vailret said softly. He looked at Delrael. His cousin shrugged and nodded slowly. "If you will help us in turn, Sardun."

The Sentinel looked at him, then turned his gaze to Bryl and Delrael, unimpressed. "Where were you when Tryos attacked? Who stood by my side to fight him? To protect Tareah? How dare you ask me for help!" Sardun's hand clenched the Water Stone again, ready to roll it and cast another spell.

"Because we have no choice, Sardun," Vailret said. He laid a hand on the old Sentinel's rigid shoulder. "The Rulewoman Melanie sent us a message—the Outsiders are trying to destroy Hexworld. They have placed a growing enemy in the east. They will play out turn after turn, putting their own plots into motion. We have to do something to stop them. You are the most powerful Sentinel left alive. We hoped you would have a solution."

"I am not powerful enough. Tareah is gone. I don't want to save anything except my daughter." A winter storm glimmered behind his eyes again. "That's why I brought the cold. Why should I be the only one to suffer?"

"You can send us on a quest to rescue your daughter. You know that we would be bound by the Rules to complete the quest. But we first need your help to complete *our* mission."

Sardun cocked his head at Vailret, helpless and pathetic. "And what would I have to do? How do you plan to stop this outside enemy?"

Vailret smiled and consciously did not look at Delrael and Bryl as he described his idea.

"If our enemy is growing in the east, maybe we can cut it off from at least part of Hexworld. You have the use of the Water Stone, Sardun, and the Ice Palace is near the Northern Sea and the far edge of the map. If you could channel a *river* from the Northern Sea down to the southern edge of the map, that river could act as a barrier. It would cut off and protect at least half of Hexworld. Make the river so wide that whatever armies or monsters the Outsiders send against us are unable to reach the western side. We'll be safe."

Delrael crossed his arms over his damp leather armor, smiling at Vailret.

Bryl scowled, looking terrified at the thought of embarking on an even longer quest. "Think of the damage such a river would cause on its way to the sea. There'd be no way of stopping it."

The aspect of destruction seemed to intrigue Sardun. The expression in his eyes went far away and he muttered to himself, lisping, "The Northern Sea would come rushing down to the ocean like a battering ram. A wall of water from the frozen seas, crashing through the canyons and mountains and grassland, pounding its way to the ocean. Think of the power, think of the destruction! A Barrier River—a whole hex wide!"

"No other Sentinel has ever left so great a mark on Hexworld," Vailret whispered to him, afraid he might sound too manipulative. "Tareah would be so proud of her father!"

Sardun's lips moved, and then he answered louder. "Yesss."

CHAPTER 4
THE BARRIER RIVER

*RULE #2: The system of quests and adventures is all-important to the
Game. Once a group of characters undertakes a quest, they must see it
through to completion. Incidental adventures are likely to occur along
the way, but the ultimate goal of the quest should always remain foremost
in a character's mind.*
—The Book of Rules

The balcony of the Ice Palace's tallest tower drooped at a
deadly slant, scarred with soot and the marks of dragon claws.
A waterfall of icicles poured from the balcony's edge.

Sardun was alone out in the open air, rooted to the ice and clutching
the Water Stone with his one functioning hand. The northern breeze
whipped around the tower, but he used the sapphire's power to surround
himself with a pocket of calm, weaving the winds away from his body.

The Sentinel stared across the geometric landscape of Hexworld. The
sight of the sprawling hexagons of terrain always filled him with awe.
And now that Tareah was gone from him, he just wanted to stare and
stare until he faded away into nothingness.

"Sardun, are you sure you'll be all right?" Vailret called from the balcony doorway. He refused to step out on the slanting ice after he and Delrael had carried the old Sentinel to the top of the tower.

Sardun did not turn to answer him. "I will do what you ask. And you are bound by the Rules to keep your bargain, to go on a quest to find and rescue Tareah."

"We'll do it, Sardun," Delrael said.

Sardun doubted they would succeed. In fact, since they were required to continue the quest, no matter how hopeless it seemed, he felt almost certain he was sending Vailret and his companions to their deaths.

But if there was a chance, if Tareah might be rescued, Sardun had to take the gamble. Too much of Hexworld's future rested within Tareah. She was the last full-blooded female Sorcerer. And she was his daughter.

Tareah.

"Leave me. I have never controlled this much power before. I would not want you standing in the backlash." He turned and fixed his eyes on Vailret. "Go—begin the preparations for your journey to Rokanun."

He turned back to the scene below, not waiting to see if they departed.

To the south, he saw the valley where the Transition had taken place. As a small boy, Sardun had been there himself, two centuries before. He had offered his ineffectual help as the adults carried thousands of motionless, bereft Sorcerer bodies—people he had known—up into these mountains in a solemn and seemingly endless procession. They had placed the dormant bodies in a frozen underground tomb in the mountains and protected them.

Years later, when Sardun had full training in the use of his own powers from the elder Sentinels, he had erected the Ice Palace over the tomb as a monument to his race. He made himself the custodian of all their relics so that all of Hexworld would remember the old Sorcerers.

He stood in the cold wind, sensing the crypt deep below, untouched even by the dragon's attack. The husks of the Sorcerers slept, empty and unchanged over the centuries—while the six powerful Spirits that had arisen from their metamorphosis had vanished from the world, ignoring Hexworld and its problems. Why hadn't *they* come to help when Tryos attacked?

He tore his eyes from the landscape and looked down at the sapphire cube in his hand. Within the Water Stone resided magic from the ancient Sorcerer race, magic that—unknown to the Outsiders—was not necessarily bound by the Rules of the Game.

Sardun rolled the Water Stone and came up with only a "2," but he didn't need a very high roll to forge a frozen pedestal from the balcony floor. Chips of ice swirled up from the rippled surface, glittering like rainbow fireflies, and wrapped his dead lower body in a cocoon that held him firmly erect on the sloping surface.

"Sardun—thank you." It was Vailret's voice, coming from the tower's doorway.

Sardun continued to stare at the smooth face of the sapphire, clearing his mind for the ordeal, but his chapped lips formed a slight smile.

At first, the other Sentinels had made pilgrimages northward to the Ice Palace, to see their fallen friends, to reminisce about the Golden Age of the Game. They brought with them their own relics, their own memories, and Sardun had collected all of the items.

But as the Sentinels died, so had Hexworld's interest in its past. During the rampant bloodshed and racial hatred of the Scouring of Hexworld, half-breeds and humans concerned themselves only with their own survival, with fighting and gaming and uncovering treasure. Some characters grew bitter toward the Sorcerer race, who had deserted them in their time of need. The remaining Sentinels vanished one by one as they used magic to end their lives.

The Sentinel Kahleb had been the first to annihilate himself in a burst of Sorcerous glory. Kahleb had remained behind on Hexworld to be with his new human wife—but only a year after the Transition, she had died trying to give birth to a stillborn child. In his anguish, feeling desperately alone and unable to make the Transition without the rest of his race, Kahleb unlocked the depths of his own magic to destroy himself and his wife's body in a spectacular funeral pyre.

But this release was more than simple destruction: Kahleb had discovered a partial Transition that liberated his own spirit, raising it up to where it could have a life of its own. Over the years, Sardun had watched as other Sentinels imitated this half-Transition, giving up hope and freeing themselves as they grew weary of life.

Tareah's mother, an old Sentinel woman named Tiarda, came to the Ice Palace one winter to gaze at the tomb of the Sorcerers a final time. She had been beautiful once, but now looked worn and strained. She refused to play games with Sardun, not dice, not even hexagon chess. Sardun never asked why she had forsaken the original Transition, but he devised a desperate plan as she mourned over the dormant bodies in the crypt. Sardun had often gone with her, looking for one body she mourned in particular, but she never pointed out any one.

Sardun was at the peak of his strength, and lonely. Tiarda had no positive emotion left in her. Sardun sifted through Tiarda's despair and apathy. He asked her to wait. The two of them might make a new hope for the Sorcerers. She reacted passively to Sardun's romantic advances— she didn't seem to care one way or another. This hurt him, but he could not let something so important slip away.

Tiarda was old, older even than Sardun, but she conceived a child, and Tareah was born. Sardun had hoped this would restore Tiarda, change her mind, but she refused to wait any longer. Sardun held the baby daughter in his arms as her mother called up the magic, unleashing her spirit in a blinding flash. She seemed to grow younger at the last instant: the gray in her hair ignited and filled with molten gold. Her face held an achingly beatific expression until the light broke through and blurred her features into a brilliant glow that faded into the air, leaving only Sardun and his baby Tareah.

He had not loved Tiarda, but the loss of yet another Sentinel struck him. Only the need to care for his daughter renewed his interest in life. He devoted himself to teaching Tareah her heritage, and her mission. Year after year, he showed her the relics in the crypt, told her of the Rules and the Outsiders, taught her the historical accomplishments of the Sorcerer race.

Sardun waited, and hoped, and built his entire world around his daughter.

Then Tryos had stolen her.

Sardun swallowed a mouthful of stale saliva and began to chart the course for the great Barrier River. Bleak, towering mountains surrounded the Ice Palace. He looked to the southeast, toward Rokanun, where his daughter had been taken. He seemed to feel her calling him, mourning for him and losing hope that she would ever be free. The gray crags extended, hex upon hex, as far as the eye could see.

The wind stroked his face, and he looked beyond the hexes of mountain terrain to the north, seeing the silvery reflection of the vast frozen sea. The morning sky had been filled with clouds, but he'd sent them away with the Water Stone's magic. Now sunlight glinted off the snow-flecked peaks.

The Barrier River would flow between the mountains, skirt the Ice Palace along its two western hex-lines, then burst into the Transition Valley, perhaps making a lake there. The river would wind through the grassy hills at the lower edge of the valley and plunge southward across the grasslands and swamps, restructuring the landscape, ripping a course through the forests and hills until it finally reached the vast ocean near the edge of the map. Sardun hoped no villages lay in its path.

As he stood out in the cold, very old and very alone, Sardun realized that he was not strong anymore—he had wept too much and had not eaten enough. But this was to rescue Tareah. And he knew where to find the power he required. He did not know what the consequences would be for summoning the sleeping magic, for bending the Rules, but he had passed the point of caring.

When the other Sentinels destroyed themselves in the half-Transition, one by one, they had liberated their spirits to roam Hexworld. Some of these spirits, which were apparently aware of themselves in a murky way, had sought out other Sentinel revenants. Over the years, the congregations of spirits had settled in places still prominent in their fuzzy Sorcerer memories, blending and seeping into the fabric of Hexworld, becoming a wellspring of Sorcerer power called a *dayid*. The Ice Palace itself harbored one of the largest *dayids*, the spirits of those Sentinels who most regretted their decision to remain behind from the Transition.

Sardun looked down. The ice pedestal sheathing his lower body made him look like a crystal tree trunk with one arm and a head. He stretched out his arm and touched the Water Stone to the ice wall of the tower. The *dayid* contained the spirits of many Sorcerers; and the Sorcerers had created the four Stones. He would find the *dayid* below and tap in to it.

His thoughts narrowed to a single focus and shot through the sapphire, plunging to the core of the Palace, to the tomb of the Sorcerers. Sardun's mind was pulled by a force stronger than gravity as his thoughts dodged the latticework of ice crystals.

Unconsciously, he let his arm fall, breaking contact with the wall as though the Water Stone had grown suddenly heavy—but his consciousness continued to descend. He dropped the Stone on the slanted balcony. It rolled twice and then stopped with the number "6" facing up, the highest he could roll.

Sardun plunged deep into a hot lake of mental fire, encountering the whispered, dazed voices of Sentinels he had known. Even Tiarda was there, if Sardun chose to seek her out.

In an instant, he communicated his need and then shot upward again, swelled with the power of the *dayid*. He released his power, channeling it through the Water Stone and launching it toward the Northern Sea.

Sardun felt the Ice Palace rock under him. The Water Stone itself looked like a blue sun burning into the balcony's floor.

He pointed his straw-like fingers and traced a winding course for the newborn Barrier River. In his mind, he saw the enormous map of Hexworld on the wall in the lower vault, and he formed a line of terrain hexagons, turning each one blue as the river made its way southward to the edge of the map.

Still the power continued to pour into him from the *dayid*.

A mountain stood partly in the way, but it crumbled to one side; blocks of ice around the sea rim catapulted through the new canyon. Water spewed into its new path, frothing and spraying.

A great wall of water churned past the Ice Palace. It spiraled between the mountains and engulfed the Transition Valley. The Barrier River chewed its way through the grassy-hill terrain, then stampeded southward, seeking a route to the edge of the world and destroying everything in its path. The river would cut off the western half of Hexworld from the unknown danger in the east. No army could cross the wide, raging river

—but that also doomed all the people, all the villages on the wrong side of the river.

Sardun saw the mighty passage of water as insignificant when compared to the *dayid*'s power, a power he fought to contain. With his heightened perceptions, he looked deep into the ice to see the hidden structural flaws, the damage the dragon Tryos had done to the Palace.

More power poured into him. He could not stop it from coming and had to release it somehow before it burst from him. Sardun turned the magic to reconstructing the Ice Palace. As swiftly as he could imagine the restorations, the improvements, the great Palace stood whole and undamaged, dazzling in the sunlight. The floor beneath him bucked and swayed as the balcony regenerated itself. The bent spire straightened.

Sardun then turned his energy inward, re-charting his own veins and nerves and muscles, restoring the dead flesh he had sacrificed in his unsuccessful battle to save Tareah.

And after he had finished, the explosive power still would not release him, growing stronger as the *dayid* itself surged to new awareness after decades of dormancy.

Temptation grew in him, ravenous, demanding that he set himself free after two centuries of waiting. The *dayid* begged him to set his body ablaze, to annihilate himself in the half-Transition. The voices of the other lost spirits called to him, beseeching. *Join us*!

But he refused. Not now that he had hope for Tareah.

The Water Stone made the *dayid*'s link more potent, more difficult to deny. Blue flames licked around the fringes of his body; his newly regen-erated cells began to nova as the process of partial Transition began to take hold. The Water Stone added its power, and the reaction grew stronger and stronger. Sardun fought to break free, but the energy fed upon itself, growing.

Screaming inside, Sardun leaped downward again, dragging his consciousness back to the *dayid* in the crypt. Using all his ability as a living Sorcerer, he severed the link, thrusting the *dayid*'s power back at it, and then fled to hide inside his own body.

He collapsed like a rotten fruit on the high balcony. The cocoon of ice holding him up had evaporated, leaving his pink, newly healed legs exposed to the wind. The smoking Water Stone had melted itself halfway into the new ice floor.

In the sudden silence, the grinding roar of the newborn Barrier River rose into the air....

These relics are free for all to see.

My only fee is that you REMEMBER.

Vailret read the placard above the tunnel leading down to the crypt of the ancient Sorcerers. Bryl waited partway down the sloping tunnel, eager but hesitant to go farther alone.

Sardun lay like a dead man on the throne room floor, wrapped in several blankets. Vailret had hovered over him for hours, looking for any sign of improvement. Delrael had agreed to watch over the Sentinel while Vailret and Bryl explored the underground vault.

"Are you coming, Vailret? Tell me now so I don't waste any more time waiting," Bryl called from the tunnel, sounding anxious.

"Don't be afraid, Bryl. They're not rotting dead bodies. They're just ... empty."

"I know that—don't patronize me!"

They carried torches down the winding tunnel. But the outside light somehow reflected through the thick ice, making a refracted blue glow ripple out of the walls.

Vailret felt as if he was deep under water. The air smelled cold and musty. Bryl hovered by his side, curious but cautious.

"Do you think Sardun put any traps in the tunnels? To stop plunderers? Someone might think this is a good dungeon to investigate."

Vailret sniffed the air, fascinated by the hypnotic light from the walls. "No, I doubt it, Bryl. This museum was supposed to be open for all to see, remember?"

Bryl seemed to take some comfort in that, but he still let Vailret lead the way.

The sloping passage opened into a huge vault bordered by shadows at the far ends of the room. They moved forward. The light from their torches reflected off the hewn ice walls, illuminating a magnificent chamber complete with stalactites of ice. Vailret stared in wonder.

Bryl went to rummage among the relics in delighted fascination.

Cases, pedestals, mirror frames—all held something Sardun considered relevant to the history of the Sorcerer race. Scrolls and manuscripts had been carefully packed and labeled. An original copy of the Book of Rules stood in a transparent case. Vailret saw weapons—one sword burned and blackened—and garments, jewelry, sculpture, paintings.

Vailret felt overwhelmed as he stopped to inspect each item. His voice rose in pitch. "This is the sword of Stiles Peacemaker!" He lifted up the blackened sword. "When he ended the wars between the old Sorcerers, the leaders of both factions cast their blades into a bonfire!" He ran his finger along the dull, twisted sword.

"And this shawl was worn by the Lady Maire on her wedding day, before the tournaments took place and fighting broke out among the guests—which was the start of all the wars. And this—ah!" He held his torch down near the faded parchment, afraid to touch it with his fingers. "It's an original manuscript written by the Sentinel Arken!"

Bryl had found a chest of colored gems and sifted through its contents. He tossed a diamond necklace back onto the pile. "Arken? Who was that?" he asked.

Carried away by his excitement, Vailret scowled at the half-Sorcerer. "Haven't you paid attention to any of the winter tales?"

"I can remember plenty of things, young man! I've seen more history than you will ever read—I know it's not all glorious wonders as you seem to think. History is a lot of *normal* time with nothing happening. You have to see the highlights of a century at a time before it gets interesting. Be glad I'm taking an interest." He paused. "Well, what does it say?"

Vailret looked down at the parchment again with wide eyes. "It's the story of the Transition, as told by one of the oldest Sentinels. It's priceless! Come here and read it with me." He hoped the magnificence of the Ice Palace would awaken a sense of perspective and interest in Bryl. "The language is a little archaic, and some of the ink is faded, but I think we can manage."

Vailret read Arken's words, anxious to see what they said but trying to go slow enough for Bryl to keep up. "'The Council had not argued so much since the wars. Bellan was red-faced and sweating (as usual) as she shouted her opinions, ranting on about how we could raise ourselves, as a race, to a higher level of existence, to escape this world, which is not *real*. She vehemently pointed out (several times, as if she thought repetition might convince us) that this would open up the new doors of power and wisdom we sorely needed. The Transition could make us omnipotent spirits, gods. This was obviously the ultimate destiny of the Sorcerers—obvious to Bellan at least.

"'We could escape our war-torn past, leaving behind our physical bodies and the scars of the long battles, and make ourselves *real*. The wars had stopped, the Sorcerer race was weak, questers had no zeal for uncovering new catacombs or seeking out more treasure—what if one day the Outsiders decided to end the Game?

"'Many of the other Sorcerers agreed with her. Finally, one baffled-looking woman stood and asked why we were even discussing this, wondering if anyone had an argument to the contrary.

"'I did. I told the Council I had discovered, by close interpretation of the Book of Rules, that none of our half-breed children could come with us. None of our beloved human wives or husbands. None. We would be abandoning them. I told them I would not leave Mika or our children behind. That gave the Council something to think about.

"'Let it be understood that I did not try to dissuade my people. Not at all. I simply wanted it to be a matter of choice, that some would choose to remain behind, either refusing to orphan their families or simply fearing the unknown aspects of the Transition.

"'We debated the matter for several years. Bellan pointed out rather harshly that we dissenters could not change our minds. Individually, we would not have the power to make a Transition for ourselves. We would be Sentinels, watching over the world and our children, while the rest of our race went to its destiny.'"

Vailret took a deep breath, looking at Bryl. "Can you imagine it?"

The half-Sorcerer seemed to be looking down and through the parchment. "Yes, my parents were there, but I hadn't been born yet. My father was a full-blooded Sorcerer, but my mother was only a half-breed. He stayed behind with her, and decades after the Transition, they found themselves at the Stronghold. Your great-great-grandfather Worael ran things then. The battles of the Scouring were still going strong."

Vailret looked at the old man in a new light, remembering how much Bryl himself had seen. Vailret waited, hoping the half-Sorcerer would continue reminiscing, but Bryl fell silent. After a moment, he glanced at Vailret. "Well, does Arken have anything else to say?"

Vailret handed the torch to Bryl and ran his fingers just above the actual parchment. He didn't want to smear or crumble the paper.

"'The Sorcerers began the journey northward to the place we had chosen for the final gathering of our race, a broad valley in the north. And I came to watch, to remember. A few humans also came, and other teary-eyed Sentinels, watching their dear friends depart and thinking of the ones even more precious for whom they remained behind. They came in small groups or large, some bringing entire families, some coming alone.

"'All the Sorcerers stood in the valley and watched the sun rise. In the center of the field sat a white canvas tent, rippling with the brisk wind from the north—the five Council members had spent days in close quarters, never leaving the tent, apparently discussing final details. The rest of the Sorcerers were told to stand ready at any moment.

"'The Transition occurred on the day of the autumn equinox. I remember that as significant—a day of balance, a day and night of equal length, halfway between the start of summer and the start of winter.

"'Together, my fellow Sorcerers pooled their powers to weave a force so strong—I cannot describe it well in words, but anyone with Sorcerer blood will have some inkling of what I'm saying.'"

Vailret paused, narrowing his eyes. He could not understand what Arken was trying to describe. He would never feel Sorcerer power or the nuances of magic—

"What's the matter?" Bryl asked.

Vailret shook his head, searching for where he had stopped.

"'Sparkling lights erupted from isolated pockets of air, growing intense, like a fireworks display. My people forsook their physical bodies, joining together in a blinding light, a flash of incredible sorcerous beauty. They … *evolved*, they became spirits. The massed ranks of the Sorcerers dropped to the ground. Empty and soulless.

"'Splotches of color continued to float in front of my eyes. I thought that something had gone wrong, that all the power had been expended, leaving nothing behind. The bodies of the Sorcerers lay slumped against each other on the ground. Everything fell silent, and even the sun seemed to have paused in climbing over the horizon.

"'Then the wind picked up. I remember how forceful it became, distinct, a rush of wispy voices, quietly mumbling faint words and phrases and whispers of astonishment. The air began to glow just outside my range of vision, taking substance, finally solidifying into six towering figures that loomed over us in the valley. The Spirits all wore hoods that cast their features into shadow. Three shone dazzling and white, while the other three cloaked themselves in darkness and mystery.

"'Those of us remaining stared in awe, but the Spirits made no move to speak. They seemed indifferent to us and to the thousands of empty bodies lying on the valley floor. The Spirits conferred among themselves briefly, and then they vanished.

"'To this day, the Spirits have had no contact with our world. This does nothing to allay the regrets of those Sentinels who now wish they had made a different decision. Sometimes I wonder if I had a right to stop so many of them.'"

Vailret stopped reading. Bryl turned away quickly, as if trying to hide a sheen of tears in his eyes.

Vailret saw a plume of breath as he let out a long sigh. "Do you suppose the old Sorcerers knew something, even back then? That they were so desperate to escape to a new reality where the same Rules don't apply? Before the Outsiders decided to destroy Hexworld." He drew in a deep breath, awed. "Then why did the Sentinels stay behind?"

"The Sentinels carried all the Sorcerer bodies here," Bryl said, muffling his words in his sky-blue cloak.

Vailret squinted ahead. "Look at them all."

The ceiling of the vast chamber dropped low. The dormant bodies lay in awesome ranks beyond where the torchlight vanished into blue murk from the ice walls. They looked alive, asleep, with a gentle dusting of frost in their hair. Vailret could imagine them being placed here by the Sentinels; he could imagine Sardun spending patient decades rearranging them into restful poses.

The chamber felt very cold. Silence pressed down on Vailret, and he thought he heard breathing, countless lungs being filled at a synchronized but maddeningly slow rate, then an equally slow exhale. The torch sputtered once, making him jump and breaking the spell.

"Come on, Bryl. Let's get out of here."

Sardun propped himself up on a shaky forearm and glared at them. "You should not have waited!"

Vailret shrank from the outrage rising behind the old Sentinel's watery gray eyes, but he eased Sardun back to his blankets. "We had to make sure you were all right."

The night before, while Sardun still lay comatose, Vailret had crept out on the sparkling balcony to gaze in awe at the Barrier River. Nearly hypnotized, he stared at the vast channel of frigid water zigzagging sharply along the hex-lines, laden with ice chunks and brownish-gray silt. He squinted, but his poor eyesight blurred the details. He had to use his imagination, just as Drodanis had taught him.

Vailret stood in silence as the cold wind blew on him, and listened to the river grinding its channel deeper. The silent stars and the aurora shone overhead.

They had fulfilled the quest Drodanis and the Rulewoman had required. They had protected themselves from whatever the Outsiders had placed in the east. Creating the River might have been more extreme than was necessary to fulfill the vague instructions—but they knew too little about their enemy. They had finished one quest, but now they had promised Sardun another. And the Stronghold was still in the hands of Gairoth.

Vailret liked the old veteran Tarne and trusted him to lead the villagers to safety somewhere in the forests. But Gairoth had the Stronghold, and the Air Stone, and all his ogre comrades. Vailret hated to think of the damage they could be doing.

Sardun had nearly sacrificed himself to create the River, and they were bound by the Rules to go on the quest to rescue his daughter. By the time Vailret returned to the throne room, the old Sentinel had finally awakened.

"Tareah could be dead by now. You must hurry." Sardun's voice seemed stronger now, and he sat up again. His lisp seemed more pronounced. "Have you copied the map on the wall—so you know exactly where you're going?"

"I've already memorized it," Delrael said, crossing his arms over his chest.

Sardun sighed. "Perhaps I kept Tareah too sheltered. She should have been out, seeing Hexworld, learning the world. If she had not been here during the attack, she would still be well."

"I would like to take a good sword if you have one, Sardun," Delrael asked. "It would increase our chances."

"Yes, choose whatever you need from the relics I keep if it will help you rescue Tareah." The Sentinel spread his hands.

Bryl moved forward, reluctant but extending the shining Water Stone he had removed from where it had frozen into the ice of the balcony. The awe on his face was plain. "Here is your Water Stone, Sardun."

The Sentinel squirmed away from the sapphire's touch, twisting his face in an expression of fear and disgust. With a twitch of his gnarled left hand, he knocked the Stone out of Bryl's hand.

Astonished, the half-Sorcerer chased the sapphire as it skittered across the floor of the throne room. "What's the matter?"

Sardun slumped into his blankets, and a violent shiver rippled through his body. "When I last used the Water Stone, I forged a link with the *dayid* below. The other minds in the *dayid* are lonely. They nearly forced me to make the half-Transition. With the Water Stone, it would have been so easy. So easy. So frightening.

"I think the *dayid* hoped that with me using the Stone and with its own strength, I could liberate enough power to raise us all through a real Transition."

He sighed. "But I refused. I may regret it in the future as my only chance to make a miracle happen. I am afraid to use the Stone again. The *dayid* knows I'm here—and I doubt if I could resist that calling a second time."

Bryl looked down at his blue cloak, flashed a glance at both Delrael and Vailret, then looked at Sardun. "I am a half-Sorcerer. I can use Sorcerer magic. I can use the Water Stone." He spoke quickly, before anyone could stop him. His eyes were bright. "This could be just the magic I need.

"Hexworld is still infested with monsters that survived the Scouring. Maybe with the Water Stone, I can protect us. That would give us a better chance to rescue Tareah."

The Sentinel closed his eyes. "Yes, take the Water Stone and take it far from here. You will remove the temptation." Sardun sounded very weary. "Use it to bring Tareah back to me."

Bryl stared at the deep blue gem in his hand. He smiled, eager and in awe.

Delrael returned, holding an ornate but serviceable sword. He strapped it at his side, against the tooled silver belt his father had given him. He straightened, brushed his hands over his leather armor, and looked prepared.

"Let's go."

Sardun insisted on seeing them off, and they made their way outside with painstaking slowness. Vailret had tried to convince the Sentinel to rest, but he would hear none of it. "You will take me to the gateway!" Sardun said. His long mustache drooped into his mouth, making him look angry and impatient. They walked down curving crystal corridors just beginning to fill with rainbows as the sun rose.

When they reached the front gate of the Palace, Sardun slumped against the repaired doorway. He looked tired, but not quite empty of hope anymore.

"Luck." Delrael waved as they set off.

"Luck—rescue my daughter!"

The sunlight was much brighter now that the ice walls no longer filtered it. Vailret shaded his eyes against the glare. Some of the snow from Sardun's unnatural cold still covered the ground, reflecting the light, but the day was warming rapidly.

Melted snow had muddied the ground. The mountain path was much easier now that they didn't have to battle the weather. The Ice Palace stood whole again, glistening like a diamond.

The three travelers hiked southward, leaving the towers behind. Bryl fingered the sapphire Water Stone in his chest pocket, as if waiting for the moment when he could use it. Vailret looked at their optimism and felt a foreboding—they seemed to have forgotten what they were going to be up against.

At the Ice Palace, without the Water Stone to protect it for the first time in centuries, the tall spires started to succumb to the returning summer heat. Tiny trickles of water ran down the great walls, freezing again before they reached the ground, and then warming once more. The Ice Palace began to melt.

INTERLUDE: OUTSIDE

The Players stared at the crystalline twenty-sided die on the table. A perfect "20" faced up.

Melanie rubbed her hands together and smiled at David. David made as if to knock all the dice off the table, but she held up her hands. "You can't do that, David."

She could see the anger behind his eyes, the *need* to beat her, and she worried about the change that had come over him. Oh, he had professed boredom with the Game in the past, but never anything serious....just complaining for the sake of complaining. They were used to that from David.

But now the urgency of stopping the Game possessed him—and he couldn't just leave. The four of them were part of the Game; they had been at it too long. David acted *addicted*, hating himself for it. Like an alcoholic, a compulsive gambler … a compulsive gamer? If he just walked away from the Game and let them continue playing, Melanie knew he would be back. He knew he would be back. And he desperately wanted to remove that option, that carrot in front of his nose.

"I think we should get different dice," he mumbled. "She's been rolling too well tonight."

"Spices things up a bit," Tyrone said. He rocked back in the chair and drummed his fingertips on his chest. "Hey, anybody want some more dip? I'll put it in the microwave."

"Are you suggesting she's using fake dice, David?" Scott raised his eyebrows. "You know those are the same ones we've always used. Besides, it doesn't make sense because we're all using the same ones. If a die's loaded for her, it's loaded for us, and we should be rolling twenties too."

Melanie stared at the map, at the colored hexagons, and she smiled. "Or maybe it's just that my characters are helping out." Her voice had a facetious tone, but David looked at her sharply.

"You're crazy."

"Oh, whose turn is it?" Tyrone stood up from his chair, scooped some of his bean dip on a cracker, and offered it to Scott, who refused. "What are you going to do with your roll, Mel?" He shut the microwave door and twisted the timer.

"Sardun succeeded in creating the Barrier River. It cuts off the western half of the map from the east."

"That won't be enough," David said. "It's just a delaying tactic."

But Melanie stared at the map. Her eyes widened. She couldn't believe what was happening. "Look!"

One hexagon of gray mountain terrain below the Northern Sea suddenly winked. It changed color to the enameled blue of the water.

Then the hexagons of grassland terrain below it also turned blue, one at a time, moving downward like a zipper. One after another, the hexagons of terrain turned to water in a line that meandered its way around the forested-hill and grassy-hill terrain.

"Wow!" Tyrone leaned across the table and pressed his face close to the map. "Look at it go!"

"Like it's choosing a logical course!" Scott said. "I don't believe this."

The hexagon of a lone village was inundated and changed without a trace. Melanie thought of the villagers, the people, their homes and fields. The River moved on until it emptied into the sea below.

Melanie sat frozen. David turned gray.

Scott jumped up and ran into the kitchen, pulling open drawers until he found the silverware. He came back to the map with a butter knife. He chipped away at one section of the new blue color.

Melanie tried to stop him, but he avoided her. "Wait, we've got to check this out. Timed-exposure paint or something? Of course not." He frowned, deep in thought. "I don't know what else to make of it."

"That was wild!" Tyrone said.

Scott squinted down. "The blue goes all the way to the wood!" He looked as if his reality had somersaulted in front of him.

David's reaction was incredible even to Melanie. She was amazed.... but David took it in stride.

"I'll stop your characters. They've made a river, but I won't give them another chance."

Melanie jabbed a finger at the map. "You're way over here. You've been spending all your time in the mountains and in the east. You can't get anything to them in time."

David raised his eyebrows. "We've got wandering monsters left over from the Scouring. I can roll up some more. It doesn't have to be part of any major plot to get rid of your characters."

"Plenty of wandering monsters in my section," Tyrone said. He rubbed his hands together. "And catacombs and good stuff. That's where they're heading next."

Scott kept staring at the blue paint. "Don't you guys realize what just happened?"

David drummed fingertips on the table. "With Tyrone helping me out for the last bunch of turns, we've done everything we needed to do in the east and in the mountains. Everything is set, all my wheels are in motion. We can get out now, and on to other things. Consider your characters doomed, Melanie."

Tyrone forced a laugh. "Sounds like you're getting personal, David."

"It is personal. A lot depends on this, you guys. I'm fighting for your lives too."

The bright blue streak down the center of the map filled Melanie with awe. "And I'm fighting for theirs."

CHAPTER 5

CYCLOPS CANYON

By setting forth the Rules in this book, we have attempted to make sense
of the way Hexworld works.
Characters must follow the Rules—we have no choice. If travelers want
to go farther than the allotted number of hexagons per day, or if magic
users want to cast more than the allowable number of spells, they cannot.
Their feet would refuse to cross the hex-line, their spells would not work.
—Preface, The Book of Rules

Even with a brisk pace, the Rules said they could cover only one hex of mountain terrain per day. No matter how fast they walked, they never reached a hex-line before nightfall. Vailret wanted to hurry, to end the quest and get back to the Stronghold and his studies, but they would have to overthrow Gairoth first. Vailret hated to be away from home—he had so much else to do besides adventuring.

Delrael seemed to know what he was thinking and raised an eyebrow. "There's some consolation, Vailret. Just trying to rescue Tareah could help us *save* Hexworld. If we give them a good show, the Outsiders might stay interested enough to keep Playing a while longer."

Around him, the mountains in the distance were indistinct and blurry. Though many of the plants had died in Sardun's unnatural winter, he could still see the colors of late spring. "Do you even know where we're going?" Vailret asked.

"Sure," Delrael said nonchalantly. "We need to get across the Spectre Mountains, then follow the mountain terrain line down toward the city of Sitnalta. No problem."

Vailret looked around. "Invisible ghosts are supposed to inhabit the Spectre Mountains, you know. No character has ever encountered the ghosts and returned alive." He paused and put a finger on his lips. "But if no one ever returned alive, then how do we know the story?"

Delrael shifted his longbow on his back. The sunlight gleamed on his oiled leather armor. "This section of the map was filled with catacombs and all kinds of wandering monsters. More likely there's a Slac fortress making off with unwary travelers."

Vailret remembered his make-believe encounter with Slac in Drodanis's role-playing game in the weapons storehouse. "Then we'll need to be even more careful."

They followed the rocky trail downhill until it disappeared completely at the sharp hex-line against forested-hill terrain. They stopped for the night. Across the line, a mixed forest of oak and pine abruptly replaced the stone crags.

The three sat around the fire sparked by Bryl's magic. They played a game of dice on a flat patch of rock, but Delrael kept winning and the others grew bored. Vailret tossed a pine cone across the hex-line. It bounced and skittered into the forest debris.

Vailret sighed. "You know, some of the old Sorcerer writings get metaphysical. I remember one that tried to explain how the hex-lines got into the world."

"How else would you have it?" Delrael shrugged. "If the landscape wasn't broken into discrete areas of terrain, the world wouldn't be very orderly, would it? It only makes sense."

Bryl yawned and looked ready to sleep.

"Well, imagine a chaotic world where grassland and forest and hills and mountains are all intermingled, no boundaries, just a constantly changing confusion."

"That's crazy," Delrael said. "It would never work. It's too unstable."

Vailret leaned back and looked at the flickering flames dancing over the wood. He thought of the message stick from Drodanis and the warning from the Rulewoman. "So who says the Outsiders make sense?"

"Let's get some sleep," Delrael said as he stretched out on the rocky ground. Vailret looked longingly at the softer leaf-cushioned earth only a short distance away across the line. But he could not break the Rules and cross into another hex.

Delrael didn't see the Cyclops until it was almost too late.

They followed a stream that cut itself deeper into a narrow valley; the peaks of the Spectre Mountains remained visible only a hex away. Sandstone walls rose sharp on either side, eaten away by the swift water, dotted with a few valiant pine trees that somehow found rootholds. On the top rim of the gorge the forest grew thicker, dark with pine trees and splashed with the lighter color of oaks. The tall rock walls loomed above them, riddled with notches and caves.

The stream turned into rapids as icy water dashed itself against the strewn boulders. Delrael stopped at the foot of a small waterfall. He tried to follow an individual bead of water as it tripped and crashed against boulders before dropping into space. Bryl leaned forward to splash his fingers in the cool water. Delrael strode back and forth until he found an easy path that led them below the falls.

It all seemed very peaceful, with only ragged birdsong and the sounds of the stream. Delrael's hunter senses suddenly sent him a dozen alarms. He heard a guttural bellow from somewhere above, but when he craned his neck to look, the lowering sun flashed in his eyes.

"Look out! Heads up there!" a voice called from the opposite rim of the canyon.

Delrael turned his head to the cliff above them. His brown hair whipped into his eyes, but he stared in amazement for a moment. Bryl also saw and pointed frantically.

A thirty-foot-tall hulk emerged from behind a squat outcropping of rock, glaring at them with one wide yellow eye set in the center of his forehead. A horn curved up from his brow, looking like a twisted root yanked out of the ground and sharpened to a deadly point. The Cyclops roared again, exposing a jumbled set of fangs, as if someone had haphazardly hammered the teeth into his mouth.

The Cyclops strained his muscles and heaved a boulder over his head. His fingers ended with obsidian claws that gouged white marks into the stone. Clods of earth crumbled off the bottom of the rock, dusting the monster's shoulders.

The voice shouted again from the opposite side of the gorge. The Cyclops hurled his boulder across the canyon at the caller, but the rock fell short and plunged into the narrow stream instead.

"Run!" Delrael said, pushing Vailret ahead of him. "Get to some shelter." He smiled as he ran, though—he felt his heart beating, felt his brain working. He'd wondered when they were going to start having adventures again. This section of the map had more than its share of wandering monsters, treasure-filled catacombs to explore, incidental adventures—just like in the golden age of Hexworld.

As Vailret and Bryl hurried toward the canyon wall, Delrael paused to search for the source of the voice. In the lengthening shadows on the rock face, he could discern another creature, a hybrid man/animal with the body of a panther and the head and upper body of a man. The panther-man held a long sword that seemed to be carved from heavy oak wood and varnished with hardened pine pitch. The panther-man thrust the sword in a scabbard strapped to his back before he started down into the gorge, scrambling for footholds on the knobby sandstone wall.

"Don't just stand there and gawk!" Vailret shouted back at Delrael. "Find some cover!"

The Cyclops bellowed as he uprooted another boulder.

"Oh, no," Bryl said.

Vailret's words startled Delrael, making him realize how unprotected he was on the canyon floor. He charged toward the stream. Delrael didn't care why the Cyclops had attacked them or why the panther-man was there—this was an incidental adventure on their quest, and they had to play along. It wouldn't affect their main goal, but it might be amusing along the way.

Another thrown boulder crashed near Delrael. He made a running leap to dive across the stream. His boots slipped on the mud of the opposite bank, and he sprawled flat on his stomach. He struck his head against the bank. The wind gushed out of his lungs. He gasped, trying to take a breath, but his chest seemed to be locked tight.

He saw blood smeared on the palms of his hands, mud down the front of his leather armor. He hoped he had not smashed his hunting bow. He scrambled to his feet then fell back roughly, in pain. His ankle felt as if it had been twisted full circle. *Typical*! he thought, ready to curse his luck. His ankle felt like a thunderstorm turned inside out.

The Cyclops had seen, and picked his target.

"Look out!" the panther-man cried from his perch halfway down the canyon wall. With splayed paws, he searched for a way to climb the rest of the way down.

Delrael saw the boulder coming at him. He *knew* it would hit him. Damn it, had he used all of his luck on dice games the night before? A harsh breath whistled through his teeth as he rolled to escape the rock. He saw Vailret and Bryl, but they were moving slowly. Too slowly. Delrael thought he could hear thunder up in the sky, the sound of the Outsiders rolling their master dice.

He wrenched his body backward, twisting his chest an extra finger-width out of the path of the boulder. It crashed to the ground, spewing up earth and plowing over Delrael's left leg instead. A ton of stone crushed down, splintering bone and destroying flesh and muscle.

Delrael screamed, but then his voice fled. Horrible seconds passed before the pain mercifully shut down the connections in his brain. He floated half-conscious in a sea of exploding splotches of color and shrieking nerves. Blood roared in his ears and spilled out of his shattered leg, making thick mud in the turf.

The Cyclops sprawled out on the rock face and lowered himself down, dropping his huge body from one jagged sandstone ledge to the next. As his obsidian claws scraped against the stone, sparks showered into the air.

Vailret and Bryl rushed to Delrael.

The panther-man leaped to the canyon floor from the last ledge and sprinted across the ground. His muscles bunched and rippled as he charged toward the descending monster.

The Cyclops dropped to the floor of the gorge and reeled to get his balance, intent on his fallen prey. The panther-man gave a loud whoop and plunged toward the Cyclops, swinging his wooden sword. Sunlight gleamed from the varnish on the blade's surface.

The panther-man slashed at his legs, and the Cyclops bellowed loud enough to shake rocks loose from the canyon walls. He fumbled with unwieldy clawed fingers, trying to grab his attacker. The panther-man sprang from side to side, weaving around the monster's bulky legs.

The brute looked up and fixed his glowing yellow eye on Delrael's motionless form. He swatted at the panther man and ignored him as he thundered toward his victim.

Vailret knelt down heavily on the muddy ground next to Delrael's mangled body. His face became the color of old cheese at the sight of all the blood, but then he turned to grab the half-Sorcerer's shoulders. "Dammit, Bryl—use the Water Stone!"

Bryl was already grabbing the gem. "I know!" He touched the flat blue facets, rubbing his fingers along the surface of the sapphire, and then plunged his mind into the mental keyhole, unlocking the power trapped within.

He rolled the Water Stone on the ground. "Come on!" The gem came to rest with the number "4" facing up. Bryl curled his lips against his teeth. Vailret hoped he really did know how to use the stone.

The Cyclops bellowed as a thick cloud appeared like a glove over his towering head. He tried to dodge it, to run—but the mist followed him, covering his face and blinding him. The tip of his veined horn protruded from the cloud. Groping around in circles, the Cyclops stumbled on boulders and tripped across the stream as he staggered toward the towering sandstone cliff face. He stubbed a cabbage-sized toe on a boulder and howled, but the thickening cloud-stuff muffled the sound.

Bryl glanced at Delrael helpless on the turf with his leg mangled and bleeding. A fury of lightning bolts burst from the hanging cloud. The Cyclops yowled, launching himself forward to flee the storm—ramming headlong into the rock face with a crunch that reverberated through the canyon.

Bryl let the cloud dissolve, and the Cyclops collapsed to the rocky ground. The monster grunted once and lay still.

Vailret stared at Delrael lying on the ground. He trembled, amazed at all the blood. Sweat made Vailret's blond hair stick to the sides of his head, but his face grew stormy with anger. He bent down to unfasten the ancient sword from Delrael's side. The injured man whimpered when Vailret moved him.

Vailret pulled the sword out of its scabbard and held it awkwardly. If he tried to use a sword in battle, the odds against him would be so great as to make it not worth the attempt. But this was not battle. The Cyclops lay unconscious. This would just be revenge. He took a determined step toward the monster.

"No. That would be needless killing." The panther man padded up to him. "I will not let you kill even the Cyclops when it is unnecessary."

Vailret confronted the panther-man for a long, frozen moment, flicking his eyes from the brute sprawled among the rocks to Delrael lying on the bank of the stream.

The panther-man stared back at him with eyes as green as leaves and moss. A long black braid ran down the length of his human back to rest against his feline fur. A pendant made of pine cones and acorns bound together with pitch dangled in the front of his hairy, naked chest.

"You're a khelebar," Vailret said.

The panther-man met the young man's eyes. "Yes. I am Ydaim Trailwalker."

Vailret glared at the khelebar. "Why would you help us and then stop before the fight is finished?"

Ydaim seemed puzzled by Vailret's logic. "When is a fight ever finished?"

Vailret turned away in angry disgust. He threw the sword back down on the canyon floor. "It certainly isn't finished yet." He stared with watery eyes at the Cyclops.

Bryl knelt beside Delrael, doing little more than straightening his hair. The man's skin was a clammy gray and glistening with the diamond dust of sweat. His shallow breaths came from between gritted teeth. Blood poured onto the ground.

Vailret cut a strip from one of the blankets and bound up Delrael's thigh. He pulled the tourniquet tight, then used a twig to twist it tighter. But the blood continued to flow. "This won't do much."

"I don't know how else to help him," Bryl said. "Do we just wait here for him to heal? The Water Stone controls the weather—it won't do anything for Delrael. I never learned any healing spells!"

The khelebar leaned over to touch Delrael's chest. "My tribe lives in Ledaygen, the forest just above this valley. We can take your friend there."

Tears streamed from under Delrael's eyelids. He shuddered violently.

"He has already lost his leg," Ydaim said. "If we get him to Ledaygen soon, perhaps our healers may be able to save his life."

"We don't have any other choice." Vailret tried to make his voice sound firm, as Delrael's had been. Bryl looked at him, afraid and confused. Together, the two of them carefully lifted the man onto the khelebar's broad back, where Ydaim held him. Delrael's left leg fell limp and rubbery, bending in a thousand places where a leg should never bend. Blood dripped down the khelebar's tan hide, marking a trail down his flank.

Ydaim Trailwalker trotted ahead, but he set each footfall down with care. "Come! Follow me."

They jogged after the khelebar, leaving the Cyclops senseless on the floor of the narrow valley.

The khelebar climbed steadily up out of the gorge. Ydaim led them directly east into thicker forest, crossing the hex at its narrowest point. He moved with quiet confidence and rarely glanced at the humans.

Bryl acted withdrawn, as if cursing himself for not acting sooner, for not being able to help. Vailret looked down to see the stream below them, a thin ribbon winding over its bed of rocks. But he kept his attention on Delrael sprawled on the panther-man's back.

He wished Ydaim would stop for just a moment so he could place a blanket over Delrael. But they had no time.

Flecks of blood painted the silver belt made by the old Sorcerer's Sentinels so many years before. Delrael's skin was cold and clammy, and sweat pasted the brown hair to his forehead. Vailret couldn't bear to look at the splinters of bone jutting from the crushed leg.

Adventuring! *Rule #1: Always have fun!* This was irrational, ridiculous. Vailret resented Drodanis and his message stick that had sent them on this mission. He resented Sardun and his daughter. And most of all, he resented the Outsiders for amusing themselves with brutality to their own characters.

"That Cyclops is going to attack the next adventurers who come peacefully through here too. And the next, and the next, just like he attacked us. It will never stop, because you don't believe in 'needless' killing."

Ydaim kept moving ahead, ignoring Vailret's anger.

"How much destruction does the monster need to cause before killing him becomes necessary?"

The khelebar loped along in silence without missing a beat. "Do not worry, Vailret Traveler.

"The healing arts of the khelebar are greater than any other you will find on Hexworld. The *dayid* of Ledaygen helps us. Our healers may be hard-pressed, but you must have hope."

"You're not listening to me! When an ogre killed my father, my uncle Drodanis was so outraged, he took a band of men out to exterminate the ogres once and for all. But his anger died too soon, and he returned before finishing the job. Now the ogres have taken the human Stronghold and destroyed our entire village. If Drodanis had completed the task he started, we would never be in that mess! You're doing the same thing— who knows what else the Cyclops will ruin? And you will be responsible because you refused to do anything about it."

Ydaim raised his eyebrows and appeared deep in thought as he continued to lope down the unseen trail. His wide paws whispered through the underbrush that encroached on the fringes of the path. "I find you difficult to understand, but I am trying. Some of our elders will be intrigued by your philosophy."

His voice held a puzzled tone. "Tell me again how the Cyclops's death will help your friend. Do you believe your friend will absorb the Cyclops's life force if you kill the monster?"

Vailret blinked. "No—don't be ridiculous."

"Then how can the killing the Cyclops help your friend in any way?"

"I'm not just talking about Delrael! What if other travelers come through here? They'll be attacked too."

"But if no other travelers pass through the gorge, then we would have killed him for naught."

"Haven't you ever heard of preventing disasters before they happen?"

The khelebar shrugged. "The Cyclops is our nemesis, yes, but I have never considered killing him just to be rid of the nuisance." Ydaim was silent again for a long time, managing to keep a good speed along the path without losing his breath. "We believe the only way to get the Outsiders to stop inflicting these senseless adventures upon us is to face them with complete indifference. One day, they will see that we no longer wish to Play, and they will leave us alone."

Vailret swallowed in his dry throat. "That won't work." Bryl stumbled along beside them, silent. The khelebar did not know what was about to happen to Hexworld—and the khelebar were on the eastern side of the Barrier River, the wrong side.

The panther-man ignored Vailret's comment. "You have strange but valid points. It is not for me to decide. I will take it up with the khelebar council and allow you to speak. But our first priority is to see that your companion is taken to the healers in Ledaygen."

Thinking he had been rebuked, Vailret silenced himself. The afternoon sun fell toward night. Each time Delrael made a sound, Vailret clenched his fists.

Ydaim brought them across a low grassy rise, and they reached another, more verdant forest, isolated in the depths of the mountains. The khelebar surged forward with new energy.

"Ledaygen! Can you feel the *dayid*'s presence?" He let out a high-pitched sound and plunged into the forest, bearing Delrael with him. Though exhausted, Vailret and Bryl rushed to follow him.

An enveloping presence folded over Vailret, and a quiet eeriness penetrated even his sense of urgency. He had spent much of his life in the forest, thinking and walking among the trees and seeing the precise details of how the Hexworld wilderness was constructed. Yet Ledaygen was somehow different.

Overall, the cleanliness amazed him. No lichens or shelf-mushrooms clung to the trees, no dead and rotting branches lay strewn about the forest floor. The trees, almost entirely oak and pine, were tall and straight, healthy, without crippled branches. The forest floor had been covered with an even blanket of dry leaves and mulch, interspersed with frequent and exactly positioned flowers and plants. Vailret saw no choking underbrush, no thick brambles or tangled vines. He drew in a deep breath of the loamy air.

Delrael groaned again. He looked even weaker now, and his skin seemed translucent with pain. Only a hair's breadth separated him from death.

"Almost there!" Ydaim Trailwalker called in a strong and hopeful voice.

The trees of Ledaygen broke away from them like parting curtains. Ydaim entered a wide, grassy clearing that overlooked a stunning panorama of the Spectre Mountains. Vailret realized they had taken the short way across the forested-hill terrain and had already arrived at the hex-line.

In one of Hexworld's rare flukes of nature, the line of forested-hill terrain did not exactly match up with the adjoining hex of mountain terrain. The hills rose upward and the slope of the Spectre Mountains plunged downward, resulting in a yawning, mismatched cliff that dropped nearly a thousand feet to the roots of the mountains. One tall, ancient pine stood alone on the verge of the cliff, straight and powerful, with boughs sweeping upward and outward to watch over Ledaygen.

Ydaim looked around the clearing and shouted into the air, "Thilane Healer!" The birds instantly fell silent, and it seemed that the trees carried his words, spreading them throughout the forest. Vailret saw other khelebar emerge from the surrounding trees, responding to the summons. The panther-people stared in horror at the injured man on Ydaim's back.

"See what your Cyclops has done?" Vailret said, intending to shout, but the forest muffled his words.

The panther-people parted to let a bare-breasted female khelebar come forward. Gray-streaked blond hair cascaded down her naked back in two long braids. Tiny yellow and white flowers had been woven into her hair and draped in a sweet-smelling garland along her neck. Her panther body was a dusty gray, and lines of strain and weariness etched her face.

"Thilane—" Ydaim Trailwalker began, but she motioned him to silence. She flowed forward to inspect Delrael before anyone else could speak. She bent down, reaching out with her fingers but hesitant to touch. Thilane inspected Delrael's bruised and scraped face, his mangled leg. She brushed a fingertip against a protruding shard of bone and drew her hand away, looking at the blood clinging to her finger.

"Can you heal him?" Bryl whispered, speaking after a long silence. "Do you have that kind of magic?"

The Healer ignored the question and frowned as she continued to inspect Delrael's leg, then felt his forehead. "He will live. That is all I promise." The harshness in her voice startled Vailret. She turned to Ydaim. "I must set to work at once. Give him to me."

Vailret and three of the khelebar lifted the man's broken body onto her dusty gray back. She winced as Delrael's blood flowed down to mat her fur.

Without another word, Thilane bounded into the thick greenness of Ledaygen, where the trees swallowed her up. Vailret set off after her, but Ydaim Trailwalker blocked his way. "She must work alone."

"I need to be with him," Vailret insisted.

Ydaim turned to the other khelebar in the clearing. "I will take these two where they may eat and wash and rest. Tell Fiolin Tribeleader that this human, Vailret Traveler, wishes to call a meeting of the council this night!"

Confusion. Throbbing pain. Anger.

The Cyclops stood, felt the smoldering bruise on his forehead. The rock wall. He remembered. Pain. He grew angrier. The clouds had cleared around his head.

He turned in slow circles. Remembered the humans. He had thrown rocks. Hit one of them. Something else. One of the man-animals. The man-animal had shouted, warned the humans. The man-animal had hurt him. The man-animals.

Pain. Fire. Death. Revenge. Pain.

Vague ideas, not real thoughts—but they were good ideas. He knew where the panther-people lived. By the trees. He didn't like the trees. He preferred rocks, caves, shadows. The trees didn't like him either. He would burn them all. Fire. It would make a very bright light.

He scraped his flint claws against the stone of the canyon wall. Sparks flew.

Pain. Fire. Bright fire.

CHAPTER 6
KHELEBAR

Trees and hills and water and sky. What do the Outsiders know of all this? They have created more than they realize.
—Jorig Falselimb of the khelebar

Thilane Healer followed a path only she could see, gliding among the trees until she reached a room fashioned from the living forest. Trunks and branches had grown together to form walls. A roof canopy of leaves filtered the afternoon sunlight with green; lush weeds, herbs, and flowers dotted the ground. In the center of the clearing jutted a gigantic stump, polished smooth on top like a flat wooden table.

By herself, Thilane removed the unconscious man from her back and placed him on the flat surface of the stump. The concentric age rings glowed brown and gold, drawing her eyes. A splash of blood shattered the beauty of it.

Delrael's leg flowed like water, bending in too many places. The man's face writhed in the pain he felt even through his stupor.

Thilane walked around the clearing, touching a tree or staring at a plant. She waited, listening for something.

"This will require the extent of my knowledge, *dayid*," she said out loud to the forest. "You make me belittle myself with the scratches and scrapes of the khelebar, but now I must tend the injuries of a human as well? He is not even of Ledaygen."

Thilane put her hands on the point where her human abdomen joined the sleek panther body. She received no answer. "I want to serve *you*!" Thilane stopped herself short of clawing the ground in her anger.

The Healer continued to mutter as she touched a young tree that formed part of the woven walls of her room. "I will heal his petty hurts, but I can do nothing for his leg." She shrugged. "I will not waste my time or the resources of Ledaygen."

A thin, painful bolt of lightning jumped from the young tree, stinging her fingers. Rebuffed, Thilane gaped in silent wonder, then swallowed twice before she spoke again. "You judge this one significant, *dayid*?" She glanced over her back at the man lying on the broad stump. "Is this to be a test of my abilities?"

Thilane smiled more with pride than embarrassment. "Well, I am significant too, and I will make you proud of the abilities you have given me." The Healer's emerald green eyes sparkled. "I promise."

The background sounds of birds and wind soothed her, lulling her as she selected a thin branch from the sapling. Without effort, she separated it from the main trunk; the branch detached itself willingly. With her fingers, the Healer massaged the bark, working it like clay and sealing the small wound to remove any scar on the tree. She sniffed the sap end of the severed branch.

Thilane returned to the motionless man and waved the twig over his face. She hummed a quiet song as she passed it over the bruises and scrapes from when he had fallen on the stream bank. The superficial blood and mud disappeared from his skin. The bruises faded. The scratches and torn skin healed.

The branch crumpled to torn, oozing pulp in the Healer's hand.

"That is for appearance only, I know." She sighed to herself. "But at times, appearances can help immensely."

She turned to pluck a branch of oak leaves from another tree, stretching up on her hind legs to reach the highest, healthiest bunch. She placed the leaves on the man's ruined leg, scattering them evenly across the protruding bone splinters. Thilane sang another quiet song, and the leaves withered, turning brown and brittle. She brushed them away, careful not to hurt Delrael, and continued her song without pausing. She laid more leaves on the leg. She sang louder. The leaves died a second time.

"Oak should be stronger than this." She held up one of the withered leaves, staring at the sunlight through its shriveled veins. Thilane frowned and tried once more, singing in her strong, harsh voice. Her words trailed off as her lungs emptied, but she wheezed out a few more notes.

The leaves still turned black and lifeless. She had taken the pain away and stopped the bleeding—but Thilane could never heal his leg.

The *dayid* refused to accept her failure.

Delrael muttered to himself, whimpering. His gray eyes fluttered open, but they stared far away. He seemed unable to focus, though he could sense someone beside him. "Am I hurt? I don't remember." He sighed, and even his breath trembled. "Vailret?"

Thilane snatched a few pine needles from an overhanging branch. "Sleep!" She crushed them in front of Delrael's face, letting him breathe the smell of the pine oil. "In sleep, the *dayid* can help restore your wounded spirit."

She watched the overpowering scent of evergreen engulf him. He melted back into a blissful sleep.

Thilane stared at his unconscious form, scowling at her failure. She pressed her lips together, nodding in silence and knowing that the *dayid* approved of her decision. Drawing a deep breath to steady herself, she smelled the forest, the power, the vibrant life.

I've never done this before. Only once in all our legends has it been successful. She padded over to a sturdy oak tree. The Healer placed her forehead against the tree and wrapped her arms around the wide trunk, pressing her chest against the rough bark.

"Send Noldir Woodcarver to me," she said, and Ledaygen took her message.

Thilane went back to Delrael again, watching him breathe, hovering over his leg. She waited.

A khelebar man entered her enclosed room so silently that Thilane would not have heard him approach had she not felt the faint tremors of recognition in the *dayid*. She turned and met his questioning gaze.

Noldir Woodcarver had black hair, unbraided and sheared off in a square mass around his shoulders. An intricate totem hung on his chest, representing a dream Ledaygen had sent him one night; only Noldir understood its symbolism. His arms were heavily muscled, but Thilane knew his hands were nimble and delicate.

She nodded at Delrael lying on the wide stump. Noldir's eyebrows lifted, but he waited for her to speak. Thilane respected him for that. She had no patience for the others, like Ydaim Trailwalker, who marred the silence of the forest with useless talk.

"The *dayid* says you must help this man."

Noldir took a step backward, carefully sidestepping Thilane's flowers with his large feline paws. "I am always willing to offer my assistance...." He let the sentence hang, asking for more of an explanation.

The Healer crossed her arms over her breasts. The spicy smell of the flower garland at her neck made her feel more relaxed, more confident.

"His leg has died. The forest will take it, and the forest must give him a new one in exchange. You will fashion it—from the wood of a *kennok* tree."

Noldir Woodcarver bit back a gasp but recovered his composure. Thilane knew how powerful, how rare the *kennok* wood was, blessed by the *dayid* and containing many secrets. She was pleased to see how quickly Noldir grasped her intent.

"Are you planning to repeat what was done with Jorig Falselimb? That was many years ago."

"Yes. The khelebar do not remember how it was done. But I need to try. The *dayid* will assist me." Her eyes burned. She wanted to relax in a meadow, look out over the mountains, smell the flowers and trees. Not surround herself with so much pain.

She drew in a deep breath and returned to Delrael's side. "Study the man's other limb and make a reproduction from living *kennok* wood. When will it be ready?"

Noldir bent down, shying from the color and the smell of the man's blood. He inspected both the whole and the damaged leg. "No sooner than dusk, I think."

"So long?"

Noldir answered in a tone of voice that convinced her he was making no excuses. "His limb is strange. I have never attempted to carve such an object."

She sighed and nodded.

"I promise," he said. "By dusk."

Thilane impatiently sent him away.

Vailret slurped cold water from the pool, drinking until his teeth throbbed. He splashed the rest on his face, gasped from the chill, then drank again before shaking the wet clumps of straw-colored hair out of his eyes.

It seemed mechanical to him, but he kept following the procedure by habit. He scooped up fine sand from the bottom of the pool and scrubbed himself. Afterward, his body ached, but he felt clean at last, and very cold.

"The water comes from underground springs beneath Ledaygen," Ydaim said. "You will find it refreshing. You may dry yourself by the fire before nightfall."

Bryl shivered as he sat naked, waiting for his clothes to dry. His wrung-out blue cloak lay spread on a sun-warmed rock. His thin gray beard and wisps of hair sent drips of water down his neck.

"Any word yet?" Vailret asked. "Is Delrael going to be all right?"

The khelebar smiled blithely. "You can trust Thilane. She will do her best."

He rubbed his hands together and looked from Vailret to Bryl to Vailret again. "Will you tell me where you are from? What is your home like?" The young man found the lush green of Ydaim's eyes disconcerting; the pupils were oval, catlike.

"The Stronghold. It's far to the west from here, many hexes away." Vailret didn't feel like talking.

"I have not heard of it," Ydaim said. His expression looked grave and serious.

Vailret shrugged. Bryl coughed twice.

Ydaim stretched out his supple feline body on the long grass beside the pool. "I would like to travel someday, but I do not wish to go far from the *dayid*. I have wandered the lands around Ledaygen more than any other khelebar. The others are content to do their appointed tasks for the forest. But I like to explore. And the *dayid* always takes me back home."

Bryl finally made a rude noise. "I am getting tired of you constantly talking about your *dayid*."

The khelebar rolled himself back into a sitting position and brushed a leaf from his shoulder. His face took on a baffled expression. "The *dayid* cares for us all. The *dayid* will offer its assistance to Thilane Healer as she strives to save your friend."

Ydaim didn't seem to have any conception of what a *dayid* really was. Vailret considered telling him but decided to hold those particular loaded dice for later. Instead, he pulled on his still-damp tunic and laced up the front. "So does the *dayid* keep your forest so clean all by itself?"

Ydaim spread his arms out to indicate all of Ledaygen. "This is the forest of the khelebar. We keep it clean because that is our covenant with the *dayid*. We live in peace with Ledaygen. All life is our friend, and we hold it sacred."

The khelebar fingered the pinecone pendant on his chest.

To Vailret, though, the words sounded flat and memorized. Flashing across his memories, he continued to see the monstrous Cyclops heaving boulders, the obsidian claws scraping sparks against the stone, the boulder smashing Delrael's leg as he tried to twist himself out of the way...

The Outsiders would consider this just an incidental adventure along the path of their quest.

He looked down and saw that his hands had clenched into fists.

"And how did the khelebar get this miraculous covenant that forces you to hold life so sacred that you can't even strike back at a monster who attacked us? Some say the Outsiders put the monsters on Hexworld just to kill and be killed."

Ydaim ignored the sarcasm in Vailret's voice. "That is exactly why we must not kill the Cyclops. We must bend and twist the Outsiders' Rules in whatever way we can. We need to show them that we own our lives and that we will do what we wish."

Ydaim withdrew his long wooden sword and held it in front of his chest. The late afternoon light made the blade's hardened pitch coating look deeply golden. Splotches of the Cyclops's blood speckled the flat surface. Ydaim sounded embarrassed when he spoke again.

"Long ago, just after the old Sorcerer wars, the khelebar were violent and warlike. We had no respect for nature. We … mistreated the forest. We chopped down trees, letting them crash wherever they happened to fall, maiming the forest. Often we left the hewn trees to rot on the forest floor, useless!"

Ydaim shuddered. "But the force of the *dayid* was strong in Ledaygen. The trees banded together and the forest retaliated against us. The trees ceased to bear fruit. The wood refused to burn. The branches tangled together and the trunks moved so close that we could not pass among them. The trees shifted their positions regularly, making all the trails disappear. The khelebar sensed that the forest was their enemy, and so my ancestors fought back, chopping down trees and salting the soil. But the trees fell backward, on purpose, crushing the khelebar."

Vailret looked around, wishing he had some way to write down the legend. He wanted to remember it for his chronicle of Hexworld. Ydaim seemed lost in his words.

"Many trees and khelebar died before the *dayid* finally spoke through Thessar, the Father Pine. You saw Thessar when we first reached the council clearing, on the verge of the great cliff."

Vailret nodded.

"Thessar spoke aloud the terms of the *dayid*'s truce. The khelebar are charged with keeping Ledaygen free of decay and sickness, free of parasites and any animals that might injure the trees. We must remove dead branches wherever they may be and see to it that seedlings grow far enough apart. Ledaygen thrives. In exchange, the forest taught us true wood-magic and how to heal, using arts previously known only to the *dayid*."

Vailret finished pulling on his clothes and shook his arms. "Then you should have no trouble at all healing Delrael."

Ydaim smiled mysteriously. "That we shall see."

Fire. Sparkling orange, burning bright. Warm fire, hungry fire, reflecting from the glassy yellow of a single staring eye.

The Cyclops stood at the edge of the forest, drawing the smoke into his nostrils. Feeling powerful. The trees were afraid of him, afraid of the fire. He scraped his fingers together, and more sparks flew.

The khelebar had spread a thick carpet of dried leaves on the floor of Ledaygen. The flames grew.

Sparkling orange, burning bright.

"I have finished my carving, Healer." Noldir Woodcarver pushed his way through the dense trees into Thilane's chamber.

She looked up at him, groggy and blinking her eyes as she broke her preparatory meditation. She waited a moment, gathering her thoughts as the trees around her flickered into focus.

"Help me, Woodcarver. I must take the man to the *kennok* tree." The words scraped out of her vocal cords, sounding harsh.

Noldir slipped his fingers under Delrael's shoulders, shifting the man to get a better grip. Delrael let out a soft, pain-filled gasp, and Noldir almost dropped him. Delrael's bleeding had stopped, but he still looked weak and drained, fluttering along the hex-line between life and death. Thilane encouraged Noldir, though, and he lifted the man onto her dusty gray back.

The Healer held him in place with one arm as they set off through the uncharted ways of Ledaygen. Noldir kept pace beside her, watching and helping hold the man. Thilane could feel Delrael's weight on her back; she could feel his blood on her fur and the echoes of his pain throbbing in her head.

She wanted to drench herself in Ledaygen's cold spring waters when the ritual was finished, lie in the numbing pool until she could feel cleansed. But she had to succeed first—the *dayid* held this man in high esteem, enough to ask her for this sacrifice. The risk. The *dayid*'s demands were not easy, but the chance to work directly with the soul of the forest outweighed everything else.

Noldir led the way to where the lone *kennok* tree grew. The trees were so rare and precious that few of the khelebar knew their location.

The Woodcarver passed through a thicket of flowers and woven vines to a place where he had left wood chips strewn on the forest floor. Thilane noticed that, in his work, he had heedlessly trampled the grass around the tree.

Then she studied the new limb itself.

Noldir had joined himself to the *dayid,* working with the wood of the small but ancient trunk of the *kennok*. He had shaped the wood like clay with the palms of his hands, stroking off the bark and smoothing, bending, reshaping according to the picture in his mind. The roots of the *kennok* tree still plunged deep into the soil of Ledaygen, tapping into the blood of the *dayid* itself. But the main part of the trunk was now in the shape of a human leg, poised erect and pointing its toes toward the sky. The golden polished wood glowed with rich coppery whorls of grain, strong but soft, and still alive.

Thilane set her mouth in a satisfied line. She tossed her braids back over her shoulders, where they brushed against the injured man. "I commend you, Woodcarver. Your work honors the *dayid*."

Noldir shrugged but looked pleased, as if he had not expected her to give any kind of compliment. "The *dayid* gives each of us our special talents."

He brushed some of the wood chips from an area of grass. Thilane knelt, and the two of them slid Delrael's body from her back, laying him beside the *kennok* trunk. Noldir tried to make Delrael more comfortable while Thilane stood back, stretching her shoulders and brushing at her fur in distaste. She looked at the sticky red on her fingers.

"He must wake now, just for a moment."

She plucked one yellow petal from the garland of flowers around her neck and crushed it in front of Delrael's nose. Noldir stepped back from the acrid odor that sent the man plunging back into consciousness.

Thilane watched Delrael blink. His glassy eyes were strange and gray, different from the emerald green shared by all khelebar. Beads of sweat popped out on his forehead. She bent down, stroking his hair. He would not know who she was.

Delrael looked startled, and then his face drained back into gray as pain washed over him. Thilane turned his head, directing his gaze to the wooden leg growing up out of the tree stump.

"Behold your new limb, Traveler. Because my own skill was not enough, Ledaygen has offered you a replacement."

Delrael tilted his head, but then he saw the clotted blood that slicked his leather armor, the bone shards protruding from the remains of his leg. Thilane caught and cradled his head as he swooned back against her.

"Sleep now," she said.

Delrael's eyes closed and he breathed deeply as she whispered him back into unconsciousness.

Thilane glanced up at Noldir Woodcarver. He seemed to be struggling to contain an expression of awe and to retain the composure he thought she expected of him.

Then she ignored the Woodcarver as she ran her fingers along the cloth of Delrael's stained and torn trousers, finding the secret of the foreign fibers in the cloth. They fell away, leaving both of his legs bare.

Thilane drew a deep breath and exhaled as she closed her eyes, humming to herself, floating into the trance she would need. Keeping her eyes closed, she extended an arm to grasp the *kennok* wood reaching out of the ground. From it, she drew strength and deepened her trance.

With her mind, she searched for the *dayid*, plunging deep beneath the soil of Ledaygen, following the network of *kennok* roots toward the heart of Hexworld itself. She saw the structure, the patterns ... she learned with awe how the *dayid* slipped between the cracks, bent under and around the Rules that confined the rest of the world. Still shutting her eyes tight, she could see through the eyes of the forest.

Her hand drifted down the polished *kennok* wood until she reached the point where the carving ended and the bark began. Thilane extended her index finger and applied gentle pressure horizontally, slicing the artificial leg from the *kennok* tree.

Eyes closed, she lifted the heavy false limb and carried it on her fingertips until she rested it on the ground beside Delrael's injured leg. She aligned the two limbs then climbed back to her feet again. On four feline paws, she padded to one of the towering black pines, then ran the palms of her hands up the trunk, brushing the bark, the rough lumps of pitch, until she encountered a branch thinner than her finger. She plucked it from the trunk, leaving no scar.

Noldir watched in awed silence. He saw that dark red sap had begun to ooze from the severed trunk of the *kennok* tree.

The Healer's humming grew louder. Then she sang a song with no words, notes that sounded like running water, chattering birds, blooming flowers. Thilane laid the thin pine branch across Delrael's thigh, just above his injury.

Her breath hissed through her teeth as she pushed down. She did not hear Noldir gasp as the branch sank into Delrael's flesh, melting through the heavy bone and severing the leg.

Moving rapidly now, Thilane opened her eyes. The green irises glowed with an unseeing power. She discarded Delrael's dead limb and switched it for the living *kennok* leg, pressing it against his stump before the blood could start. The Healer wrapped her fingers along the seam, and her voice broke into a different, more powerful song that resonated in the air. The trees seemed to be singing along with her.

"Melding of flesh and tree. Merging of bone and wood. Joining of sap and blood. Bring the two together as one. Life of tree and man blend together. Meld. Merge. Join. One!"

A flood of energy from the *dayid* seared through her nerves, leaping across the barrier into the *kennok* wood.

The Healer gave a sharp cry and stepped back, blinking her eyes and seeing the forest again. Her hands trembled with exhaustion. Noldir Woodcarver stood beside her as she fought to bring her mind back through the murk of the trance. Noldir reached out a hand to steady her, but she pushed him away and bent over Delrael's motionless form.

She had attached the *kennok* limb. A sharp line marked the boundary of skin and wood, but that would fade as the man's body accepted his new leg. She smiled to herself.

Only a small amount of the man's blood spattered the grass. She ran her fingers along one of the grass blades, straightening it and wiping off the red smear.

Thilane gave the crushed, dead leg to Noldir. "Take this ... and bury it."

Delrael fled from bizarre dreams, unable to force himself awake. Something held him imprisoned with his nightmares, but locked him away from his pain. He saw a giant, one-eyed monster hurling boulders. He remembered running. Hybrid man-panthers. The huge rock flying at him. And pain. A great deal of pain.

"Roll the dice again!" he moaned and turned his head. He had better luck than this. "It's not fair." His leg felt very strange.

He lifted his eyelids, expecting to see something or someone he recognized. He didn't. He was in a thick forest somewhere. He could smell it. He could hear the sounds of wind and night birds. Everything seemed to be dark, but he was not cold. In a disorienting moment, he wondered if he had somehow landed in the Rulewoman Melanie's forest, by her Pool of Peace. He expected to see his own father there, waiting for him.

Then Thilane Healer stood over him. Her garland of yellow flowers swayed, and her face looked lined and weary. Her breasts were tanned and dusty-colored, like her pale fur. He remembered her from somewhere.

Questions ricocheted back and forth in his mind until he remembered everything. The Cyclops, the canyon, the khelebar, the boulder—his leg. He winced with a pain that was not there but should have been.

"I am Thilane Healer of the khelebar." She spoke in a quiet yet harsh voice. "Your leg would not heal, so I replaced it."

Delrael looked down at his left leg—and saw rich yellow wood laced with feathery ripples of copper-colored grains. The Healer held on to his shoulders, squeezing hard enough that her fingernails made impressions in the skin. He closed his eyes and clenched his teeth, leaning his head back. "It's not fair." Overhead, the leaves rustled in the night. "Look at it," Thilane said.

Delrael felt the words choke in his throat. His real leg was gone, discarded and replaced with something of wood. He was a fighter. He *needed* his dexterity. He needed to move, to attack, to quest, to explore. If he could do nothing interesting, the Outsiders would erase him from the Game.

"Look at it!" Thilane said again.

He turned his eyes downward, looking at the serpentine wood-grain patterns that seemed to move by themselves. He did not want to think of it as part of him.

The Healer shook her head. She took his *kennok* leg in her hands, massaging it. "Time. Give it time. I can feel the warmth in the wood." With one fingernail, she tapped against the wooden knee. He heard a light ticking noise. "Can you feel this?"

"No." He drew in a deep breath. He wanted to go back to his nightmares again. "Of course not."

"There's magic in Hexworld. You just need to know how to use it."

"That spell isn't in any book. Ask Bryl." Delrael wasn't sure, but it seemed right to him.

Thilane crossed her arms, accidentally bruising the yellow flowers around her neck. He smelled the burst of perfume they released. "Hexworld has magic the Outsiders don't even know about."

She kneaded his left foot, massaging the wood, working with the toes and bending them slowly at the joints. Delrael watched in wonder as he saw the *kennok* wood become flexible.

"Trust me," she said.

Delrael closed his eyes and concentrated on breathing for several minutes. Thilane offered no conversation of her own. "Where is Vailret?" he finally asked.

The Healer stopped her work as she scowled up at him. He was frightened of the stare behind her oval green eyes. "Your friends are gathering a council of the khelebar. Your Vailret is upset because you were attacked by the Cyclops."

Delrael saw the monster towering on top of the gorge, his brick-red skin gleaming in the sunlight, his one yellow eye like a great torch as he found his target. And hurled the crushing boulder down—

"Why *did* he attack us?"

Thilane shrugged. "Because that is what he does. The Outsiders put him there as a challenge to us. We refuse to accept it. The *dayid* gives us other tasks than to amuse childish Players."

Thilane moved Delrael's ankle, working patiently until the foot became limber and soft. Her strong hands continued to massage, pushing on the false calf muscles, and finally, with a tremendous effort, bending his knee.

Delrael reached forward, tentative. Thilane guided his hand, touching it to the *kennok* wood. To him, the polished skin seemed hard as oak, yet warm somehow.

"Where are my clothes? My silver belt?"

"Nearby. Enough talk. Now move your toes."

"I can't. It's only wood."

"It is *kennok* wood! Now move your toes."

Delrael stared at his toes, and they seemed to stare back. He closed his eyes and concentrated. But he couldn't think how to move muscles that were not his.

"The *kennok* trees have been in this forest since the beginning of the Game. Some say the Outsiders do not know they exist—they are the wellspring of the true magic of our world. But they are rare. And only once before, in all our chanted history, has this ritual been successfully performed—for Jorig Falselimb, a great leader of the khelebar."

Thilane looked around in the shadowy darkness. "Jorig saved Ledaygen from a blood-mad wolf pack that haunted the Spectre Mountains. A saliva-fever had driven all the wolves into a frenzy—and Jorig stood alone with the *dayid* to face them.

"The *dayid* took away Jorig's individual scent, making him smell like the pines, the oaks, the grass, the woodland flowers. The wolves were confused, but the great black leader of the pack found a *part* of the scent that was the khelebar, and he attacked that part of Jorig. The wolf bit off Jorig's arm. The black wolf died in a spasm of his own blood-fever, and the rest of the wolves fled.

"But the *dayid* was grateful to Jorig, and it showed the khelebar Healers how to make a false limb from the living *kennok* wood. After he became accustomed to it, Jorig used his wooden fingers to play a flute and to shoot his bow." She looked up into the night with a dreamy, distant expression on her face.

Then she whirled to shout at him, "Now move your toes!"

Startled, Delrael saw that, in reflex, his toes had moved. He felt a surge of surprise and relief.

Later, he did not want to sleep. The night went on and on. After an hour of intensive practice, Delrael used his leg clumsily. He could rotate his foot; he could bend his knee and move it. He still could not feel any sensation, but Thilane assured him that even that would come back, in time. Already, the seam where the *kennok* wood joined his leg had grown less distinct as the elements of tree and man mingled together.

Thilane pulled forth an aged wooden knife with a blade polished and hard as iron. "We shall see if the acceptance is complete." Delrael watched the edge of the blade and envied its craftsmanship; the sharpness had been honed with infinite patience and devotion. Thilane reversed the knife and tapped the man's leg with the wooden hilt. A hollow sound rang in the still forest air. "Can you feel this?"

Delrael concentrated. "I don't think so."

"And this?" Thilane flipped the knife in her hand and chopped the blade down hard into the *kennok* wood.

"Ow!" Delrael sat up as a slice of pain echoed through his leg.

"Good." Thilane hid her smile.

Vailret stood in the clearing and watched the night shroud the surrounding hexes of mountain terrain. Thessar, the tall and ancient Father Pine, loomed silent on the verge of the cliff-discontinuity. Over the sound of the wind in the trees, Vailret listened to the forest settle down.

The khelebar began to arrive in the clearing, surrounding a large, bare circle where all the plants had been removed. A heap of wood—the dead branches of Ledaygen—lay within the patch of dirt. Flames from a new fire worked their way deeper into the pile.

Ydaim had told him that some of the khelebar were Treescavengers, whose purpose was to find and remove the dead and diseased branches. They used no tools, but somehow they scrambled to the tallest branches and removed the wood. "The *dayid* guides them," Ydaim had said.

Vailret had looked with awe around the forest. The aura of Ledaygen seemed to penetrate even to him, and he could sense the magic, but he could not touch it.

He just hoped the *dayid* could help Delrael.

Bryl sat by the fire, shivering and trying to warm himself and his damp clothes. The old half-Sorcerer rubbed the Water Stone, looking distant. Vailret watched him, trying to imagine being able to use the magic himself.

He drew in a deep breath, smelling the cool tang in the air, an after-taste of smoke from the fire, the spice of pines and the plentiful dried leaves on the forest floor. Delrael might be dying....the Outsiders had effectively stopped their quest in its tracks. The khelebar had lived with the threat of the Cyclops for years and had done nothing about it.

Vailret rehearsed his line of attack as the panther people arrived.

The gathered khelebar looked at Vailret and Bryl, curious. Vailret wasn't sure what he wanted from them. He knew he was playing into the hands of the Outsiders by fighting back against the Cyclops. This was just an incidental adventure—they should ignore the monster and push on as soon as Delrael had healed.

One of the khelebar, an older male with close-cropped hair streaked with gray, stepped into the pool of firelight and paced back and forth.

Ydaim Trailwalker sat beside the two humans, like a sponsor. He tossed his black braid behind his back and leaned over to whisper in Vailret's ear, "That is Fiolin Tribeleader. He will hear your arguments."

The other panther-people tightened their circle like a slipknot around the bonfire. Over the roar of the flames, Vailret heard insect sounds in the forest. The bonfire spilled orange light over the cliff.

Fiolin Tribeleader turned to face the rest of the circle, silhouetting himself against the blaze. "Ydaim Trailwalker, you have called us together in council. For what purpose?"

With an excited gleam in his eye, Ydaim raised himself to his feet, broadening his shoulders. He brushed the pinecone pendant before he spoke. "The man Vailret Traveler has not asked for just a council, Tribeleader, but a war council."

Ydaim held his ground when the other khelebar muttered in astonishment. Fiolin maintained his cool expression, keeping his thoughts hidden. "Against whom will the khelebar go to war, after so many years of peace? And for what cause?"

Ydaim Trailwalker gestured to the two men. Vailret made ready to speak, but Ydaim continued. "The travelers speak against the Cyclops— Pain-Giver, Life-Taker. The black smoke of burning, *living* trees coats the walls of his cave like dark bloodstains. I have seen it in my wanderings. And he preys upon helpless questers such as the man Delrael, now called Kennoklimb, and these two here."

Vailret stood up. His elegant speeches melted away, leaving him weaponless to convey his anger to the mellow expressions of the khelebar. They stared back at him from the firelit shadows. Their unblinking emerald eyes made him feel as if he had stumbled into a jungle and was now surrounded by patient wild animals.

He swallowed and spoke. "Obviously, you must do something about the Cyclops." Bryl watched him. "He is destructive and dangerous. Why have you let him go unpunished for so long? He will keep hurting other characters if you don't do something."

"He maims trees," Ydaim added.

The khelebar remained silent, waiting for their Tribeleader to speak. Fiolin mused for a moment. "The Cyclops has long been our enemy. Do others agree that we should try to drive him away now that he has harmed the man Delrael Kennoklimb?"

Vailret fidgeted. He had hoped they would consider destroying the monster, not just chase him away.

One of the khelebar stood up. She had dark brown hair and a mottled panther pelt. Fiolin nodded to her. "Speak, Stynod Treescavenger."

She faced the Tribeleader, not looking at Vailret. "The Cyclops is a challenge for the khelebar to face. The Outsiders placed him here. His only purpose is to attack and destroy and eat—we must endure him as best we can." Her voice grew hoarse and angry. "If we remove him, the Outsiders will only send something worse."

"And what if the Outsiders lose interest in that?" Bryl asked. Vailret gave the half-Sorcerer an appreciative nod.

"We happen to know the Outsiders *are* bored with Hexworld. They have already begun the destruction of the world. The Rulewoman Melanie has given us a quest to prevent it if we can."

One of the other khelebar, Noldir Woodcarver, nodded. "Ah, then that is why the *dayid* demanded that Thilane Healer save your companion."

Fiolin brooded a long moment, distracted and troubled. The firelight and the night sounds of the forest insects seemed to speak to him.

"The *dayid* is uneasy tonight—I can feel it. Perhaps it sees the evil things that may come of this council."

A gibbous moon hovered over the eastern outline of the Spectre Mountains; Lady Maire's Veil draped, glowing over the north. But Fiolin stared at a hazy orange glow nearby, rising from the treetops at the far fringe of Ledaygen. As he gazed without speaking, the other khelebar also turned to look.

The Tribeleader motioned to a blond-haired khelebar standing near him. The young panther-man was deeply tanned with tigerlike whorls on his fur. Each of his arms bore an armband on the bicep, and a necklace of stones hung at his throat.

"Tayron, my son, go find the cause of that orange glow. It may be a sign from the *dayid*. Maybe it will help us make our decision."

"Yes, Father." The young panther-man turned to bound into the dark mass of surrounding trees, vanishing from sight.

Fiolin Tribeleader stilled the soft mutters around the bonfire. He turned to stare at Vailret. "The khelebar have not harmed a living being since the Scouring of Hexworld."

"The Cyclops is a killer," Vailret said, surprised at how calm his voice sounded. "By your inaction, you caused Delrael to come to harm. You won't accomplish anything by slapping the monster's hands and telling him to stay in his cave."

Vailret stopped, letting the silence hang like a poised sword over the council. The other khelebar waited, watching their Tribeleader. Fiolin avoided looking at Vailret and sat back down in the firelight. "Perhaps we should wait for Tayron Next-Leader to return."

Vailret pursed his lips in impatience.

A long time later, they heard a khelebar plunging through the forest, reckless and crashing branches and undergrowth. Tayron Next-Leader burst into the cliff clearing, scratched and wild-eyed, gasping for breath.

Vailret had never seen a khelebar out of breath before, nor had he seen such an expression of horror and despair. Tayron gasped, scattering tears instead of words.

Fiolin pounced to his feet. "What is it? What have you seen?"

Tayron sobbed but managed to speak. "The forest! It is on fire! Ledaygen is burning!"

CHAPTER 7

A FIRE IN LEDAYGEN

RULE #8: Magic users—i.e., those with Sorcerer blood—may attempt to use only a specific number of spells per day. Table A-3 lists spell allowances, calculated according to the character's percentage of Sorcerer blood, also taking experience into account.
—The Book of Rules

The khelebar sat stunned. The heartbeat of the night fell silent, interrupted only by the insects. Vailret could hear the soft crackle of the bonfire and the whisper of a breeze through the interlocked trees.

"Can you not hear me?" Tayron Next-Leader choked on his words, aghast at his own people. "Ledaygen is *burning*!"

Fiolin broke from his shock and drew himself taller as he pointed to four of the khelebar. "Ydaim Trailwalker, you and three others go scout and tell me the extent of the fire. Quickly! We must know how fast it is spreading."

Ydaim glanced back at Vailret, then bounded with the others into the mass of trees. The four khelebar became dark ripples in the forest, loping toward the orange glow.

Fiolin Tribeleader continued to motion at the other panther-people. "Aratok Treetender,

Stynod Treescavenger—find everyone else in Ledaygen. Tell them to come here. The khelebar must be alerted!"

Stynod had to shake the other khelebar man out of his shock before they both ran into the forest.

Bryl moved over to Vailret, leaning forward on the damp grass. His eyes were bright in their nest of wrinkles. "I wonder how serious this is."

Vailret stared into the bonfire. "It'll be bad enough." He turned a heavy gaze at the half-Sorcerer as the implications popped one by one into his mind. "Think about it—the Cyclops nearly killed Delrael. Now there's a forest fire." He heaved a deep breath, frightened. "I don't know how we could have hoped to hide it after we made the Barrier River.

"The Outsiders know what we're doing. And they're trying to stop us."

Delrael moved in tight circles, flexing his *kennok* limb with difficulty. "I can move it."

Thilane Healer paid no attention to him. Troubled, she paced about the clearing, back and forth. She had been silent for a long while, sniffing the air. Delrael watched her back, the tight skin against her shoulder blades, the muscles wrapped around her sides melding into the panther body.

He limped around the clearing once more and rested on a boulder; the rock felt cool as he sat on it. His *kennok* limb felt tired. Deep night penetrated Ledaygen, broken only by the moonlight.

"Something is wrong in Ledaygen." Thilane touched a tree trunk, closed her eyes, then shook her head, as if amazed to be talking to herself.

A few seconds before Delrael heard anything, Thilane glanced up and stared into the trees. Rough sounds of passage came through the forest, too careless to be a khelebar. But Stynod Treescavenger burst into the clearing. Her eyes were wild and her dark braids undone. Flecks of sweat streaked down her face and chest.

Thilane waited in silence as Stynod caught her breath in great gulps. "Ledaygen burns!"

The Healer bit back an outcry. Delrael could see the pain drive like a sword through her side. But he had helped fight grass fires in other villages to the south of the Stronghold. "How far has it spread? What kind of help do you have?" he asked.

The Treescavenger shook her head, motioning them toward the trees. "Go to the council clearing for your answers. I have no time." She set off into the forest again, moaning to herself. "How can I bear to tell any others?"

She fled the clearing, fueled by her own fear, and vanished into the thickness of the trees.

More khelebar converged on the council clearing, their faces filled with silent horror. Vailret watched them, amazed at how helpless the graceful panther-people now appeared. Left untended, the council bonfire had burned low, turning red as the moon rose higher in the sky.

"Delrael!" Bryl stood up as Thilane Healer led the man out of the trees. Vailret whirled, grinning.

Delrael stopped at the edge of the clearing, sweating and breathless. He placed a hand on Thilane's dusky back and rested. The Healer didn't seem to mind.

Vailret and Bryl ran forward. Several khelebar glared at their happy outburst, but Vailret ignored them. Delrael smiled wryly and took another limping step forward. The Healer kept pace with him.

Vailret gave Delrael a careful hug as Bryl hovered next to him, grinning. "You're all right!"

Delrael lifted his hand from Thilane's back and steadied himself. "Well, not quite as good as new, but ... different. It'll take some getting used to."

Thilane looked at the three of them in turn. "You can thank the *dayid* for challenging me to heal him. *Kennok* wood is rare and precious, but the *dayid* holds all of you in great value. Perhaps you will save us from this fire?" She snorted and went to join the other khelebar. Around the circle, Tayron Next-Leader described the blaze as they waited for the scouts to return.

"Look." Delrael lifted part of his mended trouser leg and showed the feathery grain of his *kennok* leg. "And I can move it." He puckered his brow in concentration as he bent the knee partway.

"It's not any kind of magic I've ever heard of," Bryl said. Vailret agreed.

"I need to sit down," Delrael said. Vailret and Bryl helped him over to the bonfire, away from the other khelebar.

Vailret felt light-headed at having his cousin back. Somehow, he could not worry about the forest fire at the moment. He smiled at his own memories, watching Delrael. "Del, do you remember when we were little? You always picked on me because you were older, and bigger, and stronger."

"Yes, but you got back at me every time with some practical joke. Molasses on the privy seat in winter. A puddle of water on my chair."

"Sand in your birthday honey roll. Your father said it was just like when he and my father were young. But it all changed when those outlander villagers tried to beat me up. You saved me."

Delrael shrugged but allowed a smile to drift onto his face. "I didn't want anyone picking on you but me."

"I was only ten. You were fourteen. And now we're a team."

Delrael propped himself up on his elbows, stretching both legs toward the lowering bonfire.

"Are you sure you're all right, Del?"

"Just give me some time. We've got a quest to finish." He rubbed a hand on his *kennok* leg.

Bryl cleared his throat, isolated from the conversation. He pointed to the gathered khelebar. "I don't think they're all right."

Vailret looked once again at the Tribeleader's haggard face. Fiolin looked filled with anguish for his burning trees.

"Maybe we can do something." Delrael reached out, and Vailret helped him to his feet. Together, they went to where Fiolin stood. His emerald eyes were glassy with tears and visions from his own imagination.

"Ledaygen will be consumed to the soil itself. We have no way to fight fire."

The Tribeleader closed his eyes, but Vailret touched his shoulder. Fiolin's eyes snapped open, piercing him with a lost gaze.

"We were going to offer help," Vailret said. "Bryl can use the Water Stone to make it rain on the fire. Delrael and I have both fought against fires before. Every summer, the grassland and grassy-hill terrain to the south and west of the Stronghold gets dry as a match. When the fires start, people of the Stronghold village work to stop them from spreading."

Delrael agreed. "Last year, it got so bad that the Sidonne village nearly burned. But we saved it."

Fiolin Tribeleader looked unwilling to embrace hope. "What power do you have that can defeat a raging fire?"

"Just common sense," Vailret said softly. "Fire is deadly, but it is no evil force. It's just fire."

One of the logs in the bonfire settled with a crunch, startling Fiolin. Some of the other khelebar now shied away from the fire, as if that too had turned into an enemy.

He squatted on the dirt of the clearing and motioned for the Tribeleader to stand beside him. "Draw me a map of your forest, Fiolin. Del, help me think of some strategy."

Fiolin hesitated, looking lost. Vailret raised his voice. "Come on! Another tree dies for every minute you waste."

When the Tribeleader saw that others had gathered to watch, he regained his composure. He sent one of the younger khelebar running for a stick and some ashes. The youth scattered two handfuls of white ash from a dead part of the bonfire, spreading it on the ground to make a smooth surface.

Fiolin took up the thin stick and sketched out the precise hexagon of Ledaygen and the surrounding hexagons of terrain. He indicated the terrain types. "This is our forest." He handed the stick to Vailret.

Vailret frowned and ran a finger along his lips. He tasted ash and wiped his hand on his trousers. Delrael watched him think. "Okay, any rivers, ravines? Rock outcroppings that might slow the fire?"

Fiolin shook his head. "Ledaygen is forested-hill terrain, but rather flat. The *dayid* draws water from underground springs that reach the surface in a few places, but we have no rivers."

Bryl joined them, looking smug. "The *dayid* always saved you before. Why doesn't it just stop the fire and protect the forest?"

Fiolin forced a smile, looking pathetic. "The *dayid* does not work that way. It offers assistance and gives hope, but the khelebar must do everything that needs doing."

Bryl shook his head, sighing. "Not much of a *dayid* then, is it?"

Vailret found Bryl's attitude puzzling. But then he remembered about Bryl's parents, Qonnar and Tristane, how they had both destroyed themselves in blazing sorcerous fire, a partial Transition, as their young son watched … all because they had failed at something. He couldn't remember much else, and Bryl himself never talked about it.

One of the khelebar began sobbing, as if he felt the burning in the forest itself. "Silence!" Thilane Healer said. "You show disrespect for the forest in its pain."

Fiolin sniffed the air. His shoulders sagged. "I can smell the smoke already. Already."

Delrael turned his head. He wet one finger and raised it. "A breeze is blowing this way. It isn't strong, but it will push the fire along." He looked to Vailret. "With the help of the khelebar, you might have enough man power to make an effective fire line, cutting down trees and digging trenches. Unless the wind changes, though, we'll never be able to set a controlled fire back into the first one—"

Fiolin gripped Delrael's arm, aghast and angry. The lines in his face made his expression look as if it had shattered. "Do not speak of such things! Chopping down trees, digging in the sacred earth of Ledaygen, starting another fire! Is the damage not great enough already? How can you think the khelebar would do this?"

Delrael controlled his own reply and thrust the Tribe leader's hand back at him.

Vailret made a disappointed noise at Fiolin. "You khelebar may be faithful to your forest, but you are blind to reason. If you're willing to take these measures now, you may save most of Ledaygen."

Vailret turned his back from the Tribeleader. Mists rose softly up the side of the gaping discontinuity at the edge of the clearing where the forested-hill terrain dropped off to the mountainous hex below.

The four khelebar scouts led by Ydaim Trailwalker leaped back into the clearing, pouring out of the tree shadows like dun-colored spears. Sweat and tears streaked the scouts' faces. The other khelebar stood up, anxious.

Ydaim crossed to the Tribeleader in three enormous bounds. He pawed at the bare ground and his tail swished in tension and fear. "The fire is raging!" He paused to swallow a mouthful of dry air, then glanced at Vailret, but his glassy green eyes showed no recognition. "Nothing can stop it."

"The trees are falling, spraying red coals!" One of the other scouts put a hand to her throat to slow down her throbbing breaths. "The flames move onward and onward!"

Someone moaned, and the sound grew as others joined in an eerie keening sound. Vailret watched them and shuddered.

"Enough!" Fiolin Tribeleader shouted, then blinked his eyes at his own vehemence. "We will not surrender so soon. To abandon hope is to abandon the *dayid*." He clenched his teeth and drew a deep breath. Vailret got the sense that he was afraid to speak further, but Fiolin swallowed and continued. "The travelers claim they may know a way to help. It will be painful to us, and to Ledaygen—but I say it is more painful to do nothing as the trees die around us."

He hung his head. "Perhaps it is a test. Perhaps it is time we show the Outsiders just what we are made of."

Fiolin drew himself up again and thrust his drawing stick into Ydaim's hand, pointing to the hexagonal out lines drawn in the ashes. "Here, Trailwalker. You have the best sense of your surroundings. Show us the extent of the fire."

Ydaim glanced at Vailret and Bryl. He took up the stick and studied the map.

"Ledaygen is a small forest, and the flames are moving rapidly." He drew a line from one vertex to another across the hexagon, cutting off about a quarter of the enclosed area. "By now, the flames have destroyed this much of Ledaygen. By morning—" He drew a second line over about a third of the hexagon. "—the fire will have devoured its way to here."

The other three scouts nodded their agreement.

Delrael swore. He shifted his hand from his silver belt to the sword given to him by Sardun, to his bow. Nothing seemed a useful weapon.

Vailret shook his head and rested his knuckles against his left temple. "The fire just rushes over your neat carpet of dead leaves on the ground. Then it can burn the trees at its leisure."

Bryl didn't seem to know what to do. "We might as well be sitting on the wick of a candle."

Fiolin hung his head in disbelief. "What you say frightens me. The *dayid* has told us to tend the forest as we do—and the *dayid* would never ask us to do something that might harm the trees."

"It wasn't on purpose," Vailret said.

"We would rather die than forfeit our bargain with the *dayid*," Tayron Next-Leader said, looking around at the other khelebar for support.

"We may well have to."

The silence held for a moment, then Bryl pulled out the sapphire Water Stone. Firelight glittered off its six smooth facets, but the gem glowed with its own sleeping blue fire. "Let me try to help with the Stone. I could make it rain or I could change the wind. I don't know what will work, but I've got four spells per day."

Delrael patted him on the back. The half-Sorcerer looked embarrassed.

"Ydaim, will you take me to the fire? We can travel faster if you let me ride on your back. And we need to get there before midnight so I can use my spell allotment for today. After midnight, I can try four more times."

Ydaim Trailwalker did not appear eager to return to the blaze, but he squared his shoulders. "We must hurry to the defense of Ledaygen." Bryl slid onto Ydaim's panther back and wrapped his arms around the khelebar's stomach. He closed his eyes for the ride. "Do you want me to come along, Bryl?" Vailret asked.

The half-Sorcerer shook his head. "Stay with Delrael. And keep convincing them to fight."

As Ydaim bounded off into the forest again, Fiolin called after them, "You are our hope, Bryl Traveler."

Several other khelebar followed, chasing fairy-lights of hope.

The shadowy trees of Ledaygen flew past. Ydaim Trailwalker loped through the night, seeing the unexpected obstacles with his green khelebar eyes.

Bryl held the Water Stone in his hand, eager now to have the opportunity to use it, anxious to feel its power. He rubbed his thumb on the slick flat facets. The forest fire offered him a chance to see exactly what the Stone could do.

He did not understand how the Outsiders could ever become bored with all this.

Bryl smelled burning wood long before he could see the orange flames peeling bark from the trees. He had to crouch low to the khelebar's back because Ydaim had stopped being careful about dodging branches. Ydaim charged forward, shouting his anger at the fire. Bryl heard the crackle of burning underbrush. His eyes stung from the thickening smoke.

They reached the edge of the blaze.

"It is nearer than before. Ah, *dayid,* help us!"

Bryl stared as Ledaygen's trees fell into the burning mass, one by one. In his imagination, he saw the end of the world, a conflagration caused by the Outsiders, tired of their Game and burning their master maps.

He tightened his fist around the Water Stone. With the power of the old Sorcerers and the dead Sentinels, he would fight back. He would not allow failure to swallow him up, as his parents had.

"Bryl Traveler, do something!" Tears streamed down Ydaim's cheeks, not caused by the stinging smoke.

The heat of the fire focused Bryl's thoughts. He stared at the rippling sheets of flame as he slid down from the khelebar's back. Holding the Water Stone with both hands in front of him, he stepped toward the fire. Tentatively, he sent a thought into the sapphire, focusing it through the crystalline facets and unlocking the Sorcerer power.

"I want it to rain!" He envisioned the storm he wanted, and what he would have to roll to succeed. The higher he rolled, the bigger the storm he could summon. If he rolled a "1," he forfeited an entire spell for the day.

Kneeling, Bryl tossed the Water Stone to the ground, rolling it on the unburned leaves. The facet showing "4" came to the top.

It began to rain. The crawling black smoke in the air clumped together to form thunderclouds that shone pale gray from the firelight and the night. A violent downpour spilled onto a swath of the flaming forest, but the droplets hissed into steam before they touched the ground.

Slitting his eyes half-closed, he let the rain continue but reached forward to pick up the Stone again. He filled his lungs with the smoky air. He felt larger, stronger.

"This time, I want to turn the wind back."

Bryl shifted his fingers to a different facet of the Stone, then closed his eyes as he tossed the gem to the ground. A thin line of sweat broke out on his forehead. A "2." Close ... but close enough.

The wind died without a whisper. The rain continued to fall. But his manipulation with the Water Stone affected only an area around him. He did not have the strength and training that Sardun had; his Sorcerer blood was not pure—and he had not rolled well. In the rest of Ledaygen, the fire continued to rage.

The rainstorm extinguished the nearby flames, leaving a black and steaming moonscape of soggy charcoaled trees and scorched earth. For a moment, Bryl felt a sense of accomplishment, optimism.

The rain sputtered and stopped as the first spell ended. A few moments later, he felt the other breeze pick up again, brushing his face with the smell of heat and burning. The blaze slowed its march but moved forward, skirting the rain-soaked area. Soon the fire would encircle them.

But he saw in Ydaim Trailwalker's eyes an adamant refusal to give up. Ydaim would fight for Ledaygen until his heart and lungs burst, and he would expect Bryl to do the same. If the half-Sorcerer succumbed to hopelessness and stopped trying, he knew the other khelebar would probably toss him over the hex-discontinuity as a traitor.

"Come. Let us try a different area with your magic." Ydaim extended his arm and helped the half-Sorcerer up onto his back. They set off again, racing toward the edge of the flames.

Since he had used one spell already against the Cyclops, Bryl had only one attempt left until midnight, when he would receive another day's spell allotment. As Ydaim carried him across the reeking wet ground, Bryl fixed his eyes on the flames like blurry hot knives slashing the trees. The forest fire might be something sent by the Outsiders to stop them from finishing their quest or as a prelude to their obliteration of Hexworld. Bryl would show them he was not ready to sit back and Play along.

Before rolling the Water Stone for the last time of the day, he looked at the moon and the stars through the interlocked branches. It would be close—midnight had nearly arrived, and he did not get reimbursed for any spells he did not use in a day.

He successfully rolled for another rainstorm and drove back the flames in a wider section. Ydaim clapped and gave him encouragement. But the fire flanked them again, and Bryl could do nothing to contain it.

After midnight, feeling enthusiastic with four new spells to use, Bryl imagined summoning a larger storm, a "6" storm with the six-sided Water Stone—but he failed. When the "1" came face up on the large sapphire, he had wasted one of his chances.

"Can't your *dayid* at least help me make a simple dice roll?" Bryl shouted, feeling cheated and afraid.

"You did not ask for help." Ydaim shrugged. "The *dayid* often bends Rules and works around them. Perhaps this is something it could do."

"Well, tell it to help me, then—I'm going to try one more time. *Dayid*, give me a six!"

The Water Stone came up with a "2," paused, then kept rolling, one facet at a time, until it stopped with "6" staring skyward.

Rain came down in sheets. A brisk wind pushed at the fire, driving it back. The storm spread out, attacking the blaze.

With the *dayid*'s help, Bryl abandoned himself into the power of the Stone. He cast his remaining two spells—both sixes—and spent hours in the world bounded by the walls of the cube of sapphire. He enjoyed the release of power. He enjoyed fighting when he no longer felt like the weak contender. With the Stone, he could work magic even though no one had bothered to take the time training him.

He watched the flames fall back as they tried to run from the rain. He extinguished the embers, snuffed the little fires. A chunk of Ledaygen smoldered in wreckage, scarred by the fire, wounded and gasping for its life.

When his last spell ended, Bryl blinked dumbly as he came up for air. Dawn shot through the darkness. Orange banners streaked across the sky above the plains in the east. Smoke from Ledaygen rose upward, clotting in the air like a dark pudding. The half-Sorcerer took a deep breath. His body sagged with exhaustion.

Vailret stood beside him, looking red-eyed and tired. "Good job, Bryl. You made a lot of progress."

Bryl blinked but waited a moment before he felt strong enough to speak. "Progress? That's all?"

Vailret spread his hands. "You fought back the fire, but it's still burning." Ydaim Trailwalker glared into the distance, clenching his fists. Without the influence of the magic, the prevailing breeze had picked up again, stronger now, pushing the fire toward them.

Bryl let his voice drop to a whisper. He held the Water Stone in his grimy hands, but it was just a colored rock to him now. "I can't do anything else. I'm helpless until tomorrow."

"Now it's our turn." Vailret indicated the other khelebar he had brought with him. "The less thick-headed among them have decided the situation is desperate enough. They're willing to try something else."

Bryl saw the other khelebar carrying oar-shaped shovels made from dead branches to beat at the flames and dig at the earth. Ydaim went forward to take one of the shovels. "Noldir Woodcarver shaped these?"

Vailret pulled off his tunic, baring his chest. He looked thin and not strong enough to fight against the fire, but he shook his head, making sweat fly from his hair. "You should have seen him—using his palms to slap off slices of wood from the ends, like it was butter."

Bryl hauled himself to his feet. His old bones creaked with weariness. Ydaim Trailwalker looked at him, then at the others and at the shovel in his hand. Bryl waved in dismissal. "I'll find my own way back to Delrael."

"We have to keep working," Vailret said. "Thilane wouldn't let Del come and help."

The khelebar seemed terrified of the fire, but their fear for the trees outweighed it. They beat at the flames on the forest floor, attacking an enemy.

Before Bryl stumbled off into the forest toward the council clearing, Vailret stopped him. The young man lowered his voice and placed a hand on Bryl's shoulder. With a nod of his head, he indicated the approaching flames. "You know this won't do any good, don't you?"

Bryl shuddered. He had hoped he was wrong, but he had seen through the Water Stone how good a grip the fire had on the heart of Ledaygen. If the Stone could not extinguish the blaze, wooden shovels would not.

"I know. This is all going to be one black hex."

Vailret took his shovel anyway and went toward the edge of the fire with a show of enthusiasm. "I have to get to work."

They labored through the morning, exhausted, until they had depleted even their adrenaline. The fire, gaining strength, pushed them steadily back.

Vailret could barely lift his shovel to beat down against smoldering leaves, to dig trenches that the fire leaped across. Dirt and sweat and soot trickled down his raw skin. A dozen glistening welts scored his back from flying coals. His soaked blond hair hung in ropy tangles, powdered with ash.

At noon, he saw the despair reach its peak. Gorak Foodgatherer, a slim, sunken-eyed khelebar who had worked closely beside Vailret, paused and stared at the flames. Without warning, he shouted and hurled his blackened shovel deep into the burning forest. Clamping his hands against his ears and temples, he screamed and ran into the blazing mass of trees, plunging through showers of hot coals. He moved like a demon, severing burning trees from their roots with his bare hands, knocking them down with his shoulder. His fur smoldered and caught fire, but he ran faster, lopping at trees and putting them out of their misery.

The other khelebar watched. No one attempted to stop him.

"We can all hear the death screams of the trees," Ydaim Trailwalker said. "It haunts us from within."

Gorak Foodgatherer burst into flame, but still he stumbled and knocked down two more doomed trees, positioning himself so the flaming hulk of one oak mercifully fell on top of him.

The khelebar stood in grim silence for a moment, then drowned themselves in work again. Vailret stared in horror, feeling his heart pound.

Ydaim turned to him, listless. "What else can we do?"

Fiolin Tribeleader scratched another line across the hexagonal map in the dirt, leaving less than a quarter of Ledaygen unburned. The fire had looped along the boundary lines, cutting the khelebar off with flames to their faces and the cliff to their backs.

Shaking with exhaustion, Vailret collapsed next to Delrael in the clearing. He glared at Fiolin. "We could have escaped before. You knew we were getting walled in by the fire—is it going to make us martyrs to your *dayid*?"

The Tribeleader refused to answer.

Helpless and disgusted, Vailret drew a deep breath of the oppressive air. He coughed, and the inside of his nose and throat burned.

The khelebar heard the roar and snap of burning trees. Their terror and helplessness grew, but they could find no outlet for it. Many congregated under the sweeping boughs of Thessar, the ancient Father Pine. They beseeched their *dayid* for help. Vailret shook his head in sadness.

Bryl cracked his knuckles incessantly, as if trying to loosen the cramps caused by clutching the Water Stone for so many hours. Delrael sat, looking helpless and dismayed, unable to do anything.

Ydaim's black braids had long since come undone. He had lost his pinecone pendant somewhere in the fire. Other khelebar wandered back into the clearing, looking broken—sweat had plastered soot to their bodies, and their emerald eyes were glazed with the knowledge of their deaths and the death of Ledaygen.

"I don't suppose you can do anything else with the Water Stone?" Vailret asked Bryl, but did not take his eyes from the flames he saw moving between the trees, coming nearer. He blinked, trying to make his vision clear.

The half-Sorcerer stared at the palms of his hands. "I've already used up my spell allotment for today. And even with that, I couldn't stop the fire. If I do anything else before midnight, it would be breaking the Rules. When Sardun did that, he paralyzed almost his entire body....and he's much more powerful than I am." Bryl stared at the sky, then at his hands again. "I failed too. This must be how my parents felt when your great-great grandfather Jarriel died of the tumor sickness."

He shook his head, and Vailret listened to his words.

"They had tried to save him for nearly a year, but Jarriel wasted away and died. I was very young then, but I remember them working, discussing what they should try next. But they failed, and when Jarriel's wife Galleri married a new husband, Brudane—oh, he was a rough man —they talked as if *my mother and father* had poisoned Jarriel.

"When my parents learned that, they wallowed in shame at their failure and went through the half-Transition, disintegrating in flames brighter than any of these—" He waved at the forest. "—right in front of my eyes. They didn't apologize or even say good-bye. I was ten years old, I think.

"How could they not expect their action to make them appear even more guilty? And they left *me* to grow up under that shadow. Among people who did not know how to train me or what to expect of my powers—"

Bryl stopped talking then shook his head. "It is useless to dwell in the past. Drodanis wasted years doing that, before he went off on his quest to find the Rulewoman Melanie." He brushed at his knees under the soot-smeared blue cloak.

The wind picked up and skimmed over the forest. Smoke rippled across the clearing, stinging Vailret's eyes. Oddly, he felt no tears there.

Swinging his *kennok* leg along with him, Delrael walked awkwardly to the edge of the hex-discontinuity and gazed over the cliff. Vailret joined him, and he stared down at the bottom of the mountainous hexagon far below. He squinted, but the details were even more blurred than usual with the smoke making his eyes raw. He saw no ledge, no narrow trail they could use for escape.

The fire glared brighter between the trees now, sweeping toward them, a hungry monster ravenous for a last morsel. The heat increased until the air was thick with it. They had nothing to do but wait.

The fire rushed along the scattered dry leaves. The khelebar stood in grim positions, muttering to the *dayid* for salvation. But the *dayid* had fallen silent even to them.

"There's extreme risk in doing this—" Bryl trembled as he hefted the Water Stone in front of him. He stood up, trying to be steady. "But if we're going to die anyway—"

"Luck," Vailret said with all the sincerity he could muster.

"Luck," Delrael added.

The half-Sorcerer closed his eyes and rolled the sapphire. The Stone came to rest with "1" staring upward and rolled no farther. The *dayid* had ceased to offer its help.

Bryl let out a cry as if struck by a blow. Eyes closed, he dropped to the trampled ground and lay motionless. His fingers convulsed, clutching the Water Stone. He still breathed. But the fire approached, and Vailret decided it might be better not to wake him.

The khelebar made no sound as the nearest flames skittered across the treetops to land on Thessar, the Father Pine, the last tree. Orange curtains of heat lapped at Thessar's green needles and the dry, flaking bark oozing with sweet pitch. The air filled with the stench of smoldering evergreen—Thessar seemed to sigh as the heat made sap boil and hiss.

The Father Pine ignited in an instant, exploding into a pillar of brilliance, burning, burning. Some of the khelebar sang their keening wail, but most stood in defeated silence.

Thessar groaned, weakened by the fire as flames weighed down its branches. The ancient pine toppled forward to crash with a horrible noise to the grassy clearing. From Thessar's boughs, the fire rushed into the grass and slithered toward the khelebar like a gigantic serpent.

Vailret swallowed hard, silent in his own awe. He took a step sideways to be closer to Delrael. His cousin stood white-lipped and staring with clenched fists.

Like a sharp hook had yanked at him, he felt his insides wrenched with pain. An instant of nausea replaced itself with utter despair and total emptiness. His head spun, and he could not understand until he heard the cries of the khelebar.

"The *dayid* has fled Ledaygen! We are forsaken!"

Some of the khelebar screamed. Vailret lifted his heavy gaze and watched in horror as five of them ran to the edge of the hex-discontinuity and cast themselves over the cliff.

The young Tayron Next-Leader turned red with disgust and pain. He shouted at others moving to the edge of the cliff, "Are you ashamed to die on the soil of Ledaygen? I will stand here as bravely as the trees and resist the fire until it consumes me!"

Delrael snatched up one of the ash-blackened shovels. "Come on, Vailret!" He lurched toward the edge of the fire, furious to do something. "All of you—we can use the shovels to beat out the fire on the grass as it comes toward us!"

Vailret ran with his cousin and began banging at the creeping flames, though his sore arms felt as if they had been skewered with knives.

"What does it matter?" Fiolin turned to him. "Ledaygen is dead. The *dayid* has left us."

"Damn Ledaygen!" Delrael shouted back. "I'm talking about us!"

But the khelebar refused to move. Reluctant and apathetic, Ydaim Trailwalker offered some help. They stood, insignificant against the towering flames.

"What about Bryl?" Vailret asked, turning to look at the fallen half-Sorcerer. He stared and the words crumbled in his mouth.

Bryl hauled himself to his knees. His eyes were glassy. He could not focus, but he seemed to be seeing through a million different minds. Power surged from Ledaygen into the Water Stone and ricocheted into his mind. His consciousness expanded outward as if to encompass the whole map of Hexworld in one glance.

He felt like a giant with his new power, towering over the council clearing. His small body shimmered with strength, and the milling panicked khelebar below seemed to be mere specks in the grass. When he saw the smoldering wreckage of his entire forest, he felt anger tighten around him.

In the back of his mind, Bryl felt the magnitude of power that Sardun had used to create the Barrier River. He grew afraid.

The grass in the clearing burned rapidly, and the already dead trees in the forest fell into festering ash as the wave of heat sterilized the soil of Ledaygen. He saw Delrael and Vailret both turn to stare at him in awe— but Bryl ignored all that. He dimly noticed the other khelebar pointing at him, shouting. Their voices seemed so tiny over the roar of the fire and the echoes of his strange strength.

He found it exhilarating.

"The *dayid*! The *dayid* has fled to Bryl Traveler!"

Bryl allowed himself only an instant to taste the churning voices of the hundreds of Sentinels whose spirits had collected together to form the *dayid*: all the tragedy and despair that had caused them to remain behind from the original Transition, the years of waiting through the violent Scouring as Hexworld fought with itself. He felt the grief that had finally driven them to undertake their own partial Transitions that liberated their spirits and sent them here.

The fire swept toward the khelebar, ready to destroy them as it had ruined Ledaygen. Bryl let the thunderous magic pound in his temples and behind his eyes. He knew that the *dayid* could not allow the khelebar to be destroyed, even if it meant casting the Rules to the wind. The *dayid* seemed willing to take whatever consequences would come.

Bryl clutched the Water Stone in his hand, shouting in a booming voice. He wondered if the sapphire cube might shatter from the force of his desperate anger.

"Water of the earth, I summon you!" Rippling with waves of energy from the *dayid*, he sent a thought through the Stone. "Save my khelebar! All water, come to the aid of Ledaygen. Come!"

The Water Stone bucked and writhed with the command. The soil beneath Bryl's feet became laden with water he summoned from the deep underground springs. Black thunderclouds gorged the sky above, dumping their contents in a heavy downpour.

Water built up in the center of the council clearing, pushing below the turf. A huge geyser of sparkling cold water blasted a pillar of white froth into the air.

Bryl laughed. Power continued to pour from the Water Stone.

The water erupted higher, beginning to whirl, rotating faster until it skipped away from the ground in a tremendous waterspout. The spout veered away from the cliff and plunged into the still-burning forest, spraying water onto the blazing trees, extinguishing the fire without damaging the tree hulks.

More cold water spilled upward from beneath baked rocks, splitting them. Smaller geysers spewed forth, detaching themselves to become cyclones that careened through the smoldering wreckage of Ledaygen until the fire had been vanquished.

The hiss of vanishing steam lingered in the air.

The glowing Water Stone slipped from Bryl's fingers as he collapsed to the sodden ground. He tried to hold on to the power, but the dissembling spirits fled like the smoke in Ledaygen.

The *dayid* left him, and died.

CHAPTER 8

WAR GAMES

We can defeat the Game if we can succeed in not fighting. The Outsiders must see that we will not Play along. Their amusements do not amuse us.
—Jorig Falselimb of the khelebar

Fiolin Tribeleader clenched his hand, and the charred wood crumbled to ash. He stared at his fingers in numb helplessness—the black dust had once been a living, vibrant tree. He gazed with reddened eyes at the desolation of Ledaygen, at the black hulks that were the corpses of trees. Steam rose from the ruins of the fire. "It's … all … gone."

Vailret dipped his shirt in a puddle of cool water. He bent over Bryl and mopped the unconscious man's face. The half-Sorcerer looked as drained as Sardun had after creating the Barrier River.

Delrael bent his *kennok* limb and sat down beside Vailret. He watched Fiolin and the other khelebar until he finally spoke out loud.

"We're still alive, Fiolin. You can help the trees grow again. Birds will come. You can plant flowers. In time, Ledaygen will be what it was before."

"Ledaygen can never be what it was!" Tayron Next-Leader said. The rest of the khelebar took no interest in the subject but stood around like character figurines.

Fiolin heaved a sigh and forced himself to look at Delrael and Vailret. "Ledaygen is dead. The *dayid* is dead. Could you not feel it? Why should the rest of us live? Perhaps I made the wrong decision. Perhaps we should not have fought at all." He stared up at the skies and shouted to the Outsiders, "What value is life now? Why don't you change the Rules?"

Tayron Next-Leader glowered at his father, surprising Vailret. "I will not forsake my hope until I have seen that not one tree still stands in Ledaygen. If my heart can bear it, I will scout every inch of this forest."

Ydaim Trailwalker squared his shoulders. "I will be proud to help you look for life in our ashes, Next-Leader. If a single acorn or pine cone remains unharmed, we will find it."

Some of the khelebar cheered, but most just stared as the two galloped off into the ashen wasteland.

When Bryl dragged himself back to consciousness, he blinked up at Vailret in astonishment, then stared into the sky. "We're still alive." He glanced at his hands, then at the Water Stone. "I remember touching the Stone, and I remember feeling … it was the *dayid*. Ah." His body shook from jolted nerves, but he said nothing more, though Vailret was anxious to hear.

Much later, Tayron and Ydaim returned, coated with a thin dusting of ash stirred up by their paws. Fiolin's son blew hard to catch his breath, but he kept his green eyes lowered. The rest of the khelebar stood, fragile and waiting to hear something that would restore their faith. Fiolin padded forward. "What have you found?"

"Five trees still live." The optimistic tone in Ydaim's voice sounded artificial.

"But they will soon die. They have given up their lives," Tayron said. "But … but at the edge of the forest, where the fire seems to have started, we found something else—"

Fiolin Tribeleader turned away as if he did not want to hear. Ydaim reached forward to grip Fiolin's bare shoulders, forcing him to face his son.

"We found the cause of the fire. We found footprints, we found sign. There is no doubt—the Cyclops has done this to our Ledaygen!" Tayron's green eyes blazed as he glared at the khelebar, then at the burned forest.

The khelebar muttered among themselves. "Didn't I tell you?" Vailret said, but he did not want to make an issue of it.

"Father, the Cyclops has burned our forest, murdered the *dayid*!"

The Tribeleader's expression maintained its mask of duty. He looked at his surviving people; saw the restless anger simmering within them.

Vailret watched his transformation, not sure if it was genuine or simply a role the Tribeleader decided to play.

"Tayron, gather up every khelebar whose task has been taken away by the burning of Ledaygen—gather them into a war party. Noldir Wood-carver! Arm every one of them with a bow and with arrows forged from the fallen trees. The dead branches will want their own revenge."

Fiolin watched their faces, looking uncertain. Tayron raised his fist in the air. "Tomorrow, we will march against the Cyclops—Lifetaker, Flesheater, Treeburner!"

Vailret joined in the ragged cheer. Thilane Healer, though, came forward. "Fiolin Tribeleader, we swore to resist the Outsiders by refusing to Play their Game. The khelebar have not fought for generations. Have you forgotten the examples Jorig Falselimb taught us? We were at peace with the *dayid* for as long as any of us can remember."

Tayron also spoke up. "The Healer is right. We have lost all our arts of war, and if we march blindly against the Cyclops, we will surely fail."

Thilane turned on him, as if he had twisted her meaning entirely. Fiolin's expression changed. He shook his head. "We have no other choice."

"Ah, but we do." Ydaim's green eyes glinted with excitement reborn. "Three among us are fresher to the game of war."

Vailret felt the eyes of Tayron Next-Leader on him. Bryl sat on the ground, leaning against Delrael and still wearing a stunned expression on his face. Delrael moved well on his *kennok* limb, but he could not go into battle so soon. Vailret shrank back as he watched the others turn to him and come to the same conclusion.

"I can't lead anyone," he said, looking at Delrael. "I'm not a fighter. I can't use magic—I can't even *see* very well!"

Delrael shrugged. "But you've read about all the old Sorcerer battles. You know their strategy. You're smart, and you can make decisions quickly. Go along and tell them what to do."

"Just like that?"

"Pretend it's a Game."

Tayron Next-Leader held one of the dark wooden arrows out for the others to see. The gathered khelebar watched as he ground its sharp point into the charred surface of a fallen log. "This," Tayron showed them its tip blackened with soot, "this is all the poison we need to strike down the Treeburner."

Each khelebar held a handful of new-made arrows. Noldir Wood-carver had worked his hands raw fashioning the shafts from twisted and burned branches, pulling the wood between his fingers to straighten it.

Following his son's example, Fiolin Tribeleader blackened the tips of his own arrows. "Ledaygen has provided us with this poison as her last service to us. We shall use it to destroy our enemy."

The khelebar pressed forward to dip their own arrows in the ashes. Vailret watched in silence, doubting that the ritual would have any real effect. But it served to stir up more anger and frenzy in the long-peaceful khelebar.

"Are you ready to go get him?" Vailret raised his voice. They all yelled their answer.

"I have selected five scouts to spread out ahead of the main party. First, we will find the Cyclops, then we will converge on him, and when he's trapped, you'll have your revenge. Give him one arrow for every tree he has destroyed."

He and Bryl made ready to lead the khelebar warriors. Though still weak, the half-Sorcerer had regained his complement of spells. He stared at the Water Stone as if waiting for an opportunity to touch the power again. He seemed to be stronger inside, tempered by his ordeal.

Vailret looked at the khelebar and tried to remain optimistic. They had been practicing with their bows and arrows. Delrael helped one after another until he, too, was exhausted. But a few hours of training would never make expert archers out of them. Vailret himself couldn't see well enough to make any long shots.

The Outsiders would probably enjoy this battle immensely.

"Bryl and I will have to ride on your backs just to keep up. We can switch off if the burden gets too great." Vailret tried to appear confident. "Tayron Next-Leader, I would like you to carry me first, so we can discuss strategy. Ydaim, can you take Bryl?"

"I would be honored, Vailret Traveler." The other khelebar watched Bryl with a cautious awe: the one who had linked himself with the *dayid* and saved them all. Bryl seemed to enjoy his position of prestige but acted as if he didn't know what to do with it.

Vailret and Bryl mounted easily and turned to face Delrael, who stood angry and dejected. Once again, Thilane Healer had refused to let him go, even with his healing leg. He waved halfheartedly. "Luck."

Thilane seemed upset at their mission and said nothing.

"This is for you, Delrael," Vailret said. "The khelebar have their own reasons for revenge, and I have mine."

The khelebar turned and Vailret motioned them forward. They moved into the desolate stand of blackened tree skeletons. Vailret made them pass slowly through the ruins of Ledaygen, trying to forge their despair into hot fury. The twisted and still-smoldering hulks of the once-majestic trees cried out to the hearts of the khelebar.

A brooding sense of relief came over him when they left the burned hexagon of Ledaygen and descended into the narrow gorge where the Cyclops had attacked Delrael. Early afternoon made the canyon bright and green. Vailret's five chosen scouts broke away from the main party and scattered to the upper walls of the gorge. "Remember, you must only *find* the Cyclops. Wait for all the khelebar. We will fight together."

Tayron Next-Leader and Ydaim Trailwalker bore the two humans side by side. Fiolin Tribeleader accompanied them. Ydaim pointed up. "The Cyclops often lurks in the rocks above, but he lives farther down the valley in a cave."

Water from the narrow stream splattered and dashed itself on the exposed rocks. On the east side of the stream, the ground glistened from where the water had surged across the gorge floor, dragged toward the hills of Ledaygen. Vailret looked in awe at the strength of Bryl's summons through the Water Stone.

The khelebar marched along, moving with the silent care they saved for the forest. Vailret felt like part of a funeral procession rather than a vengeful foray.

The keener ears of the khelebar detected a commotion on the jagged bluffs above. Ydaim reached across to touch Vailret's shoulder and pointed at the rim of the canyon. The rest of the khelebar stumbled to a halt. Shading their emerald eyes, they peered up at the gorge walls.

One of the scouts, Stynod Treescavenger, burst into view. She flailed her arms at something hidden in the jumbled terrain. Her mottled pelt blended well with the rocks, but her dark hair whipped from side to side as she moved. Stynod snatched her new bow and nocked an arrow. Her shouted challenge drifted on the wind, made faint by distance. Vailret squinted, trying to see what was happening.

The Cyclops emerged from the shadows of an outcropping, crouched like a brick-red behemoth. He tossed his head, brandishing his horn. He glared at the khelebar with his watery yellow eye.

"Treeburner! Lifetaker!" Stynod shouted, letting her arrow fly. The shaft struck the Cyclops in the shoulder. "Let the poison of burned Ledaygen destroy you!"

Vailret made a fist, grinding his teeth together in exasperation. "Idiot! You can't do any harm by yourself!"

In annoyance, the Cyclops knocked the arrow from his warty skin. He reached forward with flint claws and snatched at Stynod, missing cleanly, though the Tree-scavenger stood her ground. She tried to fit another arrow to her bow. The Cyclops grabbed again, this time raking his claws across her panther ribs. As she fell, the Cyclops snagged her body and picked her up. The monster roared at the khelebar below and hurled Stynod from the bluff face. She did not scream. Her body struck the ground in front of the advancing party.

"I said we all have to attack together! We can't do anything from here," Vailret said as he stared at the Treescavenger's broken body. "Stynod has ruined it for us! Come on!"

He urged Tayron ahead; Bryl and Ydaim followed, but the other khelebar stood motionless, appalled at their dead companion.

The Cyclops picked up a huge rock and raised it over his head. "Move!" Ydaim added his shout to Vailret's warning.

The first boulder came crashing down, narrowly missing the khelebar. They scattered, looking for shelter. "Stay in single file!" Vailret shouted, realizing the limitations of the Cyclops. "He's only got one eye —he can't judge distance! Don't give him a big target."

A second boulder came down like thunder, harming no one.

Only Fiolin Tribeleader stood alone, staring and weeping over the body of Stynod. He drew himself up and glared at the monster; for a moment, Vailret thought they made eye contact.

"Lifetaker, Treeburner—I curse you with all the power of the *dayid*." Fiolin shouted into the wind. He held a charred arrow in each hand, wielding them like a talisman.

Tayron seemed to know what Fiolin was doing and wheeled around, running toward him. Vailret held on to the Next-Leader's waist.

The Cyclops also saw the Tribeleader standing alone and unprotected. He found another boulder and cast it down.

Fiolin saw the rock coming at him, but he made no move to avoid it. Vailret watched the older khelebar stand still, waiting.

The giant stone struck Fiolin Tribeleader, crushing him to the earth. Mud and blood sprayed into the air, spattering Tayron Next-Leader as he ran toward his father.

The Cyclops lifted another of his giant stones, but a thin bolt of lightning struck the monster's head and skittered along his shoulders and chest, leaving a jagged black mark smoking on his skin. He howled in pain and surprise and dropped the boulder on his foot. Smaller rocks bounced off the canyon wall as the boulder rolled to the rim, then fell into the ravine.

Bryl scrambled to pick up the Water Stone. The half-Sorcerer's face seemed as tight as a drum skin over the front of his skull, but flushed with excitement.

Ydaim shouted at the khelebar to regroup. They fired arrows at the Cyclops. Most of the shafts fell short, bouncing off the rock face, but several struck the monster's legs and side. He ran away, crashing among the rocks until he disappeared behind the edge of the cliffs.

Vailret stumbled off Tayron's back. The Next-Leader seemed to have forgotten about him. Tayron thrust the boulder away from his father, leaving the older khelebar exposed and mangled on the turf. Fiolin's emerald eyes filled with tears that oozed down his cheeks. His teeth chattered.

"Father!" Tayron's words whistled out of his throat. He shouted for two of the other khelebar to come to him. "He still lives—take him to Thilane Healer! She can save him. She has the power—I know it."

The burning anger in Tayron's eyes stopped Vailret from voicing his doubts. A male and a female khelebar picked up their Tribeleader between them. Fiolin's blood slicked their hands.

Tayron grabbed a fistful of arrows. "We shall destroy the Lifetaker!" His voice cracked with emotion. The khelebar rallied around their fallen leader and the body of Stynod Treescavenger.

Fiolin stirred and wheezed through punctured lungs. "No. Enough killing." But Tayron did not hear, and Vailret chose not to repeat the words for him. The two khelebar tending their dying Tribeleader looked at each other for a moment, then bore him away.

Tayron removed one arrow from his quiver. His jaws ground together so tightly, the muscles looked like straining ropes. He ran his fingers along the burned wood of the shaft, then dipped the sharp tip in a pool of his father's blood on the ground. Before the blood had dried, he thrust the doubly poisoned arrow into his braid of blond hair.

By unspoken agreement, Tayron Next-Leader took command of the war party. Vailret signaled to another of the panther-men and scrambled on his wide back. Tayron charged off down the gorge with the rest of the vengeful khelebar in his wake.

Noldir Woodcarver stared at the toppled hulk of the Father Pine. He paced around the dead tree, pausing, frowning. He inspected the char marks, the rough patches where the intense heat had eaten through to the heartwood.

Delrael watched to distract himself from thinking of the battles the others were now fighting. The pungent odor of wet ashes still hung in the air—"the smell of tree blood," Thilane called it. The thought made Delrael uncomfortable.

Before the war party departed, Fiolin Tribeleader had summoned Noldir to the council clearing. "You shall make a monument out of Thessar's remains—the Father Pine will be a memorial for our dead Ledaygen."

Noldir stared at the fallen tree, seeing into it. His eyes glimmered with determined pride.

"You've been just looking at it for hours," Delrael finally said.

The Woodcarver glanced up at him. "I cannot carve contrary to the desires of Thessar. I must find out what it wishes to be, but it eludes me—ah!"

He clapped his hands. "No wonder I could not see it before. Thessar is practically shouting to me that it is upside down! Delrael Kennoklimb, help me."

Thilane Healer watched for a moment, then came over to help. The three of them effortlessly rolled the hulk of the ancient Father Pine. Delrael blinked his eyes in wonder—he had felt the new power sparkling through him for an instant. The blackened log seemed eager to move and floated like a dandelion seed until it came back to rest on the scorched grass.

"Look!" Thilane paused, then replaced her excitement with a show of dignity. She nodded at the depression where Thessar had fallen—a small seedling, rumpled and nearly crushed, straightened in the sunlight.

"Thessar knew!" she whispered. "When the Father Pine fell, he sheltered this seedling with a hollow in his trunk!"

Noldir called to the khelebar who had remained behind. "A tree still lives! A seedling! Ledaygen is not completely lost!"

Thilane turned away, though. "The *dayid* does not live within it."

Delrael tried to offer comfort. "Maybe when you get enough trees to grow again—"

"Yes," she said. "And maybe the Outsiders will feel sorry for us and magically make the forest reappear all by itself. I prefer not to count on miracles. If a miracle was going to happen, it should have stopped Ledaygen from burning in the first place."

Delrael tried to hide his anger. The Woodcarver spoke against Thilane. "But a miracle *has* happened—Thessar has given us a new seedling."

Thilane said nothing and plodded back into the burned forest. She and the lesser Healers tended the five dying trees, though they knew their efforts were in vain. She walked away, and Delrael watched her bare, weathered back with its wealth of corded muscles.

Troubled, Noldir turned back to the hulk of Thessar. He plunged his hands up to the wrists into the charred trunk, sculpting a wooden gravestone for Ledaygen.

Delrael watched the Woodcarver, fascinated with his work but impatient to be doing something else, to be continuing their quest southward. He walked into the dead forest to find Thilane.

The skeletal branches of the trees closed over him. The gray ash muffled all sound like tainted snow. He came upon one of the Treescavengers who was methodically removing every twig and scrap of wood from a large area and piling an immense mound of debris near the path. The Treescavenger gathered branches, uprooted tree trunks, picked up the smallest twig.

Delrael watched her work. "Want some help?" His leg no longer bothered him, and he enjoyed feeling it as he moved.

The Treescavenger took no notice of his question. Delrael helped anyway, carrying loads of fallen branches to the growing mound. He wiped a wristful of sweat off his forehead, leaving a charcoal smudge on his skin. "So why are we carrying all this wood away?"

The khelebar stopped and looked up at him with eyes as blank and empty as the sky. She blinked and fumbled with her words. "That is my work. The *dayid* made me a Treescavenger, and I must collect whatever dead wood I find." She went back to her task again, widening the radius of the cleared circle. She faltered, pondering, then she heaved another branch. "That is my work."

Delrael waited a moment, uncomfortable, and then slipped off into the deeper forest. He knew where Thilane would be working with the two other Healers.

After passing through the wreckage of trees and brush, he reached a place where the ashes had been trampled and the broken branches moved away. Delrael guessed that this was one of the first places where Bryl had used the Water Stone against the fire. Somehow, two trees had survived here. Two Healers stood beside each other, watching Thilane touch one of the burned trees.

The oak was huge and very old, surviving because of its immense size. Delrael looked upward through the dizzying crosswork of black branches. A few areas near the top of the tree appeared undamaged. The other surviving oak was a mere sapling, blackened and scarred—but Thilane insisted it still lived. Delrael didn't know how she could tell, but the Healer expended most of her effort there.

Thilane looked up from her work, removing her palms from the thin trunk and pressing the side of her head against it, listening to the tree. Her garland had wilted. Ledaygen had no more flowers to offer her.

She pursed her lips when she saw Delrael but continued her ministrations. He waited, hesitant about interrupting. Finally, he asked why she had not seemed excited about Noldir's discovery of the pine seedling. "At least you have a start now, a tree from Ledaygen."

The other two Healers heard Delrael mention the pine seedling and looked to Thilane in surprise, but they did not speak. Thilane kept her attention on him.

"Ledaygen was a forest of pine and oak. Both! Because of Thessar, the pines may now return—but *what of the oaks*?"

Delrael fidgeted. "Can't you heal one of these?"

Thilane shook her head and pointed at the large oak.

"That tree could have survived its fire damage, but it is old and has already surrendered. This one, though," she ran her fingers along the surviving sapling, "has an extraordinary will to live. How can it cling to life when it has endured more than any of these others? But it, too, has been mortally wounded. It will be dead—dead, like the rest of the forest."

Delrael looked at the emerald eyes of the other Healers, but they avoided his gaze. He spoke quietly to Thilane. "Why can't you bring in other trees? Start over?"

"Stop being so stupid and optimistic! If we brought outside trees, our home would be just another forest. It would not be *Ledaygen*. Better that Ledaygen be dead and remembered than absorbed as part of more forest terrain." She clamped her wavering lips together and drew herself straight. "And now we shall have only pine."

Thilane stepped away from the charred sapling and sank to the forest floor. She tucked her great paws beneath her belly, then reached out to run her fingernail along the peeled bark. The other Healers stopped their own work and watched her.

Delrael felt uneasy. Thilane smiled at something he could not see. Tears made tracks through the settled ash on her cheeks. She reached behind her neck and undid the long braid of gray-streaked hair that ran like a mane down her bare back. She turned and hissed at the two Healers, "Yes!"

They both took a half step backward in surprise.

"It is decided," Thilane said.

"What is?" Delrael asked.

The Healer turned. Her eerie eyes stared through him, seeming to see the ghosts of the forest. "Ledaygen has a new Father Pine. I can provide a new Father Oak. I must heal this young tree."

"But you said you couldn't—"

"I can. You must remember how we Heal."

Thilane would say no more, but rose and marched around the blackened oak sapling, contemplating. One of the other Healers took Delrael by the shoulder and pulled him away, silencing his questions with a stern gesture. Her eyes glittered with a mixture of dread, enthusiasm, and hope.

You must remember how we Heal.

Delrael watched Thilane, thinking of how she had treated some of the khelebar burns by laying green leaves on the injury; the leaves had turned black and charred.

Noldir Woodcarver had told him how she had treated Delrael's bruises and smashed muscles with twigs and branches, which had somehow become crushed and mangled in exchange.

She had brought his *kennok* wood leg to life by exchanging his flesh leg and burying it in the forest.

He frowned. None of it seemed to be "healing" at all—just an exchange of wholeness and injury.

Then he knew what she meant to do.

Thilane leaned up against the hunched sapling, embracing the thin trunk and holding it between her breasts. Her fingers fluttered up the charred bark, reaching toward the top. She began to hum to herself.

"Don't, Thilane! Please!" Delrael tried to run to her, but the Healers reached out and grabbed him. "She'll die—she'll burn like the trees!" he shouted at them.

"That is her choice," one of the Healers said.

"That is her *right*," said the other.

"It is her duty." The first Healer turned to watch Thilane. "Only she has the power to do this. For Ledaygen."

Delrael gritted his teeth in despair. He wanted to call out Thilane's name again, but he just watched her instead.

She swayed against the tree trunk, smearing soot over her skin. She hummed louder, invoking a rite that only she seemed to know. Her lips sang a song in the language of the wind, the language a dying tree might understand.

Sparks flew from her hair as it drifted upward, alive with static like a wreath of gray flames.

Thilane Healer stretched her arms still farther upward, reaching for the lost *dayid*, and then she let out a low keening. Her body burst into an incinerating white flame, burning from the inside out. She writhed as a living torch for a long, hideous moment until she crumbled to the ground. A dust of fine ash scattered with the wind of her departure.

Delrael fell to his knees, sickened and sobbing. The *kennok* limb bent easily. He wormed out of the stunned grip of the other two Healers and crawled to where Thilane's ashes lay. He took the ash in each fist and let it run back out like sand to the forest floor.

He sat stunned, then looked up. The nearly dead sapling, the new Father Oak, now stood fresh and green and explosively alive.

The war party tracked the Cyclops down the gorge, harrying him, firing volleys of arrows. The khelebar remained unfamiliar with their weapons and missed most of the time. At least Noldir Woodcarver had provided them with more arrows than they could possibly use. Vailret rode along, trying to see details in the shadows with his weak eyes.

Tayron Next-Leader went ahead, oblivious to the other khelebar in the party.

Vailret didn't know how they could kill the monster. The Cyclops had disappeared among the rocky bluffs again. The khelebar could keep pursuing him, and the monster could keep throwing rocks—the chase would go on forever. But he did know that the Outsiders would have set it up properly: They had given the Cyclops countless boulders as weapons, they had provided the incentive to the khelebar, they had provided the battle, and they would also provide the solution. Vailret had to find it.

"We have to drive him back to his lair," he said to Tayron. The Next-Leader turned to him, but Vailret kept his face firm and confident.

Without questioning, Tayron signaled for four others to locate and flush the Cyclops once more.

Riding Ydaim, Bryl appeared refreshed but still weak. He left the Water Stone in his pocket, not touching it—but he seemed ready. The war party marched on.

The Cyclops roared and leaped over the edge of the gorge, grabbing at the cliff wall to slow himself. His claws scraped on the rock and sparks flew. The monster stumbled but regained his footing.

Tayron launched himself forward with a yell. The Cyclops bounded down the canyon. The other khelebar surged after, recklessly shooting arrows at the monster's heels.

"He's leading us there," Ydaim said.

The gorge branched. The narrow stream continued down the main canyon, but a side ravine went a different direction. The Cyclops splashed across the stream, spraying water onto his brick-red skin, then he lumbered toward a gaping cut in the rock wall of the ravine. A few wisps of steam leaked from inside the cave. In the dim light, they could see branchings of the cave as it plunged into the earth, filled with gems and abandoned chests of treasure.

The Cyclops seemed ready to fight at any moment, but every time he turned, a fresh round of arrows pierced his hide and sent him howling in the other direction. The monster ran toward the cave with all the speed his great legs could muster.

"Shoot your arrows!" Tayron shouted. "We will not stop again until he lies dead, to avenge the blood of Ledaygen and the blood of my father!"

The Cyclops reached the dark opening and stood within it, glaring at the attacking khelebar. His horn jutted out, yellowed by the sunlight. His single eye glowed all by itself.

The khelebar shot another volley of arrows, most of which clattered against the stone walls. The Cyclops snarled at them, as if he had thought they would retreat once he had reached his home. Huge boulders lay strewn around the entrance, and he stepped back into the sunlight to pick one up and heave it toward them. "Stay in single file!" Vailret said. The rock fell short. The khelebar shot again. "His eye!" Bryl shouted. "Hit him in the eye!"

"They can't even hit *him*," Vailret said.

Then Vailret saw that above the opening to the monster's cave, the gigantic boulders had fallen together in a jumbled arch. Boulders, just like those the Cyclops threw as weapons, but this time, they were stacked against him. A few stray khelebar arrows pinged against the burden of rock, and bits of gravel pattered down to the dry riverbed.

He was about to point this out to the war party, when he saw Ydaim Trailwalker taking painful aim with an arrow larger than the rest. Ydaim closed his eyes, exhaled a long breath, and released the arrow.

The Cyclops screamed with an agony that chilled Vailret to the bone. The arrow shaft had sunk deep into the corded skin of his throat. Dark-brown blood gushed down his chest, and the monster ripped open other gashes from clawing at the wound.

The khelebar yelled in triumph and kept shooting arrows. A dozen shafts stuck out of the monster's rough hide. Bryl slapped Ydaim on the back. "Yes!"

"I was aiming for his heart," Ydaim muttered.

The Cyclops bashed his fists against the walls of the cave. More stones and dust trickled down from overhead. Vailret heard the boulders groan as they settled against each other.

"Bryl, the rocks!" Vailret indicated the jumbled arch. "Use the Water Stone."

Bryl looked at him with uneasy eyes. "But, I—"

"You've still got three spells left."

The half-Sorcerer took out the sapphire cube and stared at it.

Tayron Next-Leader planted his wide panther feet, scoring the dry ground with his claws. He pulled the arrow from the braid in his hair—the arrow dipped in the ash of Ledaygen and the spilled blood of Fiolin Tribeleader.

"This is poison." Tayron took three steps closer to the thrashing monster and aimed. "Lifetaker—I will take your life."

Bryl blew on the Water Stone. "All right, come on!"

Tayron shot his arrow. It struck the Cyclops squarely in the center of his chest.

The Water Stone showed a "3." Bryl struck down with a massive bolt of lightning onto the precarious archway. Vailret waved a triumphant fist in the air.

The Cyclops touched the arrow protruding from his chest and stiffened as if the life had been ripped from his body. As dead as Ledaygen, he slumped forward. Then tons and tons of collapsing stone tumbled upon him from above.

The rumble and hiss of settling rock drifted toward silence. "We have killed once again," Ydaim said, standing next to Tayron.

The Next-Leader's words were amazing in their strength and calmness. "We have always known how to kill. By our inaction for all these centuries, we played a part in the killing of Ledaygen." He drew a deep breath of the dusty air. "We have failed to see that total peace can be as deadly as total war."

Some of the khelebar went forward to the rubble, cautious. Tayron undid his long hair and let it fly free. He put one massive paw on a broken boulder and turned to the other khelebar.

"We will plant trees here."

Tayron rushed the war party back to Ledaygen. His lips were dry and his eyes were glazed and hollow-looking.

Vailret sat astride the Next-Leader's back again, and he leaned forward to speak to the khelebar. "Thilane helped Delrael, remember?" Tayron did not answer.

They marched toward the remains of the great forest. Some of the khelebar stared with a new pride, some wept as they carried the body of Stynod Treescavenger, some looked stunned and uncertain. But when they passed the black hex-boundary into Ledaygen, Tayron stopped in baffled wonder. The other khelebar looked around, emerald eyes wide and glistening as they talked among themselves. Some of the khelebar ran ahead. Vailret sniffed the air but failed to notice any difference.

"What is it? Why are they so excited?" Bryl asked.

Ydaim Trailwalker beamed at him, amazed. "The *dayid*! It is a miracle! The presence is faint, but I can feel it."

Vailret frowned. "I thought you said the *dayid* died?"

"Nevertheless, it has returned."

The war party entered the clearing where the other khelebar had gathered. The new Father Oak stood vibrant and green, filled with life. Some of the party saw the tree and stared.

But Delrael sat dejected on a burned log, looking worn and empty. Soot smeared his face, furrowed with the tracks of tears, but he had stopped weeping. Near the reborn oak lay Fiolin, crushed and dying. The two lesser Healers hovered over the Tribeleader, doing what they could.

Tayron Next-Leader saw nothing but his father on the still-warm ash of Ledaygen. He threw his charred arrows to the ground with a clatter, demanding the attention of the Healers. "Where is Thilane Healer? Why is she not tending the Tribeleader?"

The other Healers cringed in surprise, but Delrael stood up, red with anger. The sword from Sardun's museum hung at his waist beside the silver belt. His leather armor was scuffed and dirty. His bloodied trousers had been washed and carefully mended by the khelebar.

"They're doing their best," Delrael said through tight jaws.

Tayron whirled to confront him. "Kennoklimb, my father will die without Thilane Healer."

Delrael continued to stare at him. "Thilane is dead—she burned herself to death just to heal a tree. And nobody tried to stop her!" Furious tears rose in his eyes again as he turned to the Healers and then back to Tayron. He hung his head. "She didn't even know Fiolin was hurt."

Tayron opened his mouth in surprise, then in despair. The others in the war party muttered to themselves. One of the Healers grasped the new tree. "She gave herself so that a Father Oak might be reborn. Her spirit has become the seed of a new *dayid*."

Tayron looked angered and stunned. Vailret pondered the Healer's words, trying to make sense of them. But only Sentinels could engage in the half-Transition that transformed them into part of a *dayid*. Was Delrael suggesting that Thilane, a khelebar, had somehow done what only a Sorcerer should have been able to do? That was patently against the Rules—only Sorcerers could use magic. But the *dayid* of Ledaygen had stretched and broken the Rules before.

Tayron knelt beside Fiolin and said nothing. His lips trembled.

The other Healer flexed her hands, helpless. "We lack the knowledge. We have used all our abilities, just to keep the Tribeleader alive, but his spirit slips away. The new *dayid* is too weak, and we have no other living trees to aid us!"

Tayron stopped listening. He removed one of his armbands and laid it on the ground next to Fiolin. "You did your best, Father. You were a good Tribeleader."

Fiolin's eyes fluttered, but crusted blood held them shut. He seemed to sense Tayron beside him. His jaws ground together, working up a small amount of saliva, and he croaked one word before he died.

"Tribeleader."

The two Healers snatched at the air as if trying to catch Fiolin's spirit. Tayron pushed his knuckles against his mouth, shuddering, before he let out a high-pitched moan. Then he fell silent, blinking his eyes several times in surprise.

"Did you feel it?" Ydaim asked him.

Tayron nodded, still staring off into the ashen wasteland. "When my father died, the *dayid* grew stronger."

"But the trees are gone!" said one of the khelebar. "We have no purpose."

Tayron Tribeleader stood beside the monument Noldir Woodcarver had made of Thessar, the Father Pine. He drew himself up, fingered his necklace of stones, and worked to restrain his impatient anger. The surviving khelebar had come to hear him speak, overwhelmed by the magnitude of the work ahead of them. The dead forest stood defeated and burned; the trees looked like desperate claws grasping at hope.

"If that is your attitude, then perhaps we are not worthy to have Ledaygen returned to us." He shook his head and turned his bright eyes to stare them down. No one would meet his gaze. "We cannot be content just to tend Ledaygen. We must make it grow once again. We must clear away the dead forest. We must heal the burned soil to prepare for new trees."

Vailret looked at Noldir's finished carving, not sure he understood its complexity—but the khelebar stared at it in awe. The dark and polished curves implied grandeur, its intricate tangles hinted at the intermeshed existence of the khelebar and Ledaygen, the bent and twisted portion signified the forest's pain and death and eventual rebirth. And at the heart of it all stood the stylized figure of a khelebar, holding the rest together. "It seems right somehow," Vailret said. Noldir nodded.

"We will not mourn my father Fiolin," Tayron said. "If we mourn for a fallen Tribeleader, then we must mourn for each tree in Ledaygen, which also fought bravely. Above all, we must give our thanks to Thilane Healer, who has made the rebirth of Ledaygen possible.

"We have no time for mourning. The khelebar have too much to do. I will set up new tasks for those who have lost their old ones. We must get to work!"

Delrael brushed at his leather armor and trousers, looking at the tarnished spots on his silver belt. Vailret knew he was getting impatient to move on. His *kennok* leg responded well, moving at his command. Delrael showed him how the line between flesh and wood was blurring into indistinction.

Ydaim Trailwalker came to them, smiling and ready to see them off. Delrael spoke up. "We have delayed long enough here, Ydaim. We have a dragon to fight, Sardun's daughter to rescue, and our Stronghold to recapture."

"If we come back someday," Vailret said, "I hope we see Ledaygen green again." He looked around, imagining the forest already growing.

Ydaim said, "Let the khelebar take hope in that."

The three travelers departed, trudging off through the desolate terrain. The khelebar ceased their work to stand in salute, then turned back to the enormous task ahead of them.

CHAPTER 9
SPECTRES

Hexworld is not real. We are not real. If by chance a character witnessed
absolute evidence of his unreality—even if he just laid eyes on a real
object—that character would cease to exist.
—The Sentinel Arken

A narrow line of peaks separated from the main mass of the Spectre Mountains and sprawled westward across their path, forming one more obstacle. The main range continued its southeasterly course before it faded away into foothills near the sea.

Before the dawn of the second day had risen over the crags, the three travelers packed their possessions. Bryl used his normal magic—unglamorous but useful—to replenish their traveling supplies. According to the map, the Spectre range was only two hexes wide here, and Vailret looked forward to finishing the hard traveling. They set off into the last stretch of mountain terrain. Delrael walked slowly on his *kennok* leg, seeming to be self-conscious of it. But as he forgot to think about it, he moved normally again.

Throughout the day, they followed a clear-cut trail over the mountains, passing tumbled rockslides, scrub brush, steep switchbacks. They climbed to an elevation where the air was cold and dry. When they reached the glossy black hex-line at dusk, a block of crags to the west drowned out the remaining sunlight.

They could travel no more than a single hex of mountain terrain, and Vailret was ready to stop for the night. Bryl and Delrael looked exhausted as well. After a full day of travel, Delrael walked with only a slight limp, but the concentration of moving his *kennok* leg seemed to drain him.

They camped at the hex-line, and Vailret found enough scrub bushes to build a fire. He piled the wood in the center of a sheltered clearing, then left Bryl to start the fire. The old half-Sorcerer had always used a trivial fire-starting spell, but this time, he rubbed the Water Stone and rolled it on the ground. Bryl laughed as a lightning bolt came down from the sky, striking the scant pile of wood. He controlled the lightning, and the wood became a roaring fire.

"Bryl—it took me an hour to gather all that wood! You just blasted most of it into ashes—now it'll never last until morning."

"No matter." The half-Sorcerer shrugged. "I can adjust the weather to make it warm here. I've got three rolls left for today."

Vailret squatted down close to Bryl, pointing a finger at the half-Sorcerer's beard. "Now look. Over the past couple of days, you've kept rubbing the Stone as if you're anxious to use it. But let me tell you something—you don't even know what you did in Ledaygen. When we rode out to get the Cyclops, did you notice that the stream in the gorge had been ripped from its bed and thrown against the rock face?

"You did that by summoning all the water to your aid—you diverted a stream out of its course from a full hex away! That Stone is not a toy—it's one of the most powerful weapons the old Sorcerers left on Hexworld. I liked it better when you were afraid of it."

Bryl stared at the young man's outburst. "I pulled the stream from its course?" He blinked in awe and looked guilty, more so from being caught than from doing anything wrong.

"Think about where the Stone came from and remember how much magic it contains." Vailret brushed his hands on his trousers.

Delrael started heating their meal of spiced grain mash on the fire. He asked out of the corner of his mouth, "What makes the Stones so powerful anyway?"

Vailret lay back and looked up at the stars. He did not feel ready for sleep. He thought about the possibility of keeping a journal of their quest, for future historians. If Hexworld survived that long.

"Well, once the old Sorcerers had made their minds up, they waited a year before they finally embarked on the Transition. And during that year, they thought about the half-breeds and humans the Rules made them leave behind.

"Most of them could see that humans had little chance against the massing Slac armies and the monsters who wanted Hexworld for their own. One more time, Arken spoke to the other Sorcerers—they knew that the Transition would require less than half of their total powers once most of the Sorcerers had joined together. Arken begged them to use that extra energy to create a gift for their children, a weapon the Sentinels could wield against their enemies—something to make future generations remember their departed forefathers.

"So the Sorcerers worked together to create the four elemental Stones, shaped like dice, each with enormous powers. The two factions that had fought each other in the ancient wars broke apart once more, this time for the good of all. One faction, those who later became the Earthspirits, created the Air and Earth Stones. The other faction, who became the Deathspirits, made the Water and Fire Stones."

He sat up against the rock and watched Delrael divide up their meal. "Wish we had the Air Stone too," Bryl said.

Delrael took the cooking meal away from the fire, frowning skeptically at it. "Well, Gairoth still has it, just like he still has the Stronghold."

He leaned forward to hand Bryl his portion of the food.

Without a sound, a tall stranger hopped down from a ledge above, landed expertly on a massive boulder, and stepped into the firelight.

In alarm, Delrael flipped the hunting bow off his back and nocked an arrow. Bryl scrambled to his feet and lifted the Water Stone, but paused before using it. Vailret froze, not knowing what to do.

The stranger had no eyes—only crusted, burned sockets.

He wore tattered robes and pointed a bulky, shining staff at each of the travelers. In the head of the staff, Vailret stared into a confusing system of glass disks held together by a pale blue glow, shifting and clicking as the lenses focused on different objects. He felt something staring right through him.

The stranger calmly set his staff upright again. "You have finally arrived. Good." He walked toward the fire, sidestepping a broken rock on the ground. "Come with me, please, or you will be destroyed. The Spectres have been awaiting you … and the Water Stone."

Vailret's shout overlapped Delrael's. "Wait a minute!"

Delrael put a hand on his sword and spat his words at the blind face of the stranger. "We're not going anywhere with you."

"Tell us what you want." Vailret tried to be calm. They needed to learn what was going on. "You have to give us some answers first."

The tall man turned his face toward the gap between the travelers. His expression grew serious. "If you resist their request, the Spectres will take away my sight once more. Artificial though it is, I value my eye-staff highly. And they will do worse to you."

Vailret narrowed his eyes, trying to spot something he might recognize on the stranger's face. "But who are the Spectres?"

"And who are you, for that matter?" Delrael demanded.

The tall stranger looked odd for a moment, as if he was trying to remember his own name. "I am Paenar. They … are Outsiders."

None of them moved. Vailret spoke slowly and clearly to Delrael. "If he's telling the truth, we'd better take heed and go. Now."

They traveled in darkness, trying to follow the blind man's sure-footed strides over the broken terrain. Paenar seemed no more troubled by the dark than he had been by their firelight. The stranger mumbled a few replies to direct questions, but he held himself tight-lipped and silent most of the time.

"What happened to your eyes?" Delrael asked. Vailret had not been able to find the courage to ask the same question.

Paenar drew to a stop and turned his burned sockets at Delrael. "I was a Scavenger. I looked at the Spectres, just a glance. And it did this."

He set off again, solemn, working his jaws as if chewing the words and wondering whether to spit them out or just swallow them.

"I scoured the world alone, searching for relics of the Sorcerers, things buried in the ancient battlefields or left in abandoned keeps. Their weapons and jewelry are more sophisticated than what your own craftsmen make, so everything I found was always in great demand. There aren't many treasure-hunters or dungeon-explorers on Hexworld anymore."

Paenar fell silent again and kept walking through the night. Vailret tried to encourage him to keep speaking. "Did you ever sell anything to Sardun?"

Paenar paused. "Sardun, in his Ice Palace? Yes, yes, I have gone to him. It was such a little thing … but I remember it made him weep with joy. I could see the tears running down his face. Just a sketch of the Earthspirits by someone who had actually seen them—it made him cry. I dropped my price a great deal because of that." Paenar seemed to be having trouble selecting his words, but he kept talking.

"I spent years sifting the dust on some of the battlefields far to the east, then I searched these mountains. I had success in some of the caves, but most were already empty from quests at the height of the Game. Then I heard that the Slac had all marched eastward, abandoning their fortresses. I didn't know why at the time, but it was true. I wanted to break into one of their deserted citadels and take whatever they left behind. No other Scavenger had ever dared that before.

"People told stories about the ghosts, the Spectres, that had haunted these peaks since the beginning of the Scouring. I have heard many stories of many things—but I chose to disbelieve the wrong tale. I came to the Slac citadel up here and watched the crumbling fortress. After I had seen no movement in a week, I decided the place was empty.

"I entered through the huge gates. I explored, and then I found the Outsiders—the Spectres—by accident. They had forgotten to make themselves invisible, because they had not realized I was there. I caught a glimpse of them … and it blasted my eyes into nothingness."

"But why?" Delrael asked.

"Because they are *real*. If I had seen more, it would have annihilated me—I suppose you could say I was lucky." His sigh sounded like a constrained whimper. "Yes, I am so lucky."

He stopped and held his staff in his hand like a mace. "They gave me new eyes. I can see." A blue glow that looked like torchlight steamed from the end of the staff. The lenses in the staff clicked again and again as they continued to focus by themselves.

"But how do they work?" Bryl asked, afraid to move closer. "Is it magic?" The tall stranger let him stare into the end of the staff for a moment, then he snapped it away.

"These mountains divide the rest of the world from the city of Sitnalta. In Sitnalta, your magic will not work—science works there instead. The Outsider named Scott has set up a region of Hexworld where characters can duplicate some of the greatest Sorcery by using machines. In this hexagon, we are on the border between the domains of magic and technology. My 'eyes' are a combination of both: the proper lenses with the correct focal lengths held together and activated by magic."

Paenar fondled the end of his eye-staff for a moment then let out a long sigh. "I can even look at them now. There are two of them—they call themselves David and Tyrone. Perhaps the Outsiders take a strange pleasure in letting me watch their machinations to destroy Hexworld."

"It's true, then," Vailret whispered. "Our world is doomed."

"Yes, and now they need you to help them get back to the Outside world before it all happens."

A fringe of dawn light set fire to the jagged edges of the Spectre Mountains, leaving the deserted Slac fortress in deep shadow. It stood in an elbow of the peaks, with spiked parapets sticking out above sharp corners. Thin arrow slits were like pockmarks on its weathered surface, and the crumbling arch of the huge gate made it look like a cave that would hide monsters. The path leading to the fortress widened into a road, paved with hexagonal cobblestones whose surface had been worn down by years of marching reptilian feet.

Vailret stared up at the towering, deserted citadel. The air was brisk, and strong winds swirled among the peaks above them. He tried to feel the presence of the Outsiders, but he noticed nothing different.

. . .

Paenar did not pause when the wide fortress gate loomed above them. He strode into the tunnel-like entrance. The heel of his eye-staff rang out in the early morning silence. Vailret reached out to run his fingers over the frost-slick blocks. The stone outer walls of the Slac fortress were ten feet thick.

Vailret had been in such a citadel before, in his imagination, when Drodanis had challenged him with the role-playing game in the darkened weapons storehouse. He hoped the outcome would be different this time.

In all the years of the Scouring of Hexworld, only one man had emerged alive from such a hell-citadel. General Doril, the original builder of the Stronghold, who had been rescued by his friend the Sentinel Oldahn. According to the legend, Oldahn had brought the mountainside crashing down around them, killing all of Doril's captured men and losing the Air Stone in the tons of rubble. But even years later, after Doril had erected the Stronghold, he had never described what he had seen while a captive of the Slac.

The blind stranger led them through musty, oppressive corridors in the citadel. The smell of stale air clung to Vailret, and he shuddered. Bryl stumbled along, clutching the Water Stone. Delrael remained silent, keeping his hands close to his weapons and looking from side to side.

The wooden doors were all reinforced with iron. Each had a small window above eye level for a man, barred or ringed with spikes: not because each was a prison cell, but because the Slac seemed to enjoy bars and spikes. Sunlight filtered through chinks in the crumbling ceiling, casting weird shadows. Vailret tried not to imagine the hissing laughter of the Slac or the screams of captives.

After the old Sorcerer wars had ended, the Slac remained in their fortresses, simmering in anger and waiting for the day they could rule Hexworld. When most of the old Sorcerers had departed in the Transition, the Slac came pouring down out of the mountains, howling and thirsty for the blood of men. But the humans fought together with the aid of the Sentinels and won Hexworld, beating the Slac back into the mountains.

Now Paenar said the Slac had all abandoned their mountain citadels and gone east—where the Rulewoman Melanie said the Outsiders were beginning the destruction of the world.

Paenar's moodiness made Vailret feel cold and terrified. He was about to stand face to face with the Outsiders, who had created Hexworld in their imaginations, who had Played all the major characters in history.

They were here, hiding, invisible. He sniffed the air, and the dank shadows seemed filled with mystery. Were they watching even now? What did they want? His throat felt thick. The back of his neck prickled with sweat. If the Outsiders forced him to look at their *real* selves, would it blast his eyes from their sockets, like Paenar—or would such a sight annihilate him completely, because he was only imaginary to them anyway?

"Why, exactly, are the Outsiders here?" he asked.

Paenar paused in midstride, as if thankful for an opportunity to delay. "They've been here since the Transition, which was supposed to be the climax of their Game. While the Sentinels were gathering themselves together, while the Slac were getting ready to come back and fight for domination of the world, while the men began their Scouring of Hexworld—two of the Outsiders came here to drop off a seed of evil that would engulf the entire map.

"They spawned a thing called Scartaris in the eastern mountains beyond the city of Taire, almost at the edge of the world. It is a blob of energy that grows and sucks the life from the land, engulfing hex after hex.

"Nothing can stop this thing from swallowing the world and ending the Game—the Outsiders don't intend to give us a chance to win."

Paenar hung his head. "Even the Outsiders can be sore losers. For almost a century, they have been hiding here, working, creating. The Outsiders David and Tyrone are here to watch a spectacular end for their imaginary world.

"Hexworld is doomed. It is already too late."

Vailret shook his head, staring at the floor. "That means the Barrier River won't save us either. Why didn't the Rulewoman tell us more?"

"But what do the Outsiders want *us* for?" Bryl asked the blind man. His thin voice echoed in the claustrophobic passageway.

An ironic smile curved on Paenar's lips. "They don't want *you*—they want the Water Stone.

They've been here so long, they can no longer return by themselves. Their ship crumbled when they turned their immense imaginations to other things. They bent and twisted the Rules they created—and now they need Hexworld's own magic to send them back. They can't return to the real world unless they use the power in your Water Stone."

Bryl stood aghast, clutching the sapphire cube. Delrael began to laugh. "After they created this Scartaris thing to destroy us, they expect us to help? Well, if they can't play nice, we'll just take our dice and go home."

Paenar turned to him. "They will not ask your permission. If you are not careful, they will simply destroy you. The Spectres toy with me but do little else. I hate them for blinding me, yet I am dependent on their power for my new eyes." He stretched out his eye-staff.

"The Outsiders are mere children in their own world, in the *real* world. All the centuries of our history have been only a few years of gaming to them. And they have tempers like spoiled children as well.

"I cannot give you any better advice, because I have none. They have doomed our world, and I would be happy to see them stranded here to share its fate. But that is not in my power, or yours. They will take what they need, whether you cooperate or not." He set off again. The foot of his staff rang out on the stone floor.

"We'll see about that," Delrael said.

The tunnel spilled out of the hivelike chambers to a wide, barren courtyard where the Slac had apparently conducted battle training. Wooden posts and crossbars had been erected in the dusty earth; blood-stained manacles dangled from them.

Sprawled across the courtyard were huge, twisted girders, coated with rust, that formed the skeletal outline of a metal ship like a dead prehistoric animal. The ship had crumbled into a shadow of its construction, not able to travel anywhere. Vailret stared at it in awe: The Outsiders had constructed it from their imaginations and had used it to carry them from their *real* world to Hexworld. But over the centuries, which had seemed like days to the Outsiders, they turned their efforts to destroying the world, allowing their fantastic ship to fade.

They needed to use the Water Stone as a catalyst to get themselves off their own maps and back to *reality*. Vailret found the irony impressive. What possible power could the magic of the Stones have that the Outsiders' own dice could not work? It wasn't fair—and fairness was supposed to be one of the cardinal Rules of Hexworld.

They stepped out into the sunlit courtyard, and awe crept up on Vailret again. A tingling in the air, a vibration, told him others were there. He looked around the dusty, barren ground, but he could see no evidence of the Spectres other than the abandoned and disintegrating ship. Vailret stopped with Delrael and Bryl beside him. Paenar stood off to one side, scowling, gripping his eye-staff so hard, his knuckles turned white.

"You are here. Now we can go home at last." The voices boomed out in the silent mountain air, echoing like thunder. They came from different corners of the courtyard. More than one speaker stood hidden on the empty, bloodstained training ground. The words themselves were spoken in a deep, rich tone that sounded like a caricature of someone omnipotent and dangerous—the voice of an angry god. Bryl clutched the sapphire Stone instinctively, protecting it but ready to use it.

"We felt Sardun use the power of the Water Stone to create the Barrier River. We felt you, Bryl, use it to save the khelebar. Now it will set us free of this world, let us go back home before it is too late."

Delrael shouted, directing his voice at the entire courtyard, "Get rid of your Scartaris creature in the east, and then we'll talk!"

Vailret cringed, wary of the anger of the Spectres. A second voice came from a different corner of the courtyard.

"We want to stop the Game. We can do that if we want. What difference does it make—you're all just part of our imaginations. A roll of the dice."

"It matters to us!" Delrael said.

Vailret put a hand on his cousin's arm to restrain him. He made his own voice sound quiet and firm. "You don't look very real to me, Spectres—I can't see you, and you can't even get home. Who's to say you're not more make-believe than we are?"

"Shall we drop our invisibility and let you see just how real we are?" the first voice boomed.

Bryl jerked out the cube of the Water Stone and gripped it in both hands, letting it glint and reflect in the bright sun. "Spectres! My mind is linked with the Water Stone right now. If you send us out of existence, I'll take the Stone with me!"

Vailret clenched his teeth to keep from shouting his enthusiasm.

"Stop!" the Outsider shouted.

"He also has the power to destroy the Water Stone," Vailret bluffed. He doubted Bryl could bring himself to harm the gem, even if he had the strength. But the half-Sorcerer gave the Outsiders no indication of that.

"You have set in motion the destruction of Hexworld, and now you're trapped. Either send Scartaris back into nonexistence and let us continue our lives, or remain here and suffer our fate."

"But we don't want to Play the Game anymore!" the second Spectre said.

"And we don't want to be wiped from the universe either," Delrael retorted. "Regardless of what *you* say, to us this isn't imaginary at all!"

Vailret drew a deep breath. Paenar had said the Outsiders were mere children in their own world. How gullible were they? How sure of themselves? Did the Rules have nuances they did not know about?

"In fact, Spectres, we think of ourselves as *real*," Vailret ventured, stepping forward. He looked to the side, making sure Bryl kept a firm grip on the Water Stone. "Look at us—we breathe, we eat, we sleep, we love, we hate, we fight. We feel pain, and we dream. How can we possibly be imaginary?"

He spread his hands to indicate the broken rocky landscape. "Look around you. Feel the cold air, see the towering mountains, the sky, the sun. You claim this is just a fantasy world you have created as a Game— but I think you've got it backward.

"I think that we concocted *you* from our imaginations. Maybe we needed someone to blame, some fictitious outside people who make all the misery and pain in our world. That way, we could soothe our collective conscience into believing there was nothing we could do to prevent the wars, no real reason for us to work toward peace, no valid possibility to make our lives better. We needed someone to shake our fists at, someone to curse, rather than at ourselves and our own frailties.

"So we invented an imaginary group of beings who make a Game of our world, playing it as we play our own small games. Until now, no one has ever seen these Outsiders; no one has ever so much as found evidence for their existence."

Vailret took a deep breath and surged ahead with his challenge. "You say you're trapped here, but how can that be? If you are all-powerful, then change the Rules—it should be simple for you. How can you be trapped by Rules unless they're *real*?"

Delrael raised a fist in the air, grinning. Paenar stood, stunned but perplexed.

"Is there a speck of doubt in your minds? Is there even one whispered thought gnawing at you? It'll take only a momentary flicker of disbelief —and then you'll be gone!" He forced himself to laugh loudly.

Bryl held up the Water Stone, looking angry. "If I could see you, Spectres, I'd give you a taste of the power you say does not exist."

Paenar, standing in silence, rapped his eye-staff on the ground. He gave a secretive smile and pointed the end of the staff off into one corner of the courtyard.

Bryl apparently knew what he meant and rolled the Water Stone in the dust. A bolt of lightning seared through the air to where the blind man had pointed. The bolt struck something, and a mammoth shriek echoed along the stone walls of the citadel. Paenar pointed again, and again. Bryl scrabbled to pick up the sapphire cube and rolled it three more times, missing the spell once but striking the Spectres twice, using his anger to pry more energy from the Stone.

The two Outsiders howled. Vailret shouted after them, "Can you feel that, Outsiders? Is that imaginary power? How can you be hurt by imaginary pain?"

He let his words sink in a moment. "I believe the Water Stone is *real*. I believe Hexworld is *real*. I believe I am *real*." Vailret dropped his voice and spat out his words, one at a time. "And I do not believe in *you*!"

"This is not possible!" the dominant Spectre voice bellowed. Then soul-ripping wails filled the courtyard, and a burst of unbearable light, as something tore its way screaming through the air, whisked off to a place not imaginable. Only a brief howl of despair was left behind, quickly fading into the mountain wind.

Vailret found himself knocked backward to the lifeless dirt of the Slac training ground. Beads of sweat dried cool on his forehead. He blinked at spots of color in front of his dazzled eyes.

Delrael whooped. He got to his feet, jumping up and down as if he had forgotten about his *kennok* leg.

"Are they gone?" Bryl asked. "Are they destroyed or just sent back to their own world?"

"I don't know," Vailret said, but his voice came out as a whisper. "Maybe I freed them from the Rules binding them here after so long. Or maybe they did disbelieve in their own existence enough to … to erase themselves."

Delrael frowned and scratched his head. "Did you believe what you were saying to them? Is it all true?"

Vailret pursed his lips. "I … don't think so."

The sound of quiet sobbing came from beside them, and they looked to find Paenar squatting on the ground with the knees of his long legs jutting up in the air. He bowed his head into his hands, trying to hold on to his dignity, but spasms rippled through his hunched back.

Bryl saw the blind man's eye-staff discarded on the ground. The blue glow in the end had died away, and the loose lenses, no longer working, lay scattered in the dry dirt.

Paenar looked up at them, unable to cry because his tear ducts had been blasted away. His blackened eye sockets stared as blind and lifeless as the cold stone of the fortress around them.

INTERLUDE: OUTSIDE

Melanie fluttered her eyelids, trying to chase away the bright spots behind her vision. The dice bounced around on the table by themselves, like popcorn, clattering against the map. The lights in the house dimmed. The dice came to rest, and everything else fell silent.

David climbed back to his feet from where he had fallen off the chair. His skin turned pale and clammy, like old cottage cheese. His eyes looked from one object to another around the room, but remained focused in the imaginary distance. He flexed his hand where an angry red welt like a burn had appeared.

Tyrone's mouth was wide with astonishment, locked in a combined expression of delight and terror.

Scott held one of the transparent dice up to the light, staring at it. "Impossible." He frowned but glared at the dice, the map in challenge. "It's just a stupid *game!*"

"Maybe we've all got overactive imaginations," Tyrone said.

"It's not real," Scott repeated.

David shook his head and sat back down again. "That's it. Enough for tonight. I can't play anymore."

"No!" Scott slammed the dice back down on the table with a vehemence Melanie thought he did not intend. Scott looked at them all, blinking his eyes behind his glasses. "They're heading into *my* section next. I've had about enough of this magical crap. Things are going to start making sense."

He closed his eyes. "They have to start making sense."

CHAPTER 10
CITY OF SITNALTA

We have sent out explorers, we have brought our measuring devices, we have collected data. There can be no doubt: Beyond a certain boundary around our city, the Rules of Physics change. Science may not be the natural order for all of Hexworld. Some characters might believe in magic ... and in certain cases, it may even work for them.
—Dirac, address to the Sitnaltan Council of Patent Givers

Vailret found some warm, stagnant water in a cistern at the edge of the courtyard. He tore down a tattered Slac banner, soaked in the gritty cistern, and went to Paenar. He tried to soothe the blind man by dabbing water on his face.

Paenar made it clear that he did not want to be coddled. He stood up, brushing himself off to regain his dignity. The blind man stood for a moment without moving, then reached down with amazing accuracy to pick up his useless eye-staff. Paenar felt the empty end of the staff and stooped, feeling around in the dust from the loose lenses. He rubbed them together in the palm of his hand, making clicking noises like the song of an insect.

With a snarl on his face, Paenar turned and hurled the blind lenses across the courtyard, skittering them against the twisted metal girders of the Spectres' dead ship.

"You fought back!" Paenar said. "You fought the Outsiders and won! All this time, I never even tried to resist them. It wasn't hopeless after all."

Bryl crossed his thin arms and put on a defiant expression. "I'm not going to give up. Failure is the easy way out." The enthusiasm made him look healthier, less old.

Vailret went over to the ruins of the Spectres' ship. It lay in tumbled parts made of glass, porcelain, and shining metal. Thin wind howled around the girders, making them hum. Nothing seemed workable on the Outsider ship, nor was it obvious how the pieces fit back together.

He picked up Paenar's scattered lenses from the eye staff and held them up to the light; one had been chipped, but not badly. Vailret tilted it one way and another—then at a certain angle, he stopped, amazed. Through the lens, he could see a different world entirely, like a window to the Outside. He saw figures, four of them, three young men and a brown-haired girl, all dressed oddly. They seemed to be arguing with each other. Strange food and drinks were scattered around a smooth table with dice and maps.

The Outsiders?

Had he glimpsed them Playing? And survived? He blinked his eyes and felt a shiver burn through his veins. But before he could shout to the others, he tilted the lens again and lost the angle. Dismayed, he turned the glass in the sunlight, squinting and trying to find the window again— but he had lost it. Frowning, he placed the lenses in a leather pouch at his side.

"What will you do now?" Paenar finally asked.

Bryl put the Water Stone back in his pocket and tossed pebbles against the towering, moss-grown wall of the citadel. Delrael took out his sword and inspected it in the sunlight, then sheathed it with a click against his scabbard. He straightened the bow on his back and slapped a hand against his leather armor. "We may as well go down with an adventure so grand that the Outsiders will wonder how they ever got bored with Hexworld after all!"

"I am awed by you all. You shame me with my own surrender," Paenar said. It seemed difficult for him to talk. "May I accompany you at least as far as Sitnalta? Perhaps I can assist you in some way, to repay you for … freeing me. I'll try not to make your journey slower."

"We can't very well leave you here." Vailret looked at the open expression of shame and helplessness on the blind man's face.

"Before we go, let's do a quick exploration of this place," Delrael said. "Come on, Vailret—who knows, there may be other captives in some of the cells far below."

Vailret stiffened, looking up at the blocky, threatening walls. "What about the Slac? I don't want any more 'little adventures' to slow us down."

"There aren't any Slac left, so come on." Delrael shrugged then grinned at his cousin. "It just rubs me the wrong way to leave a place like this unexplored."

Bryl stayed with Paenar out in the sunshine where he could rest, but Vailret remained close by his cousin as they entered the massive fortress. They hurried through the stifling corridors, taking turns poking their heads inside open rooms. The hinges groaned when Vailret and Delrael pulled open heavy doors. "Think we'll find any food?" Delrael asked.

"Would you want to eat what a Slac eats?"

"I see your point."

They went down a broad staircase leading underground. Vailret's uneasiness grew. "Hello!" Delrael shouted. "Is anybody here?" His words pounced on the walls and rattled down the twisted corridors.

"Be quiet!" Vailret whispered. "Let's go back—I don't know if I can remember my way out anymore."

"Of course you can. We'll go just a little farther." Vailret hung back and Delrael finally sighed in impatience. "What's the matter with you?"

Vailret felt defensive but kept his anger in check. "I'm a little nervous, that's all."

Delrael pursed his lips. "With all we've been through, Vailret, I know you're not a coward—what's so frightening about an old empty fortress?"

Vailret looked at him in surprise but saw only puzzlement. "I thought you would understand. Didn't you do the role-playing training game at the Stronghold? In the weapons storehouse with your father?"

"Sure—I had to go rescue a jewel from a tribe of worm-men underground. Everybody's adventure is different."

Vailret flicked his glance around the confining walls. Sick-looking green moss crawled up from the corners. "I fought to the death in a Slac fortress. Just like this one."

It took a moment for Delrael to realize the relevance, then he shook his head. "That was only a game."

"*All* of this is only a Game. Just different players."

Subdued, they moved forward, entering a drafty dining hall with dozens of splintered boards on skewed wooden trestles. Dust, cobwebs, and cracked wooden plates littered the room. They passed through the hollow-sounding hall and wound their way down another set of steep and chipped stairs. Only a slight unevenness of Delrael's echoing footsteps gave any hint that one of his legs was not normal.

The doors on either side of the passageway became noticeably bulkier, with heavy bolts on the outsides. This looked familiar to Vailret's imagination. Delrael threw open a door that had sagged on its hinges and found a fallen bed and some straw that had rotted almost to dust over the passage of time. The next cell contained a skeleton.

"The Slac have been gone too long," Vailret said. "Even if there were survivors, Paenar would have found them. Can we go now?"

"Let me just see what's on the other side of the big door at the end of the hall."

Delrael went down the haphazard flagstones until he reached a tall door blocking their way. He moved smoothly, ready to jump into action. He seemed to have forgotten about his *kennok* leg.

Vailret kept looking from side to side. Something told him he had been here before; it seemed too familiar. Delrael wrapped his fingers around the door's studded crossbar and knocked it out of its cradle. He grunted as he tugged on the door. "Vailret, help me here!"

The two men pulled the door open, and a dry, sour smell flooded out. Delrael stood peering inside with his hands on his hips. "Would you look at that?!"

Vailret looked over his cousin's shoulder to see a wide gravel-covered arena. Stone benches ringed the lip of the circular wall around the sunken pit. Skulls and bones were scattered on the gravel.

"See, there's nothing in here." Delrael stepped into the arena. He picked up a stone and threw it across the bloodstained gravel. It bounced and pattered, then everything fell silent again.

"Del, I think you should come out of there...."

"I wonder what they did here?"

They heard a snorting sound and the scraping of gravel, as if something with large, clawed feet were charging toward them—but they could see nothing. Delrael cocked his head to listen as the angry grunts and snorts came closer, swifter. He touched his sword hilt, frowning.

Vailret jerked his cousin back out of the doorway and threw his shoulder at the door. He winced at the shock, but he jammed the crossbar back onto its supports. Then he panted with relief.

"What do you think you're doing?" Delrael brushed his chest armor, scowling.

Something smashed against the door. A few tendrils of dust leaked through the crumbling roof, but the door held firm. They heard a roar and then another crash. After a moment, the creature from the other side gave up and retreated in silence.

Delrael looked at Vailret, astonished. "What was that? How did you know?"

"It's an Akkar. They're invisible. And you didn't listen to me."

They left the abandoned Slac fortress behind, crossing a hex-line into pleasant forest terrain by late afternoon. Though the forest seemed cluttered and untended after Ledaygen, the air was warm and filled with the scent of trees and plants.

"It'll be wonderful to sleep in terrain like this!" Delrael said.

Paenar turned his head to listen to the background noises in the forest, to feel the leaves and the air on his face, to smell the wildflowers and evergreens. He still carried his useless eye-staff, but the path was clear and he could follow at a good pace if he kept a hand on someone's shoulder.

"I was such a fool to remain with the Outsiders so long. Why couldn't I see this before? Now it's my fault Hexworld is doomed."

"The Game isn't over yet, Paenar," Vailret said. "The Rulewoman Melanie wouldn't have told us to fight if there wasn't a way to win. Watch out for this branch—it's hanging low."

"Maybe we just need to find some new way to approach the problem," Bryl suggested. "Paenar, what were you saying about Sitnalta and how magic won't work there?"

"I didn't say it wouldn't work. Nothing on Hexworld is absolute, only a set of high or low probabilities. It is like an imaginary dice roll. But the chances of magic working are drastically reduced in Sitnalta, just as the chances for technology are greatly increased." Paenar rustled against a branch but ignored it as he kept talking.

"The Sitnaltans think only of the future, trying to do everything better than they did the day before. When I brought them items from Hexworld's past, things I had scavenged from the mountains, they told me they had no interest in anything that was so shamefully obsolete."

Delrael got a twinkle in his eye. "If they are so good with technology, do you think they could fix the Spectres' ship?" He chuckled to himself. "We could use it to send Scartaris right back to the Outsiders."

Bryl snickered. "Wouldn't that be a wonderful surprise!"

Paenar shook his head. "You have seen the condition of the ship—it could never be repaired. Barely anything remains of it."

Vailret rubbed his lips, pondering. "No ... but I'd bet the Sitnaltans would love to have a look at it, nevertheless. Maybe we can use that as a bargaining chip if we need anything from them."

In her tower room on the edge of Sitnalta, a young woman stared at the wide blackboard. Chalk dust from her furious writings and erasures covered the floor, her garments, and her body. She bit her lip, deep in thought, and tasted chalk.

She had patented her inventions in her own name, Mayer, and collaborated on a fifth, though none of them had been particularly useful. But this contraption—a calculating machine—would earn her a name beside the two greatest living characters in Sitnalta, Professors Verne and Frankenstein. If only she could see a trick that would allow her to mechanically solve the equations—

Mayer stared at the blackboard, baring her teeth and demanding of herself why the numbers would not balance. She reached up with her lump of chalk and intuitively altered a variable, replacing it with an equivalent expression. And suddenly, everything worked.

"Eureka!" Mayer turned to shake her fists in the air and went to the window, grinning.

She saw the four travelers walking toward the gates of the city. She gawked for a moment and then had the good sense to pick up her "optick-tube"—two mounted lenses that magnified distant objects five-fold. Mayer scrutinized the four characters carefully: One was very young—blond-haired and just past boyishness; the other young man was more muscular, obviously a fighter, wearing leather armor and carrying weapons, but he seemed to be limping. His gleaming silver belt looked rather gaudy.

The other two characters were older. One was thin and white-bearded, smaller in stature than the others, and wearing a blue cloak. But he looked intelligent and shrewd, perhaps even a professor or a great inventor in his own land. The other stood tall and gaunt and seemed to have been blinded in a terrible accident. She was familiar with industrial accidents, since some of the early Sitnaltan steam-engine boilers had exploded—but her father Dirac had developed the pressure-release valve that made steam engines safe for everyday use.

Mayer mentally constructed a detailed analysis, drawing conclusions from the evidence she had seen. Then she reached for the speaking tube, putting the cuplike brass end to her mouth and shouting the news into it. She pronounced her words carefully and kept the sentences short and clipped. Her voice would be muffled as it bounced around inside the speaking tube until it exited the other end, probably awakening the old man who sat at the telegraph station.

Within minutes, all of Sitnalta would be alerted to the visitors.

Mayer replaced the end of the speaking tube on its hook and leaned out over the windowsill. The brown-haired fighter looked up at her, cupping his hands around his mouth. "Hello up there!"

Great Maxwell! Had they no better way of announcing themselves?

Mayer picked up her own megaphone and blew some chalk dust from the mouthpiece before she spoke down at the four travelers. "Welcome to Sitnalta. Please wait for the gate to raise completely before entering. Thank you."

She threw a lever that dropped a counterweight, which turned a gear, which turned a larger gear, which caused the heavy sheet-metal gate to ratchet upward in its tracks. Mayer took one last look at her equations— now that she knew how to solve the problem, she didn't want to leave. With a sigh, she went down to meet the strangers.

The wall surrounding the city of Sitnalta was made of stone blocks cut in perfect rectangles, equal in size and with sharp corners. Vailret ran his fingers along one of the cracks—it put even the careful work of Skon the stonecutter to shame. Paenar cocked his head at the odd jumble of distant clanging, hissing, and whistling noises from within the city. The air held strange smells.

Delrael leaned heavily on Vailret's shoulder, barely able to walk on his *kennok* limb. As they had approached the vicinity of Sitnalta, the *kennok* magic had begun to fade, leaving the fighter burdened with a cumbersome and rigid wooden leg. Delrael had shown him how the dividing line between flesh and wood now stood dark and distinct again. Vailret didn't know what to do, other than leave the area as quickly as they could.

After the woman in the tower had called to them, the heavy metal gate clattered upward, opening the city of Sitnalta to their view. Bryl led blind Paenar, and Vailret supported Delrael, thinking how unlikely a fighting team they must appear to be.

But Vailret forgot all that when he passed through the gate into the city.

He and Delrael stood amazed, bombarded by the sights. Even Bryl seemed impressed. Paenar remained aloof and silent.

The main road was paved with colorful hexagon-shaped cobble-stones, each formed perfectly and laid in dizzying geometric patterns. Many of the shining buildings were two or even three stories tall. Except for Sardun's Ice Palace and the Slac citadel, Vailret had never seen such enormous structures, certainly nothing made by humans.

A thin woman stepped out of a tower doorway and walked toward them, looking stiff and businesslike. She had short dark hair, bright fast-moving eyes, and a sharp nose. She wore garments dyed more colorfully than any natural pigment Tarne had ever used in his weaving.

For a moment, Vailret thought of Tarne and hoped the old veteran was keeping the other characters safe while Gairoth held the Stronghold. He wondered how long it would be until he got home again.

"My name is Mayer. I am the daughter of Dirac." The Sitnaltan woman paused, waiting for something, then she scowled. "My father invented seventy of the greatest inventions of all time."

"We're pleased to meet you," Bryl said as cordially as he could. They introduced themselves.

Mayer swept her arms out to indicate Sitnalta. "We don't get many visitors here. We like to hear about how far ahead we are of the rest of Hexworld."

Surprisingly, Paenar snapped at her. His hand clenched Bryl's cloak, leaving fingermarks. "Or perhaps you need to learn about some of the things you lack."

Indignant, Mayer glared at him, but looked disconcerted when Paenar's empty eye-sockets met her gaze. She turned abruptly and motioned for them to follow her. She opened the wide doors of a shed near the gate, sliding the doors along polished tracks. "I can show you more of Sitnalta."

In the dimness of the shed, Mayer pushed and tugged a large wheeled contraption, a steam-engine car, out onto the hex-cobbled street. When no one moved to assist her, she shouted, "Don't just gawk at me, you barbarians! Help me get the vehicle out. Great Maxwell! How do you expect us to travel?"

As Vailret helped push, the iron-shod wooden wheels of the vehicle rumbled on the cobblestones. In the full light, Vailret thought the machine looked magnificent. A shining silver boiler took up most of the car's back, but the chassis rode low to the ground, balanced so that the heavy water-filled boiler did not lift the front wheels up in the air.

Mayer touched the metal of the tank and jerked back her hand, blowing on her fingers. "Good—pressure's still up, and the fires are burning. Someone must have just used it." She dumped coal from a bucket into the orange maw of a furnace beneath the water. Steam hissed out of a pressure valve in the back of the boiler.

"Come on, seat yourselves! We're wasting the pressure buildup."

Delrael hobbled to the side of the vehicle and swung his stiff leg up into the seat. Paenar climbed in without any assistance after Bryl had led him to the car. Vailret hopped into the back, near the boiler.

Even before they had settled in, Mayer twisted a crank that released steam through the piston chambers, turning the gears. She jerked locking pins out from the wheels, and the car rattled forward over the cobblestones.

Vailret grinned in excitement. Thick white steam belched from the mouth of their smokestack. Mayer pulled a rope that caused a shrill whistle to blast, hurting their ears. The steam-engine car clattered over the streets. Mayer wrestled with two steering levers that pulled the front wheels one way or the other.

"This is marvelous!" Vailret said. "It's like magic."

Mayer corrected him sharply. "Not magic—technology."

The pressure valve in the back of the boiler popped open, shrieking out excess steam, and then closed itself again. Paenar sat in silence, bouncing up and down as the car rumbled along the cobblestones.

The steam-engine vehicle traveled too swiftly for Vailret to take in all the wondrous things around them, but Mayer pointed out the more prominent structures.

"We create all of our materials there, in the manufactories." She pointed to massive buildings where smoke stacks dumped thick steam and black smoke into the air. "That one makes ingots of steel for us to use in our inventions. We also harvest natural gas from underground, and mine minerals from the sea. You'll find a great deal of gold used in some inventions, since gold is abundant in the sea water."

As the car passed by, other Sitnaltans stared at them from the windows of tall buildings. Mayer pointed at the web of wires stretching from house to house, connecting all the buildings together.

"Over those wires, I was able to inform all of Sitnalta of your arrival. Instantly." Mayer smiled to herself.

"I could do the same thing with a sending or a message stick," Bryl countered.

"But you would need magic. Our telegraph runs on *electricity*."

"And he should be ashamed of using magic?" Vailret said.

"I certainly would not be proud of it. The Sorcerers nearly destroyed Hexworld with century after century of their senseless wars. And then they abandoned us with only a few worthless Sentinel representatives to help out."

She turned and looked up at the tall buildings. "All you see here in Sitnalta *we* have done. Human characters—with no help from Sentinels. Magic may be the crutch of the Sorcerers, but we have developed science, we have invented tools and machines to do everything the magic used to do. We have discovered the true scientific Rules by which the world works. We can well be proud."

Bryl muttered to himself, "I'd like to see her create the Barrier River with a machine!"

But Vailret gazed around in awe. What she said struck him on a sore spot—these were human characters, and they had accomplished much of what he had always thought impossible. Perhaps he could learn from them, study how they worked their miracles and be able to create a different kind of magic by himself. Even without Sorcerer blood.

Mayer pushed down on a pedal at her feet and released another lever, bringing the steam-engine vehicle to rest. Vailret heard a different hissing that had been hidden by the din of their own car. "Look there!" Mayer pointed down another side street. "One of my father's inventions."

They saw a three-wheeled contraption with a wide spinning brush under its belly. The machine chugged along, driven by a smaller steam engine, hissing and whistling to itself from its pressure valves. The wide rotating brush scrubbed the cobblestones, devouring all the dirt and grit from between the cracks.

"Sitnalta has ten of those machines to keep our streets clean."

She released the foot pedal, engaged the gears once more, and they rolled onward.

The vehicle reached a broad rectangular plaza that stood empty in the early afternoon. An ornate fountain spurted in the center of the square, running an elaborate water clock. Mayer pulled the steam-engine car to a halt and squinted at the level of water in the clock. She locked the pins in the wheels and hopped out, running around to the back of the boiler and opening a red valve that spilled the excess steam pressure into the air. The car made a sigh as it shut down, but steam burbled out of the smoke-stack for several more minutes.

Vailret could think of nothing to say; his mind had been over-whelmed by the marvelous sights and Mayer's enthusiasm. He climbed out of the car and went to the fountain to see better, staring at the spraying water and at the clock. His ears still rang from the steam engine's loud noises.

In the pool, four large, clumsy-looking mechanical fish puttered around and around in perfect circles. He stuck his hand in the water, but the mechanical fish paid him no heed.

"The leaders of Sitnalta will be here momentarily," Mayer said.

"The leaders?" Bryl asked. "Who runs the city?"

"The people of Sitnalta decide for themselves what we will do. We are a weighted democracy. Each character has at least one vote, but those who have done the most for Sitnalta have the most votes. It is very fair—the ones who work hard for our city have a significant say in the decisions we make, and those who have done little, say little. In an ordinary democracy, the vote of a vagrant is valued as highly as that of a great inventor. And that just isn't logical."

"Why don't you tell us how you determine these weighted votes?" Paenar seemed to know the answer already.

Mayer looked at him as if he had asked something obvious. "By the number of inventions a character has contributed, of course. My father Dirac has designed seventy new inventions for the betterment of Sitnalta, and therefore, he has seventy votes. I have five, soon to be six."

"But what about the characters who aren't inventors?" Bryl asked.

Mayer snorted. "Useless people—who cares what they think?"

Paenar smiled to himself.

At some unheard signal, dozens of characters emerged from the doorways of buildings around the square and filed toward the fountain. They stared at the travelers but talked little among themselves. The other characters wore bright clothes similar to the ones Mayer wore, but some characters were covered with grease or wore work-smocks. One woman's hair looked singed; perhaps a new invention had backfired on her.

Mayer smiled and motioned to a rotund man striding toward them. The man had a bald crown and shaggy reddish hair sticking out around his ears. "This is my father, Dirac, who has designed seventy inventions."

"If she says one more time how many inventions he's done—" Delrael grumbled.

"You were early, Mayer," Dirac said, still smiling at the travelers. "Did you run short of things to show our guests?"

"No, Father!" Mayer looked at the water clock for defense, but she said nothing more.

Dirac gazed at them with a distant expression on his face, then he extended his hand to each of them, beaming. "I am pleased you've come to Sitnalta. We'll have time to discuss many things."

Paenar's blindness did not trouble Dirac at all; he reached out, guided the blind man's hand into his own grasp, and shook it. Paenar seemed to dislike the Sitnaltan's touch.

Before they could say anything to him, Dirac turned and waved two other men over to join them. "Allow me to introduce the greatest inventors in all of Sitnalta—Professors Frankenstein and Verne. I cannot begin to tell you the great wonders these men have brought to us."

Frankenstein was a young, haggard-looking man, with dark brown hair and intense, bloodshot eyes. He nodded cursorily to the guests but went back to brood with his ideas, as if incapable of making light conversation.

Verne, on the other hand, blinked in surprise at being personally introduced to the visitors. Verne had a great bushy beard and tangled gray hair hanging over his ears. He scratched his head and extended a hand to each of the four, smiling politely. A peculiar, haunted quality lay behind the eyes of both professors, as if they had the dreams and nightmares of several lifetimes locked within their skulls.

Verne rubbed his hands together. His voice had a strange accented lilt. "Monsieur Dirac himself is not a trivial personage either. He has—"

"We know," Delrael interrupted, "seventy inventions to his credit."

Dirac looked pleased, paying no heed to the sarcasm in Delrael's comment. "You must be hungry," he said, interrupting Verne. "We were about to break for our midday meal."

Both professors slipped away and stood back to observe the crowd. Dirac led the travelers over to stone benches ringing the square. Delrael lurched, nearly unable to walk on his *kennok* leg. Vailret helped him, but Delrael acted frustrated at himself.

After watching the water clock, everyone turned to face other sets of doors around the square. Wheeled carts shuttled out of the building, bearing individual plates heaped with steaming food.

Dirac sat down on the bench next to Delrael and Vailret, elbowing his way into a place of honor. Delrael absently rubbed his thigh, at the line where the *kennok* wood joined with flesh. The carts came around, and the Sitnaltans each took a plate and began to eat. As Vailret tried to choose between several different entrees, he noticed how every plate appeared the same, so carefully arranged. But after days of pack food—

They ate in relative silence. The smokestacks of the manufactories had stopped exhaling great gray clouds, and many of the background noises had also fallen silent. Off on another bench and oblivious to the others, Frankenstein and Verne argued over the fine details of some new invention.

Delrael scraped the last remnants of food from his plate into his mouth, finishing well before anyone else. After swallowing his food, he spoke to Dirac. "I don't understand one thing. We arrive at your gates as perfect strangers, your daughter invites us in and gives us the grand tour, now you introduce us to all of Sitnalta and give us a good meal. But nobody's even asked us why we're here or where we're going. Isn't that a little strange?"

Dirac wiped his mouth and looked flustered. Mayer watched her father, waiting for him to answer. "We assumed you had heard of our great city and came to see its wonders for yourself. That was Mayer's hypothesis."

Bryl laughed so suddenly that he choked on his remaining food. Delrael also chuckled, while Vailret looked at the Sitnaltans in surprise. Paenar shook his head.

"Your city is marvelous, but we are on our way to the island of Rokanun," Vailret said. "We need a passage across the sea."

The other Sitnaltans muttered. Frankenstein and Verne stopped their discussion to pay attention.

"The dragon Tyros is on Rokanun. You don't want to go there." Dirac placed his hands on the table then smiled at them again. "But don't worry —you are safe here."

"You don't understand," Bryl said. "We want to find the dragon."

Dirac shook his head as if to dismiss them. "Not another one of those silly treasure quests? I thought they went out of fashion years and years ago."

"We have to rescue someone. We promised," Delrael said.

"But why would you want to go there now?" Dirac frowned, puzzled. "It is only a matter of time before Sitnaltan technology advances enough to destroy Tyros. Why bother risking your lives?"

Paenar stood up, exasperated, and put his fists on his hips. "Are you Sitnaltans so wrapped up in your little world that you see nothing else?" He glared at the gathered characters with his empty eye-sockets.

"All of your inventions will be worthless soon—the Outsiders have decided to end the Game. Our world is about to be destroyed, and I'll bet you didn't even know!"

He pointed in the general direction of Delrael, Bryl, and Vailret. "These people are fighting—they did not give up. They will not surrender. But Sitnalta is ignoring the danger."

Across the table, Mayer bristled and glared at him. Dirac folded his hands on his paunchy belly with patronizing interest. "Oh? Please tell us more of this danger."

Vailret looked at Delrael, who raised his eyebrows and nodded.

Vailret set his jaw. "We received a message from the Rulewoman Melanie herself, telling us about some enemy growing in the east. We traveled northward to ask for Sardun's help, and he created the Barrier River that cut us off from the threat. In exchange, we agreed to rescue his daughter Tareah, who has been kidnapped by the dragon on Rokanun. But now we have learned that Scartaris is not just a normal enemy. Not just an army. I doubt that the Barrier River will be enough to stop the destruction."

Someone laughed. Other Sitnaltans muttered about "barbarian superstitions." Professor Verne tugged on his long beard. Professor Frankenstein chewed on his lip.

Mayer rolled her eyes upward. "Do you mean that Sardun, the great Sentinel, could not fight off a dragon?"

"Sitnalta has not been able to destroy Tyros either," Paenar pointed out.

Mayer fell silent.

"The Outsiders have decided to end the Game. I know, for I have been with them. They blasted away my eyes when I glimpsed them at their work." Paenar stared at the gathered Sitnaltans, offering his empty eye-sockets as evidence of his story.

Professor Verne stood up, scratching his head. "This great energy force to the east—what exactly is it? And where, exactly, is it located?"

Paenar turned his head in the direction of the inventor's voice. "Northeast of here, in the mountains beyond the city of Taire. The Outsiders have named it Scartaris—it will absorb all the energy on Hexworld, breaking the hexes from the map and sending them to drift as barren chunks in the universe."

Verne scratched his head again and said, "Hmmm." He looked at Frankenstein, and his younger partner shrugged then nodded. Professor Verne drew a deep breath. His eyes looked distant and watery.

"We did not announce our recent findings because we had insufficient data to form any conclusions. Some of our monitors have detected a powerful energy anomaly in the extreme northeast of the map. Frankenstein and I were at a loss to explain it—but these travelers offer a hypothesis that fits the data."

He crossed his arms. "In the absence of evidence to the contrary, good scientific practice suggests that we not scoff at the claims of our guests."

Dirac fidgeted, but even he did not dare to disagree with the great Professor Verne.

"Well then," Delrael said, "are you going to help us or not?"

The wind picked up, stretching the tether ropes taut as it tugged at the huge gas-filled balloon. Vailret stood on the ground, looking up at the bottom of the woven basket bobbing in the air. The balloon was constructed of bright red and white cloth, sewn tightly and waterproofed, covered with a mesh of rope that attached to cables leading down to the passenger basket below. Bright white numerals "VI" had been stenciled on the basket.

Verne had explained how simple the concept was: a giant sack filled with a gas even lighter than air. It would float, allowing them to travel through the air. But Vailret wasn't sure he wanted to trust his life to something so flimsy.

"What does the 'VI' mean?" He pointed at the basket.

Verne smiled sheepishly. Frankenstein said, "Our first five attempts did not have sufficient integrity."

The fighter and the old half-Sorcerer stood in the basket, staring down at the gathered crowd. The basket swayed against the ropes as the two passengers moved about. Even with his uncooperative *kennok* leg, Delrael had hauled himself up the rope ladder, using his arms and moving from one sagging rung to the next. Bryl scrambled up afterward, glancing down too often and looking ill. He appeared frail and spidery as he climbed into the basket.

From the ground, Vailret raised his hand in a farewell wave. Paenar had instinctively turned to face the proper direction. If Verne's intuition was right, the great balloon would take Delrael and Bryl over the hexes of ocean to the island of Rokanun....

"We have sent up test balloons," Verne had said, "small and unmanned, of course. We used detectors in them to measure the prevailing winds, and if you reach the correct altitude, you should be able to go directly to the island. The detectors failed once they'd gone a sufficient distance from Sitnalta, but we did gather enough data to be confident in our results."

"The detectors failed?" Vailret said in alarm.

"Oh yes, but we saw no evidence that the balloons failed," Verne added quickly.

"Now don't get sidetracked, Jules," Frankenstein said. "It's important that they understand this. You see, the winds move in different directions, different *streams*, depending on the altitude." He nodded to Delrael and Bryl. "You will have to control your altitude by releasing some of the ballast in the sandbags strung along the gondola. I suspect that the time of day will also affect your altitude, as the sun heats up the gas in the bag, causing it to expand."

Verne nodded. "As the days pass, some of the gas will leak out of the balloon too. You will have to drop sandbags just to maintain your flying height." The professor stared up at the colorful balloon. His eyes sparkled.

"I created this balloon for a grand adventure, for a journey of exploration that would change the way Sitnalta thinks." Verne's voice sounded wistful. "I dreamed of all we might see and do, all we might learn from such a quest. But I am too old, and the others are too frightened to go far from Sitnalta, where the Rules of Science do not hold true."

Frankenstein had looked at the four travelers with an intense light in his eyes. "No one would volunteer to test this balloon. We would have no control over its direction of flight, nor could we be sure of getting back. By using data from our regional monitoring devices, we calculated the extent of the technological fringe around our city—a lower limit, you understand, because once we place monitors near the fringe, we cannot rely on the readings they give."

The younger professor squinted at the balloon. The wind yanked at it, testing the ropes holding it down.

"We do not dare cross the fringe in that balloon. Imagine what would happen if, flying high in the sky, you passed over a hex-line, and suddenly, the very physical principle that allows the balloon to fly becomes uncertain. The balloon would fall like a stone."

"That has not been proved!" Verne cried defensively. "This balloon has nothing mechanical in it, no invention or technology that can fail—I say it will work over all the world, and we should not isolate ourselves here when we could be embarking on extraordinary voyages!"

"But no one would test the hypothesis," Frankenstein said, relating a story instead of arguing. "Until now."

Delrael had not been able to take his eyes from the towering balloon. He craned his neck upward, looking at the bottom of the basket; he tugged on the sturdy tether ropes.

"We can't all fit in that," Bryl observed.

"No," Frankenstein said. "Only two. Perhaps you can risk three, but then the odds grow worse for you."

"No!" Verne insisted. "It must be a fair test, under ideal conditions, until we know more parameters. Only two may ride, and two will remain behind. Otherwise, it will influence the results of the experiment—we have to know. An overburdened balloon may crash, regardless of how the technological boundary affects it."

"I concede your point," Frankenstein said.

Dirac rubbed his hands together. "You asked for our help, and two of you may take this balloon. The others will be quite safe here."

Verne fished in his pocket, withdrew a ticking timepiece, and handed it to Frankenstein. He pulled out the pair of dice he had been looking for. "If you wish to choose who remains behind, you are welcome to use my dice." Frankenstein produced a small gadget used for automatically shaking the dice.

Vailret shook his head, putting his hand on Bryl's wrist to stop him from taking the dice. "Let's think about this. We have to choose carefully, not by a throw of the dice."

After a moment of silence, Paenar volunteered, "I wish to remain behind. I must ... ask something of the Sitnaltans." He refused to say more.

Delrael stared at the balloon, then looked down at the half-Sorcerer. His gray eyes looked troubled. "Bryl, you have to go. Your Water Stone is the only real weapon we have against the dragon."

But Vailret watched the way his cousin moved, the pain as he kept rubbing his thigh. "Del, how's your leg?"

Delrael turned to him, then looked down at his leg. He rapped the *kennok* wood and it made a hollow, solid sound. "I can't feel it or bend it at all. There's no magic here to keep it alive." His face turned grayish. Vailret suddenly realized that his cousin was genuinely frightened but had kept it all to himself. "I'm afraid it's going to fall off."

"That settles it. You have to get out of these science-ruled hexes— now. I'll stay behind with Paenar. Maybe I can learn something here." They had clasped hands, saying goodbye.

Axes came down, severing the tether ropes. The red-and-white balloon shot into the air as if propelled by an invisible bowstring. Delrael and Bryl leaned out over the basket, waving, but then drew back inside, clutching the ropes as the balloon rose higher.

Vailret watched the balloon rise above the city until it became only a blur in his vision. He felt alone in Sitnalta, surrounded by strangers who had an alien perspective on life itself.

But then he saw how sluggish the great colorful balloon was, how it drifted at the mercy of the wind currents. If a fire-breathing dragon saw them approaching, Bryl and Delrael would be helpless. And Professor Verne had warned them that the invisible gas within the balloon was extremely flammable.

CHAPTER 11
PAENAR'S EYES

Everything on Hexworld operates by the Rules of Probability, the roll of the dice. The most unlikely events may conceivably happen, or the most obvious and ordinary things may not happen at all. With sufficient data, we can predict a likely outcome, but we cannot know.
—Professor Verne, *Collected Lectures*

Purple twilight welled up, accompanied by a salt-smelling mist from the nearby sea. The mist infiltrated the streets of Sitnalta, creeping around walls and into the clusters of buildings. Vailret stared out the window of his quarters on the second floor of a building. After an evening meal, the Sitnaltans had left him and Paenar alone in their room. Now that the strangers had lost some of their novelty, the city dwellers had other things to attend to.

Below, Vailret could see characters climbing on ladders to light gas streetlights on every corner, racing against the dusk. Weblike patterns of already-glowing lanterns sparkled on the winding streets. Other than the subdued conversation of the lamplighters, he heard none of the industrious din of the daytime. Sitnalta had stopped for the night.

Vailret smelled the sea mist, thinking of Bryl and Delrael soaring away in Professor Verne's balloon.

Paenar lay brooding on a resilient cot against one wall. The blind man listened, sniffed the air, and paid intense attention to everything. It made Vailret uneasy.

But any character who had gazed upon the Outsiders and survived.... well, that gave him a right to be a little odd.

"Vailret," Paenar asked without turning his head. "You seem comfortable with others. Have you always … been with people?"

The young man stepped back from the window, closing the shutters against the oncoming night. He considered the question for a moment, wondering what Paenar was driving at. "Well, I grew up in the Stronghold and I played in the village just at the bottom of the hill. Plenty of other characters around."

Paenar lay motionless on the bed, saying nothing. Vailret became uncomfortable enough with the silence that he spoke again. "Delrael can strike up a conversation with just about anybody, though. He's got a good charisma score—but I don't think any of that goes very deep. He doesn't like to have to depend on people."

"What about Bryl?" Paenar asked. "You worked well together against the Spectres."

Vailret shrugged. "Bryl doesn't open himself up to anybody. I guess he's a friend, though he is rather strange. But he's sharp and willing to help out when you force him. Especially now. I think this quest has been good for him, to make him feel useful again."

Paenar sounded desolate. "I wish I had known people like you. Before." The blind man sat up, facing Vailret.

"I became a Scavenger because I wanted to be away from people. I wanted to be alone. My father was cruel and forced a family's worth of work out of me. My mother allowed her children to be beaten as well as herself. Both of my parents were killed when our dwelling burned down —Father was too drunk on spring cider to wake up, and Mother ran back to save him. The other villagers came out to watch my home burn, but no one tried to save it.

"Later, the woman I wished to marry chose a richer man instead—he was an excellent gamer and had won most of his wealth through dicing. She did not love him, but she expected me to understand that simple love could not keep her fed. The others in the village taunted me because of it."

Vailret fidgeted, not sure he wanted to hear the blind man's confession, afraid it might forge a bond between them.

"So I became a hunter and a wanderer. Early on, I encountered a band of the Black Falcon Troops. They were perfect examples of how bad human nature can be, aiming to kill every non-human race on Hexworld, even the friendly ones. I was ashamed of my own people—even I did not have such wholesale hatred. I just wanted to be left alone.

"Later, I found I could be useful by uncovering artifacts from the old Sorcerers. I did not need the coins the artifacts brought me...but I did need an excuse for my life, a purpose. I wandered along the Spectre Mountains, up to Sardun's Ice Palace and down to Sitnalta. Then I stumbled upon the deserted Slac fortress and the Spectres. Now my eyes have been taken from me, and our world is doomed, and I am still alone.

"But just watching you, your attitude and your ambition to do something—that stirs things in my heart. It feels strange."

Vailret fidgeted, embarrassed and awkward that a stranger had opened up to him so much. "So why did you volunteer to stay here in Sitnalta? When we were deciding who would ride in the balloon, you said you needed to ask for something. But you've made it quite clear you don't like these people."

Paenar stood up from his bed and unerringly strode over to the window. He opened the shutters and breathed the damp air. Vailret could see that mist had swirled down the streets, making the gas lights look like glowing pools of butter.

"I will challenge them to make me new eyes."

Bryl clutched the edges of the balloon basket so tightly that the wicker bit into his fingers. He didn't like being so high in the air, especially not when the craft's own inventors refused to ride in it.

The balloon ropes creaked with the weight of the passengers and the shifting temperatures of the air. If he was going to gamble, Bryl preferred to do it with dice, not his life. The half-Sorcerer kept his fingers crossed, hoping the contraption would hold itself together. He thought he could hear the gas leaking out even now. He knew they were going to fall.

Since the wind pushed them along at its own speed, the air around them was calm. Though they could detect no motion, the three clustered hexagons of Sitnalta's city terrain soon dropped away. The buildings grew smaller, the people looked like black specks, as the balloon pulled away in smooth silence, moving with a deceptive speed that made Bryl dizzy. He could still hear the clanking sounds of Sitnalta in the still air, snatches of conversation carried up in a pocket of wind, the noise of the manufactories.

Delrael moved from one side of the basket to the other, peering at the world below. The balloon swayed, making Bryl ill, until he begged Delrael to stand still.

Below them, the jagged edge of land met the sea, giving way to an interlocked network of blue hexagons of water. In the other direction, the island of Rokanun showed plainly against the blue of the sea, three hexes distant.

Bryl had no way of telling whether they continued to rise or not. The sea below seemed so far away that he could no longer tell the difference. Through the holes in the wicker of the basket, he could see the long drop beneath his feet. He tried shutting his eyes, but that didn't help at all, just left his imagination open to picture worse things. By watching the line of Rokanun, he noticed they had begun to drift in the wrong direction.

"Trial and error, I guess," Delrael said. "We know we were heading in the right direction a while ago. Maybe if we go up a little higher, we'll reach an airstream to take us toward the island. Or when the day starts to cool, we should drop down again. That's what Professor Verne said."

Delrael untied the end of one of the sandbags and let the sand run out. Bryl leaned over to watch the tan grains pouring down, vanishing in the distance before he could see them hit the water. He thought he could feel the balloon jerk upward again.

"Not so much! Be careful."

Delrael tied the sandbag again.

The afternoon swept on, the sun fell toward the western edge of the map. The towering dead volcano on Rokanun, Mount Antas, jutted up like a festering elbow on the far side of the island. Gulls flew far below them in the still air. Bryl kept an eye out for soaring, fire-breathing, fang-filled, scale-covered—

"Look!" Delrael flexed his *kennok* limb, climbing on the edge of the basket. "I can move it again!" He seemed so relieved, he wanted to dance. But the gondola was crowded with a cumbersome metal tank in the corner. The tank contained enough of the mysterious buoyant gas for their return journey.

The half-Sorcerer widened his eyes. "If the magic in your leg works again, then we must have passed the technological fringe....and the balloon isn't going to fall apart on us!" Bryl wiped his forehead and sat down in relief.

Hours later, Rokanun loomed below and in front of them. The balloon puttered aimlessly in the eddies around the great island. They could not control its course and hung suspended over the first hexes of grass terrain on the shore of Rokanun. With dusk coming on, they began their descent.

Delrael bent to the task of letting the lighter-than-air gas escape from the balloon. He scrambled up the rope mesh around the balloon's body, using his *kennok* leg with ease. He opened sealed flaps on opposite sides of the fabric, just as Verne had taught him, allowing the gas to escape and keeping them from going into a spin.

The red-and-white balloon sagged inward, settling toward the ground. Bryl sat in the basket, yelling against the hissing sound and trying to be useful by directing Delrael to adjust the rate of their fall by opening and closing other flaps. Stray winds drove them closer to the shore as they came down.

The basket struck the brown beach grass, knocking Bryl to his knees. The balloon was still buoyant and bounced upward again in a gust of wind. Everything seemed to be moving so slowly. Bryl grabbed the side of the basket and held on until his fingers cramped. Delrael rode on the fabric of the balloon itself, sliding to the ground as the red-striped bag settled like a giant floating blanket. Bryl crawled out from under the cloth, gasping for breath. He stood up and brushed himself off.

The ocean crashed against tall rocks near the shore of a hex of grassland. The winds were gusty, but the air felt warm. All around them, the island of Rokanun was eerie and empty.

"Help me get the balloon over by that big rock where we can hide it. Sort of. We should be able to move it while there's still some gas in it." Delrael grabbed a fold of the waterproofed fabric and tugged with both hands, flashing red with the effort. "And then we're going to get a good night's sleep while we still can. Tomorrow, we'll go rescue Tareah."

Early the following day, Mayer led Vailret and Paenar back to the central Sitnaltan square. The fountain sent its feathery jet of water into the air. The water clock filled slowly and regularly, marking the exact hour of the morning.

Mayer had arrived at their doorway at sunrise, just as the city began to stir. Vailret had been sound asleep, comfortable in a real bed for the first time in weeks. Paenar had been sitting and thinking on his cot. He opened the door immediately after Mayer's knock.

"My father has asked that I show you more of our city." Mayer did not seem pleased with the chore. "Though I have my own calculations to continue."

"Are you sure we wish to see more?" Paenar asked.

Mayer raised her eyebrows at him. "Yes, I am sure."

The clanking, industrious sounds of Sitnalta filled the air as the three walked across the hex-cobbled streets. Paenar held on to Vailret's elbow.

"Let me start by showing you something important." Mayer pointed to a low building with a massive, ornate doorway that had artificial columns standing on either side. It looked like an ancient Sorcerer villa. "Inside is the one thing that fills all Sitnaltans with pride."

"What is it? A listing of your father's seventy inventions?" Vailret remarked.

Mayer glared at him.

They entered the small building with lush draperies and ornate furnishings. Propped on a pedestal against the far wall stood a leather-bound book with yellowed pages. Two curved brass pipes protruded from the wall, jetting blue gas flames that cast a glow on the volume.

"This is the original book, written by the great inventor Maxwell, in which he derived the first set of the Great Rules, the equations dealing with electromagnetism."

She looked at Vailret, expectant, but he did not know what she meant. Mayer scowled. "It is also Maxwell's treatise and charter for Sitnalta, with his hypothesis that we cast off magic and superstition because these have brought only pain and destruction to Hexworld. The Outsider Scott changed the Rules in this area of the world, allowing human characters access to technological discoveries. Have you never found it unfair that you could not use magic, just because you weren't born a Sorcerer? Magic is for the few—technology is for everyone."

"Technology works only if you live in Sitnalta," Paenar said.

Vailret pursed his lips, embarrassed, and he did not want to answer. He hated to admit Mayer had a point. "Yes, I have thought that was unfair. I'm not a magic user, but I've studied more than most Sorcerers have."

Mayer smiled at him. Vailret couldn't tell if she was being condescending or not.

"When we adopted Maxwell's hypothesis, we agreed to focus our efforts on the furtherance of science, the development of technology, and the betterment of the human race. We have chosen to isolate ourselves, to avoid involvement in any wars. Let me tell you a secret—" She lowered her voice. "We are working to develop a way that we can activate our own Transition! Mechanically! Without magic."

Her eyes glittered. Vailret thought it was a grand dream for human characters. But none of that would take place if Scartaris destroyed Hexworld.

She reached her thin fingers toward the enshrined volume but did not touch it. "Every person in our city has an annotated copy of Maxwell's great book. It has been printed time and again, but this is the original manuscript, in the handwriting of Maxwell himself." Mayer's voice was filled with reverence.

Vailret smiled at her, chiding, "So you've given up superstition, eh? Your attitude toward that old book sure reminds me of religious awe."

Mayer turned red. "You are confusing reverence and deep respect for a silly superstition."

"Is there a difference between unquestioning reverence and silly superstition?" Paenar asked.

"Yes, most certainly!" Mayer snapped. "Come with me."

She hustled them back out into the sunshine. Angry, she continued to talk out of the corner of her mouth.

"We spend our time thinking. Ideas are our greatest product. One of Sitnalta's scholars has suggested a logical reason for the existence of the hexagon-lines on Hexworld—that they are manifestations of an orderly, crystalline structure in the crust of the world, like the equal angles on a gemstone. Just think of it! The intuition and imagination that went into such a hypothesis, and of course it makes sense."

Paenar remained silent, but Vailret nodded to himself. "I never thought about it."

"Well, we did."

She led them into the main room of another building. Dozens of people stood along tables that stretched from one wall to the other. Shoulder to shoulder, the characters picked up dice and rolled them into individual rectangular wooden bins. After each throw, the Sitnaltan made a meticulous notation of the results on a pad beside his or her station and picked up the dice again for another throw. The rumble and clatter of dice hitting dozens of wooden boxes struck Vailret's ears like thunder.

"We are gathering data," Mayer said, raising her voice. "One day, we will learn the true mysteries of the Rules of Probability. Ah, then the world will be in our grasp!"

Mayer put her hands on her waist, kneading her hipbones with her long fingers. "And would you mind telling me why you must see Professor Verne and Professor Frankenstein? They are very busy, you know."

Paenar stood expressionless and immobile. "I prefer to tell them myself."

Mayer appeared frustrated from their reactions and attitudes throughout her tour. "You must show proper respect for them! We have strong evidence to suspect that the two professors are actually being

Played—directly by the Outsider Scott. They are important. Important to us and important to the Game. The professors are not here to answer your every whim—"

"This *is* important, Mayer," Vailret decided to intervene. She acted frightened when she spoke of Verne and Frankenstein. "I promise." He tried to smile at her. She didn't seem to know how to react.

She turned away and walked off, leaving them to follow.

At one of the doorways, she stopped and lowered her voice. "Since you don't want to go where I wish to take you, I must not be an adequate guide to our city." Mayer looked smug. "I have more important work waiting for me. If you have any trouble finding your way back to your quarters, use one of the speaking tubes and call for help."

She hurried off and turned a corner before Vailret could think of anything to say.

"Typical," Paenar said.

Vailret frowned, puzzled. "I just think she's not used to anyone who isn't amazed by their inventions. I am impressed at the opportunity their technology offers, especially to someone who can't use magic—like me. But she doesn't know how to defend herself against any questions we raise. She's afraid of us."

"Let us hope we can get something better from the professors."

Vailret and Paenar stood baffled at the mad confusion in the workshop of Frankenstein and Verne. Incomplete machines lay in piles of gears and sheet metal, half-assembled or half-dismantled, surrounded by the smell of grease. Rambling equations had been written all along the walls, extending beyond the blackboard and onto the bricks themselves.

Professor Frankenstein crouched low over a table under the bright light of a gas lantern, dissecting something on a mounting board. At his side lay an immense open book in which he made meticulous notes. From where he stood, Vailret could see intricate and detailed sketches of parts of the body and the brown stains of dried blood on the paper.

Professor Verne sat on a lab stool away from the worktable, puffing on a pipe and gazing off into space. Coils of gray tobacco smoke floated around his beard, giving the inventor a surreal appearance. He twiddled his thumbs and blinked at the two men as they entered. He stood in surprise. "Welcome, travelers! Forgive me—I was deep in thought."

Frankenstein glanced up from his dissection, stared a moment, and turned back to his work.

Verne's eyes sparkled. "Ah, do you bring news of the balloon? So soon?"

Vailret fidgeted. "We came to see you at work."

Verne spread his hands. "Well, as you can see, Victor and I work well together. We were born with complementary skills. We make machines to mimic living things—he deciphers how the living things work, and I invent gadgets to function on the same principles."

He scratched at his beard then set down his pipe on a slanted work surface. It slid down, and Verne tried to catch it but only ended up with a handful of warm tobacco ash. He stared at the pipe, perplexed, then took great care to balance it properly.

"Victor, remind me to invent a pipe stand."

Frankenstein did not look up from his work. "We already have. It goes before the Council of Patent Givers at the next meeting."

Verne looked pleased. "Do we have any in production yet?"

Frankenstein shook his head. "Low-priority item."

"Too bad." He sighed. "Well, as you see, we have a great many inventions in the mill right now. Some are from Victor and myself brainstorming. Occasionally, though, we cannot take full credit." He looked sheepish.

"I get ideas from dreams too—someone, perhaps even the Outsider Scott himself, comes to me as I sleep and puts suggestions in my head. I remember him clearly when I wake—he looks very young, brown hair, and *freckles*, by Maxwell! Whoever heard of an Outsider having freckles!"

Verne shook his head. "Well, he does have good, workable ideas. In fact, the Outsider Scott suggested how we might make the great balloon your friends are riding and how to obtain the lighter-than-air gas to lift it. We take a large battery, you see, and discharge electricity into seawater. The electrical charge breaks down the water into its most primal forms, two kinds of gas, which—"

He blinked his eyes, then chuckled. "My, my, I do go on, don't I?"

Paenar interrupted, as if he could wait no longer. "I wish to give you a challenge, to test your talent."

"Our record of past inventions speaks for itself," Frankenstein said. "We are not interested in tests."

Verne raised an eyebrow. "One moment, Victor." He turned to face Paenar. "What is it you wish?"

Paenar stood glaring at them with his cavernous eye sockets. "I need you to make me a new pair of eyes."

Frankenstein looked up from his dissection; Verne removed the pipe from his mouth again.

Paenar continued. "When I gazed upon the Spectres, the reality of their existence seared away my eyes. I can do nothing to help save Hexworld if I must be led around by the hand like a child. For the sake of our world's future, you must help me."

"It cannot be done," Frankenstein answered. "The eye is a most complex organ, directly connected to the brain. Creating a mechanical pair of eyes is not possible."

"I thought you would say so," Paenar said bitterly. "But the truth is, I have already had a pair of artificial eyes. The Spectres made them for me." Vailret handed him the leather pouch and he strode forward to the table, careful not to stumble on the clutter on the floor. With a sound like rolling dice, Paenar emptied a handful of glittering lenses onto the wooden surface.

"Made from these. They were arranged in a staff and activated by magic. I was able to see perfectly. Can your technology do this for me, or is simple magic superior?"

Verne pursed his lips, but Frankenstein shook his head. "We lack the time to finish the dozens of inventions we have already designed. We have many more we'd like to work on, ideas to explore. These mechanical eyes would benefit no one but yourself for now. Sitnalta has little demand for them. We must set priorities."

The blind man stood stiffly. Vailret said what he knew was on Paenar's mind. "We have our bargaining chip—and it's rightly yours. Use it."

The blind man relaxed and spoke to a point in space somewhere between Verne and Frankenstein. "When the Spectres came to Hexworld from the Outside, they traveled in a gigantic ship constructed from their own imaginations. Vailret has also seen the great ship and can vouch for the truth of my statements.

"Their ship is still there. And I know where it is." He paused to let them think of the implications. Both professors showed expressions of captivated interest.

"The ship does not still function as it once did—but imagine what you could learn just from the structure of such a vessel? You could determine how to build your own model and perhaps rescue the people of Sitnalta. When Hexworld is finally erased, you can gather all the people together in your ship and whisk them off into *reality*.

"Surely that is worth the price of one man's eyes?"

Frankenstein and Verne stared at each other for a long moment with a glitter of fascination in their eyes. Without speaking, Professor Verne relit his pipe and took a long puff, lost in thought. Frankenstein flipped the pages of his huge volume of notes, scanning through the diagrams and observations, looking for any work concerning eyes. Both inventors wore feverish smiles.

Vailret did not have to ask their answer.

At dawn, Delrael and Bryl left their sheltered spot in the rocks near the shore and stepped back out into the raw wind. They heard only the background noises of rushing waves and whispering beach grass. Delrael could feel a tension in the air, a subdued fear that kept everything quiet. The sounds of a few gulls only added to his sense of eerie loneliness, the solitude—he knew that he and Bryl were probably the only two characters on the entire island, except for Sardun's daughter.

They set off across the first hexagon of grassy terrain. According to their map, the island's northern shore was bounded by a row of grassland hexes and then forest, except for the cluster of mountain terrain surrounding the towering volcano on the eastern end of the island.

Pushing themselves, they were able to traverse three full hexagons of grassland by nightfall, when the Rules forced them to stop at the black hex-line. On the other side, they saw forbidding mountain terrain, jagged and inhospitable. The next day, they would climb the side of the volcano, looking for some way inside to the grotto of Tryos the dragon.

The grass was soft and the night warm, but Delrael had trouble sleeping. He could see the looming dark blot of the dead volcano against the skyline, obliterating the scattered stars. He watched the night and the tattered aurora, wondering if the stars were really out there, or if it was just a screen to keep all the characters from seeing the Outside.

Bryl had kept himself uneasily silent for most of the day. Now he heard the old half-Sorcerer tossing on the ground and guessed that Bryl slept as little as he did. All night long, Delrael felt the eyes of the dragon hanging over him, waiting for them to draw closer.

The next morning, they picked their way among the rock jungle of the volcano's slope. Monolithic blocks of sharp lava lay scattered like enormous betting chips along the zigzagging path. The rock was gray and lifeless, free even of lichen stains.

At last, Delrael looked up into the bright daylight and saw the sheared-off top of the cone drooping at its lip. He stopped and wiped sweat off his forehead. Despite the protection it gave, his leather armor made him feel hot and stiff. He waited for Bryl to catch his breath.

"We may have to climb all the way to the top to get inside. Tryos probably keeps all his treasure in a lower grotto, and we should find Tareah there." He sighed and shifted his long hunting bow on his shoulder. "But, then, I would not be surprised if we found a secret passage leading inside to the treasure chamber. The Outsiders seem to enjoy that sort of thing."

"Let's hope Sardun's daughter is waiting for us, and the dragon isn't!" Bryl waited until Delrael set off again and then followed close behind. He sweated from the exertion, but he did not complain.

Just past noon, they rounded a corner and came upon a narrow cave broken into the wall of the volcano's cone. Two gray-brown boulders bordered the opening, and Delrael stopped. He felt the cool breeze and smelled the brimstone stench drifting out into the sunshine.

"What did I tell you?" Delrael said, smiling to himself.

He noticed how the rocks around the entrance had been partially melted, turned glasslike from blasts of heat. "I think we should try it. I don't like being exposed out here on the mountainside."

Inside the cave, they stumbled over two ancient and burned skeletons lying just out of the light. Melted items of stolen gold were clutched in their blackened hands.

Bryl gulped, but Delrael was unimpressed. "Cute," he said. "Such a subtle reminder."

The cave was deep and winding, burrowing all the way into the interior of the volcano. Their footsteps echoed as they worked their way deeper into the catacombs of the dragon.

When he had the afternoon to himself, Vailret went to Mayer's tower workroom. Verne and Frankenstein had summoned Paenar to their laboratory for some tests of his eyes. Professor Verne had had an inspiration during the night, another sending from the Outsiders, though this time, the professor insisted he remembered a woman's presence instead of the familiar freckled boy.

The Rulewoman Melanie? Vailret wondered. Without giving further regard to Vailret, the two professors had attached probes to Paenar's arms, his temples, his eye sockets. Frankenstein checked his notes, impatient, as if nothing happened fast enough for him. After a few moments, Vailret slipped out the door.

He strolled by himself through the crowded and impressive streets of Sitnalta, trying to understand how some of the wonders had been accomplished. He sat on one of the stone benches near the fountain and listened to the falling water, staring at the ornate water clock and trying to figure out how to read its gauge.

Finally, Vailret decided to go see Mayer, in part because he enjoyed discussing things with her when she could keep from being too defensive. She would explain things to him, but she did not have the patience to make sure he understood what she said. Vailret had grown to like Paenar more over the past day, but the blind man was still too intense at times.

Since he could see Mayer's tower on the edge of the city, he had no difficulty making his way through the streets. The tower was blurry in the distance, and he did not have the skill with directions that Delrael had, but he still felt confident as he made his way past the manufactories and tall buildings, pumping stations and generator shacks to the outer wall of Sitnalta.

He stood at the base of the tower. He wondered if he should knock or shout up to the window. He stared at the brass end of the speaking tube dangling beside the door; in the end, he decided just to trudge up the stairs and find her.

Mayer stood in the wide, drafty room, staring at her chalkboard. Equations went on in endless lines. He watched her wrestle with something in her mind. Chalk dust covered her hands; a white smear on her cheek and streaks in her short dark hair showed when she had run fingers through her hair in frustration.

A cool breeze gusted through the open tower windows, scattering some papers on the floor. Mayer turned, muttering to herself, and saw Vailret. She jumped in surprise.

"I didn't mean to startle you like that," Vailret said.

She scowled and bent to pick up her scattered papers, chasing one around the floor and keeping her face turned away from him.

"I didn't want to break your train of thought," Vailret continued. "I just got here. You looked so intent on what you were doing."

After a pause, Mayer sighed and looked at him again. "I'm frustrated because I can't solve this. You wouldn't understand."

"I'm not stupid, you know. I've spent years studying the history of the Hexworld campaigns."

She frowned. "History doesn't matter. You don't make progress with your head turned in the wrong direction."

"You can't know where you're going if you don't know where you *are*. And you can't know where you are if you have no idea where you've been." He held up his hand in a truce. "Why don't you just try to explain what you're doing?"

"You'll just criticize it."

"No. I'd really be interested."

Her expression softened, but Vailret doubted she believed him. "If this works, it will be a calculating machine. It will take some of the tedium out of long but simple mathematical problems," she said, and gave many examples, the relevance of which were lost on Vailret. But he kept nodding and listening.

Mayer regarded him for a moment then turned back to her equations. "I said you wouldn't understand."

Vailret stared out the tower window, looking at the path they had traveled from the mountains. "Look, I admit I don't understand all you just explained. But you have to remember that, out there, beyond your technological fringe, none of this stuff works anyway! It would be wasted effort for us to learn it."

The intensity in her eyes surprised him. "But it would do you good! If you insisted on using technology, then perhaps the Rules would change around your Stronghold as well! The more we Sitnaltans develop science, the farther out the fringe extends. If you want to be proud of your humanity, cast off this dependence on elite Sorcerer magic. Make your own magic, with science!"

Vailret tried to look open and receptive. "We're too busy trying to survive. We're now safe from wandering monsters. We have developed hexes of fertile cropland—"

"Well, if you didn't spend so much time on those meaningless quests to get treasure or exploring catacombs, you might have time to devote to it."

Vailret sighed and shook his head. "We haven't done that since the Scouring, and that's been more than a century. The Game isn't like that anymore—and that's part of the problem. The Outsiders got bored with all the run-of-the-mill quests, and then they got bored with our daily life. We can't win."

A racket of loud bells clanged from the tops of tall buildings. Others shouted the alarm. Mayer joined him at the tower window, craning her neck to see. "Here it comes," she said. "You'll find this interesting."

A large black shape winged out of the north, skipping over the updrafts. The thing soared toward the city, growing larger and larger.

Vailret recognized the shape from some of the terrified descriptions scrawled by survivors of the old Sorcerer battles. "A dragon?"

"Yes—Tryos, returning to his island. He will probably attempt to attack Sitnalta first." She shook her head. "He never learns."

The dragon beat his huge batlike wings and drove forward, circling low over the city. Mayer grabbed her optick-tube and pulled on Vailret's sleeve. "Come with me and watch."

They rushed up a winding staircase to a platform on the roof of the tower. The sounds of the streets and the manufactories seemed far away. He could see all three hexagons of the city and took a moment to orient himself with the landmarks he remembered.

Tryos floated over Sitnalta, taking no action. The dragon's wings creaked in the wind, making a sound like leather stretched taut over a frame.

Mayer tugged on his arm, pointing Vailret's attention elsewhere. "See that tall ziggurat, the pyramid over in the southeastern hex? Watch."

Atop the stepped pyramid, Vailret could barely make out the blurry shape of a small device. He squinted, but it did no good. Mayer handed him the optick-tube.

He stared at it, turning it one way and then the other. "What do I do with this?"

"Don't be ridiculous. You look through it."

Vailret put one end to his eye but could discern nothing. Mayer snatched it from his hands and turned it around. When he stared through the lens, his perspective shifted in a dizzying jump. The top of the ziggurat leaped out at him, distorted but so close that he almost dropped the tube. He removed the end from his eye and blinked at it. Lifting it, he stared through the tube again, finding the pyramid's top platform.

In a shelter sat a Sitnaltan woman beside a strange device. It looked like a dish mounted on an axis and pointed to the sky. A box with levers and buttons rested against the pedestal, coming into view as the woman wrestled with the dish to turn it toward the dragon. Then she sat back in a firmly anchored chair. She strapped herself in. The woman flipped one of the switches.

"What is that woman doing?"

"Just watch." Mayer gave him a confident smile.

The Sitnaltan woman fastened something over her ears before she lifted a microphone to her mouth. A booming voice echoed into the air and through the winding hex-cobbled streets. "Tryos of Antas! Depart at once. You know the consequences."

Provoked, Tryos wheeled in the air and came flying toward the ziggurat, scooping the air behind his great wings. He thrust his spined head outward, drooling flames down his chin.

Through the optick-tube, Vailret watched the Sitnaltan woman adjust the face of the dish once more. Vailret felt anxious, knowing she could not escape the dragon's attack.

Tryos swallowed a cavernous mouthful of air, feeding the furnace inside of him. The Sitnaltan woman spoke into the microphone again, appearing calm. "You have been warned, dragon."

Tryos swooped down for his attack. The woman reached forward to flip a second switch on the control panel.

A destructive explosion of sound erupted outward, a roar of noise that blasted the dragon backward into the air as if he had been hit with a catapulted boulder.

The Sitnaltan woman slammed back against her chair. The pulses of sound continued to hammer forth. Tryos spun in the air in reverse somersaults. He tried to scramble away.

The device stopped itself automatically. Beaten, Tryos limped across the skies, fleeing Sitnalta.

"That is our Dragon Siren, small enough for a single character to lift, and powerful enough to defend our entire city." She smiled, smug.

"Impressive."

"The dragon knows he is defeated. He will go back to his island and sulk. We will not be bothered for a time. But he always forgets and comes back."

Through the optick-tube, Vailret watched the huge monster flap out across the blue glinting hexagon of ocean. Vailret swallowed to himself and handed the optick tube back to Mayer.

"I hope Del and Bryl are ready for him. He's not in a very good mood."

CHAPTER 12
THE WRATH OF TRYOS

Creative adventurers use the situation, use the setting, and use their
imaginations to solve any crisis. While pitched battles and direct combat
techniques are always acceptable, they are sometimes less satisfying than
a truly innovative approach to a problem.
—Preface, *The Book of Rules*

Delrael moved down the winding lava tube, feeling his way around broken corners. All his senses were alert, waiting for something horrible to spring out at them. The half-Sorcerer had used his own meager magic to make a floating torch, though he hated to waste a precious spell when they were about to enter the dragon's lair. But magic did not work against dragons anyway. Shadows puddled against the rough walls.

In the old days, such catacombs would have been filled with wandering monsters, treasure, secret doors, and passages. Now it was different, though. Delrael just wanted to reach the grotto, find Tareah, and get back to the balloon as fast as possible.

Once away from the entrance, the air became chilly, locked away from any warmth or light. The heels of Delrael's boots slipped on a patch of ice still preserved in one of the shadowy rock pockets. Delrael reached out and grabbed a knifelike corner of broken lava, cutting his palm.

For hours, they wound their way downward toward the heart of the volcano. Delrael did not want to think about how hard it would be to climb back up. Bryl muttered about how his knees ached, how hungry he was getting. They paused for a short rest, then trudged downward again.

The air smelled heavier, damper. Occasionally, Delrael saw a reddish-orange glow bound past the jagged twists and turns of the tunnel. Bryl doused his fire spell.

The reddish light grew brighter ahead of them. Delrael picked up his pace, impatient to get to their destination, to whatever adventure awaited them. He could smell his sweat in the armor, the claustrophobic thickness of the air.

They rounded a corner, and the passageway opened up. Light washed over them, carrying with it a gush of harsh sulfur smell. Despite his own admonition to Bryl, Delrael broke the silence by letting out a gasp of amazement. He stepped into the grotto, wide-eyed.

Half the room in front of him brimmed with mountains of treasure: gold, gems, pearls, coins, jewelry. In a smaller chamber off to the side stood several large statues—two leaning against each other and another on the floor, chipped and in disarray. A beautiful tapestry had been tossed in the corner, snagged on a sharp rock. Delrael saw painted hexagonal tiles, colored pottery, a bust of some forgotten old Sorcerer general.

"Vailret would love it here," Bryl said.

On the far edge of the treasure vault, sunlight shone down from the opening of the cone. They had descended to the level of the hot and smoking lava pool at the bottom of the volcano. The sound of burning and escaping gases filled the air, making Delrael's ears ring. The huge treasure grotto had been hollowed out just above and beside the simmering lava—Tryos had made a home protected from any human invaders who wanted to steal his treasure. "The dragon doesn't seem to be home," Delrael said.

He moved forward, dazed, like a Sitnaltan automaton. Taking treasure wherever it was found had formed part of his way of life, part of the society of Hexworld, for as long as the Outsiders had been Playing. But he had more important things to do now. If times changed, allowing more leisure to quest for treasure, he might come back. Someday.

Delrael hiked his bow up on his shoulders and stepped forward, ignoring Bryl. "Hello!" he shouted. "Tareah?" His voice echoed in the grotto.

Bryl wandered off again toward the Sorcerer artifacts in the separate chamber.

Delrael heard a clinking sound, coins rattling against each other. He froze and eased his bow from his shoulder, holding on to the string and ready to reach for an arrow.

Then he saw the young girl, Tareah, sitting up groggily from an exhausted sleep, lying on the piles of gems and trinkets, the softest bed she could find. The girl half-slid down the mound of treasure in a clatter and jangle of coins. She rubbed her eyes and stared at the man in silent disbelief, saying nothing.

Delrael thought she was the most beautiful little girl he had ever seen —she looked to be about ten years old, but she was Sardun's daughter and the only full-blooded Sorcerer female left on all of Hexworld. Her brown eyes were dark and wide, captivating, though laced with blood-shot lines and puffy from too many tears.

Fawn-colored hair hung to her shoulders, tangled but once curled. She wore a pale blue gown of some shining material, now dirty and tattered. Apparently bored, Tareah had bedecked her body with jewelry, rings, necklaces, bracelets, earrings, a circlet around her head. She dropped some of the heavier pieces off when she stood up, still staring at Delrael.

The young girl's voice was husky. "I knew someone would come. I didn't expect it to take so long, though. I was beginning to lose hope."

"Your father sent us here." Delrael didn't know what else to say. "We came to rescue you."

The hissing of the lava drowned out most of the background noise. "Bryl, I've found Tareah!"

"According to my studies," Tareah said, "people have stopped questing for the most part, now that the Transition has taken place and the Scouring is over with. My father must have had trouble finding someone to rescue me." Tareah's eyes brightened. "Tell me your names. Have I read about your adventures before?"

Something in her manner, a confidence and smoothness in the way she moved, did not hint at the awkwardness of a young girl. Then Delrael remembered that this "young girl" was actually older than he was.

For thirty years, Sardun had held his daughter in the body of a child, afraid to let her grow up before the probabilities of Hexworld could spill forth another full-blooded Sorcerer male. They had kept waiting and waiting for the Outsiders' dice to roll in their favor.

"I'm Delrael, and that's Bryl. We're from the Stronghold. Your father didn't seek us out. We went to the Ice Palace to ask *him* for help. He was … in a bad state, but he's better now. We agreed to try to rescue you."

Tareah's eyes became glassy and distant. "He tried to save me. I remember—the dragon blasting his way through the palace walls, clawing through the ice. My father used the Water Stone to fight back, but he was afraid. He didn't want to harm me."

"Well, even the Ice Palace is rebuilt now. And he's waiting for you to come back."

Despite everything they had encountered, Delrael had succeeded in reaching Sardun's daughter. And she was safe. They had nearly finished the quest imposed on them by Sardun. They needed only to get Tareah back to the Ice Palace. And then go fight against Gairoth.

"Bryl! Let's get out of here before Tryos comes back."

The half-Sorcerer knelt beside the toppled, chipped Sorcerer statue in the smaller art chamber. Tears streamed down his face. "I remember some of this."

Tareah turned to Delrael. "That was an original sculpture, created by some Sorcerer lord in the peaceful days *before* the first wars. Centuries and centuries and centuries ago. Somehow it survived everything intact, all the battles, all the Scavengers, the weather, the years—"

Bryl stood up. "And now Tryos tossed it here like a piece of dirt! These chip marks are fresh."

"All these treasures should be in the Ice Palace, where they can be appreciated. Where they belong!" Tareah swallowed further words and nodded formally to Bryl. "You are Bryl, son of Qonnar and Tristane, who were in turn the children of Cocker and Hellic, Karril and Junis. I could go further back, if you like."

Bryl blinked at Tareah. "How do you know all that?"

Delrael eased them both toward the tunnel opening. "The balloon is a day's journey from here. And we have a long climb."

Tareah shrugged. "My father made me study all the Sentinel genealogy. We needed to follow every thread of Sorcerer blood. He even considered you for me, but decided you were too old."

Bryl gasped out a brief chuckle. Delrael took Tareah by the hand.

"Do you know," she said, "that you're the first humans I have ever seen? For thirty years, I have been alone with my father in the Ice Palace. I have studied a great deal, but I don't have much practice in social activity. I'd never been away from the north, until the dragon took me. I didn't try to rescue myself—I had nowhere to go. Besides, I knew you would come. It's too good of a quest for the Outsiders to ignore it." She looked back at the artifacts. "If only we could retrieve these works of art. And some of the treasure too—Tryos should pay for his careless damage."

"Where is Tryos?" Delrael asked. He felt a greater sense of urgency as they remained in the grotto. His luck was strong, but he did not want to abuse it.

Too late, they noticed the jagged shadow covering the sunshine from the volcano's opening. A sound like a blacksmith's bellows thrummed in the air as the shadow descended.

Tryos the dragon had returned to his lair.

Just before absolute terror set in, Bryl realized how foolish he had been. While gawking at the treasure, he had not seen the obvious. For a dragon to have gathered and kept such a hoard, he must be more powerful and more intelligent than any other treasure-seekers, human or otherwise.

The half-Sorcerer turned to run toward the tunnel. The Water Stone seemed worthless now. "Come on, Delrael! We have to hide!"

Delrael grabbed him, though, and held his arm. Bryl struggled, wanting to scream—this was a *dragon*, one of the creatures that had caused so much havoc in the Sorcerer wars, the dragon that had defeated

Sardun—but Delrael held tight, shaking his head. The fighter looked at the open cut on his palm and wiped it against his leather armor. "He'll know we were here. We'll have to talk our way out of this."

Bryl felt cold fear creep under his skin. "What are we going to do?" The dragon's armor-plated body dropped into view, glittering green and black depending on the light. Immense parchment wings, brown and leathery, slowed his descent above the lava. Bryl smelled dry heat and a reptilian mustiness. Tryos heaved himself into the grotto, using claws and the elbows of his wings, until he stood up in the chamber.

Tareah's eyes hardened, and Bryl took a close look at her for the first time. "Keep behind me," she said. "He won't harm you if he thinks he might damage me, his treasure."

Tryos took one step forward, thrusting his wings behind him. The size of the dragon was terrifying: Bryl had to stare several seconds just to absorb the entire monster. He felt a gagging fear, and his eyes watered and stung, making Tryos waver in front of him.

The dragon sat back on his haunches and wrinkled his nose ridge. He curled a huge barbed tail behind him. His reptilian eyes tried to adjust to the dimness in the grotto, now that he blocked out the lava light. When Tryos blinked, eyelids as big as barn doors slammed shut and then opened with an audible click.

Tryos snorted, making flames flicker in and out of his nostrils. Smoke blew back into his face, and he sneezed, exploding a great gout of flame onto the smooth rock floor. Bryl did not move or breathe. Tareah stood beside them, crossing her arms.

Then the dragon spoke with words louder than a volcanic eruption. "Who isss here?" Tryos narrowed his eyes and craned his snakelike neck toward them. His voice was thin and nasal; his words were clipped and imperfect from his armored lips.

Bryl held on to Tareah's shoulders. She flinched. Delrael stood tall like a proud fighter from the ancient wars ... like General Doril, or his own father Drodanis.

"I sssee you! Sssstealing my treasure!"

"No, not at all," Delrael said. Bryl marveled at how rich and controlled the fighter managed to keep his voice. But he could see

Delrael's white knuckles and how his hands trembled with well-contained fear. "We don't want your treasure."

"Then why are you here!" the dragon demanded, eyes blazing. "Why don't you run?"

"We, uh, came to see you, Tryos!" Bryl said, his brain trying to function as fast as his mouth. He and Delrael would have to work together now for their lives.

"Yes, we journeyed many hexes just to see you." Delrael rubbed his leather jerkin and preened himself. Bryl had a terrible fear that they were both tangling themselves deeper and deeper.

"For what purpossse?" Tryos leaned forward to glare at them. Hot and rotten breath swirled the air. "Why sssee me?"

"We needed to ask you something—" Bryl started, but his wits ran dry. He turned to Delrael, pleading. Through the exchange, Tareah held herself quiet, as if afraid that anything she said would be counted against them. She appeared to have perfect confidence in Delrael.

"What? What would you asssk?" The reptilian tail twitched, slamming back down with enough force to crush a human head.

Bryl's shoulders sagged in defeat. His lips remained dormant, despite his hope that they would speak of their own accord.

"Ssspeak up!" Tryos said.

Then Delrael cleared his throat. He slapped his hands together, getting down to business. He took a step forward. The dragon's eyes shifted to the man, and Bryl felt as if a knife had been taken away from his throat.

"We need your help, Tryos."

The dragon blinked in surprise, drawing himself back.

"Would you please help us?"

Bryl wanted to pull his wispy hair out in frustration. But Delrael spoke with great force, pretending to know what he intended all along.

"Tryos, you are our last and only hope. An evil ogre and his dragon have captured our Stronghold. You are much larger, much greater—we know you could defeat this enemy dragon!"

He turned around, spreading his hands to indicate the piled treasure. "You obviously understand the joy of personal possessions. Gold, jewels, things of value. That's what Hexworld is all about, right? Quests and adventure, build up the highest score you can before you die."

Tryos bobbed his head up and down. "Be bessst. Get ahead. Be Number One dragon. Better than all others. Bessst!"

Delrael nodded. "Will you help us regain what is right fully ours? The ogre has a treasure pile of his own—we'll give it to you."

Bryl felt stiff from standing in terror for too long.

Then Tryos snorted, raising one jagged eyebrow ridge. "Ogre? Dragon? Who isss thisss dragon? What isss hisss name?"

"The ogre is Gairoth. He lived by a cesspool in the swamp terrain," Delrael answered. "The dragon is Rognoth—"

"Rognos! *Rognos*!" The dragon went into hysterics, launching himself in the air, blasting angry fire at the walls. "He isss my brother! Foul! Bad! Runt of the hatching!"

Bryl cringed, astonished at what Delrael had unleashed. But at least the fury had been deflected away from them.

Tryos brought himself under control, snorting and grinding his fangs together. He settled back to the ground, but his tail pounded an impatient rhythm on the rippled stone floor. His eyes blazed with green fire.

"Rognos isss a disssgrace! Black sheep! Shame to my hatching! Worm! I hate him—*Rognos*!" Tryos hurled another battering ram of flames at the ceiling.

"Thisss Ssstronghold—bigger than my Rokanun? Rognos have more land than me?"

"Oh, much bigger, I'd say. Hexes and hexes, as far as you can see. And no one to stop him." Delrael sighed. "It's a shame."

Bryl cringed, afraid of what ideas might be tunneling through the dragon's mind.

"Kill Rognos! He isss bad!" Tryos roared, overpowering both of them. "Show me the way to Ssstronghold!"

Bryl tried to be optimistic, tried and failed. If Tryos came back to the Stronghold with fire and thunder, it might scare off Gairoth's ogres— they should never have been fighting together anyway. It went against their nature.

That left Bryl and Delrael to contend with Gairoth—and Gairoth had defeated the half-Sorcerer before. The ogre had no doubt mastered the Air Stone by now.

But Bryl had the Water Stone this time.

Even with the wildest of advantages, even if they somehow defeated the ogre army and got rid of Gairoth and Rognoth—what if Tryos did decide to make the Stronghold his new home? The problems got worse and worse ... without even considering that the Outsiders wanted to stop Playing Hexworld.

Tryos flapped his wings and stomped a clawed foot on the hardened lava floor. "I will kill Rognos! Now! Take me to Ssstronghold."

The dragon crawled forward, slogging his way through the treasure pile, scattering coins and gems. He heaved himself up and curled his tail around to them like a long, scaly ramp. Delrael took Tareah's hand and marched forward, maintaining his confident facade. He led her toward Tryos. She looked skeptical, still not believing that her rescuers had come.

Tryos glared at them with his slitted eyes. "Treasure ssstays here. You sssaid you did not want treasure!"

Delrael covered his expression of shock with a muffled cough. "But we must take—"

"Leave treasure here! Come back later. Now we go kill Rognos!"

Bryl touched the fighter's arm to keep him from arguing. He turned away from Tareah's sad face. "We'll have to come back for her."

Bryl climbed the dragon's wide tail, pulling himself up the sharp ridges as if they were steps. He motioned for Delrael. The man turned to Tareah, picked her up, and gave her a hug. She looked surprised for an instant, then responded. "We'll come back for you," he said into her ear.

"I can't rescue myself," Tareah answered. "There's nowhere to go. I could walk out, but I'd never get off the island."

Then she spoke quietly to him. Bryl heard most of the words, but over the hissing of the lava pool and the rumbling of his own breathing, the dragon would not have heard.

"One thing to remember—Tryos is vicious if he thinks you're trying to trick him. But he's very bad with directions. He goes off on his forays and spends more time trying to find his way back than in treasure-hunting."

Delrael nodded and turned to scramble up the dragon's tail. He used his *kennok* leg without thought. Bryl wondered if they should have told Tareah about the balloon, but he didn't think any one person could handle the balloon alone.

"Luck!" she called.

Bryl tried to wave, but Tryos shoved his way back to the grotto entrance and spread his wings, making the half-Sorcerer cling to whatever handhold he could find.

"There's the Stronghold!" Delrael shouted to make himself heard over the rushing cold wind and the heavy beat of the dragon's wings. He pointed down to where he could make out the fenced-in hexagon of the Stronghold proper and the scattered dwellings in the village. Everything seemed flat from this height, like a giant map. He had to find Steep Hill by following the outline of the stream that skirted the hill and zigzagged along the village, separating the dwellings from the unclaimed forest terrain.

Delrael stared over the curved edge of the dragon's wing to look down at the Stronghold. This was worse even than being in the balloon. "Somehow or other, we got here."

During the night and all the previous day, Delrael and Bryl had taken turns crawling up to Tryos's ears to tell him he had veered off in the wrong direction again. But now they could see the forested hills, the stream, the grassland, the fields, the village. The jagged shadow of Tryos skimmed over the ground at an angle below them.

For two full days without stopping, Tryos had flown north and west, fueled by his anger and hatred toward Rognoth. They flew higher and faster than Professor Verne's balloon had gone, and the landscape flowed under them like a mosaic of hexes. The wind numbed Delrael's ears. "Land isss big!" Tryos said.

"Yes. Too bad it's all Rognoth's!" Delrael called back. Tryos narrowed his reptilian eyes and sped forward.

Bryl and Delrael sat on the dragon's wide back, tucked between two of the great plated ridges along Tryos's spine. As they had passed over the wide, shining Barrier River, Delrael felt proud of himself and what they had done. He pointed it out to Bryl, a gleaming silver channel a full hex wide, two in some places.

Bryl sat, wind-blown, with haunted-looking eyes. He chewed his nails in fear. They would soon be confronting Gairoth. Delrael was concerned too ... but he felt the most alive, the most *real* when he engaged in quests and battles.

They had been gone for nearly a month, but below them, Delrael could see that the scattered crops around the village had not suffered severely. Other than a proliferation of weeds, the fields could take care of themselves for a few weeks in the summer. The crops had been tended after all, despite Gairoth's presence—he thought of the veteran Tarne leading groups of characters out of the forests under the shelter of night, pulling weeds by moonlight. Delrael felt proud of him.

The thatched roofs of the village remained intact, with only a few unrepaired patches where the wind had torn shocks of straw from the frames. Delrael had expected to see all the dwellings burned to the ground by the invading ogres; he wondered what could have kept the ogres so busy that they had had no time to release their destructive tendencies. Did Gairoth rule them with such an iron fist? And, if so, why did they tolerate it instead of simply wandering back to their own homes in the swamps?

Tryos curved his neck and swooped downward. The ogre-infested Stronghold and the deserted village waited for them. Delrael rubbed his father's silver belt for luck. He wished he had been able to retrieve his old Sorcerer sword—it would do nothing against the dragon, but perhaps against Gairoth...

Circling the area, Tryos let out a blood-curdling scream of challenge. Delrael had expected to see the ogre army scattering for cover at the appearance of the enormous dragon, but the Stronghold seemed deserted. Tryos landed within the hexagonal stockade near the center of the training field. Wood shavings and mulched tannery refuse, originally strewn on the ground to cushion the falls of trainees, blew in the air, stirred by the bellows of the dragon's wings.

Delrael leaped to the ground. How could he have imagined an entrance more grand? It was like the golden age of the Sorcerer wars.

With weak knees, Bryl scrambled off the back of Tryos. He felt very old again. The dragon barely paused, however, and turned to them with his spotlight eyes.

"I go find my brother! Rognos! Kill him!" Blasting fire at the overhanging black pine trees on the hill, Tryos launched himself into the air, flapping his immense wings and stirring up a great breeze behind him. He didn't even seem tired. "You get Gairos," he called back.

His horny claws glinted with silver hooks as he pulled his limbs upward and tucked them close to his armored belly. "I'm sure glad he's on our side," Delrael said.

"For the time being," Bryl mumbled.

Delrael took a deep breath and turned. He could feel eyes staring at him from the windows of the outer buildings and the main hall. Everything seemed too quiet, too deserted, like a baited trap.

The Stronghold had suffered from the ogre occupation. The two main storehouses were smashed, and the grain pits under them had been nearly emptied. Siya's garden plots were trampled and torn. Some of the outer dwellings looked disheveled and poorly used. The weapons storehouse seemed intact, probably because ogres had no use for tiny human weapons. Several of the windows in the main hall hung open with shutters knocked off the walls. Delrael could imagine Gairoth and his ogres ransacking everything to seek other treasures like the Air Stone.

The training area where Tryos had landed was packed and pounded but relatively unharmed; maybe the ogres slept there, sprawled out on the mulched ground, snoring under the starlight. A few of the wooden sword posts had been knocked over in splintered stumps. Both of the hanging sacks had been torn down, and their straw stuffing drifted loose on the ground. The front gate of the Stronghold wall lay smashed on the ground, untouched since Gairoth's victorious entrance a month before.

Then, suddenly and silently, things stirred in the confines of the main hall. Two dozen ogres, virtually identical, emerged from their hiding places behind the woodpiles, in the ruined storehouses. They glanced at the sky to see if the great dragon would return.

The door to the main hall crashed open. Gairoth emerged.

The wind stopped, but the great ogre said nothing. His bulky iron crown held the pyramid-shaped Air Stone, gleaming with transparent power. The ogre had grown even larger than Delrael remembered him.

Gairoth took a step forward with an ominous slow confidence, and even the ground seemed to shake. His big bare feet dug into the ground of the training area. The low sunlight of the afternoon shaded him, casting odd shadows on the gnarled muscles of his arms. He carried his club like an uprooted tree, ready to smash an entire forest.

When Gairoth emerged into the direct light, Delrael could see his skin was dry and peeling in places. All the ogres looked dejected and uncomfortable. The cultivated land around the Stronghold was much different from their festering swamp terrain. The air held less moisture, the ground was firm, the insects were not as persistent. Gairoth did not look to be in good spirits.

A cold look of hatred poured over the ogre's face. "Delroth!" He smashed his club on the ground.

Delrael pulled his bow off his shoulder in a flowing motion. It fit nicely into his hands. He nocked an arrow. "Leave the Stronghold now, Gairoth. Enough games—we have important things to do."

"We'll call our dragon back!" Bryl said from a safe distance. He removed the Water Stone from where he had hidden it in his sleeve. The half-Sorcerer wrapped his fist around the sapphire, turning his knuckles white and letting a misty blue glow seep between them. It made him feel strong. He was a different person now than when Gairoth had tormented him before. "If I don't get you first."

Bryl's voice became shrill with anger and hatred. Delrael remembered what the ogre had done to the half-Sorcerer in the swamps, feeding him to the giant jellyfish in the cesspool, forcing him to teach how to use the precious Air Stone.

Gairoth turned to stare at him, then his single eye gleamed with excitement. He fumbled with the Air Stone in his crown and pulled down the diamond shaped like a four-sided die.

"More shiny rocks! Do more tricks, Magic Man!" The ogre stumbled forward, panting in his eagerness to snatch at the sapphire.

"This is the Water Stone, Gairoth! More powerful even than the Air Stone you possess."

The ogre slapped his thigh, leaving a wide red mark on his flaking skin. "Haw! Haw!"

Bryl spoke without his edge of confidence. "I warn you—I am more than half Sorcerer. You are a corrupted bastard child born from a Sorcerer father and a stupid ugly ogre mother!"

Gairoth snarled at him. "You be nice to Maw! She loves Gairoth! Maw be mad if you say nasty things about her!"

Bryl squeezed the Water Stone, making it glow a brilliant, blinding blue. Then he rolled it on the ground. "Come on—give me a three or better!"

The face glowing "3" gleamed on top.

Above them, a massive cloud curdled in the air like black milk. A rip of angry thunder buffeted their ears as a bolt of blue lightning lanced to the ground, blasting in front of Gairoth's feet. The sand turned to slag, and some of the wood shavings burst into flame. Gairoth howled and lurched backward. All the other ogres jumped in simultaneous surprise, though the lightning had not struck near them.

"Give me the Air Stone, Gairoth. Now!" The thunderhead still rumbled over them. "Take your mob of ogres and leave here! Give me the Stone, and I'll let you leave unharmed. But hurry, before I lose my temper!"

Bryl snatched up the sapphire, sliding his fingertips over the facets as if they were covered with oil. Two more bolts of lightning crashed down on each side of the ogre.

With a roar of fury, Gairoth flung the Air Stone on the ground. It bounced once into the air then dropped to the mulched tannery refuse. He also rolled a "3."

"Haw!" Gairoth snatched up the Stone and popped it back into the setting of his iron crown. He raised the spiked club over his head, gripping it with both hands, then he smashed it down on the ground.

As the club struck, the Air Stone gleamed like milky ice. Gairoth split into two identical ogres, each mirroring the other. With another roar, both ogres—one real, one illusion—brought their clubs down, splitting a second time and doubling their numbers. Four Gairoths, then eight, then sixteen.

"Haw! Haw!" all sixteen ogres bellowed, echoing their laughter from sixteen throats. The rest of the ogre army stood motionless, watching.

Delrael fidgeted, gripping his bow. Then he remembered how ineffective arrows had been when Tarne and the other villagers tried to defend the Stronghold against the invading ogres. Bryl scowled, bringing his eyebrows together. "You're not any stronger, Gairoth. Those are just illusions. Except one."

The mirrored ogres echoed their response. "But you needs to find the *right* Gairoth! Haw!"

Bryl had only three spells left.

Delrael pulled his bowstring tight and shot an arrow at one of the Gairoths, and the shaft passed through the illusion to strike against the far wall of the Stronghold stockade. He rapidly fired a second arrow, exposing another false ogre. "I can find the real one, Bryl—all I have to do is hit him. You watch, and then do your stuff!" He bent to fire a third shot.

But the other three dozen ogres let out a battle cry and charged at Delrael, waving their gnarled clubs, spears, and massive swords. Delrael was startled, but he ignored them for a moment more, firing a fourth arrow, striking one more imaginary Gairoth.

Delrael turned to face the oncoming ogres. He tried to back closer to the Stronghold wall, casting quick glances behind him to make sure he did not stumble. One of the broken stumps of the wooden sword posts got in his way, but he sidestepped it. He nocked an arrow and shot it at one of the approaching ogres. The shaft plunged into the monster's chest, but the ogre snapped it off with barely a grimace. The ogre batted away Delrael's second arrow as well. Delrael reached back into his quiver. He had only a handful of arrows left.

Bryl blasted right and left with lightning bolts, searching for the real Gairoth, but then the thundercloud dissolved and the spell was over. The illusion ogres milled about, making it difficult for him to remember which ones had already been exposed.

"Haw! Haw!" Gairoth could take the half-Sorcerer anytime, but he seemed to be enjoying the game.

Bryl cast the Water Stone again. He rolled a "1" and failed.

Delrael shot another two arrows, striking two different enemy ogres with little effect. The monsters pushed forward, swinging their weapons, moving with deliberate slowness. Some struck the ground with their weapons in a childish threatening gesture. They curled their lips into eager snarls, succeeding in making themselves even uglier.

Delrael bumped into the corner of the weapons storehouse. A shiver went down his spine as he remembered his personal training, the role-playing game, where he had fought against the worm-men to steal one of their sacred earth-gems. In that make-believe game, he had died—he didn't want to die again, not here, or anywhere.

The ogres kept coming.

Sixteen Gairoths lifted their spiked clubs, flexing muscles as strong as pulleys. They let out a volley of hideous, echoing laughter. "Haw! Haw!"

Rognoth heaved himself back out of the smashed wall of the village smokehouse. He ran a purplish forked tongue over his fangs, trying to sandpaper away some of the yellow scum. After snapping down five hams and a dozen or so hanging sausages, he didn't know how he could feel more satisfied.

Before fleeing the village with the rest of the characters, Lantee the butcher had packed his best-cured meats and taken them into the forest retreat. But he had been forced to leave some of the hams, sausages, and sides of bacon in the smokehouse. The butcher and his wife had barred and hammered the door shut.

But in the hot and humid air, the delicate smells of meat drifted to Rognoth's sensitive nostrils. He had already devoured every edible thing in the Stronghold's two storage pits. Though he did not particularly care for grains or vegetables, he found them to be tolerable if consumed in massive quantities.

Fed properly for the first time in his life, Rognoth had grown enormously in the month he and his master had inhabited the Stronghold. His body had doubled in size and tripled in girth. When he walked, his belly dragged on the ground. His stubby, arthritic wings spread upward like the straining fingers of a dying man.

The dragon's neck had swelled enough that the rusty iron collar became a constrictive ring around his throat. Rognoth had been unable to breathe; he stumbled around in a daze, seeing black blotches in front of his eyes. Gairoth had finally wrenched the collar free with his two massive hands. The little dragon could now draw in lungsful of air, feeding the sputtering furnace in his chest. He could smell the wonders of the world, especially the wonders hidden in the smokehouse.

Rognoth had not bothered with the bolted door, letting his clumsy momentum carry him through the wooden walls. Part of the roof fell down on top of him, and sausages tumbled from their ropes on the ceiling beams.

Two sausages and one ham beyond being comfortably fed, Rognoth lurched out of the shed, blinking his eyes in the afternoon sun.

"Rognos!" a second dragon bellowed. "Come here, you bad boy!"

Tryos soared overhead, beating his thunderous wings against the updrafts, scouting the surface of the ground. He circled the stone-filled trench surrounding the hexagonal stockade wall, then glided down the slope of Steep Hill to skim over the village, dragging razor claws on thatched roofs.

With a whimper of terror and shock, the obese little dragon scuttled back into the smokehouse.

Tryos saw the movement and swooped down. "A-ha, Rognos! You disssgrace!" With a snap of his long neck, Tryos strafed the roof with a gout of flame. Lantee's smokehouse burst into roaring flames. Rognoth waddled away, urgently dragging himself from the burning wreckage.

"Sssuch a disssappointment! You are no dragon!"

Tryos swung around again with flames gushing from his mouth. Rognoth crashed through the split-rail fence around the butcher's corral for animals to be slaughtered. He galloped on stubby legs, scraping his belly on stones and weeds, and leaped into the shallow stream just as Tryos struck again. Steam poured into the air and hot mud splattered upward. Some of the scales on the little dragon's back shattered from the heat.

Rognoth charged through the underbrush on the far side of the stream, into the hex of dense forest terrain. Above the forest, Tryos flew low, rustling branches as he grazed the treetops. At odd moments, Rognoth caught glimpses of Tryos up through the covering of leaves. The large dragon belched a wave of fire, clearing away the trees and leaving Rognoth naked and unprotected. "You should not have ssstayed with Gairos!" Tryos pulled up higher, for the deathblow.

Rognoth yelped and saw his last chance for escape. He pumped his stubby wings and launched his barrel-like body into the air. The little dragon zoomed across the treetops, fueled by the threat of flaming death. Rognoth shot forward with surprising speed, like a giant reptilian bumblebee.

Tryos used his great wings to push himself forward in pursuit. Barely able to fly at all, Rognoth could not perform elaborate evasive maneuvers. He flew northward in a straight line that, he hoped, would take him farther than Tryos was willing to follow. The gigantic vengeful dragon beat his wings but could not close with his little brother.

After more than an hour of dodging in the air, Rognoth was exhausted, but his will to survive kept the wings beating. Gravity tried to pull him crashing to the mattress of leaves and branches below.

Tryos, on the other hand, had been flying without rest for two and a half days, covering the immense distance from Rokanun to the Stronghold.

Panting and wheezing, Rognoth dropped low to the treetops of a hex of forested-hill terrain, trying to hide again. Tryos blasted the trees into cinders, but he had begun to lose his breath, and the flame was weak. Rognoth squealed miserably and forced his wings to fling him forward again, heading inexorably northward, as the hexagons of terrain flashed by under them.

Delrael backed against the splintered wall of the weapons storehouse. The ogres converged on him. He had only six arrows remaining, but they had no effect anyway. He needed to find the way out—Vailret said the Outsiders always made sure a situation had some solution.

But if the Outsiders knew of the quest to stop Scartaris, might they not just remove the troublesome characters once and for all?

Bryl struck another illusion Gairoth with a weak lightning bolt, but the one-eyed ogre guffawed. Bryl's third spell faded out, leaving him helpless again. He had only one spell remaining, one more roll of the Water Stone.

Delrael screwed up his courage and determination. He was the head of the Stronghold. He was supposed to keep the other characters protected. No matter what his father's orders said, no matter what the Rulewoman Melanie had told them, Delrael had failed in his most important job of keeping the villagers safe.

He made up his mind then. Gairoth was the main threat, not these other ogres. Without the one-eyed ogre to lead them, the others would never remain together. Within days, they would probably fight and kill each other off. Tarne and the other villagers in the forests might be able to retake the Stronghold.

Bryl had one spell left against Gairoth. He might make the Water Stone count—if he could only identify the real ogre among the illusions. And Delrael had six arrows.

Ignoring the advancing ogres, Delrael shot down the line, one arrow after the other, using the skill he had absorbed from years of training. He struck four illusion Gairoths, watching the arrows pass through them to skid against the dirt of the training ground. Then the fifth arrow stuck in the ogre's shoulder.

"Oww!" Gairoth howled, and his illusory counterparts flickered.

Bryl's eyes lit up with a surge of last desperate power. The Water Stone bucked in his hand, and he threw it to the ground. He didn't even look to see if his roll had been successful.

A ball of pale lightning appeared in the air, glowing and bobbing as it moved across the distance. Gairoth tried to duck, but the ball of lightning popped against him, singeing his hair and blistering his skin but causing no real harm. Bryl had rolled only a "2." The ogre shouted in pain.

Delrael's wrist flowed as he reached up to snatch another arrow out of his quiver—his last arrow. The oncoming ogres had hesitated for a second. He needed to deprive Gairoth of the rest of his power.

Delrael shot the last arrow.

The point struck the heavy iron crown with a thunk. The crown dropped to the ground and bounced on the packed earth. The Air Stone popped out of its mounting, gleaming on the ground.

The mirrored Gairoths winked out of existence, leaving the one-eyed ogre standing alone. Gairoth roared with pain and surprise.

Delrael could do nothing more. He cringed then balled his fists. He waited for the rest of the ogre army to plunge forward to beat him with dozens of clubs, to stab him with spears and swords...

"Come on, then!" he said, wishing the tears would stop glinting in his eyes and blurring his vision.

The oncoming ogres faltered, wavered in the warm afternoon air, and dissolved into nonexistence.

Illusions, every one of them.

Bryl dived forward, landing on his chest and scrabbling for the fallen Air Stone. Gairoth lurched at him, trying to grab the diamond for himself. But the old half-Sorcerer's fingers touched the facets of the diamond first; he snatched it up, tossed it across the field—and he vanished, surrounded in an illusion of invisibility. The Air Stone also winked out of sight.

Delrael blinked in surprise. Only a moment before, he and Bryl had been facing two dozen ogres and sixteen identical Gairoths. Now, in the entire Stronghold, he could see only himself and the one-eyed ogre. And Delrael had only a sword.

Gairoth turned red with anger and frustration. His burned skin, already peeling and cracking from being too long away from the swamps, looked blistered and painful. He swung his club blindly in the air, furious with the world, wanting to strike something, punish something, kill something.

He saw Delrael standing alone by the weapons storehouse.

"We won, Gairoth. Fair and square. You'd better leave now." Delrael crossed his arms for emphasis, trying to appear tough.

"Delroth!" Gairoth thundered forward, his eye blazing. He ran forward with his club. His bare feet kicked up the mulched wood shavings. "You be dead meat!"

Delrael had no time to duck inside the storehouse for even another dagger. He stood, wishing he could run, wishing he could just defend himself better. He was a *fighter.* But he could not use bare fists against Gairoth's battering-ram club.

Before the ogre could swing his club down on Delrael's head, another pounding came from outside the stockade wall just behind the weapons storehouse. The pounding reverberated in the air, and Gairoth stopped as a hoarse woman's voice shrieked his name. "Gairoth! You deserve a spanking, Gairoth!"

The ogre dropped the end of his club, letting it thump against the ground. His mouth hung open, dumbfounded. Delrael was afraid to make a move toward the storehouse.

"Gairoth! Do you hear me, boy?" the harsh female voice demanded.

"Maw?" the ogre asked quietly, astonished.

A crash struck the double-walled barrier, and Delrael stared as the upright logs shuddered with the strain. Another crunch, and the wall buckled inward. The logs splintered, and the cement-hard mud between them sifted down.

A huge female ogre flung the broken logs aside as if they were tooth-picks and strode into the Stronghold. One ham-like hand rested on her hip and the other held a flat-ended club that looked like an oar for a warship. She had lumpy eyebrows perched on a jutting forehead, and her skin looked as smooth as gravel. Each breast seemed fully as large as her head, and probably contained as much cerebral matter. Her hair was long and ropelike, tied with an incongruous pink ribbon that looked like centuries-old Sorcerer silk. Her buckteeth bit down on flabby lips.

"There you be!" She cracked the flat end of her club against one leathery palm. Her mouth was huge and yawning when she spoke, making "Maw" seem a terribly appropriate name. "You gonna get a whopping like you can't imagine! Look at you! Playing high and mighty in a"—she spat the word—"*human* place like this! Now get on home!"

Gairoth bowed his head and shuffled toward the torn hole in the wall. But his Maw stormed forward, threatening to crack him with her club. "What you be, an animal? Go out through the front door! And to think I raised you! Such a disgrace!"

Sheepishly, the ogre turned instead to the massive gates, which Delrael now saw had never been smashed down at all—yet another facet of Gairoth's Air Stone illusion. The ogre glared at Delrael, but his Maw smacked him for the delay.

Delrael listened to their stomping footsteps diminish down the hill path. Then he realized he was in total silence, alone in the Stronghold. Everything was over, finished, the final turns taken.

Bryl winked into visibility beside him, grinning so broadly, his wispy beard protruded from his chin and his wrinkles folded into themselves. He seemed exhausted but delighted. He held the Water Stone and the Air Stone in his hands.

"I thought you were out of spells," Delrael said. "You used four."

Bryl smiled. "When I have *two* Stones, my spell allowance is determined by a different table in the Book. I get a bonus, five spells each day instead of four. Gairoth didn't know that."

Delrael chuckled and clapped a hand on the half-Sorcerer's shoulder. "Good thing Gairoth's Maw came at just the right time."

"Let's give credit where credit is due." Bryl held up the glittering diamond. He turned to look at the section of the Stronghold wall that the ogre woman had smashed. It stood intact, untouched.

"His 'Maw' will follow him most of the way back to the swamps, maybe even make him take a bath in the cesspools. She'll tell him to be good, because he can never know when she'll be watching."

Delrael saw Bryl's eyes glittering with delight. "Making illusions is easier than I thought."

Delrael looked down and saw that Gairoth's iron crown had also been false, just a twined circlet of straw. The attack had never been real; the ogre army had never been real. Ogres don't work together! It all gave him a headache.

"At least it's nice to feel completely safe again."

The arctic winds howled around the mountains, slicing like frozen knives. Tryos's ears ached. His body felt leaden and sluggish—reptiles weren't made for cold such as this. Snow splattered against his eyelids, smearing his vision. He felt ready to fall from the skies out of sheer exhaustion.

CHAPTER 13
MOUNTAIN OF THE DRAGON

Science and magic cannot coexist in the same area. Their Rules are
contradictory: Science says you can't get something for nothing, magic
says you can. We have to choose how we want to play the Game.
—Professor Frankenstein, *Published Notes*, Selected Excerpts

Vailret leaned forward, squeezing his fingers against Dirac's polished drafting table. "It's been six days!"

He stopped himself from making a fist and smoothed out his voice. "Please give us a boat or something. We have to try to rescue them."

"The time for waiting is past," Paenar said. "We must do something. We must make a difference!"

Dirac flinched from the stare of Paenar's new eyes. The two professors had designed a pair of goggles filled with exotic oils and floating lenses sandwiched between two wafers of transparent crystal. A wire connected the goggles to a small galvanic battery that had been surgically implanted at the base of Paenar's skull.

After the invention of the eyes and a simple operation, the blind man had turned around in awe, staring at the clutter of the professors' workroom, looking at every corner, every shape, every shadow. Paenar smiled, stretching his arms upward and ready to challenge the world. "Now I don't feel so helpless!"

But in Dirac's workroom, Vailret felt the helplessness return. Many of the trappings of an inventor remained in Dirac's laboratory: the chalkboard, the drafting table, the scrawled equations waiting for answers. But everything was too ornate, and too clean, merely for show. The drafting table looked oddly like a desk, and the equations on the chalkboard appeared to have been there for a long time, unaltered. Vailret could not remember having seen chalk dust on Dirac's fingertips. Mayer had never mentioned how long it had been since her father's last invention.

"Your companions volunteered to be subjects in a scientific experiment." Dirac sat on a three-legged stool behind his drafting table. He folded his pudgy fingers together and rested his elbows on the table's clean surface.

"They were to test Professor Verne's balloon. Since six days have indeed passed, we can draw only two conclusions—either the balloon failed and they have been killed in its crash into the sea....or they reached the island of Rokanun, and Tryos the dragon has destroyed them. Either way, your friends are dead." He cracked his knuckles and sat up straight.

"I can imagine other scenarios," Paenar said.

Dirac smiled deprecatingly. "I suppose we cannot expect you to understand the Rule of Occam's Razor. You see, when more than one hypothesis fits the facts, the simplest solution must be the correct solution."

Dirac stood up from his stool; it creaked as he lifted himself. He picked up a piece of chalk and walked to the blackboard, studying his equations, but ended up writing a short reminder note to himself instead.

"There." He blew on his fingers to get rid of the chalk dust then smiled at Professor Verne, who stood watching by the door. Verne had accompanied Vailret and Paenar, ostensibly to monitor the functioning of the blind man's mechanical eyes; Verne had known full well what the two men intended to ask. He made it clear, though, that he would not argue for or against them.

Paenar stood cold and motionless, as if he knew his presence made Dirac uncomfortable. "Give us a boat, and we will see for ourselves."

"You owe us that much," Vailret said. "Our friends risked their lives to test your invention."

"The Sitnaltans owe you no debt, young man. You have no contract, no written agreement that requires anything of us. You are our guest—do we demand that you repay us for the food and shelter we have freely given? Do not insult me by making similar demands in return."

He rubbed his hands together and smiled at them again. "You are welcome to remain in Sitnalta. Perhaps in time you can be taught the rudiments of mathematics and make yourselves useful to the community."

"Oh, stuff your platitudes," Vailret snapped.

"Don't you understand?" Paenar gripped the sides of the drafting table, making Dirac take refuge behind it. "The Outsiders have already set the wheels in motion! They have thrown Scartaris here to grow and grow, sucking all the life from Hexworld! You can't just ignore this—it won't go away!" He hung his head, but the anger returned to his face. "Apathy is the worst of all sins, and you are guilty of it!"

Dirac gave him a self-satisfied smile. "You are extrapolating a great deal from a small amount of data, gentlemen. We have only a few ambiguous measurements from Professor Verne's apparatus—hardly enough information to concoct such a doom-filled hypothesis. Don't you agree, Professor?"

Verne remained silent for a moment, tugging on his great gray beard, and then he frowned. "You are showing very little scientific objectivity, Dirac," he said quietly, and turned to go. "But, then, perhaps you are no longer an inventor."

Before Dirac could reply, Vailret turned his back on him and followed Verne without a word. Paenar looked as if he wanted to shout some more, but he scowled and moved in Vailret's wake.

Dirac recovered himself and called, "Have a nice day!" as the three men disappeared down the hall.

"Follow me," Verne said. Vailret blinked when they emerged into the sunlight, and Paenar adjusted his mechanical eyes. The wind had come up, whipping the ocean's damp scent through the winding alleys.

"Why bother?" Paenar said. "You may as well go and enjoy yourself. Play a game or two. We don't have much time left."

Verne stared at Paenar's artificial eyes. "Follow me," he repeated and turned to stride down a hex-cobbled street.

The professor stumped away from his workshop at a brisk pace, as if always two steps behind where he wanted to be. Vailret grew curious about what Verne had in mind. Paenar followed, fuming and angry, impotent in the face of the end of the world.

"Dirac is too quick to dismiss theories he does not like," Verne said. "One of Maxwell's golden rules says that we must search for the truth, whether it be pleasant or unpleasant."

He stopped and shrugged. "Besides, my data supports what you have said about Scartaris. If nothing else, I trust my own data."

Verne led them out to the seawall around Sitnalta. Part of the wall had been battered away by the choppy water, and now many Sitnaltan engineers scurried about designing and constructing a new section of the wall, adding supports. A large spidery apparatus used elaborate systems of weights and counterweights to raise gigantic stone blocks, positioning them in rows along the wall. Puffs of steam and groans of stressed metal drifted into the air against the rumble of the ocean. Vailret could smell the salty, fishy mixture of the sea mixed with oil and smoke from the machinery.

Verne indicated the damaged section, speaking in a tone of amazement. "Several weeks ago, the ocean attacked our wall. The day was clear, and the sea was still as glass—but a huge fist of water surged up from the sea, as if … called by someone." He shrugged. "None of our theoreticians can account for it."

Vailret saw a vision of Bryl, possessed by the *dayid* of the khelebar forest, calling on all the water in the world to come to their aid. Vailret shuddered but did not volunteer the information to Professor Verne.

They descended a steep, rime-covered staircase on the seawall, reaching a network of docks that stuck out like insolent tongues into the water. The cold wind blew in their faces. Vailret found it refreshing after Dirac's stuffy reception.

On the docks, two men operated a vibrating generator submerged in the choppy water in an effort to lure fish into complex electronic traps. The fishing engineers soon gave up in disgust, covering their equipment with a canvas, and walked off the docks, leaving Professor Verne alone with his two companions.

Verne led them to the end of one of the docks and pointed to a large mechanical object floating in the water, tied up against the pilings in front of them. He whispered, filling his voice with a childish sense of wonder. "This, gentlemen, is the *Nautilus*."

It looked like a huge motionless fish, nightmarish and prehistoric. Jagged ridges ran down its long body, jutting like fins from crucial steering points. Thick gaping windows gleamed translucent at the waterline. Vailret sensed it was some kind of boat, and yet more than a boat. Paenar cast his mechanical eyes over the steel-plated hull and made a satisfied noise.

"Frankenstein studied thousands of fish, trying to figure out how they worked, how they swam, how they submerged themselves, how they remained under water. We used his results to create those frivolous toys in the fountain around our water clock, little mechanical fish that swim around and around, aimlessly. But I took his information one step further and combined the physics of the fish with the practicality of a boat. So this is not just a boat, but an underwater boat for submarine travel!"

Vailret looked at the *Nautilus*, not anxious to step out on the rocking, spray-covered hull. The round hatchway looked like a lidded eye on the front end of the ship. "Does it work?"

Verne tried to sidestep the question, then faced it squarely. "Yes, Frankenstein and I have taken it for several test runs near the shore. Oh, it is beautiful under the water, a world one does not normally see. My *Nautilus* will take you out toward Rokanun." He sighed and turned his eyes away.

"But this is not an exploitation of a simple law of nature, as the balloon was. The *Nautilus* is pure Sitnaltan technology, rooted in science and conceived through my own inventiveness."

Paenar understood and turned to Vailret. "He means we will not be able to cross the technological fringe beyond the city."

"No, I mean you may not be able to cross it," Verne said. "Nothing is absolute on Hexworld—it depends on the roll of the dice, the Rules of Probability. Once you cross the fringe, the probability that machinery will fail increases exponentially. You always have a chance to make it, if you try enough times."

Vailret frowned, looking at the gleaming metal fish. "Does this mean you're giving us permission to take the *Nautilus*? Why didn't Dirac say anything about this?"

"I'm not certain if I can give you permission. But I can show you how to pilot her, and I can assure you that I will not be here to stop you if, say, tonight you wished to take her and go."

"Why are you dancing around your words?" Paenar said.

Verne shoved both hands in his pockets. "I am a prolific inventor—I cannot remember how many certificates I have acquired from the Council of Patent Givers. But I am also a Sitnaltan. Since we rarely encounter strangers, and since none of our devices will function far from the city anyway, the question has never arisen if one of my inventions belongs to *me*, because I invented it, or if it belongs to the people of Sitnalta, who have constructed it and manufactured the materials.

"So, you see, if I were to ask Dirac about giving you the *Nautilus*, he would say the ship belongs to the city and not to me." His eyes sparkled. "However, if I do not ask the question, then the issue will not be raised. And no one will deny you the right to take the boat."

Vailret digested the logic and grinned. "Admirably devious, Professor. You are shrewd in other ways besides being just a great tinkerer!"

Verne stepped on the narrow deck of the *Nautilus*. He lifted up the round metal hatch and climbed into the control room. Vailret saw panels filled with switches, dials, and other controls. It all looked exotic and exciting.

The professor paused, looking up at the sun's position in the sky. He withdrew a ticking timepiece the size of an apple and cracked it open, nodding. "We should have sufficient time. Would you like to learn how to pilot her?"

~

To celebrate the liberation of the Stronghold, Jorte dug up one of the last vats of the previous year's spring cider outside of his gaming hall and broke open the top. He took a wooden rod and stirred sediment from the bottom before everyone dipped cups into the cool brown liquid. Jorte waddled over to a table to drink and enjoy himself for the first time in a month.

Early in the afternoon, the veteran Tarne and several other villagers had crept out of the sheltering forest. They had seen the dragon in the sky, heard the loud battle inside the stockade fence. But now the Stronghold stood silent and ominous. Tarne hoped the ogres had killed each other. The gates were ajar and somehow intact again. He climbed Steep Hill alone, standing in front of the open gates, not knowing what to do next.

And Delrael rushed out to greet him.

After the word had spread, the other villagers flooded back into their old homes and buildings like a long awaited sigh. Lantee the butcher and his wife stared stricken at their demolished, empty smokehouse. Others were relieved that the destruction had not been greater. Most drifted off to Jorte's gaming hall, not yet ambitious enough to start the job of putting their lives in order before the harvest.

For two days, they assessed the damage to the land and recovered from their shock. After his battle with Gairoth, Bryl seemed to be held in higher esteem by the villagers. Delrael stood with Tarne and Bryl inside the Stronghold fence, looking out over the landscape visible from the top of the hill. Tarne pointed to one of the cleared hexagons of cropland. "Our harvest this season will be poor. We tried to come out at night and do the weeding, but that was risky. The storehouses are empty.

"It's going to be a hard winter for all of us."

Delrael looked across the cleared land, past the beginning of the hexagon of forest terrain, but he said nothing.

"If the game lasts that long," Bryl muttered.

A reptilian shriek sliced through the air. Delrael crouched, letting his fighting instincts take over. Tarne and Bryl looked up to see the huge form of Tryos sailing overhead.

The dragon flapped his wings, splaying his piston-like legs so that he landed with grace on the flat training area. He beat his wings a final time and folded them across his back, ignoring Tarne and focusing his attention on Bryl and Delrael.

"Finished!" Tryos cried in his high-pitched, clipped voice. "Rognos far from here! Never come back. Never."

"Very good, Tryos," Delrael said. "Gairoth is gone too."

Tryos blinked his eyes and bobbed his head up and down. "Isss good! No more Rokanun for me! Ssstay here now! Home of Tryos!"

Tarne stared, but Delrael ignored him. Bryl fell silent, standing back from the discussion.

"No more Rokanun?" Delrael asked, speaking in a slow and careful voice.

"Nah! I have thisss land."

"Okay," Delrael fidgeted, looking first at Bryl and then at Tarne. He got no encouragement from their appalled expressions. "But what about your treasure? All those years you worked to gather it, surely you don't just want to leave it there for robbers?"

Tryos lifted his head, snorted smoke. "They would not dare!"

Delrael crossed his arms over his leather jerkin. "Who do you think you're kidding, Tryos? If you stay away, it's a treasure for the taking."

The dragon turned his blazing eyes away. But Delrael smiled. "You could, of course, bring your treasure here. Look at these big empty storage chambers we have—wouldn't they make a great start for a new set of catacombs?"

The dragon cocked his head, extending his long reptilian neck into the musty darkness of the storage pit Rognoth had gutted. "Pah! Smellsss like grain!" His voice echoed in the chamber; then he lifted his head back out again, blowing dust from his nose. "But they make good cavesss. I bring my treasure here."

"We'll help," Delrael volunteered. "Can we go right away?"

The dragon turned around in circles, then slumped to the ground, stretching his neck out and plopping his chin on the dirt. "Nah—long flight." He closed his eyes. "Tired now."

Within moments, low rumbling sounds of the sleeping dragon drifted into the air, drowning out the faint noises of the villagers still rejoicing in the gaming hall.

In their private room in Sitnalta, Vailret, and Paenar discussed everything Verne had showed them. All afternoon, the professor had bombarded them with instructions, filling the *Nautilus*'s control room with his accented voice.

Paenar remained rigid on the edge of his cot, staring at the blank wall. They sat listening to the steam-engine vehicles chugging into storage bays to let their boilers cool until morning. The manufactories had closed down for the night. Vailret waited for the gas streetlights to be lit and for the Sitnaltans to go to sleep.

"Our plan has one big flaw," Vailret said, disturbing Paenar from his daydreaming. "We have even less to fight with than Del and Bryl did. At least they had the Water Stone."

"We'll manage," Paenar said, but the bulky goggles masked his real expression. Lenses floated in their oils, hypnotic in the shadowy light. Vailret shook his head.

"Against a dragon? How? Neither of us can even fight with a sword or shoot an arrow. Not that it would be terribly effective against Tryos anyway."

Paenar spoke slowly in the new silence. "*Sitnalta* has a weapon that's effective against the dragon."

They stole down the steps of the Sitnaltan ziggurat in the darkness, lugging the heavy Dragon Siren between them. Vailret sneaked a glance at the streetlights of the jagged cobblestone streets below them. The sleeping city remained silent, but Vailret felt eyes watching them from the blind windows.

"I'll go first," Paenar said. "My eyes can adjust to the dark."

Vailret obliged, following behind and watching where he put his feet. "It seems like we're betraying Professor Verne by stealing the Siren."

"Heroic decisions are always questionable … until you win." Paenar shifted his hold on the Siren. "You'll never be remembered if you don't take chances."

"I'd rather be alive than be remembered, if it comes down to a choice between the two."

After reaching the base of the ziggurat, they hurried through the deserted streets, dodging puddles of yellow lamplight. They stood on the bank of the seawall, listening to the crash of restive waves below them. They stumbled down the worn steps to the docks below. The metallic dish of the Siren dragged at them, but they gritted their teeth. Out of breath and sweating in the chill air, they reached the swaying hulk of the *Nautilus* on the docks.

Then Mayer stepped out of the shadows. She had wrapped herself in a thin cloak, and looked cold and blown, as if she had been there waiting a long time. She pressed her lips into a thin line and tried to look haughty.

"First my father turns down your request for a boat, then Professor Verne spends the afternoon showing you the *Nautilus*. Did you honestly think I could not extrapolate what you intended to do?"

Vailret regained his composure and answered her coolly. "We are trying to help our friends, since you Sitnaltans seem quite willing to ignore the rest of Hexworld. Professor Verne graciously offered us the use of his *Nautilus* after your father refused to help. We're not trying to hide."

Mayer laughed sharply. "Who could suspect you of trying to hide, when you creep to the docks in the dead of night?"

"The tide is at its best point now." Paenar sounded smug. "Professor Verne told us so."

"No doubt he 'graciously offered' to give you our Dragon Siren as well?" She flashed an angry glare at Paenar. "Or perhaps you barbarians have no moral restrictions against stealing."

Vailret and Paenar said nothing.

Mayer's short dark hair whipped about in the wind like the barely seen waves, but the tone of her voice changed. Vailret suspected she was addressing something different entirely. "What is it you know? I can see it in you. Any idiot can recognize that Sitnaltan ways are superior to your primitive life in the outside world—yet you don't admire our city. It's almost as if you ... flaunt our technology. What do you know that we do not?"

She seemed honestly curious. Paenar fidgeted. Vailret pondered on the silent dark dock. "I can see and accept some of the advantages your way of life has—especially since I have no Sorcerer blood. In Sitnalta, all humans can use the magic of your technology. But you haven't even made an effort to see if perhaps we 'barbarians' do some things better than you.

"You tinker with your calculating machines and your street-cleaning engines, but when faced with a problem your technology may not be able to solve—Scartaris—you dismiss it as something not to be considered."

Paenar cleared his throat and placed a large hand on Vailret's shoulder. "We are going to fight against Tryos, and then against Scartaris—it is not likely we will win. But we are trying anyway. Your science has made you blind to the fact that sometimes you can win the impossible fight. Many dice rolls are not likely, but they are *possible*."

She hardened her expression. "If you take the Dragon Siren and lose, then Sitnalta will be defenseless."

"Or," Paenar countered, "if we take it and win, you need never fear the dragon again. Then your greatest inventors can start to work on the problem of Scartaris."

"After we're gone," Vailret said, "go and talk to Professor Verne. Let him show you his data and his extrapolations. Be objective. Ask yourself if there isn't a remote possibility that the threat truly exists. Then scrap your frivolous gadgets and invent something to stop this thing! If we fail, all of Hexworld could be depending on you."

As if that settled the discussion, Paenar slipped past her and clambered on board the *Nautilus*, lugging the Dragon Siren down into the control room. Vailret stared at Mayer for a moment in silence, then surprised himself by shaking her hand. He jumped onto the deck of the sub-marine boat and slipped down the hatch without another word. He closed the hatch above him.

Mayer remained on the dock looking flustered and confused, as if puzzled that the confrontation had not turned out as she had planned.

The *Nautilus* slipped away from the moorings, churning water into foam behind its propellers. The ship poised for a moment on the surface, nosed out into deeper water, then sank beneath the waves like a giant predatory fish.

~

The next morning, Tryos smashed his tail on the packed dirt, let out a yowling yawn, and demanded that Bryl and Delrael "Wake up!"

Delrael had slept in his own creaking bed for the first time in a month, but it seemed as if he hadn't dozed for more than a few minutes. When Bryl came out into the morning sunshine, red-eyed and wrapped in his blue cloak, he seemed too tired even to be afraid of Tryos.

He and Delrael sat on the great dragon's back and watched the ground drop away with each thundering beat of Tryos's wings. Tarne stood watching them with a defeated expression on his face.

The journey back to Rokanun took two days. The dragon followed a drunken course, losing and then recovering his path. The island and its tall volcano reared up at them from the mosaic of clear blue hexes of ocean. Tryos made a beeline for the wide crater opening. Heat and fumes from the boiling lake of lava hissed up at them as the dragon swooped into his treasure grotto.

Tryos scraped the hardened lava floor with his claws and moved his head from side to side, loosening up. He folded his wings and stood tall in the grotto, admiring the gleaming hoard. Bryl and Delrael climbed off, stretching and looking around. The dragon strutted among the jewels and gold, crunching treasure under his feet.

"Ahh. Good thing I not leave thissss!"

Bryl acted eager for another look at the old Sorcerer objects, but did not want to make Tryos suspicious. Delrael found Tareah in a corner by the shadow of the treasure, trying to remain unobtrusive. She looked frightened, determined, but very weak. She had been feeding herself with supplies from a trivial Sorcerer maintenance spell, like Bryl's, but she needed more.

"You came back," she said with a sort of wonder. "Now we can go back home." Delrael clasped her shoulder and gave her a reassuring hug. He found himself feeling deeply sorry for her—Tareah had been isolated for all three decades of her life, with only Sardun for company. He had no doubt she would be inept in dealing with other people, unpracticed, and not accustomed to being totally alone either. No one came to visit the memories in the Ice Palace anymore. Delrael could imagine her loneliness.

Tryos had blasted his way into her sheltered world, taking her and leaving her with no one on whom to depend. No one on the entire island.

Delrael smiled and felt warm inside, wondering if she would see him as a brave prince come to her aid. Just like in the old days of the Game.

But when he hugged her, Delrael noticed how much Tareah had grown, more than an inch in five days. Delrael blinked and stared at her, doubting that he could be mistaken. He was usually quite good with spatial relationships.

Tareah had filled out, adding a year to her apparent age. Perhaps because she had been far enough away from Sardun's sorcery for so long, her body was making up for lost time.

Delrael interrupted the dragon's silent inventory. "You will need to work a long time to move all your treasure, Tryos."

The dragon bobbed his head. "Many trips!"

"You'll get done sooner if you start sooner. You'd better take a load and go right away."

Before Tryos could sputter anything else, Delrael continued. "I know. It will be hard work, but well worth the effort."

Bryl stood by the fighter. "Delrael and I will stay here to guard your treasure. We promise. Don't worry."

Tareah looked at him in disappointed alarm.

Tryos narrowed his eyes and glared at the half-Sorcerer, assessing him with a piercing reptilian stare. "How do I know you not take treasure for yoursssselfsss? No tricksss!"

Bryl turned his eyes from the dragon's horrible stare, cringing, but he looked down at the jewels and gold and reasserted his outward calm. "Did we steal any treasure the first time you caught us? And didn't we find Rognoth for you so you could punish him? And didn't we take care of Gairoth too? And didn't we find you a big new land to live in?"

Tryos hung his head and fidgeted under Bryl's high-pitched outburst. "Yesss."

"Trust us." The half-Sorcerer smiled broadly.

"I come back sssoon—not long! Wait here!"

"Of course."

Like a monstrous reptilian shovel, Tryos opened his huge mouth and scooped up an indiscriminate mouthful of his hoard. He lifted his head with some effort, straining his muscles against the great weight of treasure. The rippling scales in his serpentine neck glittered rainbows from the reflected gold and jewels. A few scattered gems and odd coins jingled back to the ground through cracks in the dragon's mouth. Tryos shook his head, letting the last few loose items fall free back to the grotto floor. A pearl necklace snagged on one of his fangs, swaying back and forth in the weird orange light from the lava.

"Don't hurry back now, Tryos—it'll be all right." Bryl waved at the dragon. "We promise."

Delrael nodded. "You could tire yourself out by flying too fast."

The dragon tried to say something but could not spit the words past the wadding of treasure in his mouth. He almost choked. Delrael didn't want to hear the question—he wanted to get rid of Tryos as soon as possible. "Don't talk now, Tryos. You can ask us next time. Have a good trip."

Flustered, the dragon stopped trying to talk and strode over to the edge of the grotto. Bryl and Delrael waved, smiling so much their jaws ached, before Tryos spread his wings and launched himself out over the lake of lava.

The dragon fell like a stone, headfirst, dragged down by the immense load of treasure. Delrael's heart leaped with hope, praying their problem could be ended so simply. Tryos's reptilian eyes widened in alarm, and he beat his wings frantically, flaring his nostrils. The dragon slowed his plunge and labored his way back up to the top of the cinder cone. He puffed with the effort, flew over the rim and into the distance.

"Let's get up the tunnel out of here." Delrael turned and ushered

Tareah toward the opening. The hiss and bubbling of the lava added a layer of background noise. "We'll have to run like mad to the balloon. I counted the hexes—we can do it in a day and a half."

Bryl tallied on his fingers. "It'll take Tryos at least four days to get to the Stronghold and back, even without resting. Once we reach the balloon, we'll need time to inflate it, then two more days to fly back to Sitnalta. Once we're up in the air, Tareah and I can summon up a good wind with the Water Stone—but the magic might not work once we pass the technological fringe." He shook his head and sighed. "It's going to be close, very close."

Tareah looked dejected and her voice sounded bereft in the empty, echoing grotto. "You promised to stay here and guard the treasure. Why did you have to do that?"

"We're not honor-bound to keep a promise to an evil dragon," Bryl said. "Are you crazy?"

Delrael looked at her, puzzled that she needed justification. "Tryos kidnapped you and he nearly killed your father. Look at all the treasure he's stolen. Do you want to stay here?"

"But you *promised.* I thought you had a better plan than … than cheating!" Tareah looked confused, torn between two loyalties. "My father made me study the Rules, all of them. He hammered into me the ethics of gaming and sportsmanship." Her eyes glittered with either tears or anger. "When you agree to undertake a quest, the Rules force you to complete it. But isn't a vow to do a quest just an elaborate promise? By the same token, how can you break your promise to Tryos?"

"You're very naive," Bryl said. "The object of the game is winning. Whether by battle or by trickery."

Delrael took the question seriously, though. Vailret would have been able to make much more convincing arguments. "Tareah, trickery is accepted Game play. I didn't make up the Rules. A precedent has been set—have you ever played poker? It's a game played with cards, not dice. Bluffing is a vital part of the play. We bluffed Tryos into believing we would stay here."

Tareah frowned at Delrael's reasoning. "Well … he did steal the treasures in the first place."

"Tryos is our opponent. We should be allowed to use every means we have to beat him. Especially when your life is at stake. You don't feel sorry for a dragon, do you?"

Delrael put his hand on her back and moved forward with her as they entered the dank tunnel and hurried upward. "Come on, your father is waiting for us."

They entered the tunnel, but Bryl stopped as if struck with a spell. His eyes became glassy and he looked around the piles and piles of gems, gold, treasures. He swallowed hard. "Wait! The Earth Stone! It's here!" He turned to stare at Delrael. "We have to find it!"

"Why?" Delrael asked, showing more impatience. "You said magic won't help out against a dragon anyway."

"It won't," Tareah said.

"It was lost for more than a century in one of the first battles of the Scouring. A *ten-sided* emerald." Bryl sniffed the air then looked disappointed. "I lost it now, but I had another vision, like when I found the Air Stone. It's here somewhere." The half-Sorcerer's eyes gleamed with a frightening expression. "We don't have enough time, Bryl," Delrael said.

"We have to find it!" the half-Sorcerer insisted. "It might help us against Scartaris. Remember what Vailret said. The Earth Stone is the most powerful of all four Stones."

Delrael shook his head. "We can't possibly ransack all of his treasure, not if you don't know exactly where to find it. Our time is too short."

Bryl closed his eyes, holding his breath as if trying to squeeze another vision out.

Tareah hardened her expression and took a step away from Delrael. "I won't go with you if you *steal* any of the treasure—that's worse than breaking your promise to guard it. You're not at all like the heroes in the legends I've read. I'd rather stay here with the dragon. At least he plays by the Rules."

"But he stole the Stone in the first place!" Bryl said.

"He never promised he wouldn't. You did."

That decided it for Delrael. Unhappily, Bryl followed as all three of them ducked into the dark lava tunnel, fleeing the dragon's lair.

. . .

Vailret looked out at an underwater wonderland. He pressed his face against the thick glass of the eyelike porthole, watching the *Nautilus* plunge forward. The ship's cyclopean headlight stabbed into the ocean's secrets, signaling that this was more than just a fish. Few of the undersea creatures showed curiosity; most fled into the midnight-blue murk.

Vailret absorbed the strangeness of the darting gleams of color, the fishes, the fronds of pale seaweed drifting like sirens' hair. A colony of winking lights fluttered around the *Nautilus*, swirling in hypnotic colorful patterns. Before Vailret could wonder at them, the strange lights vanished like extinguished candle flames.

Paenar glanced out the ports only cursorily, impatient to arrive at Rokanun so he could fight Tryos. He turned to the stolen Dragon Siren, inspecting the simple controls and making certain he knew how to work them.

The sub-marine boat flashed through the water, driven by its churning screws.

Three hours after midnight, a huge black wall loomed up through the water, cutting across their path like a guillotine blade. Vailret sat drowsy at the controls, wishing he could rest for a while. He blinked and saw the black wall moving toward them.

For one sick instant, he forgot how to bring the *Nautilus* to a stop. Professor Verne had shown them, but Vailret had no time to try any of the controls. He let out a cry of despair. Paenar stood up so quickly, he hit his head on the low metal ceiling. The other man ignored the pain and lurched toward Vailret. Both saw the black wall and knew they could never stop the boat in time. The *Nautilus* struck the blackness.

Everything went dark for an instant, and then they were through, traveling as if nothing had happened. Paenar dropped back into his seat; Vailret blinked, dizzy. The air in the *Nautilus* seemed close and stifling, and he wondered if the air pumps were still working. Perhaps they had passed beyond the technological fringe—

"It was just the hex-line!" Vailret cried. "That's all! The line probably goes all the way to the sea bottom." He laughed. Paenar stared at him in shocked realization for a moment, and joined Vailret in relieved laughter.

They had traveled the distance of a full hexagon in barely four hours.

According to the map, from the Sitnaltan docks to the closest shore of Rokanun was only two hexes if they navigated correctly, but they intended to use the speed of the *Nautilus* as long as they could, trying to circle half the island to reach the dragon's lair on the opposite end—if the sub-marine boat continued to function that long.

They cruised through a second hex-line just after morning light turned the dark ocean a murky green. They had altered their course to follow alongside the island, and the ramparts of the rising volcanic ocean floor stood like blocky shadows in the wavering distance off to their right.

"We'd better rise closer to the surface," Vailret said. "No telling when we'll pass the technological fringe, or when this machine will stop working."

Paenar took the controls and brought the *Nautilus* nearer to the surface at a gentle angle. The sounds of the engines made a stuttering pop, then resumed smoothly.

The *Nautilus* began to break apart late in the afternoon. Twice during the day, the engines had stalled, but the two men managed to start them again after several tries. The sounds of the screws were more sluggish, whining and clunking, but neither Paenar nor Vailret knew anything about the workings of the Sitnaltan engines. The *Nautilus* labored on the surface of the ocean, crawling forward.

Thick oily smoke oozed around the sealed door of the engine room. At the same instant, some of the floor panels split apart, popping rivets and letting harsh seawater squirt up through the deck. The ship lurched sharply to the right, toward the brooding island.

The engines sounded as if they were shredding themselves in howls of torn metal. The hot propellers churned the water around the tail of the *Nautilus* into a steaming froth.

Seawater gushed through breaches in the hull. Smoke from the dying engines made breathing and seeing impossible.

"This machine has served its purpose," Paenar shouted over the noise and stood up to unfasten the hatch over their heads. He turned his face to Vailret, peering through the smoke with his mechanical goggle-eyes. "We must swim to shore. By the sound of those engines, the *Nautilus* might explode."

Vailret cried out, choking, "—reef!"

As Paenar stuck his head out the hatch, a powerful blow struck the ship, throwing him back to the floor. Vailret half-caught the other man, keeping him from dashing his head against the instrument panel. A black elbow of rock punctured the hull of the ship. The *Nautilus* groaned to a halt.

Paenar clambered to the hatch again as foamy water spurted into the compartment. He peered outside, wiping sea spray from his goggles. "We've caught on a reef. It will be tricky going, but I think we'll be able to walk to shore."

Vailret coughed and struggled out of the hatch, dropping to the rugged rocky shelf. Choppy water washed over his boots. Rokanun lay not far from them, but a careless blow from an incoming wave could easily sweep them away.

"The Dragon Siren!" Paenar scrambled back into the ship. Vailret crawled back to the top of the hatch, leaning inside. He urged the other man to hurry and helped him lift the Sitnaltan device out of the hatch. Paenar tossed up a coil of rope, and Vailret caught it, wondering how the other man could be calm enough to think of such details.

Panting, they struck out as fast as they could, dodging the crashing waves on the slippery rock, lugging the Siren between them.

With a small explosion, the engines of the *Nautilus* started themselves again. The powerful screws drove the armored ship relentlessly forward, ripping open its side against the rough rock and sending it plunging into the deep water again. Vailret turned, watching as gouts of smoke spewed into the air from the open hatch and the breaches in the sides. The heavy hull split wider, and the *Nautilus* slipped beneath the waves, struggling to right itself, like a dying prehistoric beast. Then it vanished completely from sight, leaving only a circle of froth, like a wound on the water's surface.

Vailret and Paenar heaved themselves up on the rough and rocky beach, panting. The crashing waves knocked both men to their knees as they tried to scramble out of the surf. They somehow managed not to smash the Dragon Siren.

Vailret shook out his stringy blond hair and looked up at the huge cinder cone looming over them. He coughed and spat warm seawater out of his mouth. "Look how far we've come."

Paenar turned to him, but didn't quite look at the young man. The expression on his face was plaintive and forlorn. "You'll have to describe it to me, Vailret."

He tapped his goggles, but the lenses hung dead in the colorless oils sandwiched between the thin glass. "The *Nautilus* was not the only mechanical thing here. I'm afraid I am quite blind again."

Tryos dared not swallow, afraid that he might send one or two gold coins into the furnace in his gullet. He flew steadily, leaving the zigzagged outline of Rokanun far behind and striking out over the honeycombed surface of the world. The dragon kept his eye on the different colors of the hexagons below, trying to match it to his dim memory of the route. But often he forgot.

He struck out over land, flying south until he stumbled upon the ocean shoreline again. He followed the shore until he came upon the mud-choked delta of the Barrier River, frothing and still cutting its channel through the forests and plains of the south. He thought he remembered the river, but the surrounding landscape did not look familiar.

The dragon continued westward. His wings felt tired enough to drop off. Anger and discouragement bubbled up inside his chest. He had tried to ask the little humans for detailed directions before he departed, but they had kept him from speaking. Were they anxious to get rid of him?

Tryos snorted because his laden mouth would not allow him to voice the comments he had in mind. He swung around. He'd just have to ask them for directions again. Though he could not find the Stronghold, he was not lost.

Dragons could always find their way home.

After only five hours of flight, Tryos flew back toward the volcano on Rokanun.

CHAPTER 14
BATTLE ON ROKANUN

RULE #13: All monsters were created during the old Sorcerer wars. Each monster has its own set of limitations, its own vulnerabilities. Some may be obvious, some may be well hidden. No monster is invincible, but its weaknesses can be very difficult to find.
—The Book of Rules

Vailret and Paenar worked their way up the volcano's steep side. In places, they had to crawl on hands and knees over the broken-glass terrain of lava rock, cutting and scraping themselves. Darkness fell, making things worse. The stars scattered tricky light on the uneven ground. The two men climbed higher, hauling the Dragon Siren after them.

Paenar's mechanical eyes flickered on and off intermittently. "They function only about one fifth of the time, I would guess." He turned to Vailret, then stopped. "There they go again."

He set off, taking the lead, but Vailret caught up to him and walked alongside.

"I can see flashes of the landscape. I'm used to it now. I just memorize what I see during that instant and keep going until my eyes flicker back to life again."

Vailret didn't know what to say.

"I can endure it, so long as it doesn't ruin my chances of fighting the dragon." Paenar shrugged, but did not look at anything. "I have to strike at least a symbolic blow for all those times when I refused to do anything."

They had traveled two thirds of the way to the lip of the cone when Vailret heard a whooshing sound in the silence of the dark sky. Paenar wedged the Dragon Siren beside a massive outcropping. Both men took cover under the overhang, hiding in the shadows.

Vailret looked up at the star-spattered sky and saw a black shadowy form swoop low over the mountain—immense pointed wings, a long tail, a jagged reptilian head. Orange-tinted smoke from the volcano drifted into the night, swirling when Tryos flew through it and descended into the yawning mouth of the cone. The shape of the dragon ducked out of sight below the rim.

Vailret's eyes glinted wide in the quiet starlight. "He's going to be very upset if he finds Delrael and Bryl in there!"

Instead, the dragon was upset because he did not see them.

Tryos sat back, his mouth full of treasure in the dark and humid chamber. He grunted, trying to call to Delrael and Bryl. He sniffed but found the human scent was cold. He plodded deeper into the cavern—the scent of the men disappeared into the narrow tunnel leading up and out of the mountain.

Then he looked frantically around. One of his treasures was missing: the daughter of Sardun, the last remaining Sorcerer woman—more valuable than any of his baubles. Tryos let out a roar of rage and betrayal, spraying the gold jammed into his vast mouth in a molten starburst on the grotto walls.

"Tricked! Tricked!" the dragon roared. In his fury, he intentionally set fire to one of the stolen Sorcerer tapestries. He forgot how Delrael and Bryl had led him to Rognoth, he forgot how they had shown him a vast new land. The only thing that mattered was their trickery.

Tryos surged out of the grotto and into the night sky. He wheeled around to the opposite side of the cone, picturing in his mind how he would make the two men writhe as he crisped them with his fire.

Delrael, Bryl, and Tareah traveled two hexes by nightfall, when the Rules forced them to stop. They had skirted lava rubble and crossed a hex-line that separated the perimeter of the volcano from the surrounding grassy-hill terrain.

Delrael stayed close beside Tareah as they traveled, seeing to her safety. The wind whipped in his face, fluttering Tareah's long hair in front of his eyes. Delrael carried his old Sorcerer sword again and his hunting bow, neither of which would help at all against Tryos.

"My bones hurt." Tareah rubbed her arms and elbows. "I think I'm growing too fast. I don't know why."

On the top of a tall rise, they stopped to rest. They had crossed a hex of grassy hills and waited on the black edge of thick forest terrain. In half an hour or so, it would be midnight, and they could push on for another day's allotment of distance. Delrael turned back to see the outline of the stark volcano etched in the haze from its inner lake of fire. Then his mouth went dry as a winged and monstrous form flew up against the fiery glow. He heard a distant outraged cry.

"Bryl! Look!" he said.

Tareah fell silent, rigid with her own fear. "Now he's come back for us." The dragon came after them, blasting the countryside with his flames. Bright orange pinpoints of fire made him appear distant, but Tryos flew at them fast.

"We have to get out of here!" Bryl turned around in panic.

"We can't go into the next hex until midnight," Delrael said, standing in a fighting stance but feeling helpless.

Tareah kept her despair in check, making Delrael proud of her. "You won't have another chance to talk with him. You tricked him, and he'll want to blast you to ashes. He'll be more intent on destroying you than he'll be on keeping me from harm."

"I'll protect you," Delrael vowed quietly. "I just wish I knew why he came back so soon."

They searched for a place to hide, a place they could defend... although they had nothing to fight with. Tryos moved erratically across the sky, searching. Delrael felt alone and exposed on the clear grassy hills.

"Is it midnight yet?" Delrael stared up at the stars. Bryl stood at the black hex-line, pushing against it—but he could not force his feet to move.

In the distance, they heard Tryos roar again. An orange tongue of flame flicked out to destroy a few lone trees.

"What are we going to do?" Tareah asked. "Have you planned for this?"

Delrael just put a hand on her shoulder. He looked at his hands, at his sword and bow.

Bryl shouted, "Now—now we can go!" He danced on the other side of the hex-line. "Hurry!"

They ran into the dense forest. The black shadow of Tryos had come much closer.

"We can't outrun him. We'd better look for a place to hide."

They found an area with a few skewed blocks of stone surrounded by thick trees. They crouched under a smooth overhang of rock. Bryl held his two Stones with sweaty hands, whispering to the gems as if praying.

"Are the Stones going to help?" Delrael asked.

"Not likely." He sighed.

"The Water Stone belonged to my father," Tareah said. "He used it to try and save me." Tareah closed her eyes and mumbled a lesson her father had told her many times. "But the old Sorcerers created dragons to resist magic, so that they could attack and leave the enemy helpless."

Bryl stared at her, thinking. His eyes were red and watery. "It makes the most sense for me to keep the Stones—if I hold both, then I get a spell bonus. After I've used up my five spells, then I'll give you both Stones and you get the same bonus—that way, we'll have ten spells between us instead of eight. It's a loophole in the Rules."

"My father let me use the Water Stone." Tareah did not take her eyes from the blue facets of the six-sided sapphire. "Once."

Her answer did not much comfort Delrael.

After only a few minutes of hushed waiting, they heard the coming of the dragon. Tryos rained fire down on indiscriminate patches of the forest as he bellowed roars of rage and challenge.

Bryl rolled the Air Stone on the ground and closed his eyes. "There, we're invisible now," he whispered. "Tryos will be able to see through the illusion if he makes the effort and if he knows where to look. But he might pass us by and never know it."

The wings sounded like the heartbeat of an immense giant, pounding the air. Tryos skimmed over the ground, sharpening his anger against the human characters who had tricked him and stolen his treasure.

Delrael held Tareah, staring up at the night sky in utter silence, too frightened to breathe. Tryos casually belched out a river of fire near them, then flew on into the darkness.

"He passed us by!" Delrael said.

"Maybe ..." Bryl whispered.

A moment later, when the dragon realized he had lost their scent, he bellowed and wheeled around, backtracking. They heard him returning seconds before he soared back into view.

"Now we're doomed for sure," Bryl said. He stared at the blue Stone and the white Stone in his hands.

Tryos back-flapped his wings, thundering the air. He hissed at the three crouched under the shelter of the overhang. "Now I sssee you! You tricked me! Ssstole my treasure!"

Bryl winced and tossed the Water Stone at his feet. He rolled a "2."

The dragon let loose a missile of fire.

The half-Sorcerer used the spell to hurl up a wall of water as a shield, feeding it with his own powers. Steam boiled from the surface of the water wall. The dragon flame struck, spattered outward, and continued to bombard the shield.

Bryl's protection held until Tryos stopped his assault to draw another breath. The half-Sorcerer sank to his knees. "If I miss a single roll, we're dead."

Another gout of dragon fire struck at them, and Bryl barely had time to roll again and get the water wall up before the flames could incinerate them. A puff of super-heated air squeezed in, and Delrael felt his eyebrows singe. The water wall strengthened, but Bryl looked drained when the dragon finally backed off again.

"I've only got two more spells left—then it's all up to Tareah." He panted with exhaustion. "I don't know if Tryos has any limitations with his fire."

"Then it's time for us to take the offensive," Tareah said. She looked at Delrael and raised her eyebrows. Her color was returning, and vigor had appeared behind her eyes, a quick-thinking intelligence forced upon her now that she had to fight. She had studied so many battles, so many legends. Now she could put it into practice. She plucked the Water Stone from Bryl's hand and stepped out from the overhang of rock.

The dragon reared back, recognizing his treasure. Delrael wanted to yank her back into the shelter, afraid the dragon might blast her for coming between him and his intended victims. But Tareah did not wait long enough for the dragon to overcome his own surprise. She held the sapphire Water Stone in front of her like an elemental talisman, then she rolled a "6."

She looked like a powerful Sorcerer queen of ancient days, swelled with magic. Balls of blue static danced in her hair as she summoned the Sorcery her forefathers had left inside the gem.

Tareah called forth a storm, blasting Tryos with gale winds, buffeting his wings and bending them back so that they almost snapped like firewood. The dragon roared, and the force whipped at his sinewy neck, twisting shut his windpipe. He tried to blast fire, but the flames came back in his face. Outraged words were torn from his mouth.

Tareah summoned lightning bolts to skitter over the dragon's scaled hide, leaving blackened intaglios on his armor. Tryos strained his wings and made a small headway against the hurricane winds. Sardun's daughter exhausted her reserves of strength. She had been sustaining herself with magic for too long. The storm started to weaken.

Delrael stepped out of the rock shelter and shot three arrows at the dragon, but they proved useless against the reptilian armor.

"Bryl, what about the Air Stone?" he said.

The half-Sorcerer shouted over the howling winds. "What can I do? Tryos will see through any illusion I can make to hide us. Wait!"

Just as Tareah dropped her storm and collapsed, Delrael caught her. He pulled her back to the rock outcropping. Bryl snatched up the sapphire Stone from the ground.

Tryos hovered in the air, stunned at the ferocity of her attack, but then he surged forward with renewed anger.

Suddenly, an illusion Rognoth appeared in the air—fat, with stubby wings, flying clumsily but looking terrified of his vengeful brother. Rognoth spurted past Tryos's face, and the large dragon's eyes nearly bugged out of their sockets. "Rognos! You too!"

Rognoth flapped his little wings and buzzed away. The larger dragon plunged after him, forgetting his other victims.

"Come on, we've got to get out of here!" Bryl said.

Tareah seemed groggy and drained from summoning the storm, but she soon regained her strength. Delrael looked at the rock overhang sheltering them. It was bubbly and molten from the dragon fire.

They ran as fast as they could into the forest.

Above them, the sky looked bruised and clotted, choked with the smoke and steam and fragments of Tareah's storm. Bryl left the weather to repair itself and focused on the ground around them. Taking back the Water Stone, Bryl drew a deep breath and rolled again. "This is my last spell for another full day."

"Luck, Bryl," Delrael said.

Thick fog swirled up from the forest floor, seeping out of the earth and blanketing them from view. The vapors rose upward, dank and foul. "Now he can't see us, or follow our scent."

Tareah no longer needed to lean on Delrael's side, but she remained close to him anyway. Her face was ruddy from excitement, fear, and exertion.

"The illusion of Rognoth won't fool him for long. He'll see through it once he starts to think."

Above them, they could hear the dragon as he returned for the kill. "Not real Rognos!" Tryos said. "Another trick! Tricksss! Kill you for tricksss!"

Delrael could not see the dragon overhead through the fog. Tryos would be looking down on a cottony bank of mist, a real mist created by the Water Stone, not an illusion.

But the dragon would find them again before long. Tryos jetted flame on the mist, leaving a burning and blasted landscape behind him. He methodically swept over sections of the fog, spewing fire on the mist, searching for them.

Exhausted, scraped, and bruised, Vailret and Paenar pulled themselves to the towering lip of the volcanic cone. Paenar slipped the knotted rope from his shoulders, and they balanced the battered Dragon Siren on the rough ground.

The top of the volcano commanded an incredible view of the entire island. Starlight reflected off the hexes of seawater that hid the wreckage of the *Nautilus*. Volcanic debris lay all around them where lava had oozed out centuries ago, hardening and crumbling into hexagons of desolate terrain. Tendrils of smoke curled up from the simmering lake of fire; splashes of orange light danced around the interior of the cone, illuminating the opposite rim.

Paenar stood up, scanning the distance. A brisk wind blew the smoke away from his face. "I see a disturbance over there." He pointed toward the central forests of the island and then sighed in annoyance. "My sight is gone again. Please look and see. Maybe it was only a mirage through the oils." His voice was flat and clipped, but quivering with anticipation.

Vailret withdrew the small optick-tube he had taken from the *Nautilus*'s equipment bunker and turned the magnifying lens to sight on the distant flashes of fire. The telescope still baffled him, but he quelled his dizzy sensations and lined up his field of view. Tryos sprang in front of his eyes, blasting flames.

He cried out in surprise. "Tryos is attacking someone—I think it's Del and Bryl! I can't make out the details."

Vailret turned the dish of the Siren toward the distant dragon. Moving desperately, he reached for the toggle switch that would allow him to call on Tryos in a thunderous voice.

Paenar placed his thin hand on Vailret's arm, stopping him. The blind man's' sinews stood out on his wrist, and his bony knuckles were white. "We need to settle this first. You know I must be the one. It makes the most sense. I want to do it."

"You'll be killed."

"So would you, if you took my place. That's no excuse." The businesslike, rigid voice melted to a more personal tone. Paenar clasped his hands together, as if to stop himself from begging.

"You must allow me to atone for what I have not done, for allowing the bad things to grow unhindered. It's the only way my conscience can survive, even if I do not."

Vailret did not know how to counter the other man's defense. Normally, he would have argued, stalled for time, but Tryos was attacking his friends. "I won't let you sacrifice yourself just to show off. Think of how much more you could do in the fight against the Outsiders."

"Think of how much more I could do? Oh? Even my mechanical eyes have failed. Going blind may be cruel, but less cruel than having sight dangled in front of me, tantalizing, and then snatched away. Twice! The only way I could regain my vision now would be to remain in Sitnalta for the rest of my life. That would help no one. I'd rather die here, fighting. You taught me how to do it. It is my right." He crossed his arms over his chest.

"Can you think of any other way? No—I have been trying ever since we left the *Nautilus*. There is no other way." He stamped his foot with finality. "Now summon the dragon, before he destroys your friends as well."

Feeling sick and defeated, Vailret bent to the switch and flicked it. He switched it on and off three times before the probabilities finally made it work. Vailret spoke, sending his voice out in thundering waves across the island.

Tareah could run no farther. Bryl's eyes brimmed with tears of fear, despair, and shreds of leftover defiance. Delrael stood beside Sardun's daughter, trying to look brave and strong. He ran a fingertip along his silver belt. "Maybe someone will remember our adventures."

They huddled together like captured rats, listening to the dragon's torch sweep nearer, then drift away, then come back closer still. Bryl handed her both the Water Stone and the Air Stone. "You've got four spells left. That's all we have now."

Tareah looked as if she had no more strength to give. But she pressed her lips together and took the gems.

For lack of anything else that offered hope, Delrael withdrew his bow. He wondered if he might be able to injure the soft inside of Tryos's mouth....but then he realized that if it could withstand furnace fire pouring out, the mouth would certainly be tough enough to deflect an arrow.

He thought of Vailret and blind Paenar back in Sitnalta, sorry that he could not have a chance to say good-bye.

It would be only a matter of time before Tryos stumbled upon them in his methodical search. Bryl could not maintain the fog much longer. Tryos would be able to see them soon.

See them! Delrael clenched his knuckles on his bow. The memory of Paenar had sparked an idea in his head. Maybe the dragon's *eyes* would be vulnerable to arrows. He hesitated. The idea made him uneasy.

But they had no other chance.

Just as Delrael nocked an arrow against the bowstring, Tryos burned away the sheltering fog. Bryl's spell dissipated, leaving them exposed.

Tryos back flapped his wings and leered down at them. His fangs glistened in the reflected light of scattered fires in the brush. He curled his serpentine neck and drew a deep breath, stoking his internal fires.

Delrael let loose an arrow. He closed his eyes, but the lightheaded feeling told him he had found his mark. Tryos reared back, seeing the shaft approach. His yellow green eyes widened in surprise—and the arrow sank all the way to the feather into his wet pupil. Steaming black blood poured out. The wooden shaft burst into flames.

Shrieking in agony, Tryos vomited fire down at the ground. But Delrael's success had galvanized Tareah into finding her own strength. She rolled the sapphire die, and the shielding wall of water leaped up around them. Steam boiled away, and the air became thick under the cramped dome.

The dragon's attack seemed to last forever. Tryos choked on his pain. Tareah let the water wall splash back to the smoking earth. Delrael took his bow again, firing once, then a second time as the dragon filled his lungs.

Tryos gave a moaning cry even before the arrows struck. The first arrow glanced off his horny lower eyelid, falling to the burning ground. But the second struck home in the other eye.

The dragon wailed in pain and dismay, blasting fire aimlessly, flying in circles as if uncertain whether to flee or to continue his attack.

Tareah looked distraught and could not watch the dragon's flight. "We tricked Tryos. He had a perfect right to be angry with us."

"We have to get out of here before he can find us again." Delrael forced himself not to think about what Tareah had said.

But the dragon took less time to recover than they needed. Before they could cover much distance, Tryos swooped down, craning his neck and trying to locate them by their sound, by their scent. His flames were tinted blue, hot enough to melt rock on first contact.

"How much fire can he have, Bryl?" Delrael said, panting. "Don't the Rules put limits on that?"

"I don't know—ask Vailret! But you can bet he's got more than we can withstand." The half-Sorcerer clamped his mouth shut to absorb a cry of exhausted despair. Tareah whimpered as she tossed the Water Stone to the ground again.

A "1." Her spell failed.

"Roll it again!" Delrael said.

She grabbed the sapphire and rolled it for the fourth time. The dome of water bloomed around them at the same moment Tryos struck. Bryl cried out. Tareah shuddered, concentrating on the Water Stone, flushed and sweating.

Under the constant barrage of fire, the ground turned a baking red, beginning to bubble. Inside the shelter, the air was hot and depleted, filled with steam and empty of oxygen. Delrael had to suck in great mouthfuls of air just to keep his lungs from collapsing. His face felt raw. He clenched his bow in despair.

The ground under their feet grew unbearably hot. Tareah looked as if she would collapse in another moment.

The dragon's blue fire kept pounding down.

"Tryos! Dragon! Come back to your mountain at once! I command it!"

The words came rippling across the night. Tryos turned away from the shrinking bubble that protected his enemies against even his most venomous fire. The dragon saw only darkness, felt only spears of pain that stabbed through his ruined eyes.

"Tryos, return to your home! Or I shall destroy your treasure!"

With a squeal of rage, Tryos flapped about in anger and confusion, not knowing whose voice cut across the night. He could not leave now. His enemies, the characters who played horrible tricks on him, were trapped. His fire had dwindled, but they would be destroyed in moments. He could picture their blackening skin, their faces; his dragon fire would burn their lungs from the inside out as they drew a final breath to scream. They deserved it. They had tricked him.

But his treasure! The voice would destroy his treasure—unless he destroyed the voice first.

With another cry of outrage, Tryos whirled in the air and shot back toward the volcano, to Vailret.

Vailret licked his lips and swallowed, preparing to talk faster than he ever had before. Delrael was the fast talker. Delrael had the charisma score to convince characters to believe him. Not Vailret. But he would have to learn.

Vailret watched through the optick-tube as Tryos flapped across the island, pistoning his wings. The dragon sniffed and swept back and forth, somehow finding his way. Vailret tucked the tube in his pocket and stood next to Paenar, trying to look brave. His heart pounded, sending blood roaring through his head. He didn't know what he would do if Tryos recognized the Siren from Sitnalta.

The dragon circled around the rim of the volcano, vanishing in the patchy smoke rising from the lava below. Tryos seemed to be searching, sniffing the air, though both men stood unhidden. Then the wind currents changed and Tryos snorted, homing in on their scent.

Seething, the dragon flapped his wings twice and landed on the crater edge. He extended his neck, snuffling. Two charred arrow shafts protruded from his cavernous sockets. Vailret drew back. Black blood smoked as it hardened over the wounds.

"Who are you?" Tryos demanded. "How will you get my treasure?" He breathed with a sound louder than purring Sitnaltan machinery, drowning all other night sounds. "You sssmell like humansss! Bad humansss! Play tricksss on Tryos!"

"Yes, we are humans. Both of us." Vailret shuffled his feet. "But you will be interested in what we have to say."

"No! No more tricksss! Humansss trick Tryos! All men bad!"

Vailret let his mouth roll the words as fast as the gleam came into his eye, trying to imitate Delrael's skill. "Ah, Tryos, all men are not your enemies—we are your friends. Those characters you were attacking? They are our enemies too! We came here to kill them. My friend Paenar and I want to be your allies."

"But one man can't hate another man!"

"All characters are different, Tryos—and some men are very bad men. Surely some dragons must be enemies?"

"Yesss! Rognos isss my enemy!" Tryos grumbled with a vehemence that frightened Vailret.

Rognoth?

"We can work together, Tryos. We can help you destroy those bad men. And we brought a weapon with us, a weapon that will destroy the enemy in a horrible way, much more horrible than simple burning with dragon fire. Those two have no defense against this special weapon—we built it just for this task."

"Where isss thisss weapon?" Tryos said. He leaned forward to sniff the Dragon Siren. "Thisss kill them? They hurt my eyes. I tired now. No more fire left. But you have weapon!"

"You will take it to them, and Paenar can use it to destroy the enemy." Vailret crossed his fingers, wishing himself luck. "You can trick them yourself. They don't know you have the weapon. That's part of the Game, remember—trick your enemy."

"Yesss! Trick them! Give weapon to me!"

Vailret turned to Paenar, and the blind man nodded. He stood rigid, his mind made up. The two men lugged the Siren over to the dragon. "To work best, Tryos, this weapon has to be mounted just at the back of your head, behind your ears," Paenar said.

"Yesss." Tryos lowered his broad head to the ground. Paenar scrambled up the dragon's plated body, hesitated suddenly as his mechanical eyes ceased to function again, then picked his way at a much more careful pace.

"Paenar, I'm going to toss up the end of the rope. Try to catch it." The end of the rope struck the blind man's chest. Paenar scrabbled for the end but missed, and it fell back to the ground. Vailret tossed it two more times before Paenar caught it and secured a heavy knot around the dragon's neck.

Together, they hauled the Dragon Siren up on Tryos's back. The dragon fidgeted. "Hurry up!" he said. "How does weapon work?"

"Paenar will ride on your back and you will fly to our enemies. When it is time, he will switch on the weapon. And then ... then that will be the end."

"Good, good! You sssmell funny—afraid? What will happen?"

Vailret swallowed hard. Paenar leaned over to the dragon's ear. "We're just anxious to see the end of our enemy at last."

Paenar lashed the Siren up against the back of the dragon's skull, knotting the ropes. Vailret watched the blind man tie himself down, secure against a fall. He felt sick inside.

"We go now!" Tryos stomped his foot on the volcano rim.

"Yesss, we go now," Paenar said with an undertone of sarcasm. He cocked his head down, but from his attitude, Vailret could tell Paenar's eyes were still not working. A blind man riding a blind dragon in the dark of night. Paenar held his hand up in a farewell salute. "Remember Scartaris—for me."

"I will. I promise. Luck—I wish you all the luck on Hexworld."

"I am ready, Tryos," Paenar said.

The dragon launched himself off the rim, rising straight up over the wide mouth of the volcanic cone.

To Paenar, it was a cruel joke for his eyesight to return just as they flew over the wide maw of the volcano. He looked down to see the boiling red lava, the corrosive smoke, the sharp and jagged rocks far below.

Inside him, his guilt and anger burned like molten iron. Since he had met Vailret and had seen the incentive the young man carried in himself, Paenar's own guilt had been nearly unbearable. He realized that some parts of Hexworld were worth saving, worth fighting for. Now he had a lifetime of apathy to repay, and not much time to do it.

The dragon beneath him was a target for his anger, a symbol of the bad things about Hexworld. By destroying , he could strike a blow against the Outsiders—he could free the city of Sitnalta to work on the problem of Scartaris; he could allow Tareah to return to her father, where she and Sardun could fight Scartaris.

But only if he destroyed the dragon.

His hand strayed to the Dragon Siren. He twisted the dish, aiming it at the back of Tryos's head so the spear of sound would pierce directly between the two cavernous reptilian ears. Paenar's mechanical eyes flickered, filled with bursts of random color, then focused again.

So far from Sitnalta and the technological fringe, chances were remote that the device would work the first time…but the Siren would work, if he tried enough times.

"Here is my weapon, Tryos," Paenar said quietly. "Do you remember it?"

He reached forward and touched the switch, stopped, and drew in one more breath. But the stink of sulfur smoke filled the air. "Give me luck," he said.

His mechanical eyes plunged him into blindness again, so that he could not see the fiery open wound of lava below. Paenar pushed the switch upward.

Nothing happened. He flicked the switch up and down, over and over again. He had to keep trying. By the Rules of Probability, it would work if he tried enough times.

It did.

Sound surrounded him with a hurricane of noise. He jerked backward, but the ropes held him in place. The pulses pounded, penetrating into the dragon's skull.

Tryos shrieked in horror, pain, and deeper betrayal—he went wild in the air, thrashing, plunging, trying to shake off the murderous Siren. But the tight bindings held it fast. Paenar was thrown back and forth like a puppet in a whirlwind. The ropes kept him on the dragon's back, but they cut deeply into his skin and broke two of his ribs.

Tryos writhed in the air, screaming, turning somersaults. The Siren pounded on, unrelenting.

The sound stopped for Paenar as his eardrums burst. The faceplate of his mechanical eyes shattered, and the many-colored oils sprayed out from the cracks, kept under pressure to suspend the floating lenses. The lenses spilled out, flying and glittering in the air.

Blind and deaf, Paenar could still feel himself thrown about in the dragon's fury. Though he could not hear it, the Siren wailed away, pummeling his bones. He felt as if his skull was being crushed within a giant fist.

He lost consciousness when he could endure it no more...

Mad with pain, Tryos soared upward, circled blind, and thrashed about in the air. He made a reckless, unseeing dive and plunged deep into the throat of the volcano.

The dragon, Paenar, and the Siren were swallowed up by the lake of fire.

Vailret dove for cover as a belching explosion within the volcano spewed a geyser of fire into the air. He stumbled, dizzy from the echoing onslaught of the Dragon Siren. Lava splattered around Vailret, but the scant shelter of a few large boulders protected him.

The Siren stopped as soon as Tryos vanished beneath the flames. The rumble inside the volcano faded away. On the side of the cone, Vailret could see dull red patches of cooling lava. Parts of the distant forest terrain gave off an orange glow as fires burned themselves out.

Vailret stared in silence over the lip of the crater, peering deep within the cone, searching. The molten light shone upward, scattering the shadows. But Vailret saw nothing of Paenar, nothing of the dragon, nothing at all.

CHAPTER 15

SARDUN'S DAUGHTER

RULE #18: Remember Rule #1—always have fun.
—The Book of Rules

The red-and-white balloon drifted off the beach, splashing the bottom of the basket against the choppy waves before it rose into the air like swollen dandelion seed. Water dripped from the gondola, running through the holes in the wicker. The balloon fought a tug of war with gravity, pulling its heavy load of passengers aloft. Delrael removed every one of the sandbags just to get them in the air.

When the metal gas tank had emptied itself into the giant sack, they heaved the empty tank over the side into the sea. Delrael watched it fall. A bright white splash bloomed on the surface of the ocean.

Delrael's face and hands still appeared raw and blistered from the dragon's attack. Vailret sat in uncharacteristic silence, looking back at Rokanun as it faded into the distance. The volcano, alone and empty now except for the dragon's abandoned treasure, stood above the rest of the terrain.

Even without the bulky canister of gas, the gondola offered little room for them to move. Tareah hung close to Delrael. Bryl acted uneasy, as if afraid a careless movement by one of the passengers could knock him out of the basket. Vailret wanted to be left alone, but no one could find privacy while bumping elbows with three other people. They all knew it would be a long journey.

Bryl and Tareah took turns with the Water Stone, not speaking much but keeping a brisk breeze pushing the balloon northward.

They drifted past the zigzagged shoreline where the hexagons of ocean surrendered to forest or grassland terrain. The city of Sitnalta rose on their right, alone and isolated from the rest of Hexworld. Without Sitnalta, they would never have reached the island of Rokanun—not Delrael and Bryl in the balloon, not Paenar and Vailret in the *Nautilus*. Without the Dragon Siren, they would never have been able to destroy Tryos.

But Vailret could not understand the characters there, and that disturbed him. The Sitnaltans replaced magic with science, then made themselves as elite as the old Sorcerers had.

When they could see the city buildings clearly and recognize the hexagon-cobbled streets, they waved and signaled that they were all right. The bright balloon in the sky would draw the attention of most of the optick tubes in the city, proving to Professor Verne that his balloon worked beyond the technological fringe. Verne must already know that his *Nautilus* had died.

Vailret leaned over the basket, looking down. "I guess we're giving the balloon an even more extensive test than they wanted. Do we have any intention of giving it back to Professor Verne?"

"I can't stop there again," Delrael said, looking into the distance as he rubbed his *kennok* limb. "I don't know what would happen."

"With the balloon, we can return to the Ice Palace much faster." Bryl reached out to touch Tareah's shoulder, but she shrugged him away. "That's most important right now."

They traveled without slowing. The balloon sailed over uncounted hexes of forest, forested-hill, grassland, and grassy-hill terrain. Drifting on the winds, they were not bound by the same distance limitations the Rules imposed on those traveling on foot. They rose over the craggy barrier of the Spectre Mountains, looking down at where the derelict

Outsider ship lay in ruins. Vailret wondered if the Sitnaltans would ever do anything with it.

Air currents swirled over the mountains, but Tareah used the Water Stone to smooth the updrafts. She appeared tired but hardened somehow within. Bryl curled up against the wall of the basket, snoring in exhausted sleep. He had used his minor replenishment spell several times to refill their packs with food and water.

Night and day passed again and again, and still they did not rest or stop. Nothing could harm them so high in the air. The balloon's height fluctuated noticeably from day to night, rising and falling. Day after day, too, they could see the red-and-white sack beginning to sag as the invisible gas leaked out of the imperfect seals of the flaps. They drifted northward, but they also drifted downward.

The travelers all felt stiff and cramped, confined in too small a space for too long, but they endured, thinking how much more uncomfortable it would have been to trudge across the map for weeks, sleeping on the ground and then crossing the rugged mountain terrain, vulnerable to whatever wandering monsters lay in wait.

Delrael and Tareah talked together. He told her heroic stories of the quests he had undertaken, the adventures, searching in dungeons for treasure and monsters. Tareah, accustomed to stories of long-dead Sorcerers, was charmed to know someone who had personally done something worthy of retelling.

Listening to Tareah's intelligent comments, Vailret forced himself to remember that the little girl had lived a decade longer than he himself had.

Tareah continued to grow, though, alarmingly. Her arms stretched out, and her body grew, and her facial features changed, becoming more mature but still retaining an expression of wide-eyed wonder at the world she had never seen. She appeared to be in her early teens, and her body filled out, making her look like a woman instead of a girl. She complained of terrible pains in her limbs and muscles, as if she were being twisted and pulled, forced to catch up with her years. Delrael tried to comfort her when he could; Tareah said it helped, which made him glow inside.

But none of them wanted to guess why Tareah was released from the spell that had held her in the body of a child for decades.

Unless something had happened to Sardun...

Vailret hung on the rope netting that held the red-and-white balloon in its spherical shape. Delrael scrambled on the other side, opening some of the flaps to release the remainder of the buoyant gas, enjoying himself. He used his *kennok* leg with natural ease.

The balloon drifted closer to the ground, skimming over the surface of the wide lake that now filled the haunted Transition Valley. The Barrier River surged through the deep canyons in the mountains, rushing from the Northern Sea along its course.

As the gas escaped, the bag crumpled, sagging inward. The basket bounced on the ground, knocking the travelers to their knees. It rocked back and forth as if it couldn't decide whether to take to the air again or not, then finally came to rest where the mountain terrain met the valley on the western side of the Barrier River. They brushed themselves off and stood on firm earth again, stretching and blinking.

"We couldn't have navigated through those mountains anyway. Not the way the balloon was leaking," Vailret said. "We can walk to the Ice Palace like we did before."

"Without Sardun attacking the weather, the trip shouldn't be too bad." Delrael looked around and started walking.

"I, for one, would not mind stretching my legs a bit." Bryl rubbed his knees.

Anxious to get back to her father, Tareah wouldn't let them rest. She glanced at the northern landscape, trying to recognize the mountain peaks and letting relief mingle with worry on her face.

They set off, abandoning the limp balloon on the cold and soggy ground at the river's edge. At the black hex line dividing the terrain types, they passed between the two towering ice sentries that guarded the winding road. The wind around them was cold and whispering, making the silence seem deeper.

Moving stiffly, Tareah went forward into the ruins of the Ice Palace, alone. Tears glistened on her cheeks. Delrael tried to speak to her, but his throat went dry. Neither Vailret nor Bryl said anything.

The once-magnificent Palace lay tumbled in pools of motionless water covered with a scum of ice as the sun set and the mountains cooled. Gigantic bluish-clear bricks lay scattered like a child's building blocks. Delrael remembered the tall shining spires, the gate, the rainbows of light penetrating the blue ice walls. A dusting of snow brushed against the larger blocks; other massive chunks of ice had left deep impressions in the half-frozen mud around the foundation.

"What happened here?" Bryl finally whispered, but no one answered him.

Tareah stared, unmoving. Delrael put a hand on her thin shoulder and stood by her at the crumbling arch of the main gate. She shuddered when he touched her, but he did not let go. The glistening rubble reflected tinges of orange as the afternoon neared sunset. "I have to go inside," she said.

"There's nothing left," Delrael said.

"My father's in there. Somewhere."

She stepped through the blind Palace gate, crossing the threshold. A burst of blue light glowed around her, and a vision filled the air: the last moments of Sardun recorded and frozen within the arch.

"Father," she said.

"It's just an illusion, a message," Vailret said. "What happened to Sardun?"

"Tareah," said the image of the old Sentinel, clothed in his gray robes and looking thin and withdrawn. "You will have returned by now. The *dayid* has shown me, shown me many things."

The Sentinel's throne had melted. In the image, the ceiling came down in chunks around him, praying slush, letting the sunlight penetrate where it had never gone before. The warmth of the northern summer slashed at the Palace like knives to draw cold watery blood.

"The Ice Palace cannot remain intact without the Water Stone. It cannot resist the weather, it cannot stand the heat of the sun."

Sardun seemed to know everything Delrael, Bryl, and Vailret had done. His voice sounded tired, and his lisp had grown heavy. "But without the Water Stone, you could not have been rescued. I made the right choice."

The wavering illusion stared at them. "The Ice Palace is melting, and I can do nothing to stop it. Nothing." Behind him, an avalanche of icicles came tumbling down. Delrael silently urged the old Sentinel to flee the danger. But Sardun's eyes filled with a far-off gleam, a shining emotion that made him want to shudder.

"The *dayid* is calling me, clamoring in my mind. The voices have not let me alone since I woke them to create the Barrier River."

His words dropped to a whisper. "The voices in the *dayid* want me to join them. With the spirits of the other Sentinels."

"No!" Tareah said. "Don't ..." Her voice sounded very small.

Delrael stood beside her, but he didn't know what he could say to comfort her. "This already happened, days ago."

In the image, Sardun drew a ragged breath, blowing steam through his drooping moustache. "I have lived far too long. It is time I leave Hexworld to those who deserve it. You, Tareah, are the last of us. Make the right decisions. Do what is best for yourself and for the memory of our race.

"Give my utmost thanks to those who have rescued you. I can withstand the pull no longer, the urging of the voices. I must join them in their loneliness, and make it better for a while."

Sardun's skin had taken on a translucent, whitish glow. The firm distinction between his skin and the air around him grew fuzzier as the light intensified. Behind him, water poured down the blue walls of the Ice Palace, breaking the bonds that held the ceiling arches together, letting an avalanche of ice boulders come raining down.

But Sardun was consumed in a flash of blinding white fire that swallowed up his flesh, the huge ice blocks, and the vision itself.

The dimness of sunset filled the air again.

Tareah stood motionless for a long moment, and then, slowly, started to cry.

~

"You'll like the Stronghold. You'll see," Delrael said, trying to convince her with the enthusiasm in his own voice. They hiked down out of the mountains, resting and discussing what to do next about Scartaris.

"I'm going to kill that thing," Vailret said under his breath. "I made a promise."

Tareah turned against Delrael, craning her neck to look into his eyes. She was tall enough now to stand face to face with him. "I'll try to like it." She wore her grief like a half-healed wound. "And I will try to help."

They crossed a hex-line into new terrain, heading back home.

EPILOGUE

Melanie stretched her arms and glanced at the clock. Scott yawned loudly.

"We played a long time," Tyrone said. "That was great."

Melanie felt delighted. At the climax, they had been shouting, rolling dice, cheering, enthralled by the adventure. She tried to see if David's expression had grown softer.

"Didn't you have fun, David?" she asked. "That was better than any of the other adventures from before."

"Yeah," Tyrone said as he carried the dishes to the sink. "You can lighten up now."

David shrugged into his denim jacket. He seemed unable to take his eyes from the new line of blue hexagons marking the Barrier River. "I don't think so."

Melanie felt disappointment stab through her. David stood up and moved toward the door.

"You don't understand," he turned back to them and said. "If we don't stop now, and stop for good, we'll never be able to quit. The Game will control us. The Game will be everything and we'll never get away from it."

KEVIN J ANDERSON

He turned to point at the changed map. "Can't you see how powerful it's getting already?"

Then he walked out the door. By the way he moved, he had intended to let it slam, but the door-closer eased it shut against the jamb.

"Well, see you next Sunday," Tyrone said as he gathered up his things and left. Scott followed him to the door.

Melanie went back to clean up before her parents got home. Of course she wouldn't say anything about what had happened.

"Yeah. See you next Sunday."

THANK YOU FOR READING ROLL, HEXWORLD BOOK 1

We hope you enjoyed it as much as we enjoyed bringing it to you. We just wanted to take a moment to encourage you to review the book. Follow this link: Roll to be directed to the book's Amazon product page to leave your review.

Every review helps further the author's reach and, ultimately, helps them continue writing fantastic books for us all to enjoy.

Want to discuss our books with other readers and even the authors? Join our Discord server today and be a part of the Aethon community.

Facebook

Instagram

Twitter

Website

You can also join our non-spam mailing list by visiting www.subscribepage.com/AethonReadersGroup and never miss out on future releases. You'll also receive three full books completely Free as our thanks to you.

WHAT'S NEXT?

HEXWORLD

1: ROLL (You just read)

2: PLAY

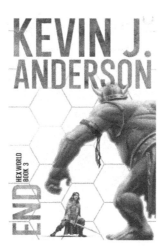

3: END

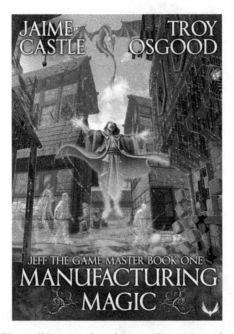

Jeff Driscoll becomes the only active Game Master for the VRMMORPG Infinite Worlds after a rogue patch turns the game into a buggy, dangerous mess. Can he fix it on his own and save the players?

GET MANUFACTURING MAGIC NOW!

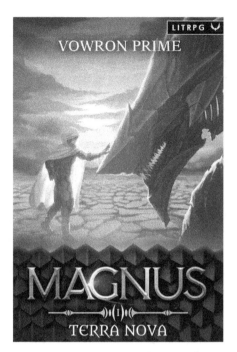

Magnus Cromwell kills for a living.

GET TERRA NOVA NOW!

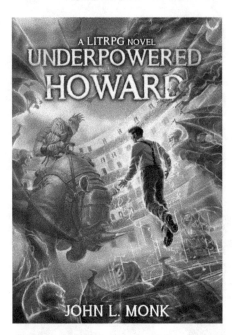

When there's no way to win, cheat, and cheat BIG. Howard, desperate to save his friends and countless innocents, hatches a plan to fix things. Using his deep knowledge of game mechanics, he'll start again as a level 0 necromancer and exploit his way to power.

GET UNDERPOWERED HOWARD NOW!

I was in my garage when the space elves addressed the whole world. Planet-wide survival reality show? Ridiculous.

GET THEY CALLED ME MAD NOW!

For all our LitRPG books, visit our website.

ABOUT THE AUTHOR

Kevin J. Anderson has published more than 170 books, 58 of which have been national or international bestsellers. He has written numerous novels in the Star Wars, X-Files, and Dune universes, as well as unique steampunk fantasy novels *Clockwork Angels* and *Clockwork Lives*, written with legendary rock drummer Neil Peart. His original works include the Saga of Seven Suns series, the Wake the Dragon and Terra Incognita fantasy trilogies, the Saga of Shadows trilogy, and his humorous horror series featuring Dan Shamble, Zombie PI. He has edited numerous anthologies, written comics and games, and the lyrics to two rock CDs. Anderson is the director of the graduate program oin Publishing at Western Colorado University. Anderson and his wife Rebecca Moesta are the publishers of WordFire Press. His most recent novels are Vengewar, Dune: The Duke of Caladan (with Brian Herbert), Stake, Kill Zone (with Doug Beason), and Spine of the Dragon.

CPSIA information can be obtained
at www.ICGtesting.com
Printed in the USA
LVHW031657010721
691688LV00001B/6